To Vee,
with best wishes
Sue Rule

GW00746457

Shaihen Heritage: Book I

Cloak of Magic

by

S. A. Rule

Bright Pen

Visit us online at www.authorsonline.co.uk

A Bright Pen Book

Copyright © Authors OnLine Ltd 2006

Text Copyright © S.A. Rule 2006

Cover design by Clive Scruton ©

All rights reserved. No part of this publication may be reproduced, stored in a retrieval system, or transmitted in any form or by any means, electronic, mechanical, photocopy, recording or otherwise, without prior written permission of the copyright owner. Nor can it be circulated in any form of binding or cover other than that in which it is published and without similar condition including this condition being imposed on a subsequent purchaser.

ISBN 0 7552 1030 1

Authors OnLine Ltd
19 The Cinques
Gamlingay, Sandy
Bedfordshire SG19 3NU
England

This book is also available in e-book format, details of which are available at www.authorsonline.co.uk

Cast of Characters

The Shaihens

Alsareth	Daughter of Caras and Elani
Brethil	Holder of Cuaraccon, wife of Jagus
Brynnen	Minstrel serving Arhaios
Caras	Heir to Arhaios and Oreath
Carastin	Youngest son of Caras and Elani
Colis	Chief of Ccheven
Elani	Wife of Caras
Ered	Chief of Hieath
Filas	Son of Rainur
Gascon	Chief of Mervecc
Iareth	Holder of Riskeld
Jagus	Brother of King Rainur
Kierce	Horsemaster of Arhaios
Lasa	Resident of Prassan Holding
Leath	Chief of Oreath, grandmother of Caras
Loia	Sister of King Rainur
Madred	Half-sister of Kierce
Onia	Chief of Ulath
Rainur	King of Shehaios
Sartin	Prince of Shehaios, son of Cathva
Taegen	Eldest son of Caras and Elani
Tilsey	Cathva's Shaihen slave
Tuli	Half-brother of Kierce
Turloch	Lord High Magician of Shehaios
Verril	Mother of Madred & Tuli, step-mother of Kierce

The Caiivorians

Cathva an' Zelt	The Emperor's daughter, wife of King Rainur
Davitis an' Korsos	Imperial Envoy to Shehaios
Girstan an' Cromed	Leader (King) of the as-caii
Hiren an' Driezi	Commander in Chief of the Imperial Army in Shehaios
Orlii	An as-caii slave
Tay-Aien	Prophet of the Emperor's god.
Tercien an' Lorca	Commander in Chief of the Imperial Army in Shehaios (Hiren's successor)
Volun	Pretender to the Imperial throne
Zelt an' Korsos	Emperor of the Caiivorian Sacred Union

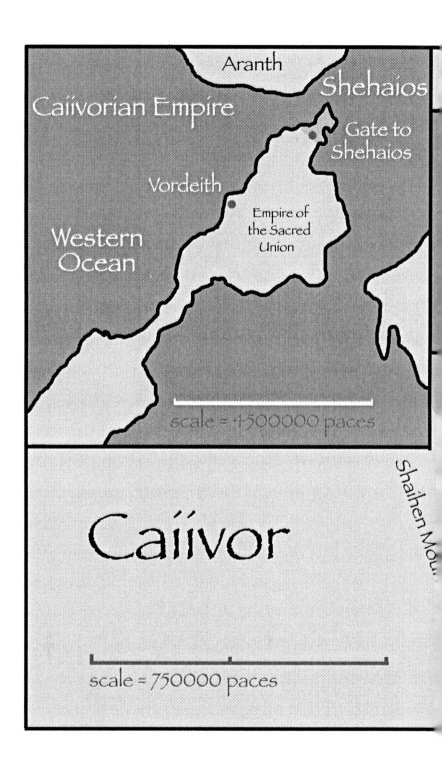

Aranth

Caiivorian Empire

Shehaios

Gate to
Shehaios

Vordeith

Empire of
the Sacred
Union

Western
Ocean

scale = +500000 paces

Caíivor

Shaihen Mou...

scale = 750000 paces

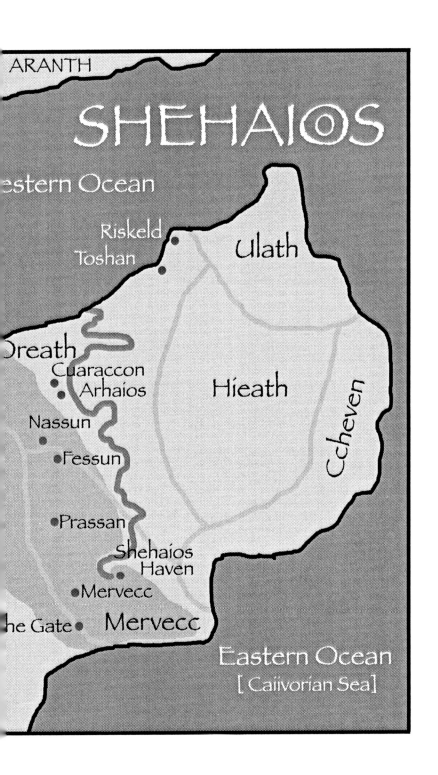

ARANTH

SHEHAIOS

estern Ocean

Riskeld
Toshan

Ulath

Dreath
Cuaraccon
Arhaios

Hieath

Ccheven

Nassun

Fessun

Prassan

Shehaios
Haven

Mervecc

he Gate

Mervecc

Eastern Ocean
[Caiivorian Sea]

Prologue

In Shehaios, you do not believe in the Spirit.

It is.

For a Shaihen to say, "I do not believe in the Spirit" is for a man to stand in front of a tree and say, "I do not believe in this tree". It will make little difference when it falls on his head.

The Spirit of Shehaios dwells in the soil of the land. It breathes the soft, moist breath of the creatures who live there. It flies on the wings of the birds and insects who breed and feed there. It flourishes in the flowers of the Shaihen flora. It lives, sometimes, in the hearts of the men and women who call themselves Shaihen and writes its name on the works of the best of them.

Part I

Introduction

They had come over the top of the world. Through the waste of snow and ice, across the barriers of golden rock that lay between Caiivor and Shehaios, they had forged their way in search of plunder.

The land that was so hard to reach was mythically rich. Game teemed there and crops grew in abundance. No-one went hungry in Shehaios. It had been worth the journey.

Twenty strong, the band of tall, battle-hardened raiders looked down on a small cluster of buildings made of the local yellow stone. A small, hairy cow stood chewing the cud in the lee of the low farmhouse, sheltering from the keen wind that whipped across the hillside. Two pigs rooted in a patch of trampled earth enclosed by a drystone wall. There was no sign of the human inhabitants except for the smoke drifting from the peak of the turf roof.

The warriors' leader, a burly man with streaks of grey in his tangled mane of golden hair, drew his sword. He raised his painted face to the gods and let out a bellow of primeval violence. His followers echoed him as they charged down the hill onto the unsuspecting farmstead.

A mile away up on the hillside, a thick-coated, wolf-like dog pricked up his ears at the distant sound. He raised his head, scenting the air. His mate, watching him, did likewise, and got to her feet. Their master looked round at the movement.

"What's the matter with those dogs?"

His brother finished checking the latest of the new arrivals to the flock before he answered.

"Maybe a bear about?" he suggested.

Both dogs were up now, and the bitch was whining and pacing. She and her mate were there to protect the flock from predators, but this was not her normal reaction. Their master caught their uneasiness. His gaze tracked her questing nose, towards the ridge that obscured the view of his homestead.

"There's something wrong. Something wrong at the Holding," he said uncertainly.

"There'll be something wrong with our stock if we leave these new-borns here undefended," returned his brother shortly.

"Stay here with the dogs. I won't be long."

With a sharp reprimand to the dogs who tried to follow him, he scrambled up the low peak beside them, and stood regaining his breath as he looked down on his farm.

He looked for some moments before he could comprehend what he saw. There were figures swarming around the farmstead. Big men, clad in furs. He

1

saw the light flash from sword blades. He saw figures dragged from the buildings; small, struggling figures, hopelessly outmatched by their captors. He saw the blades cut, and slash, swing and fall again. All in the distance, beyond his reach, like some nightmare.

He staggered back, horror stealing his strength and his balance. He half fell back down the hillside until the momentum of his descent overtook the weakness in his legs. He passed his brother and the dogs running as he had never run in his life.

"Attack!" he gasped.

"What—?"

"We're under attack!"

With a curse, his brother ran after him, the dogs loping ahead. They knew as they ran that there was nothing two men armed with knives and sheepdogs could do. These were raiders from beyond the edge of the world, and tales of their butchery preceded them across the mountains. The farmers of the Shaihen hills had thought they were safe. They had thought the mountains would protect them, and the fearsome raiders would never come.

But come they had.

Chapter 1
Twelve Stones

Darkness was no hindrance to the rodent. It scavenged by night, its mind tracking the world around it through its long, sensitive nose and its highly tuned network of whiskers.

The young man lying comfortably beside his campfire, high in the mountains above the foraging rat, noted the conflicting information reaching its senses as it paused to interpret what they were telling it.

Its myopic eyes saw a shoulder of rock reflecting the night sky overhead. Its whiskers warned it of something living, a meat-eater, an enemy. Its memory recognised the dilemma, and decided there was no danger. The big creature was not hunting. Not interested.

The rat scurried underneath the scaled foreleg and picked at the rank remains of the sleeping dragon's last meal, which were lying beside its head.

Not having any desire to cultivate a taste for rotting meat, the man drew back from his communion with the small scavenger, and briefly scanned the thoughts of the sleeping dragon. It was, as the rat had already ascertained, deep in a blissful stupor, its mind sated with contented dreams of easy and plentiful meat.

Content with his reconnoitre, Kierce turned his full attention back to the spread of painted pebbles laid on the ground beside him. He knew the rat was right. Until the dragon's stomach began to send a complaint to its brain, it would remain happily oblivious to the world around it. Dragons were not ambitious creatures.

Neither was his opponent.

Kierce gave a grunt of satisfaction as his companion cautiously placed three more stones on the grid marked out in the dust beside them. The firelight flickered on a picture of a sword, a crown, and a rock: truth, authority and strength. Exactly the stones he would have expected the heir to Arhaios Holding and future Chief of Oreath to play.

"Pay attention, Caras!"

Kierce laid a single stone in the centre of the grid, and lay back with a triumphant smirk. It bore the figure of a man, the piece in the game that turned the value of all the others on their heads.

Caras cursed in exasperation.

"When did you get to be this good, Kierce? I used to be able to beat you at least one time in three."

"Practice," replied Kierce. He scooped up the twelve stones from the ground and tipped them into a leather pouch. "I practice winning."

"You cheat," grumbled Caras.

"Against you? Never."

3

Kierce grinned. He knew very well that Caras still couldn't tell when he was lying and when he was joking.

Caras got to his feet and stacked more wood onto the fire.

"Well, my mind wasn't on the game."

"Any other excuses? Could it just be that the heir to Arhaios is a crap twelve-stones player?"

Caras shot him a baleful look.

"If you mean I spend less time playing it than you, then I'm guilty. Idle sod."

"Much underrated, idleness. You should go in for it more yourself, Caras."

Kierce stretched contentedly on the ground by the fire and pulled the thick furs over his shoulders against the chill of the spring night. He watched the play of the flames in front of him, letting his mind drift. No predators at all to pit his wits against tonight. He didn't need to cheat. Caras was risibly predictable.

His gaze shifted to the friend he had grown up with, ridden the fields and forests of Shehaios with, wrestled and vied with throughout their childhood. They were same age almost to the day, but Caras looked older. It was partly his hair, which had turned a uniform iron grey almost overnight when his parents died a few years back. It was also the worried frown that was beginning to carve a habitual furrow on his broad, blunt face.

Kierce knew what worried him at the moment. They had both been present when the minstrel brought the message to the Holding, the two youngest among the elders gathered to hear the news from the Palace. The announcement of the King's marriage did come as something of a shock, but Kierce still felt Caras was taking the responsibility of his position too seriously.

Just how difficult could it be to take part in a wedding feast?

Kierce rolled onto his back and stared up at the vast original of the faint and distorted map of stars and scudding cloud the rat had seen reflected in the dragon's skin. The title which gave Kierce ti' Gaeroch the right to sit among the elders of the Holding sat more lightly on his shoulders. Since the day four years ago when his father came out second best from an argument with a bear, Kierce was Arhaios's Horsemaster, responsible for the supply and training of the Holding's transport and power supply – the horses for which Oreath province was famous.

He had inherited his father's title earlier than he anticipated, but he had never expected anything else. His mother had died before he was a year old, and from his earliest memories he had lived his father's life, out on the hills and grasslands west of Arhaios among the herds of wild horses, watching and learning their language. When he brought them back to Arhaios, Shaihens trekked for days to barter for them.

Kierce enjoyed his life, and the company of the other creatures who shared the life of the Fair Land. He also liked to make the most of the limited time he spent among his own kind.

He began to contemplate a new calculation. They were three days out of Arhaios; they could reach the Haven in another ten. But it would not be unreasonable to take three weeks on this journey. Possibly more. Another eighteen nights, at least; eighteen Holdings, eighteen warm and hospitable welcomes for the future Lord of Oreath and his companion.

Or ten days camped out in the Shaihen mountains, watching for wildcat and bear. Not to mention the occasional dragon.

He thought it was an adult female. Asleep, certainly, but it may not stay that way.

He looked across at his stolid companion frowning into the fire, the lurid light deepening the strong lines of his face and teasing subtle echoes of its own fierce colours from the day's growth of beard on his chin.

"I think you're making me work unreasonably hard, Caras. Why are we sleeping out here tonight when there's a Holding a few miles north we could have got to before dusk? I could have played against someone capable of giving me a decent game. We could have found … all sorts of entertainment. It's not often I get to see the beauties of our more distant Holdings." He grinned, leaving Caras to interpret "beauties" in whatever way he chose.

"It took us out of our way," said Caras. "I want to get to the Haven. I want to know what's behind this announcement of Rainur's. It makes no sense to me."

"I thought that's why you wanted to visit as many Holdings as you could on the way. Find out what they think here on the borders." Kierce paused reflectively. "Not that they seem to be doing much thinking. They're losing stock to Caiivorian raiders, they've seen hunters who are not Shaihen hunters. But they still think the mountains will protect them. Their strategy makes about as much sense as your twelve-stones tactics, Caras. I suspect you can trust Rainur to be more subtle, at least."

"But now of all times, when we've got Caiivorians raiding our borders as never before, why has Rainur decided to *marry* one?"

Kierce thought he definitely could detect a subtle stirring in the dragon's dreams.

He dropped his voice into a passable imitation of Brynnen the Minstrel's sonorous tones.

"The great eagle brought tales of the peerless beauty of the Princess Cathva from far across the mountains. The King heard the tales, and could know no peace until he had seen such beauty for himself. So he journeyed to the fabled Imperial City— ." He broke off and looked up. "How much do you want to know about the fabled Imperial City?"

Caras just threw him an exasperated glance.

5

"Quite right. Let's get on with the voluptuous beauties of the Princess. Like the sun rising upon the mountains was the face of the Princess Cathva to the King—." He frowned. "Her face. Why does the man look at her face?"

Caras smiled grudgingly.

"It does go on to mention breasts like golden fruit, I think."

"Ripe and perfect, no blemish on her skin. Breasts are all very well. Legs lead in a much more interesting direction. Did he mention her legs?"

"It's not a partnership between a man and a woman, it's an alliance with the Caiivorians," Caras cut in impatiently. "You know it is."

"You mean you've got me to come on this journey on false pretences? The fair Princess Cathva is not more beautiful than the morning sun?"

"By all accounts she is, but it wouldn't really matter if she had a face like the rear end of a dragon. She's a daughter of the Imperial family."

"And there you have it, Caras," said Kierce with a yawn. "He's not marrying a Caiivorian, he's marrying the Caiivorian Emperor's daughter. There's a difference."

"She's still not of the Spirit. She's still a Caiivorian."

Kierce sighed. Caras would not stop gnawing this bone. The image teased him as he let Caras's troubled thoughts ripple over his own mind without touching him.

There was something very dog-like about Caras. It always made him smile. He liked dogs. But he didn't want to be pack leader himself. The weight of responsibility Caras felt resting on his shoulders made Kierce shudder.

He knew very well the real reason they were not enjoying the hospitality of a Holding tonight.

"And you might still be good company," he said lazily. "On the other hand, you might be just the heir to Arhaios."

Caras scowled at him.

"Time we got some sleep," he said, abruptly. "We've a long way to go yet."

Kierce paused, still contemplating the night sky. *Further than you think, Caras.*

Caras thought he already lived in the land of the Spirit; the Fair Land, the Whole Land, the Home of the Free. Kierce could see what went on inside peoples' heads.

"Your duty is to go there, Caras. There's nothing to stop you enjoying yourself on the way."

"That's very easy for you to say," retorted Caras. "Since you don't give a damn."

"I can give a damn without having to worry at it every minute of the day. Worry about it when we reach the Haven. It might look different by then."

"Yes, well. I'm not sure we agree what enjoying ourselves involves, these days, anyway."

"Not sure we ever did." Kierce grinned at his companion. "Stop being such a pompous ass, Caras. Tomorrow we stop at a Holding, agreed?"

"Not if you're going to abuse their hospitality."

"I don't abuse anyone's hospitality. I haven't fought anyone, I haven't insulted anyone, and if I've cheated anyone they haven't found out before we left."

"You know perfectly well what I mean."

"No idea what you're talking about. Fair Elani not satisfying you, Caras?"

"My marriage to Elani is fine," snapped Caras. "It's an arrangement you should try."

Kierce looked mildly surprised.

"Well, I'm always happy to oblige a friend, and you know how much I've always admired Elani—."

"I was referring to marriage. Partnership. Something that lasts longer than one night."

"A fine institution," said Kierce. "You are without doubt a fine institution, Caras."

"Go to sleep," muttered Caras, throwing his furs over himself in disgust.

Kierce smiled. Tomorrow, he would need to determine exactly how close that dragon was. The need to mate was the only desire other than food that could awaken her, and one appetite was much like another to a creature with no imagination. A hungry dragon was a dangerous dragon.

Chapter 2
Encounter with a Dragon

The life of the heir to Arhaios Holding was not a pampered one. Arhaios was a prosperous farming community in the northern foothills of the Shaihen mountains, and had been so for many generations. Its origins were buried somewhere deep in its soil. Its Holder, Caras's grandmother, managed the distribution of its wealth amongst her community; she did not appropriate an undue measure of it to herself and her family.

Nevertheless, Caras ti' Leath was used to the luxury of a roof over his head.

He awoke on a hillside scoured by driving rain to find himself alone. The covers beneath which Kierce had slept were stowed under a rock in a wrapping of oiled cloth. Caras wrung out his own sodden blanket and packed it away disconsolately. Sometimes, it almost seemed as if Kierce could do it on purpose.

He had not chosen Kierce for this journey out of sentiment for their boyhood friendship. The fur that protected Kierce from the cold was proof of his invincibility in this wilderness that was his home for so much of the year. It came from the bear that had taken his father's life.

The tale of how he achieved it was different every time he told it. There were those cynics who put his achievement down to sheer luck – the bear's carcass bore distinct signs of a wolf-kill.

Caras knew Kierce well enough to know the two truths could co-exist. It was a wolf-kill and it was Kierce's kill. Kierce not only understood the creatures he lived among, he seemed able to speak back to them. He used some to help him hunt others, he used their senses to warn him of danger, to alert him to potential food, the presence of water or a treacherous patch of ground. Or a change in the weather.

Caras had grown up with Kierce; he never thought to wonder how he did it. All Shaihens had some such skills, and though it was generally acknowledged that Kierce was in a class of his own, better even than his father, Caras was used to him being quicker and smarter than he was. That was just Kierce. Who else would he ask to guard him from the dangers he would encounter on the mountain route to the King's residence in the Haven?

The Horsemaster returned, clutching a handful of small eggs, while Caras was coaxing life back into the fire.

"Breakfast."

"Thanks." Caras took the proffered eggs. "You might have woken me."

Kierce shrugged.

8

"Awake and wet, asleep and wet, what's the difference?" He glanced across at the two horses huddled grumpily, tail to wind, just below their camp. "The horses agree with me. Precious little shelter and sod all to eat up here."

Caras scowled, and set a pot of water on the fire to boil. He watched it moodily, conscious of the clinging dampness of his garments.

Kierce was right. They would be better to travel lower down, over easier ground, and rest themselves and their horses overnight at local Holdings.

But it was only this journey that had made Caras realise just how much distance there was between the boy who had discovered the world around Arhaios with him and the man he had become. Caras was not at all sure he liked the man Kierce had become. Not in the company of other human beings, at any rate. Though he had to admit that there never were any upsets or arguments, Kierce always won the games of chance and the girls always smiled at him.

Always smiled at him. Caras couldn't understand the attraction. He would not have described Kierce as a handsome man. He conceded the possibility that the mobile face and the dark eyes full of humour held some appeal, but the Horsemaster was small and slight, hardly what Caras imagined a woman would look for in her perfect man. Unlike the tall, muscular heir to Arhaios.

It was possible his disapproval was less outraged morality and more sheer jealousy.

Without any discussion of the matter, they descended to the high pasture just above the tree line to continue their journey. The rain cleared as the day progressed, and by afternoon they were riding through spring sunshine, the green of the new year's grass sparkling beneath their horses' hooves. Caras's mood improved with the weather. They had crossed out of their own region of Oreath into neighbouring Mervecc, and if they kept up a steady pace they should be at the Haven within ten days. The air was sharp and clear after the rain, the hillside jewelled with flowers and dotted with the sheep of the mountain Holdings. An occasional hare bolted at their approach. The Fair Land stretched away around them.

Kierce was riding ahead as usual, his heavy travelling cloak disguising his shape so that horse and man looked more than ever like one dark creature moving across the bright hillside. Caras felt the sudden hesitance in his own horse's pace at the same moment Kierce checked and cautioned to Caras to do the same.

Caras gave him a questioning look, and Kierce pointed towards a tooth-edged rock a few paces ahead of them, lying among a heap of other rocks beside the path they were following. A long, low finger of it stretched out in front of Kierce's horse. Caras frowned at it, and gradually began to see that it was not a rock. It was the same texture and pale gold colour as a rock, but it was in fact a twelve-foot long somnolent dragon. The obstacle in Kierce's path was its tail.

Kierce dismounted and climbed across the boulders scattered around the dragon. Caras watched anxiously. It was notoriously hard to awaken a Shaihen dragon, but Caras would still have preferred to put some distance between himself and the monster. He couldn't tell when it might feel peckish.

Kierce crouched down beside the two-foot long jaw and slid his hand beneath the dragon's head.

"Kierce—," began Caras.

"Come here," said Kierce. "I'll show you something." He smiled at Caras's hesitance. "It's quite safe. I'll warn you if she's about to wake up."

Caras reluctantly left his horse and approached the dragon. As he got closer, he saw that Kierce held a sac of soft, swollen tissue suspended beneath the dragon's throat.

"Now, if you were a male dragon, the scent held in here would drive you mad with desire." Kierce glanced at Caras and grimaced. "Even you, Caras. From the state of this one, she's going to send a wake-up call to every male dragon in about a ten-mile area the minute she stirs. They only do it once about every five years, but unfortunately…"

"This one's five-years old?"

"More like fifty, but you get my point. I don't think we really want an army of sexually aroused dragons following us, do we?"

"When's she likely to stir?" asked Caras in alarm.

"Can't tell for sure. Could be another couple of hours, could be a day or more. Either way—." Kierce drew a small earthenware bottle from a pocket hung at his belt, and squeezed the dragon's scent glands carefully over it. A glutinous secretion dropped slowly into the bottle.

"Isn't that going to wake her?" Caras enquired tentatively.

"Let me concentrate, Caras," said Kierce carefully. "If I spill this, I'll have every male dragon for ten miles in amorous pursuit of me."

When his task was completed, he moved slowly away from the dragon. He picked up a handful of wet mud from a nearby puddle and packed it into the neck of the bottle before driving the stopper home.

"That should do it. Shall we go before she wakes up?"

They remounted, and continued their journey. A mile or two further on, however, the horses began to show signs of agitation. Kierce uttered a mild expletive.

"What?" queried Caras, with an uncomfortable feeling that he knew. Sleeping dragons were something of a joke. Wakeful ones were a very different matter, and the scent of the two men and their horses was undoubtedly still fresh in this one's nose. Dragons were not fast or cunning hunters, but they were persistent. They only gave up if they came across some carrion on the way which was sufficient for their purposes. Other predators seldom argued with a dragon.

"She's woken up," Kierce confirmed. "I knew she wasn't far off, but I was hoping we'd have a bit longer than this."

"Is it just her? Or does she have suitors?"

"Just her." Kierce sent his horse into a canter. "I think."

"You think!" exclaimed Caras, following him.

Kierce only laughed.

Caras looked back across his shoulder. He couldn't see anything. He allowed his horse to stretch out across the mountain turf, catching up with Kierce.

"How do you know it's the dragon?"

"Can't you smell it?" replied Kierce with a grimace. "The horses can!"

Caras threw him a startled look as the sleek form of Kierce's black stallion shot suddenly away from him.

"Enjoy the journey!" yelled Kierce.

Suddenly, the savage need to match Kierce surged over all other considerations. Caras drove his horse forwards, leaning low on its neck. The whipping mane tangled in his hands; he breathed air filled with warm, pungent sweat. He felt the power ripple through the horse's body as it strained to catch up with its companion, and he was back in his youth, following Kierce's skills and intuition, revelling in the ride into a world that, compared to Kierce, he only half understood.

He was almost level.

"Tired of this yet?" Kierce shouted.

"My horse soon will be."

Kierce flung him a disparaging glance.

"Too much weight to carry on his back."

Nevertheless, he checked the pace a little, racing alongside Caras. They could only outrun the dragon for as long as the horses could keep running. Not long, at this pace.

"What are we going to do?" asked Caras. "You ever fought a dragon?"

"No," replied Kierce cheerfully. "Don't think I'd recommend it. Let's try inviting it to dinner."

He turned downhill towards the dark line of trees below. Both the sure-footed Arhaien horses took the broken ground in their stride, and they reached the forest with Caras barely a head behind Kierce. Once they plunged into the tangled gloom of greenery, however, Caras had lost the contest. Kierce continued at barely diminished speed, twisting and ducking beneath branches as if he ran on his own feet and threaded his own body through the crowding trees. After one salutary whack in the face, which almost unhorsed him, Caras took it somewhat more cautiously.

By the time he caught up with Kierce's horse, Kierce was no longer with it. Caras checked in the slight clearing where the black stallion stood blowing from the run, and turned aside. He knew what Kierce was doing.

He took a spear from the pack behind his saddle, led both horses into the shadow of the trees at one side of the clearing, and waited.

Conscious of the pursuing dragon, the moments seemed to pass extremely slowly, but it was not an altogether unpleasant tension. With the sharp tang of pine in his nostrils and eyes and ears awake to the sounds of the forest around him, Caras was suddenly aware how long it had been since he last hunted with Kierce. He had forgotten how it felt.

He heard a crashing through the undergrowth and readied himself, the spear poised in his hand. He had no doubt that Kierce had already killed, and his pride demanded he too make a contribution.

A group of small deer broke out of the trees and bounded across the clearing right in front of him. It was an easy shot, and he had no difficulty bringing down a good-sized buck. As the rest of the herd fled into the forest, the black stallion raised his head and trotted off purposefully in the opposite direction. Caras let him go. It was more than his life was worth to interfere between Kierce and his horse.

He dismounted to retrieve the deer, and he was still in the process of doing so when the black stallion reappeared through the woods with Kierce on his back and a deer carcass across his neck.

"Oh, you remembered what to do with that weapon, then," Kierce greeted him, with a satisfied smile.

Caras ignored the jibe.

"Where's the best place to leave them?"

"Back along the track. The more forest between us and the dragon the better. I want plenty of other prey distracting her next time she wakes up, or she'll follow us to the next Holding – and I don't think that would make us very popular."

"Right." Caras hefted his own kill onto the horse, and turned back the way they had come. "How far?"

"Until we meet her coming the other way. She won't go for a moving target with fresh meat under her nose. Dragons never take anything but the easy option."

They travelled single file back through the trees. They were nearly at the edge of the forest again when a tremendous roar, pitched so low they felt rather than heard it, shook the ground beneath their feet.

Caras halted.

"Far enough?" he suggested.

Kierce paused and sniffed.

"Probably."

Caras unloaded his deer and dragged it forwards between the trees. As he returned to the horses and Kierce deposited his kill with Caras's, the dragon materialised through the gloom of the forest. Both men paused and watched it, Caras marvelling that such a huge creature could be so difficult to see. It appeared almost out of nowhere, its semi-transparent skin rippling with the changing colours of the woodland around it as it headed towards them at its characteristic, indefatigable lumbering run.

Dragon skin was a delicate membrane covering the rock-hard carapace that protected their bulky bodies. Caras had once seen an image, brought by a Caiivorian trader, of a man wearing a cloak of dragon-skin, his arms outstretched so that he looked as if he bore iridescent wings on his back. It was extraordinary, but it made no great sense to Caras. Wings or not, the man could not fly. Dragon skin was fragile, translucent and as useless for practical clothing as it was for wings – it turned brittle and lost all its colour within a few days of removal from the dragon's body. Since dragon meat was reputed to be as foul a thing as anyone could wish to taste and dragons were only found in Shehaios, it was also difficult to obtain. Killing a creature for its skin alone was not an act that made any sense to a Shaihen. Life was taken to sustain life. Not for any other reason.

"Kierce…" Caras suggested deferentially, since Kierce was still standing beside the deer carcasses watching the dragon.

"She won't be remotely interested in me —." began Kierce and broke off with a sudden exclamation of horror as the dragon opened its long snout to display its magnificent set of ridged teeth.

A noise like an earthquake surged over them, resonated through their bones and shook their teeth in their heads. Kierce recoiled from the dragon, his face contorted in disgust. Caras turned his head aside as the reek of the dragon's breath reached him. A smile began to break across his face as he looked back at Kierce, stumbling towards his horse, choking and retching.

Kierce so rarely misjudged an animal, Caras found it reassuringly human that he could still get it wrong. Even his horse edged back from him in disbelief, throwing up his head and curling his top lip at the appalling stench that accompanied his master.

"I can do without comments from you," muttered Kierce, swinging himself onto the horse's back. "That's the last time I invite a dragon to dinner."

They turned away from the feeding dragon, Caras shaking with laughter.

Kierce regarded him with some chagrin.

"Careful, Caras. Anyone might think you were starting to enjoy the journey."

Caras shook his head.

"It's too long since we've done this."

"Speak for yourself."

"I was," Caras admitted. "Nothing like the threat of being eaten to make you appreciate being alive."

Kierce grunted.

"So long as you're not a deer."

"Or a dragon," added Caras, reflectively and then, in answer to Kierce's wry look, "Wake up, gorge yourself on whatever falls over in front of you and go back to sleep again? Not much of a life, is it?"

Kierce laughed. "And foul breath to go with it. No Caras, when you put it like that, it isn't much of a life!"

By the time they had made their way through the forest and picked up the direction of their journey again, the day was beginning to draw to a close. They came over a ridge above the tree line once more, and found themselves looking down on a small huddle of yellow stone buildings grouped around a yard. Smoke drifted from a hole in the turf roof, forming a peaceful and inviting scene in the cool of the waning day.

"Now with a bit of luck," said Kierce. "There's our dinner."

"If they let you in. You still stink of dragon."

"Well, maybe they'll throw me a haunch or two through the door. It's the only way I'll catch any more meat until it wears off. Every creature for miles is going to run from me." He turned towards the Holding. "Come on, let's try our luck."

They rode down the slope towards the Holding. It still looked very quiet. It occurred to Caras that in most Holdings at this time of day there would be people returning from fields or folds, people attending to the domestic stock before the night fell. Kierce evidently shared his misgivings. A few yards short of the Holding, he came to a halt.

"Something doesn't smell right here."

"That's you."

"Apart from me." Kierce hesitated. "Stay here, I'll take a look."

Caras shrugged. "Take a look if you like, I'll go on to the house, see if it's anything we can help with."

Without waiting for Kierce to reply, he rode forwards and dismounted outside the farmstead's boundary wall. As he entered the yard he saw a dark-haired girl, just old enough to be a woman, come out of the house carrying an empty basket. Caras strode cheerfully towards her.

"Good evening, my lady. We're travelling to the Haven, and wondered if we might impose upon the hospitality of your Holder for the night— ."

He broke off as the girl dropped the basket, grabbed his shoulders and pushed him away.

"Go!" she whispered, urgently. "Get out of here – you're in great danger!"

Caras fell back a step in surprise, then put his hand on the girl's arm.

"Why? What danger?"

She threw a distracted glance across her shoulder. Caras followed her gaze, and saw someone else emerge from the house behind her.

Caras was considered a big man by Shaihen standards, but the figure that loomed behind the girl was a head taller than he was and looked twice as broad. His long and tangled fair hair hung in knotted braids and he wore plaid wrapped around his loins beneath a loose-fitting woollen shirt. Caras hardly needed to see the tattooed imitation of a wildcat's stripes on the man's forehead and nose to know that he was looking at a Caiivorian tribesman who belonged on the other side of the mountains.

The Caiivorian started as he saw Caras. He was half undressed, armed only with a heavy dagger not much different to Caras's hunting knife. He drew it instantly. Caras began to back away, taking the girl by the hand.

"Come on!"

"It's too late…"

The girl hung back. Caras glanced over his shoulder and saw Kierce ride to a halt outside the yard entrance.

The Caiivorian shouted something, and started towards them.

Caras clamped his hand firmly around the girl's.

"Come on!"

He turned and ran for the gate, pulling her with him. He was only half-aware of the hunting spear flying past him as he fled, but he heard the Caiivorian's roar of pain and fury. Out of the yard, he swept the girl onto his horse, and leapt up behind her. Only then did he look back.

The Caiivorian lay on the ground screaming curses at them, Kierce's spear through his thigh. Other men of his kind were tumbling through the door of the Holder's house.

Caras drove his heels into his horse and let it run. He was aware of Kierce loosing another spear before he turned to follow, and then both of them were away as fast as the horses could carry them across the darkening hillside into the safety of the mountains.

He wrapped his arm around the girl to keep her secure.

"Do they have horses?"

She shook her head. "A couple of ponies. Nothing to match these."

"The Spirit protects us."

They let the horses gallop until they could run no further, then turned and began to climb. There was no sign of pursuit, but they pushed on until the weary horses began to founder on the steep, broken ground.

Exhausted, they halted in the shelter of a rocky outcrop. Spatters of rain came down on the gathering dusk. It was going to be another cheerless night. Caras dismounted and helped the girl down. As Kierce swung off his horse in front of him, Caras saw him stumble as if one leg had given way beneath him.

"It's nothing," snapped Kierce, before he could speak. "Do what you can with this place. I'll see if they've followed us. Don't light a fire until I come back – just in case."

He turned back on foot down the way they had come. Caras watched him with some concern, aware that he still seemed to be favouring one leg. By the time the gloom swallowed him up, however, he looked as if he was moving with his usual assured agility.

Caras turned back to the girl. She was shivering – whether from fear or cold he couldn't tell – and her breath was coming in shuddering gasps just short of sobs. He fetched a fur from his pack.

"Caras ti' Leath, of Arhaios," he said, taking her hand gently as he wrapped the warm covering around her. "Mervecc is wilder than I remember it."

"Lord Caras!"

He had never heard his name uttered with such a weight of anguish and relief. She sank down onto the ground, tears welling in her eyes, her hand locked on his forearm.

"Oh, Lord Caras, you don't know what's happened to us."

Caras folded her into his arms as she gave in to the sobs wracking her body.

"It's all right," he said, soothingly. "We'll look after you. You're all right now."

He held her while she wept as he had never heard anyone weep before, let alone one so young. She wept for the broken heart of her Holding, her family and herself, all of them ravaged by the men who had swept down on them from the wilderness they had believed all their lives to be their protection.

In stumbling, half-coherent words she described to Caras the killing of her mother, grandparents, siblings and cousins. The Holder's pregnant wife and her elderly parents were the only adults in the house when the Caiivorians fell on it. Everyone else was out on the land, about their work. Lasa, the girl he had rescued, was the eldest of the children and the only one they spared. Caras did not need her to tell him why, nor how they had used her.

Kierce returned while Caras still sat with her, but he did not interrupt, even to reproach him for the rudimentary attention he had paid to their horses. He joined them silently and set about building a fire, from which Caras deduced that they were out of immediate danger.

The girl told them how her father and uncle came running back to Prassan, their Holding, as soon as they realised what was happening there; how they gathered their people and attempted to drive off the Caiivorians. She told him how frightened she had been that they would all be slaughtered as those they were vainly attempting to rescue had been. The Holder lost two more of his people in the unequal fight before he cut his losses and fled back into the hills. She did not say what she had felt as she watched them leave, knowing what fate they left her to.

Kierce brought them a meagre meal made from the grain and dried meat they carried with them, augmented with an infusion of herbs. Caras's nose also detected a modest contribution from the leather bottle of distilled malt barley liquor, which Kierce usually guarded with single-minded jealousy.

"We'll take you to them," said Kierce, handing her the bowl of hot broth.

"Do you know where to find them?" asked Caras.

Lasa dipped a spoon into the bowl and stirred it listlessly. She nodded.

"There's a cave in the hills. When we're up on the high slopes with the stock, we sometimes shelter there. People used to live there. It has pictures in it—." She broke off, and collected herself. "I think that's where they would go."

Caras hesitated. A cave in the mountains hardly seemed a fit refuge for a girl who had suffered what Lasa had suffered, but neither was this wet hillside. He couldn't trust that the next farm they came across would be in friendly hands either, and they were still several days from Mervecc Holding.

"At least she would be with her people," said Kierce. "We can't take Prassan back, Caras. Not just the two of us."

"How many are still at your Holding?" asked Caras.

"Too many to fight! Please, Lord Caras. They will kill you!"

Lasa gripped his arm fiercely. He read the renewed rush of fear in her eyes, and knew it was fear for him. The title of Oreath was one of the greatest and oldest seats on the Holders' Council; he was well aware that Lasa knew who he was, but he was touched that she thought he might be brave, or foolhardy, enough to hurl himself blindly on a Caiivorian sword.

"It's all right," he reassured her. "But I need to know what your people are up against. How much help they'll need."

The girl released his arm in some relief.

"There are about twenty or thirty most of the time. Sometimes more. There were more when they first came. There are only ten there all the time, the ones who—." Once again, she had to break off and collect herself. "The rest come and go. And there's a boy, he's there all the time too. I think he's a kind of captive, I'm not sure. He's Caiivorian, he used to tell me what to do, but they … they were always hitting him, too, and shouting commands at him, though he … it seemed as if he had … grown used to it. They hit him, he hit me. But at least he didn't—."

She broke off and clamped her teeth over her lower lip.

"Eat," said Kierce, gently. "No-one's going to hurt you any more."

She looked at Kierce uncertainly. Caras watched the fear ease from her face as her eyes met Kierce's eyes.

Even this girl smiled at him. She had no doubt heard of him. The songs which conveyed news between the Holdings of Shehaios sang the praises of Kierce ti' Gaeroch's unsurpassed skill in his calling, his affinity with the mountains, his ability to sense danger and his skill as a hunter.

Kierce smiled back, the man the wolf cubs played with.

"The victory is in surviving, Lasa. Eat."

"That … scent … Have you … ?"

"It's very difficult to slay a dragon, and kind of pointless. You can't eat it, you can't wear its skin. I didn't kill it, Lady Lasa, I fed it. I'm afraid dragons have no manners."

He moved back and laid a hand on Caras's shoulder.

"Though more, perhaps, than some Caiivorian tribes," he murmured. "You'd better stay with her. You make her feel safe. Tomorrow we'll take her to her people."

"And then we'll take this tale to the King at the Haven," said Caras. He tossed the dregs of the herb tea onto the fire where they hissed angrily back at him. "And to his Caiivorian Queen. I'd like to know just what it is Rainur is marrying."

Chapter 3
On the Edges

The icy wind howling through the caves sheltering Prassan's people mocked Caras's attempt to sleep. It had been a day's long, damp climb through the mist to find the fugitives, and he lay half awake in the darkness feeling the unforgiving nature of this land in his bones. The songs of the people who lived in the mountains were full of flight and survival. They lived here, on the edges, because it was where they had ended up.

Shehaios was a rich land, and even here they could find good living. But not without their Holding; their crops and stock, their shelter, and each other.

He rose with the first hint of grey light which filtered into the cave, to find one of the women already tending the cooking fire, and Kierce cradling an earthenware beaker of something that smelled hot, flowery and good.

"How do you do it?" grumbled Caras.

Kierce smiled.

"She merely took pity on a soft lowlander. There's a potful, I'm sure she'll spare you some." He hesitated. "It's about all they can spare us. There's nothing we can do here. We should move on."

"I intend to. The sooner the better."

Kierce's words tipped the balance of indecision that had dominated Caras's sleepless night. His instinct was to stay and help these people, but it was not the duty of the heir to Oreath to get killed in a border squabble. The best thing he could do for them was to take their story as quickly as possible to the man who could do something to help them – Gascon, Chief of Mervecc. And Rainur, King of Shehaios.

Caras did not share Kierce's confidence in Rainur. The people south of Shehaios's golden mountains were alarming and unfathomable strangers; making an alliance with them was an alarming and unfathomably strange thing for his King to do. It was not a sudden, magical love affair, he was very well aware of that. King Rainur, his brother Jagus and his sister Loia had all lived in the south while their father was King. Loia died there, and Caras had heard Jagus tell Loia's tragic story along with many other alarming tales of cruelty and injustice from the mighty Caiivorian Empire of the Sacred Union, that stretched away southwards beyond his imagination.

The Shaihens' King was neither a warrior nor their ruler. Shaihens were ruled by the Spirit. Nothing else. They answered only to life itself. All Caras really knew about the people of the south was that they killed each other. They always had, they probably always would.

He could not see how or why his own people should have anything to do with them.

He gained the cook's permission and ladled the scented tea into a cup.

"What do you think, Kierce?"

"This is very good tea," said Kierce.

"About all this!"

Kierce shrugged. "We saw the signs. Now we see the kill. The Caiivorians are not just coming, they're here. As for the ones we'll find in the Haven ..." He grinned. "I can't really tell you if the glorious Cathva is more beautiful than the morning sun until I've seen her, can I?"

"Kierce, do you ever think about anything else—?"

"You ask me why Rainur's marrying her," interrupted Kierce. "I'm beginning to ask myself why she's marrying him."

Caras floundered for an answer, and not only because Kierce was taking the conversation seriously. It was difficult to grasp the idea that anyone should not wish to move from Caiivor to Shehaios – Arhaios was the centre of the world and Shehaios a warm pool of life around it.

"She comes from the heart of the Empire," continued Kierce. "From the Imperial Royal Family, no less. I always got the impression they regarded Shehaios as beyond the edge of the world. That's why the Empire never conquered us. Nothing to do with heroic Shaihen resistance. They just never got around to it. Couldn't see us past the Caiivorian tribes south of our mountains. We didn't argue with them, they didn't argue with us." He regarded Caras with dry amusement. Caras was rather fond of the idea of heroic Shaihen resistance. "So why is this pampered Royal Princess marrying so far beneath her? What does she – or more to the point, I suspect, her father – want from Shehaios?"

"Well – what is it?"

"I was asking you," said Kierce, carelessly. He drained the tea. "I don't know. As I said, I'll wait till I see Cathva. I'm just going to check on the horses."

He left Caras brooding over his tea and went outside into the chill dawn.

A few minutes later, Caras jettisoned his drink as he heard Kierce's voice raised in a sharp challenge. It was echoed by one of Prassan's men, and then one of the women. Caras shot out of the cave and saw Kierce sliding and stumbling down the steep path in hot pursuit of a figure dressed in furs and plaid. For a Caiivorian, he was small, little taller than Kierce. He threw a wild glance back over his shoulder, and the face Caras glimpsed was that of a child, perhaps twelve or thirteen years old.

Caras started after them as Prassan's lookouts came leaping down from their higher perch. The Caiivorian boy had a head start on all of them, and he moved over the steep terrain faster than Kierce. He reached the flatter ground below the last rocky climb to the cave and ran for the hollow where they had left their horses. Vaulting the crumbled stone wall, he snatched loose the tether of the nearest horse and swung himself onto its back.

Kierce scrambled down the last of the rocks as the boy turned the horse, cleared the wall and set off across the rough hillside. Caras paused in his descent, knowing the chase was over. The horse the boy had picked was Red Sky, Kierce's stallion.

Kierce came to a standstill. He watched the fleeing Caiivorian for a moment, stilling himself, steadying his breathing. Then he threw back his head and whinnied.

The call shook through his body, focussing his mind on the running horse. Caras, and the people of Prassan, faded into the background as the strength of the animal flowed through him. His muscles flexed to the jarring of pounding hooves. He caught the rhythm of the reaching strides, felt the stranger on his back; unwieldy, alarming, a rank scent in his nostrils. He felt the stallion's pace hesitate at the familiar call of the *not-horse,* his master.

Kierce's human mind closed with the horse's, and drew him to a halt. He felt the boy's heels thump frantically against the horse's flanks, his hands jigging on Sky's neck as if he could push him on. Torn between conflicting commands, Red Sky plunged forwards.

Kierce called again, and felt the instant response, the violent sideways swerve of the horse's body. Red Sky flung up his head. Kierce's frame shook a third time with a shrill equine cry, this time resonating from the stallion's throat.

He felt, rather than saw, the boy slide off his plunging mount.

Danger – enemy – defend!

The stallion swung on his haunches and faced the threat to a herd that did not exist.

Kierce saw through the horse's eyes as the boy checked in front of him. He saw him feint to one side, and both Kierce and Sky mirrored the movement instantly.

A zephyr of the Caiivorian boy's fear blew across Kierce's mind, sending a shudder down his spine. He tried to close it out, but he was aware of it now.

He hurled the sense of threat into the instincts of the horse, those sparks of neural energy humans called emotion. Sky's upper lip curled back to bare his teeth, his ears flattened against his head. The boy dodged; the horse dodged, breath blowing hard through his flared nostrils. He twisted in half-rears, every sense focussed on his enemy, looking for a chance to strike.

The boy's terror bounded towards Kierce like a boulder crashing down a mountain. All he could see was some uncanny link between the will of the man and the behaviour of the horse, and a million superstitious explanations flooded his imagination. Kierce braced himself to hurl back the images. He felt the urge to flee tugging at his own instincts. If he channelled that fear to the horse, Sky would be halfway to Arhaios before he could even begin to get back in control.

Sky stood up on his hind legs, forefeet stabbing the air.

The boy lost his footing and fell face down in front of him, shrieking for mercy.

Kierce instantly switched the messages he was sending into the stallion's brain. Sky came back down, and stood scraping nervously at the ground with one hoof. Broadcasting calm and reassurance, Kierce began to walk towards him.

He was aware of Caras coming up behind him, but he didn't take his eyes off the horse. Ignoring the prostrate Caiivorian, he stood for a moment beside the trembling animal with his head lowered. As Sky's panic receded, Kierce reached out to stroke him, his expert fingers grooming the sweating black neck like another horse's teeth. Sky's nose sank down slowly, until Kierce could reach his favourite spot, behind his ears. The horse's soft breath warmed Kierce's own ear, and he felt a delicate nibbling pull the tail of hair tied at the back of his head.

Kierce pushed the horse's head away gently, and as he turned he saw Caras haul the shaking Caiivorian to his feet.

Words and sobs tumbled incomprehensibly out of his mouth. Kierce frowned, trying to catch their meaning.

"Don't let the devil take me, please, don't let him have my soul, please don't let him take my soul!"

And so on. He spoke in the common language, heavily accented. Kierce knew the words, but he struggled to understand them. One thing he was not going to do was to look for the answer in the boy's mind. The terror swilling about in it was not something he wanted to go anywhere near. He stayed loosely joined to the reassuringly familiar mind of the horse beside him.

Devil. He sought for a translation into his native language. *Devil – darkness – unknown.* It didn't help him much. There was little unknown in Kierce's world. He had grown up protected by a father who had taught him to understand the creatures around them, not to fear them. He had learned respect for claws and teeth, of course, and even his father had been wary of the night hunters, but that was not fear as this boy knew fear. What *devil* was it he was so afraid of?

Caras seemed equally baffled by the babble. He gave his captive a shake.

"Stop talking gibberish boy, or I'll conjure a *devil* to catch your tongue."

It was the kind of glib threat Caras would have scolded his children with. Kierce threw up a hasty mental barrier at the look of abject terror the boy turned in his direction. He didn't seem scared of what they were going to do to him so much as what he thought they had already done to him.

He saw Caras look round as one of Prassan's women joined them.

"What do you want to do with him?"

For an answer, the woman drew her knife.

"No!" said Caras. "He's a child, you can't just cut him down in cold blood. You don't even know if he's with the men who raided your Holding."

The boy twisted in his grasp towards the woman. He tore at his coat, struggling to bare his chest.

"Kill me!" he cried.

Caras held him tight and the boy closed his eyes in terror.

"Don't let the enchanter take my soul. Let me die. Let me go. Please, my lord, I beg you, show mercy!"

"Do you know what he's talking about?" asked Caras.

"Shaihen magic," said the woman, shortly. "They've no idea what it means." She lowered the knife. "I don't think you've met many Caiivorians, have you, Lord Caras?"

Caras shook his head.

"Yesterday I met my third, I think. The others were traders, but they rarely get as far as Arhaios."

"Well, I don't think I've met a Horsemaster as impressive as your Lord Kierce. I have to say his reputation is justified, but to these savages … We meet these strange, ignorant people all the time when we go to market in Mervecc. They think themselves very clever, yet they don't seem to understand the simplest of things. Like how we speak with other creatures. They seem to think it's all done by some malevolent, mystical force that they can't understand. The King is mad to be marrying one of them, they are all profoundly stupid. Tell him I said so, Lord Caras."

"I will. And I think I might take this wretch with me to tell it."

The woman hesitated.

"He knows where we're hiding. We can't let him go."

"Oh, I don't think he'll go far if he has an evil spirit guarding him. And if I know Kierce, the idea of playing the *devil* until we get to the Haven will suit him down to the ground."

The mention of his name reminded Kierce with a jolt that he belonged with the people who were talking. He smiled a little grimly to himself. He could see from his companion's face that Caras liked this idea, and once Caras had an idea in his head, there was little prospect of shifting it.

He gave a slight sigh at the thought of containing that immensity of fear. But they had to do something with the child; he was a danger to Prassan.

"What was it he was scared of?" asked Caras.

"The enchanter," said the woman. "It's their name for the Magician."

An alarm sounded in Kierce's head. He did indeed belong with these people, and this was the very reason he rarely risked such an overt display of his mental abilities. Once they were recognised, he knew responsibilities would be foisted onto him.

Of course Caras had no idea. He never did.

"I doubt they'd use it to Lord Turloch's face," he said. "I wouldn't." He glowered down at his prisoner. "Do you hear, boy? Run from me and the enchanter will flay your soul like tanned leather."

The boy whimpered and cried again for mercy. He scrabbled at his shirt, pulling it open to reveal a tattoo of a flame inside a circle, marking the centre of his chest like a target. Caras seized his shoulders.

"No killing. But no betraying these people to your savage friends." He forced the boy to turn and look at Kierce. "You see him? You understand?"

The boy seemed to dissolve into jelly. Caras was holding him upright; Kierce could see that if he were to let go, the child would fall in a formless heap at his feet. Kierce's hand, still resting on Sky's neck, began to tremble. He snatched it away, flexing his fist.

"Don't bother to ask me, will you," he said, tersely. "That's enough, Caras. The stupid boy believes it."

"He's meant to believe it."

Kierce felt a shadow fall across his face. He looked up abruptly.

Above them in the grey sky, the sun caught a flash of gold off the plumage of a huge bird, flying at enormous height. Kierce glanced at Caras. He was gazing up at the sky, his mouth open in astonishment. He had never really believed it existed, either. The young Caiivorian in his grasp looked from his captors to the mighty bird overhead, and fell once more to his knees.

So, he could see it, too.

Kierce knew what they were looking at. Nothing else was that size or that blazing, red-gold colour. It could only be a phoenix, semi-mythical symbol of Shaihen magic.

According to the stories, it was only ever supposed to appear in the presence of the Lord High Magician of Shehaios; but as usual with Shaihen stories, it was hard to tell reality from the imagination of generations of storytellers.

A shiver of foreboding touched him. What storyteller could send him such a signal but the master storyteller, the creator of illusions, the Holder of Shaihen magic? Kierce knew the power of his mind was more than other men held. He had spent so long believing he could escape the inevitable, it filled him with dismay to think that the summons might have come.

He watched until the golden figure was lost in the brilliance of the sun, following it long after Caras closed his eyes against the dazzling glare.

"No," he answered the question in Caras's mind with unaccustomed sobriety. "I have never seen one before."

"What?" said the woman from Prassan, who had not taken her eyes off the Caiivorian captive, nor put away the knife in her hand. "What were you looking at?"

"Didn't you see it?"

The woman shook her head with a slight frown of irritation.

"I was watching this wretch."

Caras looked at Kierce with concern.

"Does it … is it … significant?"

Kierce forced himself to smile, and gestured towards the boy huddled on the turf at their feet.

"If you think so, you'd better get down there with him." He caught the Caiivorian's arm and hauled him to his feet. The Caiivorian choked off a scream as Kierce touched him, and Kierce released him quickly, thrusting him back towards Caras.

"If you want to live, you'd better do as Lord Caras tells you, boy," he instructed, gruffly, and walked away.

Chapter 4
The Princess

The Gate to Shehaios was a pass through the heights set towards the western end of the towering sweep of green, gold and white that made up the mountain range marking the border between Shehaios and Caiivor. The road that led to it wound up from the swamps and forests of the north Caiivorian plains in a twisting ascent of some two thousand feet in the space of a few miles.

The snows of the higher peaks still towered over the road when it reached the top, where two iron-bound oak portals which looked as if they had been made by giants marked the entrance to the Fair Land. They stood permanently open, watched over benignly by a small fortress set into the mountainside above them. Beyond that, the road plunged into Shehaios through a sheer-sided chasm, nearly a hundred feet deep, covered by a lofty, naturally formed roof of translucent golden slate. Sometimes, it lit the road in a golden glow. At dawn, early in the year, when the sunlight refracted through the crystals of rock at the right angle, it split into a rainbow shower of colour.

The heavy ox-cart bearing King Rainur's betrothed through this spectacular accident of nature lumbered to a halt at the peremptory command of its occupant. Princess Cathva pushed open the narrow door of the stuffy travelling cabin, stepped outside and stood looking in awe at the world around her.

Her closest friend, ally and confidante, her slave-woman Tilsey, climbed down behind her and smiled at the expression on her young mistress's face. Tilsey was a Shaihen. She was coming home.

"I told you it was," she said.

"What?" said Cathva.

"Beautiful."

"It's more than beautiful." Cathva spread her arms and watched the colours dance on the rich sheen of her travelling robe. "It's like magic."

"Yes," said Tilsey.

"And it's mine," breathed Cathva.

"You belong here," said Tilsey, gently.

Cathva didn't hear her. She was watching the light rippling on the armour of her advance guard as they caught up with the unscheduled halt. She had not dared believe Shehaios was what Tilsey and Rainur told her it was. She liked to think of herself as a student of beauty, but she knew enough to know there was no such place as the Fair Land. Shaihens were minstrels, notorious for exaggerated claims and overblown language. They could speak the same tongue as the rest of the Empire well enough, but they still managed to use more words and more ways of pronouncing those words than anyone else could be bothered with.

The contrast between the rain swept wastes of the north Caiivorian realms she had just travelled through and the clean, soaring grandeur of the mountains made her breathe again. The easy, if slightly eccentric, welcome of the Shaihen guards at the border fortress eased her growing fear that she had made the most dreadful mistake deciding Rainur was an acceptable solution to the unfortunate requirement for a husband. Cathva's opinion of the feuding warbands of Northern Caiivor was much the same as Caras's – the wars they waged against each other seemed to her a foolish and brutal means of achieving what was achieved in the Imperial City of Vordeith with poisoned words and a discrete dagger here and there. She had begun to have the most terrible fear that Shehaios was going to be just another squabbling kingdom. But no. She was standing in a rainbow. This was what she was to be Queen of.

"It's mine," she repeated in delight. She turned to Tilsey, light and graceful – even in her child-like delight, Cathva never lost the perfect poise and bearing of an Imperial Princess. "I can't wait to see the Palace. Tell me I won't be disappointed, Tilsey. It's not another of those grim damp bastions we've been enduring for the last month?"

Tilsey smiled. "It's certainly not that. But neither is it the Emperor's Palace at Vordeith. It's … Shaihen, my lady. You will learn what that means, after you've been here a while."

"I can see what it means," said Cathva, turning her face upwards to let the colour play across her closed eyelids. "And it's mine."

"We had better move on, my lady, to reach Mervecc by nightfall," said Tilsey. "It's still three days travelling to the Haven."

Cathva could see the captain of her bodyguard riding back towards her. Orcen was more nervous of her progress through these barbaric territories than she was. She climbed back into the fetid coach and sat gazing through its small window as the oxen took up the strain. It was going to be all right. She had played her hand well. Her marriage was going to leave her more powerful, not less – normally a queen would not expect to hold any power except her ability to bear heirs, but Princess Cathva did not see herself as a normal woman. Princess Cathva was her father's favourite, she had sat by the Emperor's feet and told him things his advisors and male courtiers could not tell him, as her mother had done until she lost the Great Man's favour. Cathva would not make that mistake. For as long as she retained the ear of the Great Man, she knew she was as powerful as any husband.

Cathva had moulded herself with great skill to her father's ideal. She never voiced an opinion on matters on which the Emperor would have considered it inappropriate for her to hold an opinion, and in her appearance she was everything a young woman of the Imperial Family should be. She was small and well formed, with delicate features that would enable her to retain a child-like innocence for many years yet. She knew every device of paint and clothing to enhance her natural beauty to full effect, just as she knew how to give her deep blue eyes the expression that could and did captivate more than one vulnerable young man's heart.

It was that, more than anything, which had put her in danger of incurring her father's displeasure. He was not above bestowing her favours as a reward himself, but her successive dalliances with young men who were patently unsuitable as marriage partners, combined with her resistance to more eligible suitors, had reached the limit of his fond indulgence. By the time she celebrated her eighteenth naming day, Cathva knew she would need to have made an advantageous marriage by the time her nineteenth came round or she was in danger of losing her privileged position.

It was then that King Rainur of Shehaios appeared at the Imperial Court like an answer to her prayers. He was not a young man, but he was considerably better looking than most of the other contenders for her hand. There was something in the slightly dreamy look in his brown eyes that reminded Cathva of the worthless but passionate young men she had delighted in – poets, minstrels and students of human beauty, every one. Unlike them, however, Rainur was an eligible marriage partner, looking for an alliance. He was a King, absolute ruler of a land which technically retained its independence from the Empire, though this was not a fact anyone would be wise to rehearse too loudly or too often in the Emperor's hearing.

Rainur and his advisor, Lord High Magician Turloch, were nothing if not wise. Cathva watched the way the Shaihen King managed his delicate relationship with the Emperor with admiration. She had seen many fail a less delicate balancing act of obsequiousness and pride. Rainur commanded her interest and respect. She fell in love with his stories of Shehaios.

She smiled to herself as the ponderous wagon lurched over the imperfections in the road. It was all going to work out wonderfully.

Chapter 5
Mervecc

It was some weeks after the Princess's entourage passed through Mervecc Holding that Caras and Kierce, their Caiivorian captive trailing in their wake, approached it across country, from the west. They dropped down onto the main road from the Gate to enter the town. It would not have been polite to do anything else, and they were outside the Chief of Oreath's territory.

Caras paused beneath the impressive arch which spanned the entrance to the Holding to adjust from the isolated solitude of the mountains. Its location as the first major settlement north of the Caiivorian border made Mervecc more of a town than any other Shaihen Holding, the point where the isolated hill farmers and the traders of the Empire met, but the soft colour and sheer substance of the yellow stone buildings seemed to welcome him with the very image of Shaihen hospitality. The Hall of Learning above his head was a grander and more solid building than the one at Arhaios, but he knew it still fulfilled the same function. As a boy, he had had toiled over the workaday skills of counting and herb lore within its more modest timber counterpart above the entrance to Arhaios. He had learned there, too, the poetry of *haios*, of all things and their connectedness.

He heard Kierce draw in a deep breath of satisfaction, savouring the zestful and not always pleasant scents of the busy Holding rather as Caras had tasted the air of the high forest. Now he came to think of it, Caras could seldom remember seeing Kierce in the Hall of Learning. Kierce seemed to acquire knowledge the same way everyone else knew how to breathe.

Caras knew what he was looking forward to in Mervecc. The other most important building in any Holding faced them, forcing the road into a sweeping curved detour around it. The Meeting House at Mervecc was typical, a dominant circular building with a high-pitched roof, set in the middle of a large open space known as a *vecce*, or meeting place. There were plenty of people in there who could give Kierce a decent game, along with any other diversions he might seek.

"I'd better find Lord Gascon as soon as possible," said Caras. "I'll leave Orlii and the horses to you."

"Thank you," said Kierce with some irony. The Caiivorian boy had become something of a millstone around both their necks on the journey from Prassan. Neither of them really wanted to be responsible for keeping a terrified child captive, but neither did they know how to release him. His own fear kept him their prisoner.

Caras suspected Orlii's welfare would feature considerably lower on Kierce's list of priorities than that of the horses, but he could not take the wretched boy with him to meet the Chief of Mervecc.

"I'll catch up with you later."

Kierce smiled. "I should be well ahead by then."

The minor irritations of his travelling companions were soon out of Caras's mind as he negotiated his way through the traffic of people into the entrance hall of the gracious half-timbered residence of Mervecc's Chief and his household. He not only wanted to warn Gascon about the plight of his border Holders; he wanted to know what he thought about it.

It was all very well for Kierce to say he just had to enjoy the King's wedding, but Caras knew that he was going as his grandmother's representative. His attendance signified Oreath's recognition of the alliance, as Gascon's presence would signify Mervecc's. Caras wanted to know if Gascon was intending to go. Gascon was nearly twenty years his senior, and for fifteen of them he had been Mervecc's Chief.

Inside Gascon's majestically proportioned house, however, even Caras's single-mindedness was brought up short by the detail that spoke of Mervecc's wealth and Gascon's pleasure in it. Even in the lowly entrance hall, rich fabrics jostled each other for space on the walls, and exotic trinkets from the furthest reaches of the Caiivorian Empire decorated corners and niches.

Caras peered cautiously at the collection of Imperial curios, and picked up a little bronze figurine of a fat goddess with astonishingly large breasts. It was gross, it should not remind him of his own beloved wife, and yet it did. There was an amazingly sensuous warmth to the cold metal that invited him into the womb-like embrace of the goddess's arms.

He turned abruptly as he heard the east door of the hall open and found himself looking into Gascon's long and lugubrious face.

He stepped forward and grasped the arm Gascon offered him, hand to elbow, in the traditional Shaihen greeting. Caras's arrival had evidently not gone unremarked; Gascon was expecting him.

"Welcome to Mervecc, Lord Caras," he said affably. "I hope you won't take it amiss if I say I'm sorry not to see your grandmother with you. I trust she's well?"

"She's very well," said Caras. "But it's a long journey for a woman of her age."

Gascon gave him a droll look. Caras was not a good liar. Leath was not coming, because Leath was not sure she approved of the King's marriage. Allowing her grandson to represent her put a diplomatic distance between accepting the King's invitation and sanctioning his extraordinary choice of bride.

"I could add, a long and a dangerous one," he went on tersely. "I have urgent news from your western Holdings, Lord Gascon, and it isn't good."

Gascon ushered him without further ado through to his own quarters, where the adornment of the hall exploded in a display of sumptuous elegance.

Caras paused in the doorway, momentarily overwhelmed by the colours and scents which assailed his senses. Gascon turned and smiled at him.

"I know," he said. "It's too much. Caiivorian traders do seem to think they need to give me things. I should tell them, but I have to admit, they have such beautiful gifts I find it hard to resist."

"Why do they give you things?" asked Caras, following him into the room and staring around him in amazement. "You mean they barter?"

He couldn't imagine what Gascon had that could be worth all this magnificence.

Gascon shrugged.

"They do good business in Mervecc. They seem to think if they don't offer me a reward, I'll show favours to traders who do. It's what they're used to. The fact that I have no favours to offer doesn't seem to have registered with them yet." The dry smile was still playing on his broad, full-lipped mouth. "Perhaps I should try harder."

Caras frowned.

"In my limited experience, Caiivorians seem better at taking things than giving them."

Gascon's expression sobered rapidly.

"Ah, yes. Your news, Lord Caras. I'd better hear it. I feared I would, sooner or later."

It was evening before Caras finally took leave of his host. He went to find Kierce to confirm that Gascon had offered them lodging in the Holder's House for the night.

He knew where Kierce would be. The Meeting House was not only a gathering place for the people of the Holding, it was a place of rest and relaxation for any visitors. The vital and exotic population he had seen passing through Gascon's house would draw Kierce like a blowsy flower seducing a bee.

As he approached it, a curious sight outside the Meeting House caught Caras's attention. Around the curve of the hall some distance from the doorway he could see a group of half a dozen dogs, lying in various attitudes of semi-wakefulness. Every half-open eye and pricked ear was focussed on something huddled against the Meeting House wall, enclosed by the canine crescent. Caras turned aside and went to look closer.

He recognised the bearskin beneath which the figure cowered before he recognised the unhappy figure itself. It was Orlii, the Caiivorian captive he had left in Kierce's charge.

Caras frowned, wondering why Kierce had left the boy in charge of a pack of Merveccian dogs, before it gradually dawned on him that Orlii was not in charge of the dogs. The dogs were in charge of Orlii.

More than once, Caras had cause to regret his rash decision to saddle them with a Caiivorian prisoner. From the moment he left Prassan's people, he had been anxious to place their problems before their Chief, and Orlii slowed them down. He had no horse, and when relentlessly bullied into riding behind Kierce, his terror was palpable. It seemed to transmit itself both to Red Sky and to Kierce himself. Kierce's sardonic good humour disappeared into a well of brooding resentment and Red Sky started behaving like a half-schooled colt, shying at nothing and jumping at his own shadow. Eventually, he jibbed and reared with such violence Orlii slipped off over his tail. After that, nothing would persuade either Orlii or Kierce to repeat the experience. Orlii travelled almost the whole way from Prassan to Mervecc on foot.

Having put a suitable distance between themselves and Prassan, Caras almost hoped the boy would run away from them, but once he planted the terror of Shaihen magic in Orlii's head, the idea of escaping from it did not dare to surface. It was only its effect on its victim that gave Caras any idea what a powerful myth he had conjured up. Once or twice, when Orlii was dropping with exhaustion, Caras did prevail on the boy to ride with him, but even then he sat shaking at Caras's back in silent misery, and Caras knew it was the horse he was frightened of as much as the men. He would not believe they were ordinary horses any more than he would believe that Shaihens were ordinary men.

Caras started forwards to rescue the miserable captive, and then paused. He hesitated to interfere with Kierce's decisions. Quite apart from the etiquette of doing so, those dogs were not far removed from their wolf cousins and Kierce possessed the very fine bearskin, currently keeping Orlii from the evening chill, courtesy of a wolf pack.

He thought better of it, and went into the Meeting House.

The noise of gossip and argument, of wagers being laid, deals being forged and alliances broken, assaulted his ears as he opened the door. The acrid reek of smoke from hearth and torches caught in his throat. It took him several minutes to locate Kierce, sitting with a crowd of strangers to one side of the ill-lit hall, deep in a complex game.

Rather than interrupt his play, Caras availed himself of Gascon's ale, and watched for a while. He had played Kierce himself a number of times recently, but he hadn't seen him play against others. He was intrigued to find out whether his own skill was deficient or Kierce really was as good and as ruthless as he suspected. It was evident from a cursory assessment that his opponents were not easy prey and the stakes represented by markers in the middle of the floor around which they sat were alarming. Nevertheless, as Caras watched the shift of fortunes played out, it was evident that Kierce was consistently winning. As when Caras played him, he appeared somehow to take control of the game, to force moves on his opponents that worked to his advantage. Caras studied him critically, but he still couldn't see how he did it.

He also became gradually aware that Kierce was not even giving the game his undivided attention.

There was a full-figured, fair young woman lounging on the arm of one of the other players of this exclusively male game. More than one disparaging comment about the intensity of Kierce's desire to win passed her lips during the course of play, and it was clear from the odd glance she flicked at him that she had taken some dislike to this visitor from Arhaios. To the others present, Kierce appeared to meet her comments with good-natured tolerance. Only Caras, who knew him, saw his interest in her and saw him glance at her with an expression Caras had seen on his friend's face before, an expression which turned him into a stranger and sent a chill down Caras's spine.

Caras went over and laid his hand on Kierce's shoulder.

"Is Gascon doing all he should?" asked Kierce, without looking up.

"Of course. Though it all seems to take a frustrating length of time."

"That's the trouble with things you don't have to do very often. When was the last time Shaihens fought anyone?"

Caras reflected for a moment in surprise. Probably fifteen years ago, when his grandmother had a slight altercation with some unruly representatives of the Imperial Army.

"Don't hover, Caras. You're putting me off."

"Kierce – Orlii?" Caras reminded him.

Kierce swore softly and gave Caras an apologetic look. "Forgot every damn word about him. Go and rescue him for me, would you? I'm a dead man if I leave this game now."

"Will the dogs let me?"

"Might lick you to death."

Caras hesitated. He leaned closer to his companion and lowered his voice. "Kierce, I still have matters to discuss with Gascon. Don't cause any trouble here."

"Would I?" said Kierce, with a brief glance at the fair-haired girl.

"I don't think she likes you."

"The night is young," responded Kierce, complacently. "Piss off, Caras, and let me play this hand."

Caras set his jaw and swallowed the angry response that rose in his throat. He turned abruptly and left the Meeting House.

He returned some time later, when the hall was almost empty and the twelve stones game was breaking up. In the course of finding their captive a more suitable place to sleep, he had fallen into conversation with two other visitors to Mervecc. They were from Ccheven, a region which sprawled most of the way along Shehaios's eastern seaboard. They came to Mervecc with alarmingly familiar stories of raids and looting. Their assailants came from the sea, attacked with the same savagery as Prassan had experienced and carried the wealth and the people of Ccheven away in their ships back south to Caiivor. Hearing their story made up Caras's mind to spend a little longer in Mervecc before he went on to the Haven. The more he heard of Caiivor, the less he felt inclined to celebrate a closer alliance with it, and the contents of

Gascon's house told him how much more the Chief of Mervecc knew about the mighty Caiivorian Empire than Caras did.

Caras returned to the Meeting House to warn Kierce, before he did anything he might wish to leave behind in a hurry.

He spotted his companion standing beside a door across the far side of the hall, and headed towards him. He was about to speak to him when Kierce went out of the door, and Caras realised that he, in turn, was following the fair young woman. He quickened his pace and went after them.

Kierce touched the girl's arm as she stepped out under the long eaves of the Meeting House roof. She turned towards him. Caras heard Kierce speak softly to her – he couldn't hear what was said, but he could guess. From her behaviour during the evening, he would not have been surprised if the girl had fetched Kierce a clout round the ear – or even on a more tender part of his anatomy – for his impudence. He was startled to see her check and gaze at Kierce as if she were spellbound. Kierce pulled her gently towards him, moving out of the doorway and into the shadows beneath the eaves. The girl made no resistance. Kierce put his arms around her and kissed her eyes, then her lips, a deep, fierce, hungry kiss. The girl's arms went around his neck, and she returned the kiss with passion, pressing her body against him like a lover re-united with her mate after a long, enforced abstinence.

Caras watched, at a loss. Kierce had never met this woman before tonight, he knew he hadn't. He doubted he knew her name. Caras was fairly sure he could tell flirtatious teasing from genuine dislike, and he was equally sure that neither the animosity this girl had shown for Kierce earlier, nor her interest in the young man she had spent the evening with, was false.

But neither was there anything forced about the eager lovemaking going on in front of his eyes now. She was stripping Kierce's jerkin from his back almost as fast as he was unlacing her bodice, careless of the relatively public place in which this was taking place. It was Kierce who was edging them back, away from the door, deeper into shadow and a shade more privacy. He pushed the bodice from her shoulder and bent to kiss her breast, and then flinched suddenly and drew back. He looked across his shoulder and saw Caras.

Caras saw the glint of his smile in the darkness.

"Get your own, Caras. I don't think I can handle three at once."

"What the hell do you— ." Caras broke off abruptly, conscious that this was not the time or place to discuss anything with Kierce. He turned and walked away from them with a flush of embarrassment warming his face. Willing was hardly a strong enough description of the wanton desire that girl was showing for Kierce and yet her inexplicable compliance made Caras uneasy. He still felt it was Kierce's lust he was seeing. He didn't like to find the word for Kierce's intentions.

He stalked away in a simmering rage that Kierce could even contemplate playing these games with the horror of Lasa's story still raw in the memory.

There were times when he didn't recognise this man he had known since childhood. The man who dined with dragons. The boy who would sit for hours winning the trust of a horse – or days winning that of a deer. The boy who could get himself accepted into the wolf pack and play with their young, lie so still for so long that the shyest creature would venture to sniff at him and see what kind of a beast he was. Who knew every inch of the hills and forests around Arhaios and the mountains beyond and loved it with a passion and understanding that perhaps only Caras, bred to be Holder of the balance, fully appreciated. But put him among his own kind and Kierce could too easily become this other person, callous, impatient and ruthless in pursuit of his own desires. Caras, being a simple man with a simple morality, simply did not understand it.

Chapter 6
Caras's Challenge

Responsibility for their Caiivorian captive took the edge off Kierce's pleasure in the opportunities Mervecc afforded him. If Orlii regarded him as something between a beast and a spirit, Kierce quickly began to regard the boy as something less than either. From Kierce's perspective, the Caiivorian was incomplete. Shaihens carried with them, subconsciously, the heritage of their land and their people, a story sung into their souls by means more profound than words. Orlii had a name, but he had no identity. He was a blank, awaiting direction. Worst of all, he looked to Kierce to give it to him.

Kierce was both goaded and irritated by the youngster's cowed reticence. He spent the first couple of days at Mervecc attempting to drive him away. Since Orlii was already terrified of his horse, Kierce made the black stallion the boy's guard, and watched Red Sky patiently ambling around the Holding in Orlii's wake. Then he tried the dogs, and the following morning enticed a large raptor to swoop repeatedly low over Orlii's head, making him believe for a few petrified moments that it was going to carry him off. Orlii bore it all in abject terror, without a murmur of protest. Wherever Kierce went in Mervecc, his shadow followed. Orlii had been born into slavery. It was fixed in his head that he belonged to Kierce, and Kierce gradually began to understand that the boy was not going to be easily dissuaded from his misapprehension.

When Caras finally sent word that they were moving on from Mervecc, Kierce was amused to see his companion approaching across the Merveccian meeting place leading a rather elderly grey pony.

"What do you call that?" Kierce greeted him, casting a disparaging eye over the pony.

"Something Orlii might actually be persuaded to ride," replied Caras. "I don't know about you, but I didn't relish the thought of riding all the way back to Arhaios with him running along behind us."

"Or of what Leath might say when she saw it," added Kierce. "Well, since we're not going to be rid of him, I suppose you have a point. Come on then, Orlii."

Without glancing at the boy, he gestured peremptorily towards Caras's purchase.

"M…master?" stammered Orlii.

"Just ride it, Orlii."

"Yes, Master," said Orlii, in a voice like doom.

He approached the horse with heavy feet, and hesitated. He half-glanced at Kierce, as if to make an appeal, then thought better of it. He mounted as if he expected it to be the last act of his life. The horse, unsurprisingly since it was a fairly old and dull Merveccian workhorse, barely flicked an ear.

Caras gave Kierce a slightly horrified look.

"He's frightened of every creature in Shehaios," said Kierce, dismissively. "You know he is."

"That's not what worries me. It's what he called you."

"The boy's a slave, Caras," replied Kierce, vaulting onto Red Sky's back. "If I've made no other progress with him, I've at least established that. He can't see himself as anything else. A slave without a master is as worthless as … I don't know. A tail without a dog." He threw Caras a look of mild resentment. "You gave him to me."

Caras absorbed this disturbing revelation in silence as he mounted and finally turned north from Mervecc. The entire idea of slavery was foreign to Shehaios. Holders served their people, and everyone served the Spirit, but that was all Caras understood by servitude. The use of "Lord" or "Lady" was the Imperial language's translation of the polite form of address for any adult Shaihen, applied to swineherd, dairymaid or the Chief of Mervecc.

Kierce knew very well that it had not been Caras's intention to enslave Orlii, or even hold him captive for longer than Prassan's safety demanded. Kierce found the reality of Orlii's subservience irritating; he could see that Caras found it distasteful to the point of being offensive.

"Make up your mind, Caras," he said wryly. "Have we captured him or rescued him?"

"He can do Prassan no harm now. A little more respect for his dignity wouldn't hurt."

"Difficult to respect what isn't there," replied Kierce. "He's happier believing he's my slave than believing I'm going to flay his soul like tanned leather."

Caras scowled. "Master!" he muttered, contemptuously.

Kierce smiled. "If you'd rather be master, I could sell him to you, if you like. Or maybe we could play for him?"

"Don't be obscene," retorted Caras. "Have you any idea how cheaply the Caiivorians hold the lives of their enemies or their captives?"

"You had an educational stay in Mervecc, then."

"It seems you had a lucrative one."

"A certain balance to be redressed. There was a lot of Shaihen gold flowing from your hands into the purses of Caiivorian traders."

"I needed to talk to them," said Caras, irritably. "They don't talk unless you're buying."

"You can hardly blame them. That's why they're here." Kierce paused, and gave Caras a slightly amused look. He could see the confusion of information cluttering Caras's thoughts with tales of feuding southern caii indiscriminately stealing stock and people from their enemies and counting it an act of heroism. Caras's view of the forthcoming alliance with these people was swinging from concern to horror. "You'd better make up your mind soon, Caras. It's only two days journey to the Haven."

"I know that."

Kierce shrugged. He held his own view on the subject, but it was not his responsibility. It was Caras's job to make deciisons for the Holding, and Kierce had long ago grown used to Caras's agonising over the right path to follow. He usually made a sound choice in the end.

The Haven, where the Council met and the Keeper of the Gate had his residence, was the site of the historic gathering of the five tribes which brought together the ancient strands of the Fair Land. In the high valley, above a spring which spilled waters heated deep in the earth onto the frozen mountain, their leaders met to declare their mutual allegiance to *she-haios,* the Whole Land. The spring, long ago enclosed by walls, was set a little apart from the centre of the Haven and it was overshadowed by the sprawling edifice of the Royal Palace which squatted on the valley floor.

Half a day short of their destination, Caras stopped unannounced by the roadside, and pulled from his pack sword-belt and sword. He buckled it on, remounted and rode on for the Royal Palace. He offered no explanation to Kierce, and Kierce did not ask.

Nevertheless, it left an air of tension between them. Among a people with little respect, and certainly no reverence, for the skills of the warrior, the sword had become a tool for ceremony and entertainment. As heir to the Holding, Caras was trained in the physical use of the weapon, but he knew very well it was the message he conveyed by wearing it that struck the most telling blow.

For a Holder to come armed into the house of another was to issue a challenge. It was a declaration of an argument which the challenger was prepared to pursue by force if the response did not satisfy him. Smaller Holders did it all the time over any number of petty squabbles, rarely resulting in bloodshed, but for Arhaios, Holding of the Chief of Oreath, to challenge the Haven was unprecedented. Meetings of the five regional chiefs of the Holders' Council were frequently tempestuous, but to take disagreements at that level as far as a formal challenge was to threaten the unity of the Whole Land.

Rainur's men came out to greet Caras as he carried the challenge down the sharp descent into their valley. Their welcome was faultlessly courteous, but they gave the two Arhaiens and their curious Caiivorian companion a very close escort. Caras was conscious of their barely contained interest in the significance of the sword at his side no less than the novel experience of Kierce's disapproval. He resisted, with just a trace of smugness, any temptation to explain. He wasn't even sure himself how far he was going to take the challenge. More than anything, he wanted answers, and Leath had warned him how adept Rainur could be at avoiding awkward questions.

The Palace of the King and Guardian of Shehaios was not one structure but a whole range of square buildings, one inside the other, separated by gardens and courtyards. Dominating the north side of the outer layer of its huge quadrangles was the Haven's unique stone Meeting House where, they were informed, the King was receiving the guests crowding into the Haven for his wedding.

Caras was prepared to take a sword into Rainur's Meeting House, but he hesitated to take a Caiivorian. They left Orlii in the care of the people who took their horses.

With each step that took them nearer to the cavernous welcome of the Meeting House entrance, Kierce's anxiety grew more apparent, until finally he stepped in front of Caras and physically barred his way.

"That's far enough, Caras," he said. "We came to celebrate a marriage, not to start a war. Take the sword off now."

"Out of my way, Kierce," said Caras quietly.

"It's enough to take it to the door— ."

Caras rested his hand on the weapon's hilt. "This is Prassan's sword."

"It's not, it's the heir to Oreath's sword. You've made your point. The news will be all round the Haven and heading for the rest of Shehaios before the end of the day. Rainur will know!"

"Rainur should have known before this. He should have gained the agreement of the Holders' Council to this alliance before it was made. He's always been too close to the Empire, now he's marrying it. He needs to know that there are those not afraid to dispute his judgement."

"Not like this. Not here. Not in front of half of Shehaios and the Princess's guards!"

Caras threw his cloak back over his shoulder so that the sword was clearly visible and pushed past him towards the hall. Kierce cursed and followed him.

"You don't have to come with me," said Caras.

"Someone has to watch your back," snapped Kierce. "Pompous ass!"

They strode into the Meeting House side by side.

A riot of dragons and heroes described scenes from the Shaihen histories on the walls of the Haven's hall. Opposite Caras and Kierce as they entered, all the stories of passion and struggle, vision and sacrifice, luck and mistakes that had brought the Shaihen people to where they now were culminated in the symbol of the union of the Whole Land, the unicorn. It reared above the entrance to the rest of the Palace complex.

The hall was crowded with people, most of them other Holders and their kin there for the celebration of Rainur's marriage. But Caras need not have been concerned about Orlii. There were a number of Caiivorians present, instantly distinguished by their height and their dress.

These were the retinue of the Imperial Princess, not the unkempt rough-clad men who had attacked Prassan. Their hair was cropped short and there were no tattoos on their shaven faces, but to Caras's eyes they were just Caiivorians. With a sense of shock, he noticed the two armoured Caiivorian soldiers standing guard below the unicorn either side of the door which led ultimately into the living quarters of the King and his favoured guests. The Princess Cathva, of course, was currently among those guests.

A gradual hush fell across the crowded hall as Caras passed through, followed like a wave by a murmur of animated comment. The Shaihens gathered in the Meeting House of the Haven could barely believe what they were seeing.

The only eyes that did not stray immediately to the sword at Caras's side were those of the King. Rainur, a slim urbane man, elegant in a finespun woollen cloak of vivid royal blue, was in the middle of the hall, welcoming another group of newcomers. He conducted the conversation with the easy lack of ceremony Shaihens would expect from their Guardian of the Fair Land. He continued to talk as Caras moved through the hall towards him, even though the guest he was addressing had ceased to listen.

"This is bad strategy, Caras," muttered Kierce, striding shoulder to shoulder with his companion as if he had every confidence in him.

"I know what I'm doing."

"Not as well as Rainur knows what you're doing."

Caras shot him a brief, startled glance.

"He knew before you did, idiot," hissed Kierce. "He takes advice from the Lord High Magician!"

Caras looked in slight alarm at Rainur, still apparently oblivious to what held the fascinated attention of every other person in the hall. But it was too late to change direction now.

He reached the King, and drew the sword. The two Caiivorian guards grasped the hilts of their own weapons almost in unison, and Kierce swung round towards the foreigners in warning.

Before any of them could do anything else, Rainur turned to Caras with a genial smile and extended his hand towards the heir to Arhaios both as a welcome and an invitation to place the sword in it.

"Ah, Caras, you bring me something from the Holder of Prassan, I believe? Thank you."

Caras hesitated, his heart beating uncomfortably but his purpose fixed. He laid the sword flat across his outstretched hands, the traditional way for a Holder to deliver his challenge. Slowly, he bent down and placed the weapon at Rainur's feet.

"This is what I bring you from Prassan."

"I will speak to Lord Gascon. Prassan is under his protection."

"That's not the challenge. The Holder of Prassan questions the marriage between the Keeper of the Gate and the kin of the people who attacked and killed the women and children of their Holding." Caras paused, aware that every ear in the hall was listening. "Arhaios awaits the answer to the question."

"Arhaios is not alone." Rainur appeared neither to acknowledge their audience nor raise his voice, but his words carried clearly to the edges of the hall. "The men who attacked Prassan Holding are rebels against the rule of the Empire of the Sacred Union. They are as much the enemies of our Imperial allies as they are ours."

"Caiivorians live by the power of the sword," said Caras. "Is that the rule you intend to bring into Shehaios?"

Rainur met his eyes calmly.

"It's you who has brought a sword into my hall, Caras."

Caras glanced defiantly at the Caiivorian Imperial guard behind Rainur. "Not the first one."

Rainur gestured to the Caiivorians to keep their weapons sheathed.

"I respect the customs of my bride," he replied. "I don't live by them."

"Do you accept the challenge?" demanded Caras.

"I will discuss that with the man who issued it."

"You won't answer me?"

"You didn't issue the challenge. Only a Holder can issue a challenge. You brought me the message from Prassan, Caras, for which I thank you, and I'm happy to discuss my answer with you as your grandmother's representative." He grasped Caras's shoulder in a friendly gesture and steered him away from the sword still lying on the floor between them. "I hope you left her well, incidentally, I'm sorry I won't see her at my wedding in person. We leave tomorrow for a day of sport in Dornas Forest, Lord Caras. Join me. It will be a good opportunity to discuss the issues that face us."

Go with him!

Caras thought Kierce muttered the advice as Rainur began to walk towards the door at the back of the hall. He found himself forced to follow as they flanked him, Kierce on one side, Rainur on the other. The escort felt like a guard, and Caras's mind resisted as his feet obeyed the invitation to move out of the limelight.

"I'm not sure talking will be enough," he said stubbornly. "And I'm far from sure Oreath will have a presence at your wedding, Lord Rainur."

"Nevertheless, I think the Chief of Oreath would prefer to hear that you discussed the matter with me in Dornas forest rather than fought my champion there, Lord Caras. Don't you?"

"I think the Chief of Oreath would like some reassurance that we are not to become a vassal of a military Empire!"

"Not here, Caras," said Rainur, quietly, with a fleeting glance at the Caiivorian soldiers. Their hawk-like eyes were watching Caras's every move from beneath their helmets. Rainur smiled. "Let the Lady Cathva show you what else this military Empire can offer us. Go through to the Holders Hall where my steward will introduce you."

Caras halted at the doorway and confronted Rainur.

"The sword remains drawn."

"Until tomorrow."

Rainur turned away and paused face to face with Kierce.

"You will ride with us, I trust, Lord Kierce."

"Thank you, Lord Rainur," said Kierce.

"And don't let him out of your sight."

"I didn't intend to."

Rainur turned back into the Meeting House and immediately engaged himself in another conversation as if nothing of great moment had occurred. Gradually, the general noise of voices rose to normal level, and Caras found himself and Kierce isolated in the doorway under the suspicious eyes of the Imperial guard.

"What did he mean by that?" demanded Caras in a fierce undertone, aware that he had been out-manoeuvred. Leath had advised him to watch and learn from King Rainur. He doubted she had meant him to do it this way.

"The King was asking me to protect you, you fool," retorted Kierce. "You think you don't need it?"

"It's him I challenged—!"

Kierce seized his arm and hustled him past the Imperial guards and into the passageway that led to the Holders Hall.

"You challenged the Imperial alliance. You challenged Rainur's authority in front of his Caiivorian bride's retinue. You're lucky he didn't order you dragged away in chains!"

"He wouldn't have dared issue such offence to Oreath ."

"Caras, you've no idea how difficult Rainur's position is. He has to maintain face in front of the Caiivorians."

Caras checked and turned to him with a scowl.

"How do you know all this? How come you know so much more about what's in Rainur's mind than I do?"

"Trust me. This was a crazy thing to do. I didn't think even you were stupid enough to go through with it – Rainur got you out of it brilliantly. For Spirit's sake, come and be nice to his Princess now and people might actually believe you were just delivering a message."

"I'm not alone in this."

"Of course you're not. That's what makes it so bloody dangerous." Kierce gave him a look of exasperation. "Caras, you need to spend more time playing twelve-stones. You really do."

Caras stared at him, suddenly beginning to realise why Kierce was so much better at the game.

When you find yourself on a collision course with a man, put yourself where he stands. If he is your enemy, you will learn how to defeat him. But you may find when you look from where he looks that you are not on a collision course at all, just approaching the same problem from different directions.

He could almost hear Leath's voice saying it, and she had said it often enough. He found himself at a loss to explain why he had not been able to hear it before he drew a sword on the King.

"I didn't do it, did I?" he said, in dismay. "I didn't put myself in Rainur's place."

Kierce's expression relented marginally.

"Not an easy place for you to put yourself in," he conceded. He put his hand on Caras's shoulder. "Just come and meet the Princess, Caras. Let Rainur sort it out."

Kierce could almost feel the charge of energy in the Meeting House lifting the hairs on his body like thunder in midsummer. The words that brushed his ears and his mind as they walked through the crowd breathed the ominous whisper of parched grass stirred by the wind of an advancing fire. Kierce was seldom frightened, but when he looked back on Caras's performance, he didn't know how else to describe the sensation he felt. If Caras had been aware, as Kierce was, of the soaring admiration inspired by the sight of the tall, powerful young man striding through the King's guests with a sword at his side and all the authority of Oreath on his shoulders, Kierce would have found it much less easy to forgive him.

Kierce's loyalty was not easily given. He lived at a distance from his people, spending his life teaching creatures to trust him and then betraying that trust by giving them to another master. His father had commanded his love unquestioningly. But there had been times when his father had had to find someone else to care for his child while he followed the herds, especially in the early years of Kierce's life. He left him in the care of the Chieftain's family. Kierce's friendship with Caras was like a tie of blood, he would always defend the man he thought of as his brother. The fact that he could see in Caras's mind how often they thought in completely opposite directions did not affect the bond between them.

But there were times when it could bring them to blows with each other. Rainur knew Caiivorians. More to the point, Lord High Magician Turloch knew Caiivorians. If their strategy for dealing with this overwhelming power beyond the physical borders of Shehaios was to make an alliance with it, Kierce did not feel that Caras had anything like enough information to dispute it at the moment. Kierce did, of course, have the advantage of reading in Rainur's mind the King's desperate desire to explain himself to Caras, and through him to his people. He felt, as always, as any reader of minds would do, the split of seeing both sides of the argument.

He scanned the Holders Hall through Caras's eyes, drawing on his companion's greater familiarity with the appearance of the Holders' Council.

Fortunately, it seemed as if none of the other chiefs had actually witnessed Oreath's dramatic arrival, though they'd all know about it soon enough. He identified the shining pate and bull-neck of Lord Colis of Ccheven, looking like nothing so much as a grizzled sea lion, standing beneath the painted silver fishes which symbolised his region. Nearby, almost lost in the crowd, was a stout, diminutive figure Caras recognised as Lady Onia, the Chief of Ulath. There appeared to be no sign of Ered of Hieath, either here or in the Meeting House, and Kierce knew Gascon had not yet arrived.

Neither he nor Caras could tell whether Lord High Magician Turloch was present. Few people ever saw Lord High Magician Turloch. That didn't necessarily mean he wasn't there.

Kierce exhaled a private sigh of relief, and looked around the hallowed Holders Hall with less anxious eyes. The wood-panelled walls were lined with Imperial soldiers. The change of atmosphere from the noisy openness of the main hall was tangible. It was impossible to ignore the armed foreign presence in the background, starkly out of place against the symbols of the seven members of the Holder's Council – the five regions, the Crown and the Magician – depicted on the panels behind them.

He was well aware that Caras was both confused and unnerved by the sight, as much as by the outcome of his challenge. He stood just inside the Hall, suddenly reluctant to mix with the distinguished company inside it. Kierce was content to let him suffer in silence, until a Shaihen man made his way over and introduced himself as the member of Rainur's household responsible for organising presentations to the Royal Bride. The ceremony this implied only served to deepen the frown on Caras's brow.

It was no accident that Rainur did not wear a crown or any other badge of office. Shaihens celebrated their land and their history with symbols, but not each other.

"Lord Rainur apologises for troubling you with this," said their guide, "but you know that the Lady Cathva is not of our people, and has other customs to our own. When she enters, please wait while I introduce you in turn. Lord Rainur asks that in courtesy to our honoured guests, you show the Lady the … respect she anticipates."

"I wouldn't expect to show Lord Rainur's guest anything less," replied Caras. "But it depends what you mean, exactly, by 'respect'?"

"She will extend her hand in greeting. She will expect you to kiss it."

Kierce sensed the dogged stubbornness stirring in Caras's mind.

"Just her hand?" he commented, guilelessly. "We could show her much more respect than that if she'd like us to." He lowered his voice and murmured to Caras, "Breasts like golden fruit, ripe and perfect …"

Caras glared at him.

"Now who's pushing their luck?" he hissed.

"The difference is I wouldn't say it to her face, Caras," said Kierce drily. He met Caras's eyes squarely. "For Spirit's sake don't insult the woman. Even if she does have a face like the rear end of a dragon."

"It is asked of all who are presented to her," explained the steward. "It's their custom."

"I've no wish to insult the lady," said Caras, stiffly. "I'll kiss her hand if that's what she wants. As long as I don't have to fall on the floor and crawl backwards. I have recently heard something of southern customs."

"The Lady Cathva is marrying into a Shaihen household. Believe me, she is bending more to our ways than we are to hers."

"I'm pleased to hear it," said Caras.

The man moved on to give his instructions to others in the honoured party, and the awkward silence returned, until a sudden harsh braying called everyone's attention to the south end of the room. Both Kierce and Caras started slightly at the noise, unused to the stridency of instruments designed to carry across a battlefield.

The liveried trumpeters lowered their instruments, and while the notes of their call settled on the hush that had fallen over the hall, the doors beside them opened.

Like a vision, Princess Cathva entered the room.

Kierce intended to watch Caras, but he found his eyes drawn irresistibly to the blaze of torchlight that heralded the Princess's appearance. It dazzled her audience, leaving the small, perfect creature in the centre of it to appear gradually, as if out of the air. She glided into the Hall, delicate as a butterfly, points of light dancing from the jewels and precious metals woven into her apparel. Her face was powdered to a pure unblemished finish, and paint accentuated her dark lashes and red lips. Such glimpses of her skin as her costume allowed showed a richer, deeper complexion than the pale flesh of her northern hosts, almost the gold of the ballads. Her hair was the most magnificent colour, a burnished dark bronze, bound in intricate tresses and studded with jewels. Her dress was a work of art in itself, encasing her in a shimmering cloth which clung to the outline of her body, shaped and lifted her breasts to a swelling cleavage where a fine, semi-transparent mesh of material made some pretence of covering the golden fruit. The rest of the dress nipped in tightly at the waist and fell in gorgeous folds to leave only two tiny feet in sculpted slippers visible.

Kierce looked at Caras. His mouth was slightly open. His eyes looked mesmerised. With a sense of relief, Kierce read the surging desire to protect this rare and perfect beauty coursing through his companion's veins. Cathva had scored her first victory.

He looked back at her. He couldn't actually see the woman at all, only the image of frail, shining perfection. A slight shudder of revulsion ran through him.

Caras jolted out of his reverie and glanced at him.

45

"You're not impressed?"

"Dazzled," said Kierce. "But one's eyes adjust."

Caras frowned at him, perplexed.

"I don't understand you. She's—."

"A beautiful costume," supplied Kierce as Caras struggled to find an adequate word. "I like a beautiful woman. Preferably with no costume at all."

"But she is beautiful."

"Oh, you can see her can you?" Kierce hesitated, studying Cathva. "No Caras. A living thing in captivity never strikes me as beautiful."

"Captivity? What are you talking about? She's of the Caiivorian Imperial family, and she's marrying our King, how does that make her a captive?"

Kierce shook his head.

"Can't you see it, Caras? Well, let's just say I don't fancy your odds if you expect our women to start following this fashion, that's all. Teaching Shaihen men to be warriors is one thing. Teaching Shaihen women to be painted puppets is a far taller order."

Before Caras could reply, they were invited forward to present themselves to the illustrious lady herself.

"Lord Caras of Arhaios," announced their guide. "Heir to Oreath."

"Lord Caras," she said, managing with a skill born of practice to address both of them. Kierce realised she was unsure which of the two in front of her was the future Lord of Oreath, and which was his servant. His hackles stirred at the automatic distinction that arose in her mind.

Caras stepped forward and kissed her hand.

"Lady Cathva," he acknowledged, "Allow me to present my friend and companion, Kierce ti' Gaeroch, Horsemaster of Arhaios."

There may have been a very slight curl to Cathva's delicately coloured lips as she turned reluctantly to accept the greeting of a man so far beneath her station; but it was nothing to the disgust that choked in Kierce's throat as he bent to kiss her hand. To senses attuned to natural scents, Cathva's perfume was overpowering.

Kierce stepped back hastily, turning the gagging reflex into a polite cough. He looked up, into the deepest, bluest eyes he had ever seen. Something other than the scent caught his breath. For that moment, he could only stare at her, his gaze striking straight through her mannered poise. She stared back at him, startled. A delicious shudder touched his body as he sensed her response. Now, he could see her.

The contact was fleeting, barely conscious. He hardly even held her hand for more than a moment before Cathva turned her attention, and her heart-breakingly glorious eyes, back to Caras.

"Arhaios is one of Lord Rainur's oldest Holdings, I believe?"

"Arhaios is one of the oldest Shaihen Holdings, my lady, yes," agreed Caras.

"And held by – your grandmother, I'm told?" A very slight and very attractive little frown touched Cathva's perfect eyebrows.

"My grandmother Leath is Holder of Arhaios and Chief of Oreath, my lady."

"It is curious to me that women hold power in Shehaios. The lady Leath must be a truly remarkable person."

"Well, we all think so in Oreath," admitted Caras, with a slightly fatuous smile. "But we are a little prejudiced. I doubt she is more remarkable than the Lady Onia of Ulath, who waits to greet you in this hall."

"You remind me of my duty even as you detain me with your charm, Lord Caras. I do hope we will speak again."

She bestowed one last precious look on him, and moved on to greet others without a second glance at Kierce. Caras let go a small, unconscious sigh.

"Caras, you're drooling," said Kierce in amusement, though his eyes also followed Cathva round the hall. "What am I going to tell Elani when we get back?"

"It makes me wonder why Rainur is actually marrying her. Does he need any more reason than the lady herself?"

"You've been listening to too many minstrels, Caras," replied Kierce. He hesitated, and added in an undertone, "Don't underestimate her. It's a very good disguise, but don't be surprised to find there is something a bit more substantial under all that paint. She may not say much, but it's not because she doesn't have much to say."

"What's that supposed to mean?"

Kierce smiled.

"That possibly you need protecting from the painted puppets as much as from the warriors."

Chapter 7
Dornas Forest

Rainur made a point of inviting both his Arhaien guests to dine with him later, as further proof that there was no division between them and the Haven. Caras did not wish to compound the impact of his dramatic gesture by spurning the King's hospitality, but he viewed with dismay an evening spent being convivial with Rainur's guests.

The animated response he met when he returned to the Meeting House confirmed his worst fears. The sword he had laid at Rainur's feet remained where he had left it, in a space of its own as if some mystic force guarded it.

The moment Caras arrived, he was the centre of a crowd agog to find out what he intended to do next.

He didn't know who all these people were, and yet they greeted him like old friends, full of opinions and advice. There was a man with such a strong Ulathan accent Caras could hardly understand him, beseeching him to take Ulath's advice on the wording of his apology.

"What apology?" said Caras, lost among the hubbub.

There was a big bearded man who wanted to talk to him about the strategy of raising an army.

"What army?" exclaimed Caras. "Why do I want an army?"

"Hieath will side with you," the man was saying. "Lord Ered has no time for this love affair with Caiivorians."

"We dislike them because they fight—."

No-one was actually listening to him. He was the focus for every passion Rainur's open courtship with the Empire stirred among his people. They talked at Caras and shouted at each other; they requisitioned his support with mugs of ale pressed into his hand. The Haven's ale. Rainur's ale.

He could see Rainur across the other side of the Meeting House, but he could reach neither him nor the food he had been invited to share. He could certainly put himself in the King's place now. He imagined some young stranger in the Meeting House at Arhaios doing this to Leath.

He'd throw the man out. He'd probably ask Kierce to summon some hungry wolves to chase him on his way.

He found himself struggling to defend the King. They did not know that Rainur was surrendering Shehaios to rule from Vordeith. They did not know anything except that he was marrying a Caiivorian Princess. She was a very pretty Princess. Most people married for love, and everyone knew how much Rainur felt the death of his first wife and the absence of any children.

Even Caras didn't really believe Rainur's marriage was a love-match, but he realised he did not have any idea of the terms of the alliance or the circumstances under which it had been made. Only Rainur and Lord Turloch knew the intentions of the Great Emperor; but Lord Turloch would know them intimately. Lord Turloch read minds.

He knew Rainur was keeping an eye on the uproar surrounding the heir to Oreath, but the King seemed content to let it run its course. He was talking to Gascon, who must have been closer behind Caras than he had thought, to be in the Haven tonight. Gascon was chatting and smiling as if they were old friends, there wasn't any hint that he was going to take issue with the King's marriage. Caras felt betrayed, but when he spared a moment to think about it, he didn't know why. Gascon had never divulged his intentions to Caras.

The Ulathan had secured his ear, and when Caras looked around, he realised it was because the large, bearded Hieathan was in animated conversation with Kierce, a band of his rebellious supporters gathered around them. Kierce was opposite him, and Caras could see the look of intent concentration on his companion's face, the light of competition in his eyes and the lurking half-smile that signalled a game of tactics in progress. What was he saying? What was he telling them?

He made a move towards them, but the Ulathan grasped his arm.

"You must understand, Lord Caras, that the strength of Shehaios lies in her unity. We all desire the same thing, our peace, our prosperity, the liberty to live as we wish. If we don't trust the King and the Magician to guard these things for us—."

Caras shook the man off in annoyance as an aggressive bellow of laughter burst from the group around Kierce.

"A Shaihen trusts himself, man," he snapped. "The Spirit breathes life into all of us, and we must all of us protect the things we love."

Kierce and his band of rebels were migrating across the hall now, bound Caras knew not where. He struggled to reach them, and found himself almost literally falling over a fight between two boys which erupted suddenly in the middle of the hall. He grabbed at the figure who rolled against his feet, as much to rescue his balance as to intervene in the fight. The boy lashed out, his fist striking ineffectually against Caras's leg. Caras saw others grab hold of the other participant, a young and rather drunk Royal steward, and took a firmer grasp of his own charge. He hauled the boy up and realised, as the size of the wriggling body became apparent, that he was holding Orlii.

Orlii turned towards him and a look of pure horror crossed his round face.

"Lord Caras!"

Caras let him go.

"Did I ... ? I struck you!"

Caras frowned, until the faint niggle of a bruise on his leg reminded him. He nodded towards the bloodied face of the steward still struggling against those restraining him.

"I think you struck him harder."

"But he's a servant!"

Caras grabbed hold of Orlii's arm again, sensing he was about to fall to his knees. At this precise moment, with all the passion and argument about servitude and freedom raging in the hall, that would not have helped.

"He's considerably older than you are, even if you are just as big. What were you doing fighting him?"

"He … he insulted you, my lord."

Him and the rest of the world, thought Caras.

"Orlii, we insult each other a lot in Shehaios. We try to avoid fighting over it." He looked across the Hall. The scrap had barely been apparent to most of the throng, involved in their own vociferous arguments. He couldn't see Kierce anywhere. "Try," he added, under his breath.

He felt a hand touch his arm, and looked round into Rainur's smiling face.

"Come," said Rainur. "You've had nothing to eat yet. Talk in a Meeting House means very little. Tomorrow we will discuss what really concerns you, and I hope then you'll understand the road that lies ahead of us. I don't ask you to like it. Just to understand that we have no choice but to set foot on it." He looked at Orlii. "Bring the Caiivorian boy with you, and allow my young champion time to come to his senses."

It was almost dawn when Caras got back to his bed in the guest quarters of the Palace, and he awoke after a brief, deep sleep to a thick head and a sun high in the sky. He groaned and fell out of the bed, groping for his boots and his cloak. He was late for his appointment with Rainur's hunting party.

Kierce had already gone – or more likely he had never been back. If Caras had not been drunk when he made it to his bed, he would have lain awake worrying about what Kierce was doing. It was becoming uncomfortably apparent to him that Kierce's ability to school creatures to obey his will was not limited to non-human life. He knew Kierce had taken control of his confrontation with the King just as much as Rainur had, just as he manipulated the twelve stones games. Caras found it worrying that a man so self-possessed and self-oriented held such power to deceive.

To his relief, Caras found his Horsemaster in the stable yard. He showed no sign of having been up all night, let alone at the same party as Caras. He seemed to derive some mirth from the sight of the dishevelled figure who approached him.

"Some night," Caras greeted him, cautiously.

"We seem to have been popular."

Caras paused. This was Kierce, his friend, the Horsemaster, who stopped him tripping over dragons. He had stood in front of the Meeting House and done everything but wrest the sword from Caras's side.

"You're going to tell me I should have seen it coming."

"I'm not sure what else you expected. Dramatic gestures tend to get peoples' interest."

"Yes, but I didn't mean … I meant to get Rainur to realise … I didn't consider what everyone else would think. For Spirit's sake, I didn't intend to incite a rebellion. If they—".

"I was talking to them to keep them away from you," Kierce interrupted, regarding his companion's agitation wryly. "I was afraid of what they might claim you'd promised them. I honestly think my fears are better justified than yours are. Don't you?"

"I'm sorry."

"So you should be. I don't cheat when I play with you, Caras."

Caras made no comment as Orlii scurried by, slopping water from a leather bucket.

"Oh, yes," said Kierce, "thanks for rescuing Orlii. I just stabled him with the Palace staff, it never occurred to me that the idiot would get involved in the fight. What do you do with the boy? He's frightened to death of us, but he's willing to stand up and fight for us." He shook his head. "Not a thought crosses that child's mind that isn't put there by someone else."

"He ate next to nothing and took most of what was left off the table when we went. He thought no-one saw him. We all knew he'd taken it. I was afraid Gascon was going to say something, but he didn't. It was appallingly bad manners."

"In Caiivor, I think it's called theft," said Kierce.

"Theft is taking … what someone else needs. Orlii was invited to eat with us."

"Yes, but he didn't think you meant it. He thought it was an opportunity to stock up against the times when no-one invited him to eat. Orlii's mind is a very curious place, Caras, it's not somewhere you want to be."

Caras frowned at the odd turn of phrase.

"What do you mean, it's a very curious place?"

Kierce slapped his shoulder. "You stick to trying to fathom out Rainur's mind, Caras. This is a very distinguished 'hunting party' we're joining. If you'll take my advice, you'll go and wake yourself up while Orlii and I get the horses ready. You need your wits in place. Whatever you like to pretend, you're here as the Holder of Arhaios and Chief of Oreath today."

Either by luck or discreet diplomacy on their host's part, although they were among the last to join the party gathered at the main gate to the Palace, they were there before Rainur arrived to signal the start of the journey to Dornas.

Kierce watched Caras take his place near the front, with the King and the other members of the Holder's Council. Since Gascon's arrival the only Councillors still missing were Ered, the chief of Hieath, and the Lord High Magician.

As they left the Haven, another latecomer joined the stragglers at the back of the group. He did not join the illustrious company around the King. He fell in beside Kierce, an unremarkable figure on a nondescript brown horse.

Kierce turned to see who was seeking his company. He was startled to see the appearance of the nondescript man on the nondescript brown horse fall away before his eyes to reveal a small, wizened figure riding an almost equally old and wizened grey unicorn.

It was only the manner of his appearance that told Kierce his new companion was Lord High Magician Turloch. Like almost everyone else in Shehaios, Kierce had never seen him before.

He threw a distasteful glance at Turloch's mount. He did not like to see a unicorn in harness. There were so few of them left and they were such fey creatures; their survival was always hanging in a balance any interference from man could tilt against them. Even Kierce, who spent much of his life in wild and remote places and could track any animal, had only ever seen three unicorns.

"Freath was an outcast when I found him," said Turloch, while Kierce was still forming the thought. "He would have died. Instead, he's grown old and fat and contented in the company of another awkward old bugger. You need what friends you can find, Lord Kierce."

Kierce shifted uncomfortably, unsure how to answer when the conversation hadn't even started. He had not realised quite how disturbing it could be to know that what you chose to say did not govern what your companion knew about your thoughts.

"You do well to remember it, Lord Kierce," commented Turloch, doing it again.

"This certainly is some extraordinary hunting party," observed Kierce.

"Oh, you knew that before," said Turloch. He tilted his round and wrinkled face up towards the young man who rode beside him and some way above him. Kierce found himself drawn to the curiously lucid green eyes. "I know you watch as I watch, Lord Kierce. It will take both of us to keep our people safe from those who don't need to hear what's said in Dornas Forest today. After that ... after that, you know very well there are other things the two of us need to talk about."

Deep in Dornas forest, the real hunters of the day had been there well before them. In a clearing, two small boars were already half roasted over a spit and the ceremonial seats of the Holder's Council were set in their traditional circle, awaiting their occupants.

Caras viewed the scene with mixed feelings. The last time the Council met, he had watched from the sidelines. This time, the seat bearing the emblem of Oreath's pale horse was waiting for him. But not in the Holder's Hall. In the forest, hidden from Caiivorian eyes. He had seen the Haven's guards dispersing into the woods as he saw Kierce ride off with a nondescript man on a brown horse, presumably to join them.

He waited to see what the others would do, particularly Hieath's chief, who had kept them all guessing until the last minute whether he was going to turn up at all.

Ered of Hieath was a large and comfortable man, made uncomfortable by his long journey to the Haven. He did not move fast. He took a long time dismounting, talking to his own party, and by the time he ambled over to the circle, most of the others were seated.

Caras quietly joined the circle. It followed the geography of the places represented at it, with the King and Mervecc at the southern end, Oreath to the west, and Hieath curving the circle north towards Ulath and east towards Ccheven. The Magician's place, between Ccheven and the King, remained unfilled, as it often did.

Once they were settled, Rainur arose to address the gathering.

"First of all, I apologise for the time, the place and the pretence. Need I explain it?"

"You need to explain why there are Caiivorians in the Palace," said Hieath.

"That's what I'm here to do. I issued an invitation to you all to celebrate my marriage to Princess Cathva and a peaceful alliance with the Caiivorian imperial family. Two of you have accepted, two wait at the edges of the Haven, and Oreath sends a proxy. It's not enough, my friends. I need your support."

"Don't you know what to do with Cathva?" said Onia. "I'll show you that, Rainur. You don't need any of these menfolk to advise you."

There was a murmur of laughter, which Rainur acknowledged with a smile.

"I don't need advice, Onia. I assure you, I've been guided in all my negotiations with the Emperor by Lord High Magician Turloch. What you must understand are the choices you're making in siding with me or going against me. Yesterday, Lord Caras brought me a challenge from a Holding on our southern border. Their Holder asks why I am marrying the Caiivorian Empire – the Empire that spawns the raiders who devastated his Holding. Caras," He turned towards Oreath, "why did you bring me the sword instead of using it against the men who attacked Prassan?"

Caras stared back at him for a moment in astonished indignation.

"There were twenty Caiivorian warriors!" he began.

"Exactly. They were too many, and too strong. If I know my Lord Gascon, the people of Mervecc are gathering even now to go to Prassan's assistance. I hope and trust they will succeed in restoring the Holding to Shaihen hands, but they will not do it without killing, and the blood ties of *caii* warrior always demand vengeance. So it starts, and so it goes on, until the rights and wrongs

53

of the original act are lost in a circle of hate and retribution. That was the circle broken by the meeting of the five tribes at the Haven."

He paused and looked around the listening Council.

"I am the Keeper of the Gate, the Guardian of Shehaios. We are a people who live in peace with each other. I can only defend that heritage by alliance with the Empire, not by declaring war on all Caiivor. Caiivor has breached our borders, and we cannot escape their wars. There are raiders living on the southern faces of our mountains, beyond the reach of the Emperor's soldiers, who plunder both the Caiivorian plains and the Holdings of Mervecc. There have been skirmishes along the east coast." He looked to Colis of Ccheven for confirmation and received a nod of agreement. "And the Western Ocean is dominated by the pirates of Aranth. How much trade does Oreath conduct with the Empire?"

"We have no need to trade with the Empire," said Caras. "Oreath's fishermen suffer no assaults."

"Nevertheless, this is a fight we can no longer stay outside. The Emperor is not prepared to leave Shehaios to become a refuge of those who live beyond his rule. If we don't invite the Empire in, they will come anyway."

"So we're to be overrun by the raiders and the outlaws, and the Imperial army?" said Ered of Hieath, with some sarcasm. "Do you envisage us having any say in this, Rainur? Or do we all roll over and do as your pretty princess bids us?"

"We retain our say in this, Ered, by employing the Imperial army to defend us from the raiders."

"We can defend ourselves," said Hieath, doggedly. "Against whatever Caiivor spews at us. We are people of the Spirit, we fight for our homeland."

Caras felt his blood stir. He almost voiced his approval, but checked himself. He saw Lasa's fearful eyes begging him not to tackle the men who had taken her Holding. Prassan's people were children of the Spirit. It hadn't been enough for them.

"Study the song of Vordeith, Ered," said Rainur. "It's a story of a people who grew tired of losing their wealthy Holding to raiding neighbours. They made it their business to be stronger than everyone around them, that's why they now they rule an Empire. To fight an enemy with weapons of their choosing is to serve the spirit of death, not the spirit of life."

"So you do see them as our enemy, Rainur," said Gascon.

Rainur turned to look at him. There was very little to show the anger provoked by Mervecc's quiet observation, but Caras could tell it was there. It convinced him, more than anything the King could have said, that Rainur spoke in earnest.

"When the song is sung in full you will learn quite what a triumph this courtship has been, Gascon," replied Rainur. "Our future does not lie in taking sides. If we don't invite the forces of the Sacred Union in, they will come anyway. If we do invite them, we retain our independence. They come and go with our knowledge and agreement."

"With the knowledge and agreement of the Royal Palace, perhaps," said Mervecc, "but the question is, Rainur, who occupies the Royal Palace after this marriage is made? The Keeper of the Gate? Or the client-king of Vordeith?"

"While I live, I am the Keeper of the Gate and the head of the Holdings of Shehaios," stated Rainur. "That is not in question. Unless it's one asked by this Council."

"And after your death?"

There was a telling pause before Rainur answered.

"I will name an heir, and the Council will take the final decision on the succession, as the history tells it."

"And will the Emperor accept it if you name as heir anyone other than the child of yourself and your Imperial Caiivorian wife?"

"Right now, we are looking at our own survival," cut in Rainur, impatiently. "Can you not understand that? Do you need to see with your own eyes the lands beyond the Gate?"

"I don't want to see with my own eyes the lands beyond the Gate brought this side of the mountains!" snapped Ered.

"We are all one land, it is all *haios*!" retorted Rainur. "I told you, I have not taken a step or a decision without consulting Turloch. What else is there for you to understand? Caras," he turned on the youngest of those present, "have I answered Prassan's challenge?"

Caras jumped slightly. This was exactly the sort of response to his challenge he had sought in making it, but he composed himself before he replied. He better understood now that when he spoke as the future chief of Oreath, his words had to be carefully chosen.

"You have answered it," he said, eventually, "and I believe what you say. But why did you have to say it here? Why not in the Holder's Hall?"

There was a tense silence.

"The Emperor does not make deals with councils," said Rainur. "He may revoke the agreement if he knew I had to have your approval for such a decision. That some of you demurred from the agreement. He has to believe that my word is law in Shehaios."

Gascon of Mervecc's long face always gave the impression he was only half paying attention to what was going on. But he responded while Caras was still deliberating, and Caras realised he was watching every nuance of Rainur's expression with the intensity of a Merveccian wildcat.

"So what happens if we don't agree, Rainur?"

"The Imperial Army is on its way here, Gascon," said Rainur. "Welcome it, or fight it. I've made my choice."

"A young and pretty one," said Onia of Ulath. "How much choice did she have, I wonder."

Caras was surprised to see Rainur look more thrown by this comment than by Gascon's accusation.

"A free one, Onia," he said. "It's not the romance the minstrels tell it as, but I wouldn't … I have every respect for the Lady Cathva. She has been an invaluable help to me in negotiating her father's agreement to this marriage, and without that marriage, we will have to fight not to surrender the government of Shehaios to the Emperor. That's what he wanted me to do. It's still what he wants me to do. We can never relax our guard against a people who don't respect the power which governs us, or they will play us like pebbles in a twelve stones game, and they will come out the winners." He paused. "When I make my promises to Cathva, and she to me, I deal us into that game. It will be up to all of us to win it. My position, my credibility with the Emperor, depends on your open and unquestioning support. I need to know who will be there. Mervecc?"

Gascon of Mervecc, prosaic governor of the merchant town, shrugged.

"I'm not about to declare war on the Sacred Union. But you're going to need a good game-player on your side, Rainur."

"Oreath?"

There was a pause. But Caras didn't think Leath wanted him to declare war on the Sacred Union, either.

"I will advise the Holder of Prassan to withdraw the challenge. I am prepared to trust your judgement, my lord, and … I'm sorry. Leath may have trusted you better."

"Leath would not come," observed Rainur ironically.

Caras met his eyes. "Indeed she wouldn't. But partly because what we're deciding here affects the future and not the past. Leath feels her age, Lord Rainur, even though she still doesn't look it."

"I'm sorry to hear it. But I'm happy to see that Oreath's future is in good hands. So," Rainur turned to Ered, "that leaves Hieath. Since, of course, any Caiivorians have to go through any one of the other chieftains to reach you, Ered."

Ered bristled. "What are you saying?"

"That you can better afford cosy gestures than the rest of us," said the Holder of Mervecc, on the southern border. "Time to stop sitting outside the Haven muttering into your beard, Ered. Time to come in and stand beside Rainur, for better or worse."

"I'm not getting married!" retorted Ered.

"We all are," said Gascon. "Shame only old Rainur gets the pretty girl to go with it."

The debate continued among the wider company over the roasted boar. The smaller Holders did not speak at the Council, but they were always entitled to be there and form their own opinions. Caras listened with half a mind to the task which he knew lay ahead of him. He had an uncomfortable feeling most of the rest of Oreath would have preferred him to leave the sword drawn. He wished he could talk to Kierce about how to tackle them. He scanned the deep shadows of the forest around them, but there was no sign of him.

To finish the day, Rainur had arranged for the provision of some trophies, in proof that it had indeed been just a hunting party that kept them so long in the forest.

The small herd edged into the clearing calmly, grazing as they went, unaware of their danger. The two who drove them were invisible to them.

It was done as a gift from Rainur to those who had come there and supported him, and they fell on it with good-humoured appreciation of the gesture. The quick and the lucky fled, others went down to feed Rainur's wedding feast.

Caras was taken almost as much by surprise as the deer were, and loosed a poor shot. It struck his quarry in the hindquarters, trapping a nerve and crippling its rear legs. It staggered for the cover of the forest, but didn't quite make it before it fell. Before Caras reached the stricken creature, Kierce was there with his knife, slitting its throat. There was no expression on his face as he did it except concentration on the efficient completion of the job.

"Sorry," Caras felt constrained to say. "My mind wasn't really on it."

"I've seen cleaner kills," said Kierce, unconcernedly. "But he's a good fat animal, he'll grace the King's table well enough." He glanced at Caras. "Are we still eating at it?"

"Yes. We are." Caras paused. "Where did you get to, anyway?"

"Watching your back," said Kierce with a smile. "And providing your quarry for you. Just as well judging by that shot. You need practice, old man."

"I wasn't expecting to actually do any hunting!"

"Then the Caiivorians would have thought you an even more strange hunting party than they already do."

"Did you see any?"

"Caiivorians? Yes. Some. We took care of them."

Caras looked at Kierce in slight alarm as he worked the knife around the entrails of the deer, dressing it fit for transport back to the Haven. It was a perfectly routine task, which Kierce had carried out hundreds of times. Yet today, Caras found his efficiency oddly disturbing.

"Took care of them?"

Kierce laughed.

"I think killing them might have been a touch undiplomatic, don't you think? I was with the Lord High Magician, Caras, we had more subtle ways of deflecting their attention."

"You were with … Turloch?" exclaimed Caras in astonishment. "I don't understand."

"You don't need to. Not your business, Caras."

"I didn't even know he was here!"

"You weren't supposed to. No-one ever knows he's there. But he usually is."

Cathva could hardly keep still while she waited for the captain of her guard to arrive with news of the hunt in Dornas Forest. She felt like a child on her naming day. She was almost ashamed of her excitement; she knew she must not let Rainur see it. He would consider it a tasteless subject for entertainment.

But she struggled to contain her impatience to hear how he had done it. He would have been subtle. And she did love a good tale of murder.

She raised her eyes expectantly as the door opened and the soldier came in. There was nothing in Orcen's expression to give the game away, but he was a stolid sort of individual and his face rarely carried any clues to his feelings. She knew he had some. He had been captain of her personal guard since she was a little girl, and he was very worried about Rainur's unruly court. She was astonished that he could not see why Rainur had invited the nobleman who threatened him with a naked blade in his own hall to go hunting. It was obvious to her. Lord Caras's doddery old grandmother made a far safer Chief of Oreath than the young firebrand himself.

"Well?" the question tumbled out of her before she could stop it. "What news, Orcen?"

Orcen saluted her with a stiff bow.

"The Chiefs of Shehaios, and the King, went hunting, Your Highness."

"Well, I know that. What happened?"

"They took a good bag of deer, and returned to the Haven. In good spirits, as far as I could tell."

"Lord Caras?" prompted Cathva.

"I believe Lord Caras took down two young bucks. I didn't see it for myself, they were out of our sight for much of the morning."

Cathva turned away from the grave self-righteousness in her bodyguard's eyes. Disappointment and dismay sank through her body. She had been so sure. What was Rainur playing at?

"I expressed my concerns for your safety to the King, Highness," Orcen went on. "I have to say I was not reassured by his response." He hesitated. "You are not obliged to go through with this, Highness. Commander Hiren's forces will be here in a month's time. I have every confidence in the Commander's ability to establish his presence here whether Shehaios welcomes him or not—."

"No!" interrupted Cathva, furiously. That was not the plan. She wanted to walk through the golden Haven as the beloved Queen of the Fair Land, not live guarded in her Palace against barbarian rebels. "No. Thank you, Orcen. I have agreed to this marriage, and I will make it."

"You are young, Highness, and when we are young, sometimes we dream—".

"Thank you, Orcen," snapped Cathva. "I am not dreaming. I trust Lord Rainur." A knock on the door saved her. "Enter."

It was Tilsey.

"The King wishes to see you, my lady."

Cathva gave Orcen a condescending look.

"That will be all, Captain. Thank you."

He bowed briefly to her and walked out without a word. His stride said it all. After all, he was the man who would stand between her and Caras of Oreath's sword.

Rainur came in smiling. He rarely looked at her without smiling, and Cathva enjoyed watching her reflection in his eyes. She was a student of beauty, who knew herself to be beautiful.

Rainur seemed particularly pleased with himself today. He didn't look like a man whose plans had gone awry.

He exchanged a cheerful greeting with Tilsey before he crossed the room and kissed the hand of his betrothed. He raised his head, and looked into her eyes.

Cathva allowed herself to melt graciously into his arms. She was pleased to find he neither looked nor smelled like a man who had been out hunting all day. He did not wear scent, as so many Vordeithan noblemen did, but his smell was clean and pleasantly masculine.

He kissed her lips, such a delicate, tender kiss that Cathva almost wanted to laugh.

Is this why your first wife bore you no children, Rainur?

It hadn't been an easy judgement, deciding whether or not to make him abide by the mores of her people, but Cathva was confident now that she had got it right. Rainur was a man of ideals, and the image of perfect, innocent maidenhood drew him far better than any license she could have allowed him. Once she let him transgress the boundaries, he might have been repelled by the superficiality of the image. Unlike her young artists, Cathva's future husband had barely touched her.

"I hope Orcen has not been worrying you with his insecurities," he said, drawing back from her and smiling into her face. He was a comely man, his face smooth, his features regular, his light brown eyes full of life and energy. The age lines made him look authoritative, not old. He wasn't old. Less than twice her age. And for all his diplomatic skill, in many ways, quite child-like. His faith in the innate goodness of people was as admirable as it was foolish. "Your captain seems to think he is still in Caiivor, not in Shehaios."

His grin suggested a shared secret, but she didn't share it.

"He has valid concerns, my lord."

"Cathva!" His tone was gently reproving. "I sent Caras to meet you. I trusted you to see what kind of a man he is."

Oh, she had seen what kind of a man he was. Such fearless eyes. She was the first to admire a handsome warrior, but you did have to be careful where you pointed them. They were inclined to go off unexpectedly.

It did not take a political genius to understand the danger of disloyal warriors, nor the power of the mob – she had heard of the riotous debate in the Meeting House last night, too. Her father tolerated debate, within the walls of Academia. Not on street corners. Certainly not in his Palace.

"The Council met in Dornas Forest today ..." began Rainur.

"I thought they were meeting tomorrow?"

"Tomorrow, their words will be reported to the Emperor. I wanted them to be able to speak their minds, as they are used to doing."

"Lord Caras seemed to need little invitation."

"Caras, to use your phrase, had legitimate concerns, but he more than anyone knows there are already Caiivorians in Shehaios. He met a bunch of raiders on his way here, that's what upset him. He just needed to understand."

Cathva stared at him in astonishment.

"You took Caras out into the forest to *talk* to him?"

Rainur's eloquence, like his extraordinarily untarnished idealism, was all a part of his charm. He spoke and acted as if he really believed in this mythical Fair Land of his, and since he was its king, he had persuaded Cathva it could have a certain reality. But there were limits to naïvety, and Cathva considered them reached when weapons were drawn.

"Of course," he said, as if it was the most obvious thing to do with a rebel. "Caras is a good man, Cathva. He's a son of the Spirit."

None of which would necessarily stop him killing you, thought Cathva.

"Orcen has worried you, hasn't he? Don't be afraid, Cathva." Rainur came over to her and rested his hands on her shoulders. "Cathva, your safety and your happiness are no less to me because there are politics involved in our marriage. You are safe here. I hope you will be happy. You already have my love."

She turned and looked into his strong face, wondering how such a clever man could be such a fool. Throughout their courtship in Vordeith, Cathva knew she had done nothing except respond to Rainur's expectations of her. She had approved him as a marriage partner, and she wasn't going to do anything to drive him away. She had listened and studied him, and made herself what he wanted her to be. He knew nothing about her.

He kissed her again, with just as much restraint as before. A little shudder ran through her. Was she really marrying a man with water for blood, whose kingdom was at the mercy of his nobles?

It crossed her mind for the first time to wonder whether her father was really trusting her to bring him news of Shehaios, or abandoning her to a rebel kingdom where her antics at court would embarrass him no further. She embraced Rainur with sudden fervour.

"Promise me you will always protect me, Lord Rainur."

"In a week's time, I will take a solemn oath to do so. But I've already promised it where it matters." He touched her face affectionately. "You have nothing to fear from Shehaios, Cathva. No-one is going to hurt you."

Chapter 8
The Eve of the Wedding

In the early evening of the day before Rainur's marriage, Kierce strode back through the Palace gardens to the guest quarters with a raging resentment clouding his mind. It was nothing to do with Caras. He had no idea what Caras was doing. For the first time in many years, it was his own future that preoccupied him.

Over the years since he began to develop his ability to share minds, it had gradually become apparent to Kierce that the powers he possessed were what others called Shaihen magic, but the consequential link between that realisation and the office of the Lord High Magician was one he deliberately refused to make. Caras was destined for the responsibilities of a Holder, he was bred to it. He would take on the Chieftain's mantle like a cygnet moulting into its adult feathers. It was not a destiny Kierce had any desire to embrace; he did not see the point of learning what Turloch wished him to learn, and Turloch seemed less than committed to teaching him.

In fact, Turloch was impossible. He talked in riddles. Kierce couldn't even keep up with the names of the lands and gods and princes whose stories and politics he waxed lyrical about. He spun patterns out of numbers, found the power of the sun in the minutest particles of matter. He seemed to have lived for ever and to know everything, from the intimate workings of the human body to the make-up of the infinite heavens.

Every Holder knew their own land, what grew and what would not grow, how many of each creature there was, the balance between hunter and prey. The Magician was the ultimate Holder, outside the authority of the Shaihen king. He drew on knowledge no other Shaihen could access to read the winds and the waters and the people and the whole, the *haios.* Turloch was scathing of Kierce's inability to pick up in a few days what Turloch had spent a lifetime devoting his extraordinary mind to. He was utterly contemptuous of some of the uses to which Kierce had turned his powers.

He was, as Kierce quickly realised, utterly contemptuous of his pupil. He didn't think anyone would be able to replace him when he was gone.

Kierce had suffered a day of Turloch's mercurial dialectics. He had endured the Magician's provocative and abusive methods of instruction until he was ready to add the word magicide to the Shaihen vocabulary. He was on the edge of his tolerance of his fellow man.

The wedding celebrations were due to commence that evening, and Kierce resolved to throw himself into them heart and soul. The spirit of distilled malt barley seemed to him to hold a greater attraction just at the moment than the Spirit of Shehaios.

Princess Cathva an' Zelt was also in the Palace gardens. Like Kierce, she was wrestling with thoughts of her future.

These formal gardens were a memento of Rainur's time in Vordeith, created to commemorate his sister. Cathva knew the sad little Shaihen footnote to Vordeithan society that was the tale of the Princess Loia. She would have been about Cathva's age when she entered into marriage, with a head full of Shaihen dreams and no idea what it meant to be the fourth wife of a powerful Vordeithan nobleman. She was dead, by her own hand, within two years of the ceremony.

The gardens created in her memory were the only part of the Shaihen Royal Palace which reminded Cathva of her home, and on the eve of her own marriage, even an Imperial Princess sought the solace of semi-familiar surroundings. She was feeling a long way from home, and very much alone.

Despite appearances, she was beginning to understand that Rainur was not – or did not consider himself – a citizen of her father's Empire. His Palace was not at all like the Imperial Court, his people barely treated him with respect, let alone reverence, and Cathva feared Shaihen servants would be the ruin of her marriage. They were woefully trained and insufferably insolent – she had found her orders disputed, postponed and revised in ways that would have parted the culprit's skin from their back in Vordeith. Her complaints to Rainur were met by his gentle insistence that Shehaios was not like other places. He had said that to her before, in Vordeith. But Cathva was only now beginning to understand what he meant.

Already, Shehaios had infected even her most devoted servant with something close to sedition. That was what had occasioned her first argument with her betrothed.

Ever since her mother's banishment, her Shaihen slave woman, Tilsey, had been Cathva's closest and most trusted confidante. Sixteen years older than her mistress, Tilsey had in many ways taken the place of Cathva's absent mother, but she had never before presumed on her closeness to say anything other than words her mistress wished to hear. Cathva had no idea where the suggestions she was making now were coming from. *Discuss* her needs with the Palace servants? *Ask* them if something can be done – even, for god's sake, how to do it? Cathva had not come to Shehaios to practice humility. She had come to acquire the mantle of a Queen.

Tilsey apologised for provoking the furious tirade Cathva hurled at her head. After all, she knew very well she had deserved it. It would all have blown over, if only Rainur had not overheard.

He took Cathva aside and told her gently that she could no longer regard Tilsey as a slave, or even a servant, if she was to become Queen in the Home of the Free. Her relationship to the people who made up the Palace community had to change. Inside, Cathva was furious at being told how to run her household, but she lowered her long lashes and demurred without question to her future husband's chastisement. She knew what it was to lose a great man's favour. Her mother lost the great man's favour.

Rainur was all she had here, and the night before she married him, Cathva was desperately homesick for the sweet, perfidious embrace of the Imperial City. She hid her face in the heavily scented alien hedges from the south of the Empire while tears of rage and self-pity disfigured her perfection.

She heard the purposeful footsteps approaching her retreat and struggled hastily to swallow the sobs. Was there nowhere in this place where anyone could get any privacy? She looked round the end of the maze as a small Shaihen man strode past her on the path. His long hair was tied back in a pony-tail, and a line of black beard traced his jaw. She recognised him at once. The experience of Kierce's deep and searching gaze was as difficult to forget as it was to forgive.

He turned as she emerged.

"Don't worry," he said, brusquely. "Rainur will like you well enough without your clothes on."

Cathva gave a small gasp of outrage. He wasn't even one of Rainur's Holders. In Vordeith, he wouldn't have been allowed to breathe the same air as her.

"How dare you!" she exclaimed, the blood rushing to her cheeks.

It was only then that Kierce realised what he'd actually said. What he meant was that her Caiivorian costume created a barrier to Rainur's Shaihen tastes as it did to Kierce's, but he realised that was not how it sounded to Cathva's Caiivorian sensibilities. He raised his hand apologetically.

"Poor choice of words, Lady, forgive me," he said, with a slight smile.

"You have no business to be here in the first place!" she went on, ignoring the apology. "I know your insolence. You're Lord Caras's servant, aren't you?"

Kierce's jaw tightened in annoyance. The word she used was part way between servant and slave.

"My lady needs to learn a little more about our people, I think."

"Don't deny it! You're groom to the Lord of Arhaios, if I call the guard I could have you flogged just for being here!"

She knew she couldn't. But she felt she ought to be able to. Shaihen servants were completely intolerable.

"I am the Horsemaster of Arhaios," replied Kierce, tersely, "And we're not in your father's house now, we're in Shehaios. You have little enough time left to understand what that means before you become one of our people, my lady, you'd better start learning fast. Forgive me for intruding on your unhappiness, and I'll forgive you for the insult."

He nodded curtly to her and turned away.

"Don't walk away from me!" commanded Cathva. Kierce, gritting his teeth, ignored her. "Don't you dare walk away from me!"

She almost saw his temper snap. He turned on her.

"All right, Lady Cathva. I won't walk away from you."

She felt his gaze lock and hold her. She felt the presence invade her, lapping over her mind. She stared at him, trembling in the grip of a power she did not understand. Cold sweat bathed her body. A thousand unseen fears fluttered at the edges of her consciousness.

An image came to her of the spring that gave life to the Haven, stars in the open sky above it glimpsed through dark clouds of night. Walls of golden stone enclosed her, and the warm, damp scent of living plants filled her nostrils. She closed her eyes. Without moving she reached for the bubbling water, leaned into its flow. She could almost feel it on her lips, warm and pungent tasting. It splashed off her face and onto her body. Its sudden touch on her skin stung. She was naked beneath it. Still aware of Kierce's physical presence, she cried out in confusion, reality and enchantment teasing her brain.

The image faded and she stood, breathing heavily, in the gardens of the Palace. She was fully clothed and quite dry. Facing her stood the slight, contained figure of the Horsemaster of Arhaios, composed, unreadable, uncommandable, a servant who was not a servant.

But he was human, and separate. The presence in her mind had gone.

She let out a slow, shaken breath.

"What did you—how did you—?"

"How did I know you were afraid your husband wouldn't want you in his bed? That you fear you can't manipulate his favour? You didn't ask me that, did you? As I said, lady, you have much to learn."

And I have the power to teach you.

He smiled, and went on his way.

She did not try and stop him this time. She was not sure what his parting words had been, whether the last mocking phrase had been spoken, or in her head, or something stirring in her own desire.

Caras was glad to accept Kierce's invitation to visit the Haven's spring, despite the late hour at which it was issued. It seemed entirely appropriate to commit their troubles to the living waters from the heart of the Shaihen mountains before their lives were married for ever to the fortunes of the Empire. He was under no illusion that Kierce also had troubles of some kind at the moment. He had been more than a little concerned by his friend's effective disappearance during the past few days, and relieved to see Kierce back to his old self at the celebrations for Rainur's forthcoming wedding, participating with gusto in the ritual of song and storytelling. Caras was still smiling at some of the barbed and pithy couplets Kierce had decorated the ballads with as they passed out of the chill night air into the muggy embrace of the Temple built around the Haven's hot spring. The walls overlapped each other like a maze, leading into an enclosed area where the people of the

Haven had dug out the natural hollow formed by the water gushing out of the side of the mountain. The warm waters welcomed the weary into a pool sufficiently large for six or seven people to bathe in comfortably.

The curved roof, made of translucent golden slates worked from the rock of the surrounding mountains, covered only the pool. The south end of the building was closed by the sheer face of the mountain, leaving the spring that flowed from it open to the sky. Woven around walls, spring, roof-pillars and pool was an abundant growth of vegetation, clinging to the micro-atmosphere created by the warmth from the spring and the enclosing building.

In the early hours of Rainur's wedding day, the temperature in the town outside was a little below freezing. Within the Temple of the Spring, it was consistently comfortable to bare human skin. Though at an hour or so before dawn, only just so.

Caras welcomed the chill in the air as he stripped off his clothes. It had been an evening of loud and boisterous celebration, and it was so easy to get carried away by the songs and the humour of the storytelling, easy to believe at that moment that his people were invincible, and immortal. He slipped slowly down into the warm water, enjoying the feel of it opening up his skin. He said nothing to the three people already there. Caras did not worship the spring, but like all his people, he revered it. The fronds of greenery and colourful blooms that surrounded it all year round were visible proof of its fecundity, and its constant flow was precious when the icy grip of winter froze everything else around it. For this warm spot, the Haven was named. The sweating of a steam lodge was fine for every day, and an excellent place for a Holder to keep tabs on the latest gossip, but this was different. It was an individual ritual, but it was nevertheless a ritual, concerned with more than just cleansing the body.

He lay in the water, absorbing the past, contemplating the future. Kierce lay silently beside him, cocooned in his own thoughts. After a while, the man and the two women who had been there when they arrived got out and left the two Arhaiens alone.

"Do you know her name, this time?" asked Caras, after a few minutes.

Kierce replied without opening his eyes.

"It's a man."

For a few seconds, until he remembered it was Kierce he was talking to, Caras felt less comfortable to be lying naked in the water beside him. Kierce met his slightly startled gaze with amusement.

"And I thought life was just for living," he said with a sigh. "I had no idea it was all so complicated."

"Am I supposed to know what you're talking about?"

"You rarely do. It doesn't seem to be a problem for you. I just wish you'd realised what you were doing, turning me into Orlii's demon."

Caras said nothing, still feeling faintly disturbed. He suspected Kierce was teasing him. He would have sworn his fondness for women was unequivocal.

"I thought you'd sorted that out?"

"I've persuaded him I won't flay him alive on a whim. He still dissolves in terror if I merely frown at him. And I can't get rid of him – he follows me around like a puppy. Quieter, but a lot less appealing." He smiled. "Don't worry, Caras. He's my slave in the Caiivorian sense, not the Shaihen."

"Shaihens don't have slaves."

"We're all slaves to our own passions. It's what makes Rainur's job so unenviably difficult. You ought to bear that in mind, hero." He stretched and closed his eyes again. "In the meantime, let's just make the most of it while we can. *Haois o caras.*" (Life from the rock).

He slid down so that the cloudy golden waters covered him completely, face as well. Caras frowned at him disconsolately. Kierce never seemed to have any difficulty knowing what went on in his head; one of these days maybe he would work out what went on in Kierce's.

Caras left the pool first. By the time he had dried and dressed himself, his companion still showed no sign of moving, except to surface periodically to breathe, rather like the whales that spouted off Oreath's coast.

"If you stay too much longer you'll turn into a shrimp," he commented. Kierce didn't answer. Caras turned to go. "I'll see you at the ceremony. Don't be late."

He had no idea if Kierce had heard him. He gave up, and headed back for the Palace for a few hours sleep. Once the ceremony was over and his duty done, he wanted to get on the road for Arhaios without further delay.

Later that morning, Caras stood sweating in the packed Meeting House, fretting at the absences to Rainur's wedding. It was well past the hour appointed for the ceremony, and Cathva had not arrived yet.

Neither had Ered of Hieath. He had been present at the previous night's celebrations, reciting histories with casuistic accuracy, but it seemed he was not going to lend his presence to the actual promise. Last night, he had set himself up repeatedly as a target for Kierce's incisive wit. Caras had been as helpless with laughter as everyone else. He fervently hoped that was not the cause of Hieath's absence this morning.

At least Gascon was there. He was standing beside Caras as they both turned towards a noise from the doorway. It was no-one they knew.

"Where is your Horsemaster, Caras?" enquired Gascon.

Caras was wondering exactly the same thing himself. Drunk or distracted in the arms of some woman, he suspected. He cursed himself for letting Kierce's philosophical mood at the Temple fool him. He should have insisted they left together.

"I'm sure he'll be here."

"I think the King is as anxious for his support as he is for yours or mine. Since you left Mervecc, I have heard nothing but stories of his good fortune." He glanced wryly at Caras. "You'd better warn him, Caras – if the Caiivorians ever find out how he does it, he may need an army of his own. They're not used to losing against Shaihens."

"Twelve stones is a game of skill," said Caras. "Kierce is a skilful player."

"Uncommonly skilful," remarked Gascon. "Oh, I like Kierce, Caras. Don't misunderstand me. I wouldn't like to see him come to any harm."

"Kierce protects me, Lord Gascon, not I him. His defences aren't easily outwitted."

Though I wish I knew where the dark unknown he was. And where the hell Orlii is.

"I don't doubt it," said Gascon. "On the subject of protection, you may like to know that I hope to have an armed force leaving Mervecc little more than a week from now."

"A week? That's quick."

"As I said, your news was not entirely unexpected. I can only hope rescuing Prassan will not bring fire down on my own Holding."

"If it does …" Caras thought of the warm, rich Holding with its throng of people. "Oreath will do for Mervecc what Mervecc is doing for Prassan, I promise you."

"Thank you, Caras. I hope I will never need to ask you." He paused. "If you wish, I will settle the matter of Prassan's challenge with their Holder. I suspect you are anxious to return to Oreath, and Prassan is, after all, my responsibility."

And it was Gascon who fed the doubts about Rainur's integrity in Caras's head. Caras gave him a surreptitious glance.

"Do you play twelve stones, Lord Gascon?"

Gascon chuckled.

"Every Shaihen Holder should study the play of the stones, Lord Caras. Youth excuses impetuousity and it needed to be said plainly. The Council in Dornas Forest was just what we needed, and I don't know for certain it would have happened without you. Rainur's very nervous of his Imperial observers."

The trumpets sounded their Imperial flourish. Cathva had arrived.

Kierce was going to miss it.

Chapter 9
Cathva and the Magician

It was some time after Caras left the Temple that Cathva arrived.

She came alone, slipping secretly out of her quarters after she had retired for the night, swearing Tilsey to secrecy. No-one must know she had come, but she couldn't sleep for wondering what she had touched in the garden that evening. It was a power such as she had never known before. She could not get the dream of it – it was a dream, what else could it have been? – out of her mind. It pulled her towards the Temple.

She didn't understand the Shaihen gods. Rainur said they had none, but Cathva didn't see how that could be so. She had heard about Shaihen magic, the force which kept the Fair Land golden and peaceful. She always found it difficult to equate the myth of exquisite beauty with the small, dessicated figure of Lord High Magician Turloch – what she had tasted earlier seemed much more promising.

Although Cathva had been brought up in the faith of her mother's people and their single, patriarchal god, her father patronised a number of the temples which populated Vordeith. She found his pragmatism much more to her taste. The immortals came by different names, who could tell which ones could be safely ignored? Cathva had always chosen the ones whose ceremonies she liked best and Rainur assured her there was nothing to fear from the Temple of Life. It was just a spring, just water coming up from the earth. You bathe in it, he said, take off your clothes and let it wash over you. It's very relaxing. Renews your spirit.

The very thought was a little exciting. Her mother's god was a harsh deity conceived under the fierce suns and the parched landscape of the southern deserts, and his laws on nakedness were strict. Women were never seen unclothed except when their men required it, and water was something to be used sparingly. It had nothing to do with the spirit. Spirits were more affected by fire, unless you were virtuous and obeyed the rules.

Rules or no rules, Cathva was used to getting her own way. Threats of fire didn't seem particularly meaningful when she was about to become a Shaihen queen.

Besides, no-one knew she was going there.

Except the one who had told her to come.

Kierce sensed with something other than hearing the fall of her delicately shod foot as she crept cautiously around the wall into the temple. He held his breath. He hadn't really thought she would come.

He wallowed in his own power as he watched her creep around the end of the walls into the Temple. He rolled the little thrill of fear she felt on his tongue, enjoying the taste of it – so different from Orlii's draining terror – and slid behind her eyes, to see it as she saw it.

Cathva's gaze went straight to the spring bursting out of the rock at the far end, a froth of silver light reflecting from the moon overhead. The murky waters of the bathing pool were obscured beneath a low mist of steam, and she barely glanced at it. There would be no-one else here at this time of day.

Though she could sense a presence. It sparkled through her in imitation of the spring's exuberance.

She slid off her heavy over-cloak in the warmth which rose to meet her, and moved slowly towards the fall, looking up, entranced, at the unique roof and the exotic flowers. She trailed her hands through the creepers that wound up the pillars as she passed them, remembering the soft, damp feel and the soft damp smell. The gently thunderous fall of the waters filled her ears. She was walking through a dream, alive to every scent and texture around her.

Reaching the spring, she leaned tentatively towards it. She licked the waters that splashed in her face, and grimaced at the taste. Laughing, she held her hands under the fall, then kicked off her shoes and stepped into the edge of the splash pool. Water soaked into the hem of her gown and cascaded over her face onto her shoulders and breasts. With a rebellious joy in her heart, she unlaced the gown, and stepped out of it.

A swathe of undergarments still hid her from prying eyes. Kierce was forced to take a careful breath to stop himself laughing. He couldn't hold this much longer.

She knelt in the shallow pool under the spouting water and raised her hands.

"Spirit of Life hold me safe!" She spoke into the rush of the waterfall, imploring the foreign gods. "Make me a powerful queen of this place!"

She heard the different sound of surging waters behind her. She spun round, startled. The naked figure of a man rose from the steamy mist of the pool, a man with the slender form, the sharp features, the black hair and close-trimmed beard of the man in her waking dream. He stood more terrible than the nightmare, unconfined even by clothing now, the creamy waters swirling around his thighs and running in silvered rivulets down his body.

Cathva gave a shriek of terror and cowered where she knelt, covering her head with her arms.

She heard him climb out of the pool. She did not dare to look at him. She knew that merely looking at a god could destroy her. The presence in her mind began to throb like her heartbeat.

"Spare me," she breathed. "I beg you!"

"Spare you? I don't know if I can do that."

His voice was terrifyingly close. She felt him touch her shoulder lightly. The impression of his fingertips on her wet skin left a slight sensation of burning.

"Fire for death," he said, softly. "Why do you wish to worship death, Lady Cathva?"

"Forgive me," moaned Cathva. "I didn't mean to offend you."

"You ask a lot," said Kierce. "When I am, after all, only groom to the Lord of Arhaios."

He caught her arm and drew her onto her feet.

Cathva choked back a shriek, though there was no hurt in his touch this time. She cowered away from him, scrupulously averting her eyes. When he let her go she did not dare to move.

Kierce began to unfasten the complex pinning of her hair.

"Are we still talking of flogging, do you think? Have you done much of that? No, you don't do it, do you, not a lady of your sensibility. You order it done. It feels good to instil fear, to command and be obeyed, without thinking. Without feeling what it is that they feel. You turn in your golden prison and heap chains on all those whose space is smaller than your own. That's a lot of people, when you're a princess, isn't it? More when you're a queen." He ran his fingers through the lock of hair he had freed. "A powerful queen of this place."

His voice sounded in Cathva's head like the waterfall, a rush of sound. Her mind hurtled around what he was saying, and couldn't stop long enough to make any sense of it. All her life, Cathva had feared only her father. With his protection, she need fear no other man. Until Kierce rose naked from the waters in the Temple of Life, and she wasn't sure then whether what she beheld was a man or a god. He was so close. *He was inside her.*

"Who … who are you?" she whispered.

He let the loose hair fall across her shoulders and began to work methodically at another lock. He ignored the question.

"People, creatures, life in general. Where are you, Lady Cathva?"

"I am in the Haven. In the Temple of the Spring."

"Why are you here?"

"I wished … forgive me, I only came here to worship the gods of this place. I meant no harm!"

He found a key pin and the rest of her hair tumbled loose from its constraints. He turned her to face the spring.

"We have no gods, Lady Cathva. We are the people of the Spirit." He seized the material of her undergarment and ripped it apart. She gasped as the warm waters fell on her bare flesh. "The Spirit knows what you hide as well as it knows what you fear. It knows when your father sends you here to paint Lord Rainur a pretty picture of life married to the Imperial family." He stripped the last of the clothing from her body and thrust her right under the falling waters. Cathva spluttered and struggled as the water hit her face, pouring into her eyes and her mouth. It tasted foul.

"Now, you're fit to marry him. Now …" he paused. His voice softened. "Now you are beautiful."

The hand still grasping her shoulder relaxed its grip. She felt his fingers begin to explore the texture of her skin.

"By the Spirit, you are beautiful."

His voice dropped so low she hardly heard him.

This was something she recognised. She held her breath. His hand slid slowly down her arm and came to rest on her hip. His other hand balanced it, mapping the narrow curve of her waist. She heard the water break on his head as he leaned forwards and she felt his breath on her shoulder. She pulled away from him, through the waterfall.

He did not try to hold her. She couldn't go far. She was trapped between the face of the mountain and his body. She pushed herself against the rock as if she could find a way out through it. Her face pressed against the warm, fragrant stone, her nails dug at the surface, scraping a thin film of slime but giving her no purchase. She waited, breathing hard, not daring to give voice to the prayers to her own god running through her head.

The rock steadied her. She wrestled her thoughts clear of the overwhelming fear. This presence in her mind was what she had come here seeking. It was this man – god – whatever he was, she sought. She knew that he was playing with her, that what she felt was the faintest touch of a wonderful, terrible power that could destroy her and still only draw on a fraction of its potential. She wanted it. She wanted it even more than she feared it.

The waiting dragged on and he made no further move. If she didn't understand what he was, she had understood the way he had begun to stroke her skin.

Cautiously, with every grain of courage she possessed, and leaning hard against the rock for support, she turned her head towards him. With nothing left to protect her, she dared to look at him.

She waited. No bolt of power struck her down. He was just standing the other side of the water, watching her, as he had watched her in the garden.

"Who are you? What are you?"

"For now," replied Kierce. "I am this place."

She turned fully to face him, her back pressed against the rock. Whatever he was, he was at least enough man to find her desirable, that much she could read. She was not used to being desired like this, stripped of her riches and her finery, but if that was what he wanted, it was a currency she dealt in. It was freely traded in Vordeith, among both gods and men.

"I will serve you," she said. Her voice, like her body, still shook with fear. "I've trespassed in the Temple of Life, and I am yours to command. But if you will make me a powerful queen of this place, I will serve you—."

He surged forwards and seized her shoulders.

"For Spirit's sake, be silent you stupid woman! Don't you ever think of anyone as an equal?"

She stared into the dark eyes that saw straight through to her deepest desire. She had thought he spoke from anger, but she saw a reflection of her own alarm looking back at her. She didn't understand.

"You serve the King," he said. "You're marrying the King."

"You have power beyond that of Kings. Does he not serve you?"

"Don't you understand, woman? Shaihens do not serve."

She watched him steadily, balanced between terror and desire.

"I am not Shaihen. What would you have me do?"

For a moment frozen in time, he did not answer.

"Sweet waters, you know what I'd have you do," he whispered.

He touched her face, pushing back the wet hair. A shudder ran through her. She couldn't tell what emotion it was. She turned cautiously and kissed his palm. His lips brushed her forehead, and closed her eyes. His body was so close, so real, so exciting. She couldn't stop herself reaching out to touch him, caressing the sinewy muscle of his back and shoulders. His mouth closed over hers hungrily. She felt the desire flood through her, and neither knew nor cared whether it came from her or from the enchanter in her arms.

When he was that close to another life, Kierce could not filter what he shared and what he did not. He felt both his own desire and her fear; he worked on her mind and her body to drown the one in the other, for both of them. Cathva was so easy, he barely needed to touch her. She had created this illusion for him; none of this was in Turloch's book of spells. Kierce doubted this was in Turloch's ken. It was very much in his. This was what he was supposed to be giving up, and this was precisely why; he knew from the moment he let humanity slip into the god-like act that he was losing control of it.

The first time he experienced the overlay of sexual union on the mental link he could forge he had been very young and very besotted with the girl in question. Neither of them had realised, at the time, that the intensity they shared was out of the ordinary. Now, he found it hard to resist a woman he sensed an affinity for, even if her passions were not immediately aroused by the small Arhaien Horsemaster. It was so easy to arouse them. It was getting less and less easy to deny himself, and now he could not stop.

The Caiivorian woman's body was unbelievably soft and perfect. It was the most beautiful thing he had ever seen, the most exquisite to touch. He could smell her own scent now, not the cloying artificiality she doused herself with, and it was strange and wonderful to him. His tongue on her skin tasted the pungent spring waters as well as the sweetness of the woman.

The dangers inherent in who they were and where they were shrieked at the back of his mind but he could barely hear.

He felt her hands exploring the physical reality of what held her with the same sense of excitement. He grasped the treacherous tendril of desire in her mind and held fast, teasing and caressing it until he knew she was his for the taking. Against the face of the golden mountain, beneath the waters of the living spring, he took her.

It was only as the passion subsided that Kierce began to realise what he had done. Not so much with regret, but with a recognition that, this time, there were going to be consequences. Something had drowned in the heady magic of the spring of life.

He looked across to the side of the pool and with a shock he found Turloch was watching him. The Magician's eyes were like chips of green ice.

Kierce did not choose when to read Turloch's mind, Turloch chose when to let him. A frission of fear ran through the younger man as he encountered Turloch's controlled rage.

He felt a sudden, sickening lurch. He stumbled and fell, and found himself sitting on the ground where Turloch had stood, looking at himself standing in the spring, with Cathva still wrapped around his body. He saw Cathva open her eyes and look into his face. He saw her start in sudden shock, and knew she was gazing into those chips of green ice. She tried to break away, and Turloch caught her roughly with Kierce's hand. She gave a small whimper as he dragged her towards the edge of the pool; before she reached it, her body sagged against the Magician and almost slipped down into the water. Turloch scooped her into Kierce's arms and dumped her beside the pool.

Kierce tried to move, and found he couldn't. Turloch was in control of both his own body and Kierce's. Kierce could only watch.

Turloch climbed out of the water, picked up Cathva's discarded shift and dried her cursorily with it. He seemed oblivious to either the sight or the touch of her nubile young body. He retrieved her gown and flung it over her, then turned back towards Kierce.

There was another sickening lurch and Kierce found himself back in his own form beside Cathva, looking at Turloch across the spring.

Now walk away from her.

Kierce hesitated and looked down at Cathva's sprawled figure with more than a twinge of guilt. He hadn't intended to hurt her. That was the last thing he meant to do.

By everyone's gods do I have to do that myself, as well? Walk away from her! And pick up your clothes. She's marrying the king in a few hours, I don't want any trace of you left here when she wakes up.

Reassured, Kierce turned away from her.

"Think I might have left a trace of me with her," he responded.

A sharp pain shot suddenly down the back of his neck as if someone had struck him between the shoulder blades.

Abuse and contempt he had tolerated. Physical chastisement was one stage beyond what Kierce was prepared to take; he lashed out in restoration of his outraged dignity, reaching almost unconsciously for the power within him.

Turloch deflected the response with ease, watching him steadily, gauging his anger.

Grow up. You've a lot of it to do. You can't go around starting forest fires like this.

Kierce shot him a venomous look, and turned away, massaging his numb shoulder.

It was more of a wake-up call than a blow. You know what it would have felt like if I'd really hit you.

"Miserable old sod," muttered Kierce, well aware that Turloch could hear him perfectly.

Turloch let it go.

Kierce dressed himself and walked round the temple to join his mentor. Turloch led the way outside without further comment.

Kierce paused at the edge of the temple wall and looked back. His mind reached gently towards Cathva.

Wake up!

By the time she stirred and raised her chilled body from the stone floor, he had gone to receive his instruction in the responsibility of Shaihen power.

Chapter 10
Above the Haven

Turloch's unicorn, Freath, was waiting for him outside. The Magician mounted the small grey animal and they set off purposefully, heading away from the Haven up into the surrounding mountains. He allowed no pause for Kierce to fetch his horse, and the pace he set forced Kierce into a loping half-run to keep up with him.

Kierce did not dare refuse to follow. He had grown up with hardly any apparent magic around him. The powers he possessed were informed by what he knew, the histories of Shehaios and the natural world. Whenever he glimpsed the pattern of connections in Turloch's mind, he felt he knew nothing at all. If he walked away from Turloch now, the Magician's death would leave him adrift in a sea with no landmarks.

Why they had to climb half way up a frozen mountain at dawn to discuss landmarks, Kierce did not know. He suspected it was part of the punishment for his indiscretion with Rainur's bride. It took all the skill and agility his body had learned over years of hunting, tracking and riding for Kierce to keep his feet on the treacherous path, and he dropped steadily further behind Turloch and Freath as they climbed the starlit hillside.

Just as Kierce's horse came struggling up to join them – a summons Kierce would not have been capable of issuing a few days before – Turloch stopped and dismounted.

"Too steep for hooves," he said, shortly, turned right off the sheep track they were following and set about climbing the scramble of rock which drew itself up another couple of hundred jagged and difficult feet.

Kierce paused and watched him in dismay.

Although dawn was touching the eastern peaks, the western face they were climbing was still in darkness. Turloch, aged though he was, tackled the craggy rock with vigour, thrusting his stout wooden cane onto the ground to help him on his way. The Magician's staff, Kierce observed, merited the same lack of respect as the other symbol of Turloch's authority, his cloak. It was a grubby and well-worn garment, full of pulled threads and small holes. Turloch cared nothing for what he looked like. He preferred not to be seen.

With a small sigh, Kierce followed Turloch's ascent a little more carefully, feeling his way to a secure footing on rock slippery with ice. At last, he joined the Magician on a modest summit. Further south, half-seen outlines of higher peaks made darker shadows against the sky, but here they were above most of the land immediately around them.

Kierce looked down. Occasional small glimmers of light showed where flames illuminated a busy Haven, preparations already underway for Rainur's wedding. He could make out the shapes of buildings and the pale line of the road that veered west and then south to the Gate. Where it led out of the Haven north, plunging down through wooded valleys into the rest of Shehaios, it was hidden from his view.

He became conscious that Turloch was waiting for him, an extraordinary little mental image like an impatient cough. He turned.

Turloch thrust the staff towards him, turned horizontally so that Kierce automatically took it in both hands to keep it balanced. It was an intricate object, made of many different woods carved and interwoven with each other so that it was difficult to tell where one ended and another began, and impossible to guess how it had been made.

"Go home," said Turloch.

Kierce looked at him cautiously and found the Magician's mind no longer quite the closed barrier it had been. He understood what Turloch meant, though he didn't understand why. He obeyed the command, and let his thoughts turn to Arhaios.

He was still conscious of where he was, of dawn breaking over the Haven behind him, but he was also now back in the Horsemaster's house at Arhaios. He was in darkness, moving confidently across a room so familiar there was no need to wait for the light of morning. He had done this himself so often, rising early with thoughts of the horses he was working with, content to get on with another day's work despite the temptation of a warm bed on a cold morning. But this was not his body moving quietly through the darkness, nor his room in the Horsemaster's house. There was another bed close by in which another figure still slept and the mind familiar with this room belonged to the eldest of the two sisters who shared it.

To Kierce, his family was his father. For the first seven years of his life, Gaeroch was all he had; the family he shared the Horsemaster's house with now was that of his father's second wife. The mind he was sharing, several hundred miles away across the Shaihen mountains, was that of his half-sister, Madred.

Usually, he had to focus hard on a person he could see to do this. Other animals were much easier. He used the skill sparingly, as a short-cut, or to tweak a game of twelve stones. Most of the time he wasn't interested in what other people thought.

It seemed to Kierce that Madred turned and looked at him as he drew back from the deceptive semi-familiarity of her thoughts, but there was no smile of recognition. She couldn't see him. He wasn't there.

Madred took after their father. He wasn't surprised that, of all the people in the Holding, thoughts of Arhaios should take him to her, but she was not the only one his mental ear was aware of. He sensed the presence of the rest of Gaeroch's family like colours in the darkness. His youngest sister was almost a blank sheet, the busyness of her skimming thoughts lost in a deep and untroubled sleep dominated by the image of an Arhaien boy Kierce recognised. Beyond the half screen in the middle of the long, low space under the eaves where the family slept, his half-brother Tuli lay deep in a drunken stupor, the alcohol damping down the disturbance of a day dominated by arguments with Madred. Kierce smiled, amused rather than surprised to find Madred's sound good sense and Tuli's pride as sole male resident of the household in conflict.

Kierce sensed Turloch nudging him to move on. An idea of where the Magician was taking him prickled at the back of his head. He did not want to go there. He gripped the staff and summoned his mind to resist.

"Elani," he said, as if the word had the power to summon her image.

But he could not find Elani. Instead, he found himself drifting inexorably into the mind of the woman who slept at the end of the loft in the Horsemaster's House, enveloped in the feather mattress that had been a marriage gift from her husband's Holding.

Kierce threw everything he could into blocking the image. He did not want to touch his stepmother. He had never wanted to touch her. Her flabby body had come between him and his father when he had been too young to understand why Gaeroch could want anyone else to love.

When he first began to sense the thoughts of others, Gaeroch was the first person whose mind he had learned to share. He was fifteen, and he had lacked the skill to avoid touching Verril through Gaeroch.

Arhaios mocked him with the memory of lying in the room where Tuli now lay, with the too-intimate knowledge of what his father and his stepmother were doing in the next room burning through his body like a fever. Once that experience had imprinted itself on his conscience, he knew he could never reveal his gift to Gaeroch. And if he could not tell Gaeroch, he could not tell anyone.

Never be afraid to look at what you fear. Knowledge is of itself neither good nor bad, but once innocence is lost, ignorance is no excuse.

He found himself trapped, his thoughts running where Turloch directed. He looked with dread, but to his relief, he realised he was touching Verril's mind, not her body. She was deep in peaceful sleep, unconcerned by the sibling rivalries filling her childrens' heads, let alone the guilty secret in her stepson's mind. Her dreams were a jumble of unfulfilled errands and gossip. She cruised blissfully along the surface of life, appalled by small things and absorbing great ones with magnificent equanimity. Gaeroch's memory, which lived permanently at the back of Kierce's own mind, was barely discernible in Verril's. She had wept copiously for her husband's death, but the wound of his passing had healed cleanly, leaving scarcely a scar on her daily routines.

You must know where you came from.

She's not my mother! Kierce thought fiercely.

Exactly.

With relief, he drew away from Verril, through the confusion of plans and hopes and dreams that made up the human life of Arhaios. He had been amid a herd of horses, sharing their senses, and he had felt then a similar kaleidoscope of life around him, each individual distinct and yet each a part of the life that was the herd. He had never before experienced the same sensation amongst humans, especially humans several days journey away from him. He knew this was the gift of the Magician. Moreover, it was not a power contained in the staff in his hands. It was within him.

He picked out a number of girlfriends, some lying alone, others not. A stray image of himself surfaced here and there, and he felt gratified to know that he was missed. He lingered a moment with one young woman who slept deep in blissful ignorance of his attentions. Her name was Roa and it was not unknown for her image to lurk in his own subconscious, but her dreams were just a confusion of banal concerns that reminded him uncomfortably of Verril. He looked in vain for any fond remembrances of Kierce the Horsemaster. He wished he could turn the lens around and look at her, but he could only look within.

His hand stroked the strands and textures of the staff, and his mind soared beyond Arhaios out into Oreath. The images and whispers of his people rolled across the land like the waves in a calm sea. Occasionally, something caught his interest and he dropped on it like a gull fishing the waters. Bright Cuaraccon, the home of the minstrels, its music still at this hour, but its dreams pulsing through him with all the excitement of the dance. Plenty of drunken stupors there, too. Less elsewhere. Dreams and plans. Working men and women everywhere, up to tend stock, start ovens, rake over embers, and start another day.

And then, at last, he came back to Elani, the first and only woman he had ever loved. He lighted on her mind like a homecoming bird, and snuggled into her dreams. She was missing Caras, and feeling the strain of comforting his children for their father's absence. Her five-year-old son was curled up asleep beside her, nightmares chased away by his mother's reassuring presence. Kierce understood him perfectly. Just to be near Elani was to feel her healing touch. Plans of reconciliation, ideas, and remedies buzzed below her dreams in a hum of invention. She knew Tuli and Madred weren't getting on. It amused her to think of Kierce as the patriarchal figure of that household as much as it amused him.

Friend, confidante, but only ever briefly, lover. No matter how hard he tried to hold on to her, he found Elani taking him to Caras.

The physical distance was irrelevant. Caras was in the Haven below him, worrying even in his sleep about the King's wedding, Imperial alliances and how best to bring the news back to Oreath, but he was such an intrinsic part of Arhaios – or perhaps more accurately Arhaios was such an intrinsic part of him – that Kierce realised the view he was looking at would not be complete without Caras.

Caras took him to Leath. Kierce was beginning to understand now that this sharing was not about his own feelings but about theirs. The discomfort he felt at being taken into the thoughts of his chieftain was less to do with her sex, and more to do with her status. If there was one woman in the world who held Kierce's unquestioning respect, it was Holder Leath.

She was awake. She seemed to be baking. Leath was given to bread-making when she was worried. Something to do with pounding the dough, or so he had been led to believe. Superficially, her mind was full of oven temperatures and the activities of yeast, but beneath that her worries were a reflection of her grandson's; what was happening in the Haven, what Caras was doing, whether he was saying the right thing. When he would return, and what news he would bring. And whether Kierce knew yet.

He started, and opened his eyes abruptly, brought up short by Leath's intuition. He hadn't thought anyone except Turloch had the first idea.

"She's not a Chief for nothing," commented Turloch. "Enough?"

"Fascinating," said Kierce. "Could I have … done anything?"

"You always want to be doing something. It's not a matter of control, Kierce. It's a partnership. Something you are woefully incapable of making." He sighed. "So tell me, what were you doing with Cathva?"

Kierce could not suppress the graphic image that came into his mind.

"You know what I was doing with Cathva."

"Physically, it was pretty obvious."

"That's all it was."

He resented that fact that Turloch knew that wasn't true. This matter of seduction was a subtle negotiation of power, he always took the object of his desire with him. If he could not persuade, he desisted. He sought to enjoy their pleasure as much as his own. But when he touched Cathva, all semblance of control over what was happening left him.

Turloch shook his head.

"A man without a mother and a woman without a father. Just as well she's marrying Rainur."

"Cathva has a father."

"The Emperor Zelt an' Korsos has sired one hundred and eighty-five children, ninety of them legitimate. He is father to none of them. I will spare you, for the moment, a vision of the Empire. I am tempted to destroy you, but you're all Shehaios will have when I'm gone."

"Ninety legitimate children? It's not possible!"

"Ten wives," said Turloch. "Let me explain the freedom of the Empire of the Sacred Union. A man's body and his labour can be bought and sold at whim. He can be sent to fight and die for something he does not believe in. He can be forced to marry where he does not love and be forbidden consummation of a love he feels deeply. He can be forced to work at something that will destroy him, with his family held hostage to starvation if he doesn't. For a woman, freedom is a word with no meaning at all. What is Elani?"

She is beautiful. She is a healer. She is my salvation. She banished Verril's image from my bed.

80

"She is Caras ti' Leath's wife."

Kierce shot him a look and a thought of angry astonishment. Her marriage to Caras placed Elani out of his reach, but it did not stop her being Elani. It was her insistence on being who she was that had drawn her away from him in the first place.

Turloch raised his sparse eyebrows.

"I am thinking like a Caiivorian for you, Kierce. Carry on. Verril?"

Stupid clumsy woman who took my father away.

"Domestic goddess. Leath."

Arhaios. Kierce shook himself in slight annoyance at his inaccuracy, but still only concepts associated themselves with Leath, not characteristics. It was like playing twelve stones. *Trust. Wisdom. Power.*

There was a brief silence from Turloch.

"Old woman. Widow. Burden."

"Rainur's making an alliance with this … ?"

"You're making an alliance with it, Kierce. The Magician holds the power to read and interpret the dreams of the people who believe in the Fair Land. You will have the power to bring them together, to make their dream reality. Tessella."

My mother. But what came into his mind was Cathva's image of delicate perfection.

"Stop playing tricks on me!" exclaimed Kierce. "My mother was nothing like Cathva, Cathva is nothing like her."

"You don't know who she was. She was never the image left in Gaeroch's memory. It's all illusion, Kierce, the way we see ourselves and the way others see us. People choose what to believe. The Magician must not make images that enslave the original. If you cannot form a partnership with what made you, it is Shehaios you drown in the spring with your libido. Do you love your land, Kierce?"

The question took Kierce by surprise, and he could not quite keep a hint of contempt from both his eyes and his thoughts. It was a ridiculous question for anyone to ask a Shaihen, let alone a Magician. His land was like his skin, it grew anew each year and he lived his life under it.

So why am I asking you?

"I don't know, Turloch. You seem to confuse my … weakness for an attractive woman with an inability to appreciate what living is all about. Seems to me you're the confused one. I don't hurt anyone. The girls always think it's what they want at the time, and they never think any different afterwards, whatever they thought before. They enjoy it, I enjoy it. What do I destroy?"

"The power you hold has touched two Caiivorians," said Turloch. "One already believes himself to be your slave and the other has given herself to your unbridled appetites. What you will inherit is the power of magic in the land of the free. What you will destroy is yourself."

Cathva was different. She wanted me... I couldn't help myself. I couldn't stop.

Kierce lost sight of Turloch's mind as his own descended into turmoil. He very much resented Turloch witnessing his confusion. He had learned to separate his own feelings from the thoughts and fears around him. It was the only way he knew how to deal with the constant undertow of emotion, not only from people but from the creatures he bent to his will, hunted, ate. And Cathva would not stay separate.

She must.

How? I can't undo what I've done.

That's exactly what you must do. If Cathva found Kierce attractive, Kierce must be a stranger to her. When Cathva awakes, she will not be sure what really happened. Keep it that way. Encourage her to think she was dreaming.

Kierce laughed humourlessly.

Powerful bloody dream.

Caiivorian dreams are. They believe more readily in shadows than Shaihens do. They live surrounded by them. They are very reluctant to shine a light on them to see what they hide. For the sake of everyone concerned, be a shadow to Cathva. Be whatever you can make her believe you to be other than a male human who can't resist proving his prowess to every passing female. Can you really get no further than that, Kierce?

You should know, Lord High Magician. He hesitated, sorting his thoughts into order. "Should I stay for the wedding, then?"

What do you think?

But I will need to be in the Haven. I will need to come back if ... He couldn't even quite think it. The weight of it terrified him. He only ever wanted to enjoy life.

The "if" was there when you entered the Temple of the Spring, and it's a "when", as well you know. You gave yourself the problem. You make sure you don't give it to Rainur. He has problems enough. And his Imperial Queen is not the least of them.

Chapter 11
The War God's Charm

Caras was furious with Kierce. He didn't need him in Mervecc, or in the Haven; he needed him on the journey, and when he came to set out on the journey home, he found Kierce had gone. Without warning, without a word of explanation, taking Orlii with him.

His anger grew from the moment he realised Kierce was not going to attend the wedding, and he was going to have to make another apology to Rainur. It coloured his view of the ceremony, so that when he looked back on it afterwards, he could remember very little about it. He remembered that Cathva looked unreachably perfect and her escort of Imperial soldiers looked formidable. He remembered the lion of the Empire emblazoned on the soldiers' black cloaks and on Cathva's gorgeous scarlet train. Caras could read symbols as well as the next Shaihen, but it appeared to him that the lion was merely there as a distinguished guest. Cathva was a small Caiivorian and Rainur a tall Shaihen; standing beside him, her escort of soldiers surrounded by the throng of Shaihens in the Meeting House, it seemed as if she was marrying Shehaios rather than binding her husband to Imperial rule.

When he sought Rainur's pardon for his companion's unforgivable lapse of manners, Rainur seemed more concerned about Caras's own safety. It was clear by then that Kierce had left the Haven, and no-one seemed to know why, or where he had gone.

"I don't think you need worry, Lord Caras," said Rainur. "I have spoken to Lord Turloch."

Caras frowned. It hadn't occurred to him to worry, and he didn't understand why Turloch needed to be involved. Leath talked about the Magician like a rather infuriating elderly relative, but to Caras he was a figure so distant and venerable as to be almost unreal. It seemed odd for Rainur to refer to him like an everyday aquaintance.

For the first time, it occurred to him that Kierce's disappearance might not be of his own volition. He studied Rainur a little anxiously. He believed the King to be an honest man, yet he was adept at presenting a pleasant face to the world. Caras was never quite sure what Rainur was thinking.

"Is there something I should know about Kierce, Lord Rainur?"

"Not that I can tell you, Caras." Rainur gave him a slightly curious look. "Forgive me, Lord Caras, I was told you were ... close to Lord Kierce?"

"I've known him all my life," said Caras.

"Then I'm surprised he was able to hide it from you. Still, Lord Kierce is, as we know, a formidable game player."

"Lord Rainur, is Kierce in danger? In trouble ? I would like to know, my lord, infuriating though he is, he's ... well, as children, we were more like brothers."

"Fought all the time," said Rainur, with a smile. "As I said, I don't think you need worry. I am confident Lord Kierce is in no need of assistance either from you or from me. I don't know why he was unable to attend my wedding – all I know is that it's not for you to apologise for his absence. Lord Turloch has already done that. My concern is that you've lost the protection which guarded your journey here. I can't offer you Lord Kierce's skill, but such escort as I can provide, you shall have."

"Thank you, Lord Rainur, but I don't think that's really necessary."

"Oh, I do, Lord Caras. I think it's essential. I want you safely back in Arhaios to plead my case with Lady Leath. Not to mention the rest of your people. I, too, have a brother, and I suspect you may well regret his existence when you get back to Oreath."

Jagus had never forgiven the rest of his family for his sister's death in Vordeith. He had married an Oreathan Holder, and Caras already knew he could as easily persuade swine to sprout wings as talk Jagus into supporting Rainur's alliance.

"Well," said Caras, "perhaps to the borders of Oreath."

Rainur's escort left him at the edges of the Oreathan forest. He still had several days journey ahead of him, but once inside his own borders, Caras finally felt able to relax. They had seen no Caiivorian raiders, and although he had to describe the King's wedding at every Holding he visited, the reception so far had been, at worst, neutral.

He rode on alone through the woodland's soft gloom, following a drovers' road carved into the hillside by generations of travellers. With every pace his horse took, he looked forward to Elani, his children and his people. He ached to be back among them. He had not been so long away from Elani since they were married.

He was anxious to take his journey as far as possible towards home, and he travelled on until he could hardly see where he was riding beneath the canopy of spring growth. He knew he was some distance from any settlements, and he was just beginning to look around for somewhere to make camp for the night when a figure jumped down onto the path in front of him.

His horse shied violently, and all he saw as he reeled in the saddle was a barelegged man in Caiivorian plaid. Caras turned the horse to face the man, reaching for his hunting knife.

Even as he did so, another body landed on his back, pulling him off the horse to fall in a tumble of hooves and dust to the ground. His assailant lost his grip slightly as they fell. Caras lurched away from him, trying to regain his feet first. He was barely on his knees before a sinewy forearm locked across his throat, and he felt the blade come up under his chin. Even as he felt the edge of cold metal on his skin, the man holding it uttered a heartfelt roar of frustration and stopped. The knife remained at Caras's throat. He knew the man holding it intended to kill him. Yet he didn't.

Caras opened his eyes, and found himself looking up the bank above the road into Kierce's face. Kierce's gaze was fixed on Caras's assailant with an almost inhuman ferocity in his dark eyes. Concentration was etched into every line of his expression, sweat shining on his brow, but he didn't appear to be doing anything. He was standing stock still, hands by his sides, fists clenched, just staring at the man trying to kill the future Lord of his Holding.

Slowly, the fingers of the hand holding the knife at Caras's throat uncurled, one by one. Caras could hear the man who owned the hand grunting with the effort of trying to make it obey his own will, but he was losing. The knife fell to the dirt track and Caras simultaneously drove his elbow into the Caiivorian's ribs and threw his considerable strength against the arm that held him. With an effort of will as much as muscle, he hurled the man over his shoulder. As he sprawled in the dust, Caras snatched his own knife free and came down after him. He didn't hesitate. Creatures who attacked him in the forest were a danger that could not wait for debate. He slit the man's throat, as he would have dispatched a wounded animal.

He was half aware of a faint gasp from the bank where he had seen Kierce standing, but his attention was focussed on the other Caiivorian. He saw him scramble into the saddle of Caras's horse and turn to flee down the roadway. It only occurred to Caras afterwards that it was probably what they had wanted in the first place, the horse and the pack it carried. He stood panting in the roadway, watching the horse take off along it. When he recovered his breath, he put his fingers to his mouth and gave a shrill whistle.

In a shower of mud and leaf-litter, the horse skidded from full gallop to dead stop, dropped his head, and let his rider fly over his ears onto the ground. The man landed on his head with a sickening thud, and lay still.

The horse danced about excitedly, still in half a mind to flee. Caras saw Kierce pick himself up – he hadn't seen him fall – and move towards the agitated animal. It calmed noticeably as soon as Kierce's attention was on it.

"It's over, Caras," he called, as he led the horse back up the track. "The other one broke his neck. You got 'em both."

"I thought I'd be safe inside my own borders!" said Caras shakily.

He brought the knife up abruptly as another figure in Caiivorian dress jumped down from the bank above them.

Kierce caught his hand with a weary smile.

"Not that one, Caras. He's mine."

Caras lowered the knife as he looked into the startled face in front of him and recognised Orlii.

"He looks like another bloody Caiivorian."

"He is another bloody Caiivorian," said Kierce. He handed Caras the reins of his horse, and turned to clap Orlii on the back, the hearty gesture belying the ashen exhaustion Caras had seen in his face. "No redeeming features whatsoever. Can't even cook. Well, not anything you'd consider eating, anyway. But he's the only Caiivorian left alive here. You're safe again." He paused and looked critically at his companion. "You all right, Caras?"

"Yes. Though I don't think I've any right to be." Caras fingered his throat tentatively. He found he was shaking, not only from the shock of the attack but from his own response to it. He had never killed a man before. When he killed this one, he realised he hadn't even been thinking of him as a man, but simply a creature who had attacked him. He had struck in sheer instinct, without thinking about it. It was only now, when he turned back and looked down at the body in its pool of blood, its glazed eyes staring from between the blue tattooed snakes curling across the Caiivorian's cheekbones above his beard, that he realised he had taken a human life. He had disturbed the *wholeness*.

The content of his stomach threatened suddenly to deposit itself on the ground. He reached rapidly for some words to quell his nausea.

"What were they doing here? I thought we were safe to ride our own forests, for Spirit's sake!"

"Prassan thought they were safe to farm sheep in the mountains," said Kierce. "I didn't look closely. I don't know what they were doing here. But for what it's worth, I'm pretty sure there aren't any more of them in the forest. Not yet. I've been tracking these two for the last couple of days – they seem to have been some kind of renegade pair living off what they could find. Maybe that's why they'd drifted so far into Shehaios." He paused. "I'm sorry now I didn't stop them earlier. I was tracking them, I didn't quite realise they were tracking you. Simply didn't occur to me that that's what they were hunting."

Caras stroked the horse's neck reassuringly and looked across at the body of the other Caiivorian, lying where he had fallen. "Just as well you were trained by an expert Horsemaster, old boy."

"Just as well your Horsemaster has a penchant for tricks," added Kierce. "I'm glad you were able to get the horse back yourself. I'm not sure I could have done it for you just at that moment."

Caras hesitated. A lot had happened here, very fast, and he was still struggling with it.

"What did you do? Why didn't he kill me?"

"Because I wouldn't let him." Kierce hesitated. It had evidently shaken him, too. He lacked his normal assurance. "I suppose we shouldn't leave them here like this."

"I don't see what we can do except leave them here at the moment. It's almost dark. Tomorrow I'll go back to the last Holding I passed and tell them what they had on their doorstep."

"If you want to."

"What do you mean, if I want to?"

Kierce met his eyes gravely. "I told you. There are no others in Oreath yet. There's a good chance you'll get away without any retribution for this. And you have to go back to Arhaios and convince them it's a good thing the King's marrying a Caiivorian."

"All the more reason they should know how close the threat is."

"Think how you first reacted, Caras. A Caiivorian is a Caiivorian." He moved towards the fallen interloper and crouched over him. He drew his own knife and ran it lightly across the bloodstained tunic at the man's neck until he found what he sought. He slipped the blade beneath a fine silver chain and jerked it back to cut the ornament free. He stood, and came over to Caras with the chain and the charm it bore staining his palm with the Caiivorian's blood.

Caras looked. The charm was a crudely shaped bull's head on a lion's body. He knew it represented one of the multitude of gods widely honoured in Caiivor. This one was especially revered among the Empire's warriors; his image was supposed to offer them protection in battle.

"I learned a few things in Mervecc myself," said Kierce, quietly. "I learned what a former soldier will, and won't, gamble. I'll take good odds those two men spent time in the Imperial army. There's some truth in the fact that a Caiivorian is a Caiivorian." He glanced at Orlii. "Didn't I say something about eating, Orlii? Stream …? Fish …?"

"Yes Master," muttered Orlii and set off obediently on his errand.

"I don't hold secrets from my people," said Caras. "Tomorrow, I will tell the local Holder."

"As you wish," said Kierce. He closed his fist around the charm. "I wouldn't tell them about this, though. Caiivorian raiders. Not renegade Imperial soldiers."

He opened his hand and let a fine cloud of silver dust float to the ground. Caras could see it glinting in the pale moonlight that was stronger now than the last light of day. He looked at Kierce with his mouth open to speak, but Kierce was already walking away.

"I'll check the other one. Just up the hill from here is a good place for us to camp. With luck, by the time we've built a fire Orlii will have caught us some supper."

"Kierce— ." Caras followed him over to the other Caiivorian.

Kierce removed a similar silver charm from the second man's body and offered it to Caras. "Did you want this?"

"No!" said Caras, recoiling from the trinket. "I'm not a warrior."

"You've challenged the King and killed your first Caiivorian," said Kierce. "Give the minstrels five minutes with that and they could probably turn you into one."

"Kierce, I'm not in the mood for this!"

"I'm not sure I was ever in the mood for any of it." Kierce crushed the charm as carelessly as he had the first one, dusting the silver off his hands. Some of it was left stuck to the blood that smeared his palm.

"I didn't intend to meet you like this, Caras. But I did intend to meet you. I need to talk to you before you get back to Arhaios."

"Good. Because grateful as I am, you still have some explaining to do. You were specifically invited to the King's wedding – you did him a great insult by not being there."

"The insult I did Rainur was a little more than you know, I'm afraid," admitted Kierce. He looked up at Caras. "You must promise not to laugh if I tell you."

"I think that's unlikely," said Caras, grimly. "I was prepared to be angry with you until you saved my life." He met Kierce's eyes. "You always draw the better stone. I always end up in your debt."

"We'll make camp, we'll eat," said Kierce. "And I'll tell you."

From the top of the bank, Caras saw there was a good view of the road, as well as the hillside around them. Kierce and Orlii's horses were already grazing a flat grassy platform by a stream, and an outcrop of rock provided protection from the prevailing wind. Who had seen this spot first, he wondered, Kierce or the men he was tracking?

Caras unsaddled his horse and turned it loose with the others before he went to assist Kierce collecting fuel for their fire.

"I hope Orlii won't take too long," he commented, as they returned to the campsite with the makings of the fire. "It would have been quicker if you'd caught the fish."

"Even a Caiivorian knows how to catch a fish." Kierce stacked kindling and turned to pull some dried grass for tinder from a hollow of the rocky ledge. Caras went to his pack for a flint.

"Doesn't he know how to start a fire then?"

"There are ways of starting fires," said Kierce.

Caras took the flint from the pack, and turned back to the fire. Kierce was squatting beside it holding the ball of dried grass. He leaned over it and breathed on it gently. A small orange tongue of fire glowed instantly in his hands.

Caras stopped dead, the makings of the fire in his hands and the living thing in Kierce's.

Kierce smiled at what should have been burning his palms, and was not. He lowered it carefully onto the kindling.

"Now you're looking at me like Orlii does," he remarked.

Caras sat down slowly, watching the small flames run hungrily over the twigs until they were a fierce red heart of heat and energy. Kierce fed more logs onto them.

"Kierce, what is going on? You disarm a man without touching him. You crush solid silver into dust in your hand. Now you light a fire with your breath. Am I seeing things? Did that man kill me?"

"No. You're still alive," replied Kierce. "Let me get around to it, Caras. It isn't easy." He paused. "I'm sorry I deserted you at the Haven. I couldn't stay for the wedding."

Caras poked at the fire aimlessly. He was uncomfortable with Kierce's apparent resolution to share confidences. Kierce was Kierce, all-knowing and untouchable. Usually, he turned every attempt at intimacy with a wisecrack.

"Get around to what? You're playing with fire to show me I'm wrong again – Rainur is making a mistake? What?"

"It's nothing so worthy, Caras." He paused. A small explosion spat sap out of the fire. "The night before her marriage, I had a slight … encounter with Princess Cathva. It was better that I … didn't stay."

A weight settled somewhere at the edges of Caras's consciousness, like a fall of snow beginning to work loose from the top of a mountain.

"What do you mean by an encounter?"

"She found out who I am."

"What do you mean, who you are?"

Kierce gazed distantly across the fire, its flames throwing the lean lines of his face into stark relief.

"I've always spoken the language of other creatures, Caras. My father taught me to. You see what I say to them, but you don't see what they say to me. I wish I could show you how different the world looks to a horse. They see either side of them and behind them – it's like having eyes in the back of your head. They're always aware of the rest of the herd. And they live their lives poised to run. It's not something that worries them, it doesn't feel like a human living in a constant state of fear, but experiencing it as a human is … wearing."

"Experiencing it?"

"Yes. Unicorns are even worse, that's why you never see one. I could never spend long with a unicorn, I'd be a nervous wreck. I don't know how Turloch does it. They're impossible creatures. Worse than deer. Hunters are easier – wolves, cats. But even wolves are always so aware of the world through their noses. It tells you so many different things. You see the world in different ways. You begin to see how it works. The connections. *Haios*."

Caras frowned into the fire. He couldn't smell malt barley spirit on Kierce's breath.

"You've lost me, Kierce."

Kierce sighed.

"Wolves see the world with their noses. Humans see the world with their minds. When you know how it works, you know how to change it. Control it."

"Do you mean … when you're with these animals, you become one? Or imagine you do? Have you been tasting the fungus that makes you better than drunk?"

"What I'm telling you is how I can make myself Red Sky's herd leader, and the man of Hesa of Mervecc's dreams." He smiled. "You see, I did know her name."

"She didn't even like you," said Caras, faintly.

"Oh, I soon changed her mind."

The word seemed to carry the weight of the avalanche. Caras struggled manfully through the mist of comprehension.

"How did you change her mind?"

"By being in it with her." He looked at Caras wryly. "Gets kind of crowded in yours. You carry your herd around with you."

Caras stared at him.

"You can … ?"

"Of course I can. I have since puberty. When I wanted to."

"I mean, read minds."

"That's what I meant, too."

"But that's …" He half expected Kierce to finish the sentence again. Why had he never noticed before how often Kierce did that? "That's the power Turloch has."

"Yes."

"And you use it for … Spirit defend me, Kierce, what do you use it for? You just killed a man!"

"No, Caras, I went to some lengths to avoid that. You killed him. I just stopped him killing you."

"And the women!" Caras got to his feet, beginning to feel as if the avalanche was tumbling down the mountain towards him. "That's just downright—". His fretful pacing came to a sudden halt. "By the Spirit," he whispered. "Cathva?"

Kierce prodded the fire and did not answer. For Caras, that was answer enough. The vision of perfect and untouchable beauty swam before his eyes.

"How could you?"

"Oh, very, very easily," said Kierce, ruefully.

Caras hardly knew what he was doing. He strode across to Kierce, hauled him to his feet and swung his fist into his face.

It connected with thin air. It threw him so off-balance, he almost fell.

"She really did bewitch you too, didn't she?" Kierce was staring at him in astonishment. "You self-righteous bastard, if you'd been naked in the Temple of Life with her, I'd like to have seen you resist the temptation."

"I wouldn't have put myself there!"

"No, you never saw past the dress, did you? You walk around with your bloody eyes shut!"

Caras launched himself at him, determined this time that he would get hold of him. He hit the ground where Kierce had been standing with the force of a catapulted stone, narrowly missing the fire. He lay, winded, wondering how he could have missed.

"Do you have to spend your life being bloody stupid?" said Kierce's voice behind him. "I'm always going to see you coming, Caras. I'm the Lord High Magician's heir."

The avalanche dumped itself on his head. He lay dazed, clawing his way back to the surface. His imagination baulked at the task Kierce asked of it. The Lord High Magician was the holder of wisdom, respected by every Shaihen from the moment of their birth. To put his feckless contemporary in such a role made a mockery of it. Kierce, trainer of horses, Kierce the joker, the gambler, the seducer.

"Turloch's far from perfect, you know," commented Kierce "And I am a very good trainer of horses. I didn't choose it, Caras. I didn't want to be Turloch's heir."

"You wanted the power without the responsibility."

"I had the power. No, I didn't want the responsibility. Now I understand I don't get a choice. The Magician is born of Shehaios. If Shehaios does not exist, neither does the Magician."

"If Turloch's named you his heir ... " Caras rolled over. "Kierce, he's older than the hills – sooner or later he's going to die."

"Sooner rather than later. That's why he finally gave in and told me. He didn't want to, any more than I wanted to hear it. Or you wanted to hear it."

"Can you blame him?" Caras sat up, painfully. It felt as if the parts of his body that had not been bruised when the Caiivorian took him off his horse had hit the ground doubly hard this time. "Rainur's walking a treacherous path – all the way along it he'll need the Lord High Magician beside him, guiding and advising him, and you've betrayed him before you start, you little piece of shit."

"It wasn't deliberate. That is ... I lost control of it, Caras, it started out as a joke."

"A joke!"

"All right, I'm not laughing! But I'm not trying to take Rainur's wife away from him. I have no more intention of splitting the Whole Land in half than you did when you started brandishing a sword in Rainur's Meeting House. I can't be in everyone's head all the time, I didn't know she'd actually believe I was a god."

"Believe you were *what*?"

"We were in a temple. Cathva's ideas of temples are ... different. Cathva gave herself to the god of Shehaios, as she saw it. I should have had the strength to stop it. I didn't. It was a mistake, but at least it didn't prevent her fulfilling her promises to the Shaihen power she should be serving. She's safely married to Rainur, she's Queen of Shehaios, and if she serves the Spirit in a way the rest of Shehaios would not quite approve of, well ... " He paused for breath. He certainly did lack his usual assurance now. Caras took some consolation from realising that something about his attack had taken the bastard by surprise.

"The only people who know it are me and Cathva, Turloch, and you."

"Why did you tell me? Once Turloch was gone, no-one would ever have known, except you and Cathva."

"I told you, because you've known me so long …"

"You can't have thought I'd find out some other way. I'm too stupid to notice."

"I was going to say, I could use a friend."

Caras sank his head into his hands.

"A Lord High Magician the King can't trust. Do you think that's going to work, Kierce?"

"He has no reason not to trust me. Unless you give him one, *caras*."

He gave the word the subtle inflection that turned it from Caras's name to the word meaning "rock".

There was a heavy silence. He couldn't help believing Kierce meant it, and he couldn't help doubting his own belief. How did he ever know whether he was thinking his own thoughts, or what Kierce wanted him to think?

Kierce turned away from him and tossed some small branches onto the fire.

"Well, you always have to be bloody right, heir of Arhaios," he said. "If you think you ought to tell him, you'd better tell him."

"And what does that achieve?"

Kierce shrugged.

"Tell me?"

"Bastard," muttered Caras. "You know I've no choice."

"I always know."

"Yes? Then how come you're such a bloody fool?"

There was a further pause.

"This … Cathva," said Caras hesitantly. "It is something … finished?"

"I'm not that much of a bloody fool. And Turloch's not dead yet. I shouldn't have let it happen. I'm the Magician's heir. I'm still human. And she is … magnificent."

Caras frowned at the wistful edge to his voice. He had seen the cynical manoevring behind Kierce's conquests in Mervecc.

"You were point-scoring, Kierce. You were winning a game. Weren't you?"

"Human male," Kierce smiled ruefully. "I suppose so. I don't know what I was doing, Caras, if you want the truth of it. But I'm not going to let Rainur's wife betray him."

"Leave her alone and she probably won't."

"I wouldn't trust her that far. First word of advice from your future Lord High Magician, Caras. Don't trust any Caiivorian further than you can throw them."

Caras looked round, and found Orlii standing behind them with a fistful of gutted fish. From the look of trepidation on his face, he had not only heard Kierce's remark but was tensed in expectation of being thrown any minute.

Caras beckoned him forwards impatiently.

"Bring the food here, boy, let's get it on the fire."

It was time, he reflected, to do something about Orlii. The fewer opportunities Kierce had to play master, the better.

Chapter 12
Arhaios

Caras had never felt so relieved to be approaching Arhaios Holding. The familiar cluster of timber and thatch on its low hill above the river valley seldom failed to move him with a sense of pride and love. As he rode out of the forest towards the gentler landscape of trees and fields rolling away at Arhaios's feet, he felt immensely grateful to have reached it at all. He felt like a man walking blind along a treacherous mountain path. He could only trust that his next step would take him further along firm ground and not pitch him headfirst into an abyss.

Caras liked his way through life clearly marked, and changes to come at a measured pace. The worst disruption to his world so far had been the loss of his parents to a fever epidemic when he had barely attained manhood, and that was a grief shared by many others in his Holding. So many deaths within such a short space of time caused Leath to establish her grandson swiftly in her daughter's place as her successor, and Caras had found himself comforted by the need to comfort others. The community of which he was a part recovered and continued as it had for generations.

But now he could see that very community under threat – from the Caiivorian queen and her armed entourage at the Haven no less than from the man who had tried to cut his throat as he rode through his own forests. His head understood Rainur's strategy, but the nearer he got to home the more he realised how little he could see of where it was going to take him. Discovering that Kierce was to become their guide on the road ahead left him groping completely in the dark. Kierce went by ways that no-one else could follow, and seldom told anyone where he was going.

Caras could not imagine ever regarding Kierce with anything approaching the reverent respect Turloch's name automatically commanded. There were some things on which he firmly believed that he was right and Kierce was wrong, and he couldn't see anything making him think any differently.

It was mid-afternoon when they passed under the stout wooden beams that supported the Hall of Learning and entered Arhaios Holding. A number of people about their daily business called a greeting and a welcome as they passed, but the Caiivorian who accompanied them created as much or more excitement. Curious glances and whispered comments followed Orlii all the way across the Holding.

The Holder's house, which Leath had invited Caras and his family to share some years ago, lay on the south side of the Holding with its back to the summit of the hill. The Horsemaster's house was downhill to the west, looking out across the plains where his stock roamed freely.

Caras drew rein outside the Meeting House where his way and Kierce's should part.

"Come with me to see Leath," he suggested.

Kierce gave him an amused look.

"Caiivorian bandits you can deal with. Your grandmother, on the other hand ..."

Caras scowled as if dismissing a fatuous comment, though in fact it wasn't far from the truth. "What I mean is ... you are going to tell her, aren't you? Who you are, I mean, not ... the rest."

"I'm not sure I'll need to," admitted Kierce. "But yes, I was intending to tell Leath. Though going by your reaction, I'd rather not tell everyone just yet."

"It ... it came as something of a shock," said Caras, suddenly conscious that he was calling on a friendship he had denied to Kierce. Though he supposed it was pointless to tell even reassuring lies to the Magician, or his heir. The thought sent a clammy shiver down his spine. He was never going to be able to think of Kierce the same way again; and knowing that Kierce knew it was less than comforting.

"I think we all need more time to get used to the idea," said Kierce. "I certainly do."

Caras looked at him curiously.

"Surely you must have known ...?"

"I was trying to pretend I didn't. Come on then, Caras. I'll hold your hand and you can hold mine."

He turned his horse towards the Holder's house, a long, wooden building with a high-peaked thatched roof. A narrow passageway split it into two halves, effectively the public and the private, the west end meeting the Holder's obligation to provide hospitality to travellers and the east end forming the family living quarters. The central passageway led through the house to the domestic and farm offices at the rear.

Kierce and Caras headed around the eastern end of the building to the stock yard behind, but before they reached the house two small figures burst out of the east door, a tow-headed little boy and a slightly older girl with a mane of wild chestnut-brown hair tumbling across her shoulders. The girl was screaming at the boy to let her go first. The boy was taking not a blind bit of notice.

A broad grin broke across Caras's face. He swung himself off his horse and abandoned it to sweep both children into his arms.

Kierce dismounted more slowly. He had to prompt Orlii to follow suit. The Caiivorian boy was sitting on his horse staring at the unrestrained emotion of the greeting between Caras and his children. Kierce paused for a moment, glimpsed very briefly the memories and hunger the scene evoked in Orlii's mind, and deliberately turned away. He did not like to share Orlii's thoughts.

The Caiivorian's ignorance offended him, and he felt enervated by the constant undertow of terror in Orlii's life. Worse than a bloody unicorn, Kierce reflected to himself.

"Go in," he said to Caras, drily. "I'll sort out the horses and join you in a moment. I'd better leave Orlii with them for now. I think we'd probably better explain him before we introduce him."

"Yes. Of course," said Caras absently, setting down his son. "Taeg, you've grown heavier since I left. What's you mother been feeding you on?"

He went into the house without a backward glance, an arm around each child.

When Kierce joined them a short while later, Caras's family had grown sufficiently used to his return to spare almost as effusive a greeting for his companion, though Kierce had to go to the little girl, Alsareth, to get a hug since she refused to move from her father's lap.

Elani was less restrained. She enveloped him in a long and heartfelt embrace, which he very much appreciated. He stored a memory of Elani like a small treasure, locked from anyone except the two it belonged to. Even Caras had no key to it, though he had won the competition, in the end. There were other things to a partnership than sex.

"You are a bad man, Kierce ti' Gaeroch," Elani remonstrated with a smile, "to come here before you tell your own family you're safely returned."

"I'm sure the word's reached them by now," replied Kierce. "If they needed telling. I should hope they know me better than to think anything else."

Elani squeezed his arm gratefully.

"Thank you for looking after him."

"Oh, I only had to fight off one dragon and a handful of bears," said Kierce airily. "Not to mention a few dozen women, of course—".

"No slander," protested Caras.

Kierce put a conspiratorial arm around Elani's shoulders.

"Get him on his own," he advised, confidentially, "and ask him to describe Queen Cathva for you. I guarantee he will blush."

"Where's Leath?" Caras interrupted uncomfortably. "We have urgent news for her."

"I should hope you have," contributed a firm, quiet voice from the far end of the room.

Leath closed the door of the small inner chamber where she kept such tallies of trade and communal exchange as Shaihen Holdings bothered to keep. She moved forwards into the light from the hearth. She was tall, like her grandson, but much more sparely built. Age marked the features of her lined face the same way the years had bleached the red of her hair to grey, but it remained a strong face.

Over the course of her long tenure of office as Chief of Oreath, many had found to their cost that Leath was not a woman to be trifled with. The story of how she had banished her own husband from Arhaios was apocryphal. His sin was avarice, but there were other unforgiveable sins in Leath's canon. Kierce knew ignorance and idleness could count among them, as well as he knew that each of the two young men who faced her could be charged with one or the other of those crimes.

The untimely death of Leath's daughter had left her little time to reflect on the wisdom of giving Oreath its first male Chief for five generations when she made Caras her heir. Kierce could see that she had been doing quite a lot of reflecting on it recently.

She came across the room, and embraced each man in turn.

"I welcome your safe return, Caras – and thank you for it, Kierce. But you won't be surprised to know that news of you has reached me quicker than you yourselves have." She paused and fixed Caras with the keen grey eyes that had a capacity to make strong men squirm. "I was fascinated to hear that Oreath had declared a dispute with King Rainur."

"I didn't exactly do that—," began Caras.

Leath laid her hand on his shoulder and steered him back towards the doorway of her inner sanctum.

"Really? Come and tell me about it. Kierce, Elani, you are welcome to join us. But perhaps the children should not."

"I'm sure I'll hear it all later," replied Elani, exchanging a sympathetic look with Caras. "Be gentle with him, Leath. I want him back."

"You shall have him, Elani," promised Leath. She turned her inquisitorial gaze on Kierce. "I've heard no songs of you, though, Horsemaster, and I must admit I was half expecting to. Must I speak to Lord Turloch again?"

Kierce met her searching eyes with uncharacteristic humility.

"No, my lady," he admitted. "I have … spoken with Lord Turloch."

"And about time you did," said Leath. "You can't keep it a secret for ever."

"You … knew?" queried Caras in astonishment.

"Oh, if you had a grain of insight you'd have known too, you clay-clod," retorted Leath. "There could be no more skilled Horsemaster than Gaeroch. So young Kierce had to have something more than ordinary skill. Why do you think I wanted him to go with you?"

"I chose—."

Caras broke off at the look of wry amusement on Leath's face. She sighed.

"Caras, I do despair of you sometimes. You really must learn to see what people really want, rather than what they say they want."

"You got that one past me, too, Leath," admitted Kierce. "I thought you wanted me to protect him."

"I do. Now Turloch's told you how you're going to do it."

"I'd rather it wasn't general knowledge yet, though," said Kierce. "Only Turloch, Rainur and Caras know. And Orlii, I suppose, but he thinks I'm a demon."

"And who is Orlii?" queried Leath. "That doesn't sound like a Shaihen name?"

"It isn't," admitted Caras. "He's a Caiivorian. We caught him trying to steal our horses at Prassan."

Leath paused and gave him an eloquent look.

"A Caiivorian. Who tried to steal Kierce's horse. I must meet this man."

"He's a boy," replied Caras. "He was a slave in Caiivor. He … he thinks Kierce is his master."

Leath frowned.

"Does he."

Kierce raised an instinctive mental barrier as the grey eyes turned back to him accusingly. Leath did not read minds. Sometimes, he felt she didn't need to.

"And which of you gave him that idea?"

"Neither of us," said Kierce. "It's the way he thinks."

"Educate him," Leath instructed, shortly. "Freedom is the life blood of the Lord High Magician, you can't afford to own a slave."

"I don't own him, he just thinks I do."

"Is there a difference?" said Leath sharply. She kept a steady gaze on Kierce for several moments, but he was proof against it. "Stop playing with it, Kierce. I know what you do with your talents. You're not a boy pushing the boundaries, you're a man. Spirit defend us, you're a Magician. Turloch's had his say. Ignore him and you answer to me." She paused for a moment, watching him, and a smile twitched at her lips. "Though I wish I could have been a magician for a moment, to watch you and Turloch meeting. I can't imagine you get on?"

Kierce returned a slightly apologetic smile. Leath shook her head.

"By the Spirit, what kind of magic are we going to get from you, Kierce ti' Turloch?"

She turned back towards her grandson, and her expression hardened.

"Well now, Caras. Time you told me what exactly you've been doing in my name."

Chapter 13
Dispute

Two weeks after Caras's return from the Haven, Lord Jagus of Cuaraccon swept into Arhaios with an escort of twelve armed men, flung his sword at Leath's feet and declared that Caiivorians would be seen in Oreath over his dead body.

He failed to notice that Orlii was in the hall at the time, in his customary place at Kierce's side.

Caras avoided catching Kierce's eye. It had taken considerable effort from both of them to convince Leath of Rainur's argument, not least because the story of the Royal marriage and its implications had spread before them like a bow-wave through Oreath. The inevitable balladic account the minstrels were telling of the heir to Arhaios drawing his sword in the King's Hall had been raising belligerent murmurs among Leath's Holders before Caras was half way home.

In some ways, it was a relief that it was Jagus he was confronting. Everyone knew Jagus was much more noise than substance. He suffered from being the younger brother of the King and the husband of the Holder of Cuaraccon. He had nothing in his own right except his own self-importance, which was, Caras assumed, what made it so precious to him. The validity of his challenge was as dubious as Caras's challenge to Rainur had been. Jagus, also, was a messenger, not a Holder.

Nevertheless, Leath insisted that Caras treat the challenge seriously. She dealt with Jagus as Rainur had dealt with Caras, offering him the hospitality of her table, sitting him down and talking to him – or rather, making it plain that she expected Caras to talk to him.

Talking to Jagus was not easy. Getting a word in edgeways was not easy.

Caras had heard the story many times before. Jagus returned to Oreath from Vordeith two years ago, and never ceased to tell everyone how hard a journey it had been. By his own account, he had suffered slavery, poverty and overwhelming persecution; it took him eight years and a heroic defiance of the odds to make it back to Shehaios alive. This very story had contributed in no small part to Caras's own mistrust of the Empire, which culminated in him drawing a sword on Rainur.

Nevertheless, Jagus left Shehaios for Vordeith with a reputation as a vainglorious braggart and it was difficult to sift the truth from the bombast in his narrative. In his version of the tale, he was unconvincingly blameless.

What Caras knew was that Jagus and his brother Rainur were both sent by their father to complete their education in the court of Emperor Zelt. Rainur studied the Imperial histories and observed the intricacies of Imperial politics, but – reading between the lines – Jagus tired easily of such things. His interest was caught more by the endless competitions of physical strength indulged in by the young men of the city.

"They laughed at me," said Jagus. "A small man. We are all small men to them, Caras, remember that. They laughed at my size, at the length of my hair and the colour of my skin, they laughed at my strength and my skill with a sword. When I left five years later, they did not laugh. I learned their games, and I beat them. In the Arena, in front of the Emperor, I matched some of their finest champions. You do not have to be a big man to be strong. Focus on a sword and the spirit of life flows through its blade. Train your body, and it strikes quicker than your mind can see the enemy. That is the only lesson we need learn from the Empire."

"You are speaking of weapons and enemies," said Leath. "Shehaios speaks to us of peace and harmony."

"I am speaking the language of the Empire, my lady," said Jagus. "I am familiar with it, and you are not. When we were boys, both Rainur and I were seduced by it. I have fallen out of love. My brother has married it."

"You think we don't need the protection of the Imperial army, then?" said Caras. "You think perhaps Kierce and I should have fought the twenty Caiivorian warriors at Prassan?"

"You could have defeated them. If you had the skill."

"I didn't," said Caras. "Nor do I wish to acquire it. I'm heir to a Holder, not a warrior."

He shuddered slightly as he remembered the last time he'd denied a warrior heritage. The staring eyes of the Caiivorian robber still lived in his dreams.

"Then you're a coward," snapped Jagus. "And you're dreaming if you think Rainur wants anything other than a taste of Imperial power."

Caras took a very deliberate draught of ale and schooled his pride. Jagus had brought a drawn sword into the Holding; he could be as provocative as he liked. It was up to his hosts to avoid the head-on collision.

"Then what is Lord Turloch dreaming of, to sanction his actions?"

Jagus scowled. Speaking disrespectfully of the King was a matter of course, but no-one spoke disrespectfully of Lord High Magician Turloch.

"Rainur is trying to deal with the Empire as a Shaihen," said Caras. "Not as a Caiivorian warlord. Surely you must see that?"

But Jagus felt no compulsion to see anything other than the view he was familiar with. The argument lasted three days, and Jagus left with the sword still drawn between them.

Neither was he the only dissenting voice. Others too had some past experiences with the Empire that left them with bitter memories. No-one else actually laid a sword at Leath's feet, but many of them talked of it.

Leath left Caras to deal with most of them. She made him argue Rainur's case until he had argued the doubts out of his own head, but after nearly two months, when the trickle of worried Holders visiting Arhaios was becoming a flood, Leath decided to call a formal council of all the Holders of Oreath to settle the matter.

It was Caras who suggested that the council of Oreath met at Cuaraccon, territory of two of his most dogged opponents. Jagus and his wife did not agree on many things these days. But on the matter of Rainur's marriage they found themselves in accord. The minstrels of Cuaraccon really preferred to sing the history of the single magic kingdom shining like a gem behind its golden mountains. The Fair Land as a very small province of a mighty and corrupt Empire did not evoke the same passion.

All the Holdings of Shehaios had their own individual character, but Cuaraccon, the home of the minstrels, was famously beautiful. Set on the shores of a lake near the edge of the western plains, the vast open skies of the grasslands tended to cast it in a permanently changing, but always dramatic, light. It was largely constructed of a local stone found a few miles south of the Holding, a pale kind of granite which contained glittering chips of quartz. Buildings made from it quite literally sparkled.

It had a tendency to sparkle on the inside as well as the outside. Lady Brethil's view of the Holder's role was to ensure that her people spent the minimum amount of time working and the maximum amount enjoying themselves. Cuaraccon was the home of debate, debauchery and delight.

In their great silver-stone Meeting House, Caras heard his own voice repeat the words Rainur had used to persuade him. It was a strong voice, trained from adolescence by the skilled orator he was destined to succeed. He threw every ounce of skill Leath had taught him into his words, Rainur's words.

They were listening. He could see that they were listening. He could see from the glower on Jagus's face that he was winning hearts that belonged in their land, with their families, not in dreams of glory.

It was obvious that no-one wanted wars. Shaihens did not want to kill any more than they wanted to die. If the Empire wanted to protect them from those who wanted to kill them, then let it do so, and rejoice.

He was still speaking when he became aware of the stalwart figure of Brynnen the Minstrel standing at the back of the hall. His head was slightly bowed in a preoccupied attitude, his hand unconsciously stroking his beard. His long, tawny hair fell across his face, hiding his expression, but Caras could sense that the news he brought was not good.

He brought his speech to an abrupt end.

"I'm sorry, my friends," he said. "We'll return to this matter. But I believe Brynnen may have something more important to tell us."

Brynnen looked up and met Caras's eyes across the sea of heads.

"A new song, Lord Caras. Well known, south of our mountains. Hard to sing. Harder still to hear." He looked around the hall. "Are you ready to listen?"

Caras listened in horror as the stark, evocative words of Brynnen's song dropped into the hush that had fallen over the Meeting House. It told him of the fierce and bloody fight to regain Prassan, the subdued celebration of a costly and hard-won victory. It told of the rebirth of hope for Prassan's people, which lived but two turns of the moon. It told of a hundred *caii* warriors where ten had come before. It sang the lament for Prassan's death; the small, hard, Holding that had clung to the thin earth for generations. It sang the lament for the death of a score of other small Holdings. And it sang the lament for Mervecc.

Gascon had brought fire down on his own Holding.

It ended with a victory. The Haven came to Mervecc's aid, and the invaders were driven off, Cathva's Caiivorian guards earning a line or two of praise to themselves. Shehaios regained the land on which Mervecc had stood, but the Holding itself was devastated. Lord Gascon lay between life and death in the hands of the Lord High Magician, while Rainur strove to pull something of Mervecc from the ashes.

"Leath has heard this?" asked Caras, in the stunned silence that followed the telling of the horrific tale.

The big minstrel nodded.

"She bid me bring it straight to you. And those gathered here. She asks that the disputes cease, now, and you return to Arhaios."

"At once," said Caras, "And then to the Haven, and Mervecc. Is there need of more fighting strength at Mervecc?"

"I think not. It's all over – this time, at least. It was a hard won victory, but victory it was, there were few enough Caiivorians left to dispute it in the end. The hard thing, Lord Caras, is that the Caiivorian invaders were mighty in their strength, but few in numbers. We were hinds before their spears."

Caras turned to the assembled company.

"Do I need to say more? We have to seek the protection of the Imperial army."

"It didn't stop this happening, did it?" demanded Jagus. "Rainur has his alliance and his Caiivorian queen, and still we lose our holdings and our people. What does the Guardian of the Gate say to that? Or is he too busy securing his claim to Mervecc as well as the Haven? How weak does my brother wish to keep us? How much does he want?"

"He wants what we all want. To keep Shehaios for our people."

Jagus and several others all began to shout at once. Impatiently, Caras raised his hand and called for silence, but he could not be heard above the din. The shock and panic engendered by the news from Mervecc threatened to reduce the gathering to a chaos that would forever undermine the authority of

Arhaios. Caras sensed it happening, but was powerless to control it. He could not make himself heard. He was trying to think of a means of getting their attention when he became suddenly aware of Kierce's unexpected presence beside him.

Kierce had kept himself apart from the internal wrangling of the Oreathan holdings. It was some weeks since Caras had spoken to him at all, though he knew he was still in Arhaios. Kierce had been about his own business. He spent all his time since returning from the Haven working to ensure the standards of the Horsemaster of Arhaios would not fall too disasterously when he left.

There was no time now for Caras to ask where Kierce had sprung from, nor would Kierce have heard over the racket in the hall if he had. Kierce gave him a slight, reassuring smile and stepped forwards. He did nothing, made no move, no signal, no sound, simply stood quietly, hands folded in front of him.

The hubbub in the hall gradually subsided as everyone turned to stare at Kierce. Holders everywhere shifted a little guiltily, like children caught out in a foolish squabble.

"The Holder of Arhaios bids that all disputes cease," said Kierce, into the hush. "Listen to her envoy."

He turned towards Caras and gestured to him to take the floor. Caras postponed all the questions about how, exactly, Kierce had commanded the attention of the uproarious crowd who had signally ignored him, and took the chance Kierce gave him.

"I speak for Leath, and for myself," he said. "We are both Holder of Arhaios – she as of now, and I in the future. I support Rainur, because if I don't I fear I may not have a Holding to inherit. It's that simple." He paused, holding their attention now. "The time for discussion is past. I don't want to see Shaihens fight Shaihens, but if you really dispute the decision of Arhaios in this, declare it, and we will fight. Otherwise, take up your sword and keep it ready to fight the sons of war who raid our borders."

He turned and left the hall, Kierce beside him and Brynnen following.

"Not that I'm not grateful," muttered Caras as they left. "But I thought you didn't want them to know you're Turloch's successor yet. Should you have done that?"

He was grateful. He also resented the apparent ease with which Kierce conjured a power and authority that had been beyond the grasp of the heir to Arhaios.

Kierce smiled and put his arm around Caras's shoulder.

"Don't worry," he said. "You saw Kierce. They saw Turloch."

"Turloch!" Caras exclaimed. No wonder the Holders of Oreath had stared.

"You think I could have attracted that much reverence?"

"I didn't know how you'd done it."

"Only way I could have done it. If they weren't listening to you, there's no-one else they would have listened to except Turloch. Won't do your reputation any harm to be seen leaving in the Lord High Magician's company, either. Only you and I know it's the future Lord High Magician you're with and not the present one."

"Well … " Caras glanced at him and tried not to sound grudging. It was after all easier to accept Turloch's authority than Kierce's. "Thank you."

"A modest illusion. Gambler's bluff. You should know I'm good at that."

"What are you doing here?"

Kierce hesitated.

"I'm on my way to the Haven."

"Cuaraccon is hardly on the way to the Haven from Arhaios."

It was, in fact, precisely in the opposite direction, though Arhaios and Cuaraccon were not far apart from each other.

"No, but it's where you were."

Kierce removed his hand from Caras's shoulder. Caras had been walking rapidly out of the Meeting House towards the stock yard where his horse awaited him, anxious to leave behind the talking and be active in answer to Brynnen's news. Kierce matched his briskness without comment. They strode on together in awkward silence for some minutes.

"Well. It was good timing," said Caras eventually. "At least I got the chance to speak. Though whether I was talking to myself or not I don't know."

"You weren't. Far from it. But I should tell you that two of them, at least, are ready to fight you."

Caras cursed under his breath.

"Two of them … ?"

"At least."

"Jagus?"

"Difficult to call. Cuaraccon has its own dispute brewing."

Caras looked at him questioningly.

"Jagus was away too long, and the novelty of his return is beginning to wear off. His wife developed a taste for younger flesh in his absence."

Caras hesitated, studied his companion briefly, and decided he didn't want to know. The attractions Cuaraccon held for Kierce were many and varied.

"So their partnership is … unstable?"

"Decidedly. Brethil is Holder of Cuaraccon; Jagus may use this as an opportunity to try and take it away from her. His arguments have their followers." Kierce looked at Caras. "People are afraid of where you're taking them, Caras. It's only to be expected."

"I'm not taking them anywhere, it's where we're going. It frightens me. All we can do is try and make it an easier journey." Caras frowned. It was blindingly obvious to him, now, what Rainur was doing. He found himself intensely irritated by the obstinate inability of some of his people to see it. "Which two?" he asked.

Kierce gave him a questioning look.

"Iareth and Brethil?" Caras answered his own question.

"The Lady of Riskeld and the Lady of Cuaraccon," agreed Kierce.

"But Brethil's not opposing it because of Jagus?"

"Almost the opposite. Jagus's opposition is pushing her towards supporting you."

"Then what is it that's pushing her away? Why are the women against me, Kierce? Don't they know what it is we're trying to defend here?"

"They're women who know Caiivorians, Caras. Brethil's heard all about the Empire from Jagus, and seen its effect on him. She's heard Lady Loia's story told over and over again. Iareth … well. We know the history of Riskeld."

Riskeld was a small Holding on the west coast of Oreath. Many years ago they had suffered a brief, traumatic occupation by Imperial troops blown ashore by hostile winds. The soldiers were returning from a campaign against the tribes who inhabited the lands across the Western Ocean from Oreath, and they failed to distinguish between the insurgents they had been subduing and the peaceful allies on whose shores the winds had blown them. Like Jagus, Riskeld held memories of Imperial violence that were long and bitter and not easily forgiven.

"I can't leave with this still unresolved," said Caras anxiously. "Yet I need to be at the Haven—."

"Do you? What can you do there?"

"I don't know. That's what I was intending to go and find out."

Kierce grimaced. "You might be able to trust the women, but I suggest Jagus needs watching from a closer vantage point than Rainur's palace."

Caras considered the truth of this with disquiet. Jagus retained the fighting skills he learned in Vordeith as a young man, seasoned now by the brutality of his subsequent experiences in the Empire. His ability with a sword was rumoured to be both impressive and deadly. Despite Caras's sweeping declaration as he left Cuaraccon's Meeting House, he realised this was not something that could be dealt with quickly or easily.

"I made Gascon a promise," he said, uneasily.

Kierce looked at him briefly, read the promise and dismissed it peremptorily.

"That wasn't a promise, it was a polite gesture. Gascon is the master of expediency, he won't hold you to that unless he has other good reasons for wanting you to raise an army. Save it until Gascon calls it in."

"If he lives to do so."

"If he lives to do so," agreed Kierce. "Caras, I have to go to the Haven anyway. Stay here where you're needed. I'll act as your voice to Rainur and his to you."

"What business do you have at the Haven?" asked Caras, a touch suspiciously.

"More than I want. Trying to ensure Gascon lives, for instance." Kierce paused. "I came via Cuaraccon to say goodbye, Caras. I'm leaving Arhaios, and it may be some time before I return. You know our conversation about the time of Turloch's death? Well, sooner seems to have arrived. And believe me, Jagus's supporters aren't the only ones who are scared of what tomorrow holds."

Caras looked at him in surprise. He never imagined Kierce being afraid of anything.

For the first time, he shifted focus from his own political problems to register a hint of the revolution going on in Kierce's life. The man who spent most of his life alone in the hills, living with the elements and working with animals was being pitched into the heart of a Shaihen society sliding rapidly into the wider Imperial world. The man who preferred to occupy such time as he spent in human company in pleasure and diversion was being given responsibility for the whole balance of Shehaios. Caras may be appalled at the idea that Kierce was the next Lord High Magician; he was just beginning to realise how equivocally Kierce himself welcomed it.

Kierce did not pursue the matter directly. He grasped Caras's shoulder.

"Take care of yourself. Jagus will walk through you if you get in his way. And the sword is his weapon." Kierce tapped his head with his forefinger. "Use yours. If you allow that bag of wind to take your life I'll never forgive you."

"What it is to have advice from a Magician," said Caras. "Thank you for that, Kierce. Most helpful."

"You're more than a match for him, idiot. Don't take him head on, go round him." Kierce smiled. "And enjoy the journey."

"Easier said than done," retorted Caras.

They entered the yard, where five horses waited outside for their riders. One was Brynnen's sturdy bay cob. The other four, dutifully attended by Orlii, belonged to Kierce. Red Sky was saddled, proof that he was embarking on a long journey. For preference, Kierce rode bareback, but a saddle made his weight easier for the horse to carry on a long distance over rough terrain. The old Merveccian workhorse had been quietly retired, and one of the three mares was saddled for Orlii. The other two carried packs holding such worldly goods as Kierce possessed.

At last the message penetrated Caras's skull. Kierce his friend, Kierce the Horsemaster, would never return to Arhaios. When he came back, he would come back the Lord High Magician. And neither of them knew quite who that person would be.

They exchanged a brief, wordless embrace before Kierce turned and called a greeting to the black stallion. The horse responded and walked towards his master. He came alongside as Kierce vaulted lightly onto his back, the movement of horse and man perfectly synchronised so that it looked like one flowing action.

"I've always wondered," said Caras, admiring the display of grace and athleticism he had so often witnessed and so rarely seen. "Why is a black horse called Red Sky?"

"Caught him on a dark night," said Kierce. "Thought he was a chestnut."

He grinned. Caras knew very well Kierce did not catch horses any more than he gave them meaningless names. He never laid a rope on them until he had already persuaded them to accept his mastery.

"It's his scent," Kierce explained. "Horses identify each other by their smell. I was watching a fine sunset after a wet day when it crossed my mind that this bright little black colt I was trying to name smelled just like earth after rain." He shrugged. "Well, he does to me. Come on, Mud."

He turned towards the yard entrance as Orlii brought the other horses up behind him.

"Kierce …"

"I'll stay clear of the Spring." Kierce spared him the trouble of finding the words that wouldn't come. "You see a man reformed beneath Turloch's scourge."

The reassurance lacked something in sincerity. Caras sighed.

"Well, I suppose I need someone to tell me when I'm being a pompous ass. And I suppose I'd rather it was you."

"I promise you, Caras," said Kierce, as he rode out of the yard, "I will never fail to tell you when you're being a pompous ass." He turned in the saddle and pulled something from the pocket hung at his belt. "I nearly forgot. I meant to give this to Tuli. Catch, or you'll have every male dragon for ten miles in amorous pursuit of you."

Caras lunged for the small earthernware bottle flying through the air and gathered it to his body as it fell safely into his hand. The thought of what might have happened if he'd dropped it brought a cold sweat to his forehead. He glared at Kierce's retreating back. Why take such a stupid, pointless risk?

What kind of Magician are you?

Chapter 14
Kierce's Inheritance

He could hardly believe it was only a few months since he had played twelve stones here. Since he made love beneath the eaves of the Meeting House to a fair-haired girl whose rational opinion of Lord Kierce of Arhaios was that he was an impertinent Oreathan dwarf.

Kierce stood in the centre of a low circle of blackened stone, the foundation and wall of the Meeting House at Mervecc. The rest, made of timber, lay around him in skeletal black ruins and a desert of choking ash. There were bones, too, the charred remains of the seventy eight people who had shared this funeral pyre alive.

Their death, and their pain, throbbed through Kierce's body in a constant dull ache. He had mastered it. He couldn't stop it.

Kierce bent and picked up a shiny, slightly flattened stone, fired to jet in the furnace. He knew by its shape that it was a gaming stone, though it was impossible to tell now what pictures it had carried. He contemplated its hidden faces. He had come here straight from jewelled Cuaraccon, full of passion and argument, songs and laughter. There had been, for Kierce, the same buzz of life in Mervecc's market place, in the strange scents of its shifting population and the constant whisper of wagers and lies and promises. If Cuaraccon was silver, Mervecc was gold.

He looked up at Orlii, waiting beyond the edge of the ruin, probably not far from the place where he had sat for several cold, miserable hours beneath the gaze of Mervecc's dogs.

Kierce tossed the stone aside and made his way carefully through the dust and the wreckage out of the building.

"What do you think of your people, Orlii?" he asked, sourly.

Orlii looked at him wide-eyed. Kierce very rarely spoke more than a gruff command to him.

"M ... master?" he stammered.

Kierce gave him a withering look.

"Foolish question. Had the word 'think' in it." He turned and swept a dramatic gesture across the scene of devastation around them. "Are you proud of this, Orlii? Does it make you feel good to have served the men who did this?"

"They ... were my masters, my lord," murmured Orlii humbly.

Kierce contemplated him a little more thoughtfully.

"But not your people. So your people were better than that, were they?"

"M ... my people, Lord Kierce?"

Kierce saw the boy's hand stray almost unconsciously to his chest. The crudely stylised flame enclosed by a circle seemed to be the only image mention of his people brought to Orlii's mind.

Kierce turned impatiently and headed towards the remains of the Holder's house. It was one of the few buildings in Mervecc still standing – it had most of a roof and almost four walls. The wounded survivors of the fight who could not be moved to the Haven or other neighbouring shelter were in there.

"Don't make me work at it," he snapped. "I've too much else on my mind to waste time reading yours. You must know something about your family. Your father, your brothers, your mother – you must at least have had a mother?"

"My mother served my masters, Lord Kierce," said Orlii, stumbling after him with a rush of relief that he had something to say.

"You were born a slave?"

"N… no. No, I don't think so. I don't know. I don't remember."

"You don't think and you don't remember," said Kierce with a slight sigh. "What am I going to do with you, Orlii?"

"Master? "

Kierce laid a hand on his shoulder and propelled him towards the ruins of Gascon's once-beautiful house.

"Spirit give me strength," he muttered. "Come and make yourself useful, child."

Turloch had called Kierce back for two reasons, though Kierce quickly realised they were in fact the same reason. Kierce saw the moment he met the Magician how he had shrunk. His skin had a worryingly translucent pallor and the brilliant emerald eyes were dimmed. It had startled Kierce that Turloch should have aged so much in such a short space of time, that he should suddenly look so close to death.

The first time he laid eyes on the ruin of what had been Mervecc, he began to get some idea why Turloch was fading before his eyes. The first time he entered the makeshift hospital, he understood with a vengeance.

He had always had to school himself carefully when he was hunting, to be sure that at the last moment he properly separated hunter from prey in his mind. When he transfixed the interloper at Prassan with his spear, he felt the weakness in his own leg. When Caras cut the throat of the man who attacked him, the sharp finality of his death dropped Kierce to his knees.

Since his last visit to the Haven and the beginning of Turloch's tutelage, he had begun to hear the voice of the land itself. Until now, he had been moving through familiar territory, a story he knew and a world in harmony. But the broken body of Gascon's Holding lay in his own bones like a dull ache. The ash dried his throat and seeped into his skin until it felt as if he had been dragged naked through a pit of sand and grit.

Almost the first person he came to when he entered the hospital was Gascon, lying feverish and semi-conscious with a cracked head and a livid scar across his belly. Kierce looked down at him, and saw what Turloch had had to do to save him from the near-fatal spear-thrust, the mess of internal organs to be healed and restored. His own guts contracted. He felt the pain of the man who loved beautiful things watching his Holding destroyed, falling on the brink of driving out the men who had destroyed it. Gascon was less a warrior than Caras was, but without Turloch's intervention, he would have died on the battlefield.

As Kierce moved on, it grew worse. He felt every wound he looked at. The burned face of a young girl made his own face burn; when he passed a man with a crushed leg he stumbled on the pain which shot through his own limb. He saw what they had seen, killing and mutilation without mercy, delight in human butchery. His breath began to come in snatches, his body wracked with echoes of suffering.

He fled, every shred of willpower holding back an urge to scream.

Outside, the feeling diminished. He paused with the sweat pouring off his face to recover himself from the pieces into which he had split.

Turloch followed him outside with the shadow of a cruel little smile on his weary face.

"*Jo a haios o. Haios o ja. Ush eloh,*" (haios is me. I am haios. We are one) observed the Magician. "To understand, you have to feel. Learning to control it enables you to heal them."

Turloch at least acknowledged Kierce's state of distress by using his voice rather than forcing him to read his mind.

"Heal them!" exclaimed Kierce, breathlessly. "I can't even get near them!"

"You can heal yourself and you can heal them," replied Turloch implacably. "But it doesn't come as easily as seducing foolish little girls. It burns up your strength. That's why we can't heal everyone or everything. The Magician would be exhausted within days and dead within weeks if Shehaios asked that of him. You use it sparingly, as you use all your powers." He slapped Kierce heartily on the back, setting Kierce's ravaged nerves jangling with signals of anticipated pain. "Still, if there's nothing more to be said for you, you're young, you're fit, you're strong. And I am none of those things. Don't sit idling here, Kierce, there's work to do."

Kierce drew himself up with an effort. "How—?"

"Well, come back in, and I'll show you."

Kierce had the abilities of the Magician, the part that was not in Turloch's gift; but he needed Turloch's guidance to control and direct them, and as the exhausting intensity of the days he spent at Mervecc soon revealed, he needed to have started learning long before this.

Nevertheless, he stayed with it. He mastered his horror, and learned to focus on what he could do, rather than what he couldn't, displaying a tenacity and self-control that would have amazed and impressed Caras. After three weeks, he elicited a complaint from Gascon that laughter hurt, and was aware of an unguarded glimmer of approval from Turloch. He counted such crumbs as a triumph. It was all he ever got.

Turloch was at first reluctant to allow Orlii near these people who had suffered their injuries at Caiivorian hands, but Orlii had the ability of all good servants to make himself invisible, even to the Lord High Magician. He obeyed without question, anticipated the needs of his masters, was there when he was needed and unseen when he wasn't. He fetched and carried and cleaned in silence, with barely a curious glance at the victims they treated. Turloch rapidly began to take him as much for granted as Kierce tended to.

Kierce watched how Orlii did it. He began to forge a curious, subconscious sense of solidarity with the boy, who served alongside his master without question. In these circumstances, they were both slaves to an overwhelming demand.

After an exhausting month in Mervecc, however, Turloch abruptly declared that it was time he seriously addressed Kierce's education, and at that point, Orlii lost them.

The nearer Turloch drew to his death, the less the incidentals of life seemed to concern him. He neither slept, nor ate. Had Kierce's stomach been less clamorous, he would have been asleep on his feet when they reached the derelict cottage on the hillside above the Haven.

It didn't look much like the residence of the Lord High Magician. It looked more like a half-ruined turf hut, with a broken door and the debris of winter gales strewn across the floor.

That, in fact, was what it was. Turloch lived at the Palace, with the King.

Kierce feared it was going to afford him little in the way of food or rest, both of which his body was aching for. They had covered the two-day journey from Mervecc between sunrise and sunset, and although they hadn't ridden it, the travelling had been even more exhausting than if they had.

No time.

Turloch didn't even wait for Kierce's weary mind to form the complaint. He put his shoulder to the lop-sided door and heaved it fully open.

It led into a single, dark room. A dusty hearth lay cold at one end, with a trivet and a cooking pot beside it. A rough-hewn wooden dresser held the promise of food, but all Kierce could see on it was a forlorn bunch of shrivelled herbs.

In the rear wall, a dim light issued from an open archway which seemed to lead into the mountain behind.

Turloch moved towards it. Kierce hesitated in the entrance, grasping some idea of what Turloch was taking him into. The Magician's store of knowledge represented a meeting of minds that crossed language, culture, distance and time. It was the heart of his power, the generator connected to the powers of communication Kierce already possessed.

Shouldn't it be better guarded?

Can you see it?

Of course I can see it.

No-one else can. Come.

I have to rest. I have to eat.

You've spent more than twenty years doing that. Now you have to work.

I have been working !

It was a waste of time. Turloch disappeared from view behind the dim light of the cave entrance.

Reluctantly, Kierce followed him. He couldn't tell where the light was coming from, but he could see clearly. He passed through the narrow entrance passage, and into a vast cavern stretching away too far for him to see the end of it. It was filled with row upon row of... stuff. Stacked from the floor to somewhere lost in the gloom above his head were thousands of engraved tablets, rolls of parchment and manuscripts, broken armour and fragments of weapons, shards of pottery, brick and stone, jewellery, bones, and objects of unknown obscurity. A low, dense level of noise assailed him, the constant murmur of thousands upon thousands – millions – of voices.

Kierce paused, rapidly recognising the need to make the same adjustment he had made on entering the hospital at Mervecc. He could not let all these stories touch him, or he would drown in it. He met Turloch's eyes as the small Magician stood waiting for him.

Now you know why I didn't bring you here earlier.

He led the way through the labyrinth of artefacts, which seemed to crowd closer on Kierce as he went further into them. Turloch rarely paused by any individual item, though sometimes he pulled a scroll or a manuscript down, opened it up and showed Kierce the image that leapt off the page. Scenes of battle and atrocity, buildings and civilisations, cloth, grain and gold tumbled in chaotic miniature in front of his bemused gaze until Turloch replaced the item that contained the words describing them. All the time, the Magician's mind was full of what he passed among and touched, and Kierce was soon struggling to concentrate on the welter of information. He followed Turloch in a daze, hour after hour lost in time and each footstep heavier than the last. His head was spinning. He had no idea where he was, when he was, where he was going or what any of it was supposed to mean to him.

Eventually, he sat down on a pile of board-bound objects he took to be piles of parchment and tried to just focus on Turloch's racing mind.

His head sagged. His eyes closed. He fell in an ungracious heap with the pile of books cascading around him and awoke with a start.

He picked himself up angrily.

"This is ridiculous," he announced, his voice uncannily loud and discordant above the strange whispering background. "It will take me months – years – to even start learning any of this."

Turloch regarded him reflectively.

"You won't ever know all of it. No-one does. You just know more than everyone else, if you know where to look. I am trying to show you where to look. You could at least show sufficient respect to stay awake."

"We have spent weeks of hard labour in Mcrvecc bringing some of Gascon's people back from the dead. I learned that. We came to the Haven without stopping, and now you haul me in here and expect me to learn what you should have spent the last – I don't know – years, at least, teaching me." He paused and glared at the Magician. "You left it too bloody late, Turloch. Admit it."

He knew why Turloch had left it too bloody late. Turloch did not believe anyone could replace him, let alone Kierce. His opinion of his heir had never been high and after the events of the night before Rainur's wedding, it had plummeted. No matter how much he might have striven to educate his heir, Turloch believed fundamentally that Kierce would always have failed him.

But in Kierce's mind, Turloch had already failed him. He had written him off without ever giving him a chance to prove himself. They were magicians of one generation and the next, and apart from their shared responsibility of power and understanding, they found little in common.

Kierce bent to pick up one of the fallen books in the silence that followed his accusation. His arm brushed against a roll of parchment, knocking it to the floor. It unrolled and a tiny grey image of a man in a highly embroidered silken gown emerged and began to recite the lineage of some southern dynasty. Kierce snatched up the parchment and stuffed it back on the shelf, silencing the mannequin.

"I'm tired, Turloch, and I'm hungry," he asserted. "And I've had enough."

Already?

I can't even begin to learn in one night what will take me a lifetime. You know that.

I don't have a lifetime. I don't have years, or months, or even weeks. You know that!

Then you will have to be content to show me this place, and leave it to me.

Kierce looked unflinchingly into the emerald green eyes. He was already and inescapably Turloch's heir, and he was beginning to feel Shehaios would have to make do with the Magician he was, not the Magician Turloch wanted them to have.

"You'll just have to trust me, Turloch. Now show me the way out of here. I'm going back to the Palace."

Turloch regarded him stonily.

"Where else am I going to be offered food and shelter?" added Kierce, belligerently. "I'm not about to start hunting my own dinner now. The state you've reduced me to I'd probably end up as something else's dinner." He stopped speaking before he remembered that it didn't make any difference. *I'll have to go there sooner or later. I'll have to meet her again.*

And you have to remember. Don't get too close. Be a shadow to her.

"Show me the way out of here," said Kierce, bluntly.

Turloch began to lead him back through the maze of objects.

It's you that's the oddity, Turloch, not me. Kierce directed the thought very deliberately to ensure that Turloch could not miss it. *Love is just what humans make out of our instincts to procreate and protect. You know that. It's perfectly natural for a human male to take pleasure in the body of a human female. I could make some sense of it if you took pleasure in the body of a human male, but you don't like anyone, do you?*

We're not free to follow our passions. When other Shaihens strike, it's with a fist or a sword, the damage is visible. If you or I strike, the fire burns down the ages. Love and hate must both become strangers to you.

You believe the Magician of life should become a stranger to what makes life worth the living? Spirit defend me from ever becoming like that.

"Kierce, you are a coarse, ignorant, arrogant fool," responded Turloch. He glanced contemptuously at Kierce. "Young men usually are. I trust you will learn that, at least."

The air outside the Magician's cottage hit Kierce with unexpected force. He staggered, and caught the dubious support of the derelict door to steady himself. The Palace, half a mile below him, seemed suddenly a long way away.

Turloch, what have you done to me?

He gritted his teeth, and pulled himself upright. All he needed was food and rest. The basics of survival were really much more simple than Turloch liked to think.

Chapter 15
The Magician's Death

When Cathva heard that Kierce was returning to the Haven because he was the Lord High Magician's successor, she understood what it was to feel as if her blood was freezing. Turloch's odd little figure had always made her skin crawl. She hated the way he looked at her sometimes, and she knew she had seen those cold eyes somewhere during the encounter in the Spring.

The experience lay festering in the recesses of her memory into something dark and horrible, a threat to the triumph of her marriage. She was ashamed of herself, to have been so foolish as to let a man trick her like that.

She strove, with some success, to put it all out of her mind, a superstitious nightmare that should never have happened. There were plenty of other things to think about – her wedding was perfect, and she quickly began to make her mark on the Palace staff. Rainur was as charming as he had ever been, and he certainly did not have water for blood, though he remained touchingly gentle with her. He slept beside her even when he did not want her. She was glad of it. He kept the ghost of the Temple at bay.

There had been no difficulty in conceiving the heir he so wished for, and although she had not yet made it public, Cathva knew it secured her place in Shehaios.

Shaihens chose their king – Vordeith chose its Emperor – but in practice, titles nearly always passed along bloodlines. Children of chieftains learned the business of being chieftain.

A child got between Rainur and herself would be the embodiment of the two bloodlines which made the alliance. It bound the future of Shehaios to the Sacred Union, yet the child would be raised a Shaihen king.

Everyone in the Palace was waiting with bated breath for the announcement of her pregnancy. They fell over themselves to make her feel at home, even to the extent of trying to act like servants. They weren't very good at it. But it was entertaining to watch them try.

She saw her own smile looking back at herself from the mirror, and it reminded her that there was, suddenly, a very large shadow over her happiness. Rainur was still in Mervecc. It was her duty to welcome the heir to the Lord High Magician and she was accustomed to doing what was expected of her, no matter how hard or horrifying it might be. She spent a moment or two longer composing herself before she sent word to arrange a meeting with Lord Kierce.

Kierce's instinct aroused him from sleep in spite of his body's protest. He raised his head and listened, then relaxed and lay back on the bed, closing his eyes with a faint smile.

"Come in, Orlii."

The door to the Palace's guest room opened quietly and Orlii crept in.

"I have bread, Master. There was a fresh batch."

Kierce laughed softly. "How do you know, boy?" He looked at Orlii in amusement. "And how in the Spirit did you get here? How did you even know I'd be here?"

Orlii looked at him with the cautious forerunner of a smile in his eyes. It was the first time Kierce had ever come close to welcoming him, let alone praising him. He came into the room and set down the basket of still-warm bread on a chest near the bed.

"I asked, my lord. They said you would most likely have gone with Lord Turloch to the Haven."

"I abandoned you in Mervecc. You could have just run away."

He couldn't. Kierce knew that what bound Orlii to serve him was in the boy's mind, inescapable. He was distantly aware of Orlii's feelings towards him transmuting from fear to adoration; he resisted, as always, any involvement with his own emotions.

The seductive aroma of the bread reminded him how ravenous he still was. He seemed to have some embarrassing recollection of falling asleep in the middle of a meal. Only for a moment, before he caught himself, but he retired before he made more of a fool of himself, too tired to assuage his hunger.

He swung himself off the bed and helped himself to the riches of the Palace bakery. He pushed the basket towards Orlii.

"Eat some, you idiot," he slurred, through a mouthful. "Destroy the evidence. Before they know you've nicked it."

"It was made for you, Master," said Orlii.

Kierce paused.

"What?"

"You slept a day round. The King's stewards were concerned—."

"A day round? A full day? And I didn't even know?"

Orlii backed off.

"My lord, you have worked hard."

Kierce swore violently.

"I never do that. Am I a dragon that I can afford to be oblivious for so long? What has Turloch done to me? Oh, for Spirit's sake, Orlii, don't run away now!"

Orlii froze where he stood.

"Tell me what I've missed."

"N... nothing, my lord."

"I've missed breakfast and supper for a start, that's not nothing. Orlii, the act doesn't do it for me any more." He looked directly at the tall Caiivorian boy with the ever-watchful eyes. "You don't think, but you don't miss a thing. It seems I might need some extra ears and eyes if I'm going to spend this long inside my mind. Yes, you would improve my temper if you offered to shave me. It would improve more if we visited the Spring and bathed properly. Yes, I can see myself through your eyes, and I look like I was last night's dinner. And the Queen wants to see me? Shit."

He ran his hands through the long hair hanging uncharacteristically loose and tangled over his shoulders.

"I'll need your help, Orlii. The last thing I want to remind Queen Cathva of is a *caii* warrior." He paused. The mere mention of her name brought back to him the scent and the taste of her, the softness of her golden skin and the soaring pleasure of her body entwined with his. He could have drowned in that spring, and died happy. "What does an Imperial Queen think a shadow looks like?"

He glanced across at Orlii. An image leapt unbidden from Orlii's infancy of a menacing, black-haired, sharp-featured figure with fanged teeth, leering through flames, his eyes shot by fire.

It looked remarkably like Kierce on a bad day.

How much of that was because Orlii was unable to separate him from his image of the Enchanter of Shehaios, Kierce couldn't tell.

"Fanged teeth and fire." He grimaced. "Well. I'll try it, Turloch." He lingered a moment on a memory of soft skin and sweet lips, and shook himself. She was Rainur's Queen, the one woman he couldn't have.

Cathva arranged the meeting with careful formality. She received him in the Meeting House, with guards and Palace staff present at a discrete distance.

Kierce viewed her with covert admiration as he crossed the Meeting House towards her. The jewels and glitter, the constricting dress and the false face no longer repulsed him; he hardly saw them. His mind was looking at her as he had last seen her, and he was so entranced by the view from that level that he was half way across the room towards her before he touched the fear in her mind.

It was so unexpected, he almost came to a dead halt. His recollection of their union was of something he had enticed her to, not something he had forced on her. He had thought he was going to have to make himself a monster. He didn't expect to find himself one already.

No-one in Shehaios had ever been afraid of him. There were plenty who disliked him, even more who found him irritating, but he was a small man who had never had the ability to physically intimidate, even if he'd wanted to. He had only ever used the power he held to win trust. He made deceit into a vocation, but crude bullying was alien to his nature. His horses did not fear him. Even the creatures he hunted did not fear him; he prided himself on his ability to get close enough to kill before they were aware of the danger.

When Cathva turned to him in terror in the temple, he had found the undignified loss of her Imperial arrogance amusing. It felt different to Orlii's enervating, ignorant terror. Now, it didn't.

He had to make himself keep walking towards the barrier of her fear. This was how Turloch wanted it to be. *Be a shadow to Cathva. Be whatever you can make her believe you to be. Other than a male human who can't resist proving his prowess to every passing female.*

It was the last thing he wanted to do. He wanted to smile and tease her until she realised that she had nothing to fear from him except her own feelings.

He took the trembling hand she extended towards him and raised it briefly to his lips.

"Your servant, Lady Cathva," he said, ironically.

She stiffened as she recognised the taunt.

"You are welcome back to the Haven, Lord Kierce," she said coldly.

He looked into her face and smiled at her. He did not grow pointed teeth and flashing eyes, but he might just as well have done. Cathva flinched away from him.

"More welcome to some than others, I think," he suggested. He let his gaze travel down her body to the shimmering cloth that covered her belly. To ordinary human eyes, it was not yet detectable, but Kierce knew from the moment he looked at her that Cathva was with child. From the signals he read in her body, it had been conceived very soon after her marriage. Or possibly just before.

It was something that hadn't occurred to him. Shaihen women controlled their own fertility, and none of them wanted the kind of union he indulged in to bear fruit. He stored it as another point to settle with Turloch, that his mentor had not seen fit to bother him with this gem of information.

"May I be among the first to congratulate you, Lady Cathva," he said quietly.

Cathva's eyes widened in horror, and her hand rested on her stomach in an unconscious gesture of protection.

"Who told you?" she whispered.

"I don't need to be told." He looked into her eyes with the grin still on his face. "I know."

Cathva took a step backwards. He knew it had not occurred to her until that moment to doubt the parentage of her child. If she feared what he was, she feared tenfold what his offspring might be.

"You … you are welcome to the Haven," she repeated, incoherently. She turned abruptly and all but fled from the hall.

Kierce closed his eyes. "So how was that for you, Turloch?"

Turloch didn't answer.

It was another day or two before Kierce could bring himself to start seeking Turloch. He had rather thought Turloch would be plaguing him again before that – when he didn't, Kierce began to worry at the continued interruption to an education he recognised he needed, no matter how much he resented it. He slept poorly, and arose early with a sense of foreboding. The need to find Turloch dominated his thoughts.

He went out into a morning of brilliant sunshine and sudden blustery showers. It was shortly after dawn, but when Kierce looked up at the hillside above the town he saw Turloch sitting with his face to the new day, the unicorn Freath lying beside him. They looked as if they had been there for some time.

Kierce left the streets of the Haven and climbed up the mountainside to join him. He had a grievance to settle with Turloch.

Had he not been so full of his own concerns, he might have been a bit more aware of Turloch's mood as he approached him, but as it was, he barged in like a fart in the heavenly choir.

It would have helped if you'd told me.

Turloch turned towards him with a slight frown of annoyance and query. It deepened when he understood Kierce's question.

I forgot.

His response was terse and dismissive.

How could you forget a thing like that?

Easily. Turloch regarded him with dislike. "It's Rainur's child, Kierce."

Even you can't know that yet! challenged Kierce.

It can be no other. Leave it alone.

The matter was closed in Turloch's mind. He was not interested in the truth.

"It's probably best that it is Rainur's," said Kierce. "Since he'll regard it as his heir from the moment it's born. I would still have liked to know. You made it clear enough that I have to keep my distance from her. You could help me a bit."

He paused, his temper somewhat restored now he had got a little of his resentment off his chest. He looked out across the Haven, bright and beautiful in the rain-washed morning light.

I thought I did it quite well.

Turloch gave him a cynical look.

You played on the fears she already had. Easy enough. The woman's life is governed by fear of the power others hold over her.

"You told me to do it!"

Turloch sighed. *Because you left little other choice.*

Kierce scowled slightly at the Haven shining below him.

Why are you here? The question came into his mind involuntarily.

It is a good day to die.

Kierce turned, slipped slightly on the wet rock and sat down abruptly. *It is?*

Turloch shrugged. *In these times, it is as good as any other.*

You can't go yet. There's too much still to do.

I have done all I can.

Kierce looked into the dull sheen that had replaced the former gem-like clarity of Turloch's green eyes. He could see in Turloch's mind the confusion of regret that he had not left enough time to prepare Kierce properly for this moment, and the persistent belief that no amount of time would ever have been enough. The dread of what he was bequeathing Shehaios was breaking his heart.

Kierce took a mental step back from the condemnation in Turloch's sorrow.

Don't go yet. Please. I'm not ready.

The thought behind a smile lifted the gloom on Turloch's soul.

He learns wisdom yet!

Turloch got to his feet and shrugged off his cloak. He gestured peremptorily to Kierce to stand beside him, and placed the cloak around him. The garment that had fitted his round body like a well-worn glove settled itself on Kierce's shoulders as if it had been made for him. He glanced down at the elegant, pitch-black folds of material. There wasn't a pulled thread in sight. Turloch picked up the staff lying on the ground beside him and placed it in Kierce's hands.

"No man to whom these things have been given has ever been ready, Kierce." He spoke aloud. "You are all I have. You are all Shehaios has. You are all you have. Prove me wrong. Inspire histories down the ages with your brilliance."

Are you being sarcastic?

Kierce found himself unable to see now through the clouds in Turloch's mind. He reached out and grasped the old man by the arm. *Don't go. For Spirit's sake, don't go!*

Turloch pulled back gently.

"It is a good day to die," he repeated.

He looked down from the hillside to the road below, the road that led to the Gate. Kierce followed his gaze. Along the road, just coming into view, was a band of about a hundred men. Armour glinted beneath their cloaks, and the sun dazzled on their helmets. They carried sword, shield and spear. They walked with purpose, step by step together, covering the ground with a steady pace. At their head was a banner bearing the same design as the one Cathva's guards wore on their shoulders, the lion of the Empire.

Kierce knew he was looking at the advance party of the Imperial army. He also knew now, as he strongly suspected Caras and the other Holders did not, the full terms of the deal Rainur had struck for the protection of the Imperial forces. The reaction of the chieftains when they discovered what they were committed to was part of the dilemma Turloch was leaving him.

A good day to die it certainly is, he thought, bitterly. *You bastard.*

Oh, I have many fathers, Kierce. So do you.

Turloch withdrew quietly and settled himself down on his ledge with his back to the mountain and his face to the sun. The old grey unicorn lay down comfortably beside him. They waited together, and Kierce also waited, watching the Caiivorian soldiers march by below and pass into the Haven. There were ten times the number who had escorted Cathva, and these were only the advance guard. In a few days time, there would be thousands of troops marching down that road.

The Lord High Magician held the balance which kept Shehaios alive. Turloch was choosing to die rather than tackle the task of holding it against such odds.

How do you expect me to do it, Turloch?

He knew the answer. Turloch didn't expect him to do it. Turloch expected him to fail.

He sat down to wait for the end. He could feel the Magician's spirit fading. He had touched an experience of death many times with animals. Once, with his father. Turloch was suffering none of the desperate anguish of Gaeroch's final moments. Gaeroch fought tooth and nail to hold on to life, and his son had shared the short, futile battle to the bitter end. If only he had known then the healing skill he knew now.

Turloch slipped slowly and peacefully into the world of dreams, the world of memories.

Had he ever really wanted to be anywhere else? Among real creatures, with minds full of the endless need to feed, preoccupied with defending herds and territory, with copulation and the raising of young. Among real people with their games of love and hate.

Why? he found himself thinking. *Why am I Turloch's heir?*

Plainly, not because Turloch had chosen him. Not because he shared any of Turloch's intellectual pursuit of perfection. The written word seemed to him a dull medium when all his senses could join his mind's engagement with the world around him. Why craft a beautiful song of love when you could enjoy the song of a beautiful body? But then, he liked life. Turloch …

Turloch didn't.

Through most of the day, he waited. The spirit passed from Turloch and Freath together as the light began to fade.

Kierce knew he should take the news to the Haven, and make arrangements for the funeral pyre. Fire for death and water for birth. In between the earth and all its life, sung in the winds.

But he did not want to walk into the Haven wearing the Magician's cloak, carrying the Magician's staff. He did not want Turloch's symbols. Turloch's power. Turloch's responsibility.

His face creased in a frown.

Why me?

He did not pursue intellectual perfection. He played games of chance. He played them very well.

He had played against a retired soldier in Mervecc. The man should have been living on a farm on a good pension; he was playing twelve stones on the borders of the Empire because his passion for the game did not match his skill. His play reminded Kierce of Caras.

When all was said and done, Caiivorian or Shaihen, they were only men.

He heard a low *whoosh* behind him. He turned, to see flames breaking out around Turloch's body. They turned swiftly from yellow, to red, to a fierce white, and Kierce was forced to step back from the rapidly intensifying heat, turning away to shield his eyes. As he did so, he heard a keening cry soar into the air above him. He looked up. This time, the phoenix was only a few feet above his head, its immense wingspan casting both him and the fire which burned beside him into darkness.

For a moment, the weight of Turloch's shadow seemed to bear down on his shoulders as if the cloak he wore encased him in iron. The unfathomable twists and turns of the staff in his hand protruded into his flesh. He gripped it fiercely and glared up at the mighty phoenix.

I am Kierce ti' Gaeroch of Arhaios. And I'm all you've bloody got!

The reborn bird soared upwards in the intense heat of the fire which was more than fire, its size diminishing before his eyes as it climbed into the mountain air. He watched it out of sight, until the speck of gold blinked out into the bright gold of the setting sun, and Turloch was gone.

Chapter 16
Jagus's Challenge

The army camped outside Arhaios was larger than the Imperial advance guard but considerably less purposeful. Its purpose at the moment, in fact, was simply to be there, outside the bounds of Arhaios. It was a show of strength by numbers since those within it held little strength within the social organisation of Shehaios, containing only one Holder and one would-be Holder. The rest were disaffected individuals, drawn from all over Oreath but centred on a group from Cuaraccon. There were more than two hundred, less than three.

It could have been worse. The Holder of Cuaraccon herself was not among them.

Over the months following the council at Cuaraccon, Caras had worked tirelessly to undermine Jagus's efforts to command the support of his people. He had not long returned to Arhaios from a journey which had taken him the length and breadth of Oreath, to every Holder who had not come to him. Finally, he had gone beyond Oreath into Hieath, to Ered's Holding. The stones of the game fell in his favour. Ered spent the meeting at Dornas muttering that no good would come of the alliance – he was still muttering, but he would not rise against Rainur. Hieath was safe at Oreath's back, and Caras had satisfied himself that the rest of Oreath was safe in support of his and Leath's leadership. He had only to deal with the King's brother, the Lady of Riskeld, and the men and women they had gathered below Arhaios.

Caras was out early to check there had been no developments in the threat across the river. He spent some time talking to the Arhaiens guarding the bridge, and he was making his way back into the Holding when he was almost bowled over by his daughter and her cousin.

He caught Alsareth around the waist and swung her into his arms. Alsa was seven years old and always hurtling somewhere.

"Where are you off to in such a hurry?"

Alsa squirmed impatiently.

"Secret."

He set her down before she slipped out of his grasp.

"Remember what I told you. Stay inside the Holding."

Alsa pulled a face. "It's only Sheldo's dad."

"Yes, well. Sheldo's dad and your dad have an argument, and I don't want any children involved in it."

Any more children, he added, mentally, with a brief glance at the golden-haired little boy waiting awkwardly for his playfellow. Sheldo was Alsa's kin, because his mother was Caras's aunt. She was also the Holder of Cuaraccon.

"You tell me and Taeg off when we argue," said Alsa.

"The trouble with grown-ups," said Caras, "is that there's no-one more grown-up to tell them off."

"There's granny Leath," said Alsa, mischievously.

"She's on my side."

Alsa turned triumphantly on her cousin.

"Your dad's naughty!" she proclaimed.

"You are most wise, Lady Alsareth," said Caras. "But if I hear you've been teasing Sheldo, I will declare a dispute with you. It's not his fault."

"I know," sang Alsa, derisively, beginning to hop away from him.

"Stay in the Holding!"

"I'll make sure she does," said Sheldo, solemnly.

Caras smiled and tousled his hair.

"Do your best, Lord Sheldo."

He watched them both run off, safe in the knowledge that every inhabitant of Arhaios would keep an eye on them. Alsa adored Sheldo, she probably would do as he told her. Caras wasn't too worried, yet. No Shaihen challenge in living memory had resulted in an actual armed fight. He remembered how appalled he had been when he thought Rainur was going to call his bluff.

Jagus, he suspected, was in for the shock of his life.

It wasn't Jagus who worried him, though. It was Iareth of Riskeld. He had talked with Iareth until he hardly had a voice left, and her opinion remained exactly what it had been when he first returned from the Haven. He could not change her mind, and Iareth was a Holder. Unlike Jagus, she could legitimately declare a dispute.

Caras made his way through the arch at the centre of the Holder's House to raid the kitchen for a late breakfast. Arhaios was big enough for other families to hold a communal table, but a significant number ate at the Holder's House, and there were a team of people whose role was to feed them. But if Alsa had already escaped, there would be nothing left for him in the family dining hall.

The hall door stood open to the summer morning, and Elani's voice called him as he passed.

"They're still there, then?"

"No change." Caras hesitated, and then went into the room. "Elani, do you think Sheldo's all right?"

"He's fine." Elani looked up from the collection of herbs spread across the low table in the middle of the small hall. "He spends so much of his time here, he hasn't noticed any difference."

"Still. I don't like having to do it."

Elani smiled.

"I don't think I'd have married a man who liked kidnapping children. He's better off with us, Caras, you know he is. Naming a ten year old as your heir …!"

"You can see why Brethil did it," said Caras, sprawling on a bench at the side of the room. "Leaving Jagus thinking he had a chance of being her heir was almost inviting him to get rid of her."

"They're as bad as each other, those two."

"Jagus doesn't know when to stop. Brethil's all right when she's sober, and I'd rather have the Holder with me. Kierce was right about that. Once they started arguing with each other, they didn't want to stay on the same side."

Leath felt particular responsibility for the problems of Cuaraccon; it was the home Holding Caras's grandfather returned to, when Leath threw him out of Arhaios. Brethil was his daughter. Cuaraccon was always a volatile community and the young lovers Brethil patronised were inclined to abuse their position as the Holder's favourites.

Her reconciliation with Jagus had been short-lived. Jagus apparently proposed that, if there was fighting to be done, Cuaraccon had need of of a strong Holder skilled in the use of a sword. Brethil, unsurprisingly, took exception to this blatant attempt to usurp her authority, and far from being allies, the two were now at loggerheads again.

"I think you can take some credit for converting Brethil," said Elani. "She's got a bit of a soft spot for her favourite nephew."

"She's got a bit of a soft spot for a lot of young men. That's her problem."

"Well. Jagus's problem."

"Not only his."

"When do you expect him?"

"Any time. If he doesn't come tomorrow I'll go to him. The longer he sits over there, the more poison he's pouring into Iareth's ears."

Elani looked dubious. "She doesn't need much. You can't confront one without the other, Caras."

"That's why I'd rather Jagus came to me. I've run out of arguments with Iareth."

To Caras's relief, it was only Jagus who swept once more into the Meeting House of Arhaios at the head of a deputation the next day. Finding Caras there to meet him, he demanded the presence of the Holder.

"My grandmother is indisposed," replied Caras, calmly. This was, unfortunately, not a lie though he wanted to deal with Jagus himself anyway. The demands of the times were taking their toll on Leath's health as they had on Turloch's.

Jagus regarded Caras warily, weighing up the situation. Leath's growing frailty was no secret. It was only a matter of time before Caras came into his inheritance, and Caras strongly suspected Jagus thought him a less formidable opponent. Leath was notoriously hard to bully. The council at Cuaraccon had demonstrated Caras's weakness.

"A sword lies between us, Lord Caras," said Jagus. "You know that."

125

"Your sword, Lord Jagus," said Caras. "A Holding does not have to answer to one man. Take your dispute where it belongs, with your wife."

Jagus glared at him.

"Don't tempt me to school your manners, young man. The lesson might come hard to you!"

"I apologise," said Caras, easily. "I had no intention of insulting you. I merely meant that the Holder of Arhaios is only honour bound to answer a challenge from Cuaraccon."

"I bring the challenge of Cuaraccon."

"I think not, Lord Jagus."

"The Holder of Cuaraccon has forfeited the respect and loyalty of her people by her behaviour. Cuaraccon is too precious to be frittered away for the amusement of foolish young men. It needs a leader who is strong and capable of defending it. I speak for Cuaraccon."

"The Holder of Cuaraccon acknowledges her fault and agrees to mend her ways," said Caras.

Jagus stared at him, taken aback.

"What the dark unknown does that mean?"

"It means exactly what I said," replied Caras, innocently. "I have been to Cuaraccon, on my grandmother's behalf, to discuss with Lady Brethil exactly those concerns about the state of her Holding and the respect of her people." He paused. "When were you last in Cuaraccon, Lord Jagus?"

Jagus regarded him suspiciously.

"The Lady Brethil wouldn't mend her ways for you or I or all the colours of the rainbow," he said bluntly.

"You do her a disservice," replied Caras. "There are things she values above her own pleasure. I have to admit that my grandmother and I have been concerned about the governance of Cuaraccon. Since Lady Brethil chose to name her heir while he is yet at such a tender and vulnerable age, we felt it best to offer him some protection against the mayhem with which you and your wife are threatening Cuaraccon."

Jagus started.

"What do you mean?"

"Your son, Sheldo. He resides at Arhaios with my children. So should there be any violence done within Cuaraccon—."

"You devious bastard!" exploded Jagus, reaching for his sword.

"Take care, Lord Jagus," said Caras. There was an echo of Leath's iron in his naturally melodic voice. "Neither you nor Brethil are fit to govern Cuaraccon, still less to dispute the wisdom of Arhaios. Raise a hand to me and I'll have you thrown down in a pit where the dogs and horses can piss on your head!"

Jagus's hand paused over the sword hilt.

"Do you know how many men I have camped outside Arhaios?"

"Not enough to take Arhaios. They came for a party, Jagus, not for a fight. They came to show me how impressive they are. I'm not impressed."

"Then perhaps you will be when we raise the rest of those who resent your high-handed manner, Caras. When Hieath rides to join us. You're right, we didn't come expecting to fight you – I came to tell you that our dispute lay not with you but with my brother. I came to offer you the chance to get out of my way. If you will stand in it, I will ride you down!"

"I doubt that. Oreathan horses have more sense. As have Oreathan people. You have no army to raise, Jagus. Hieath will not come to your aid. You will not take the Holding of Cuaraccon from your wife. What you will do, I don't know and I don't much care but I suspect you have heard the news of Turloch's succession from the Haven?"

"Your lackey the stable boy," said Jagus with a contemptuous snort. Caras wondered that he apparently saw nothing ironic in deriding Kierce in Imperial terminology. "Should I fear him now as well?"

Caras shrugged slightly.

"You seemed fairly in awe of him last time he spoke to you."

"In awe?" sneered Jagus. "Of Kierce? I think I might recall that!"

"When he told the council at Cuaraccon to let me speak. After Brynnen brought the news from Mervecc."

"That was Turloch! It was the Lord High Magician who spoke to us then."

"Yes, it was. It was Kierce." He paused. "You're not a Holder, Jagus. You must accept what Shehaios demands of you. Brethil governs in Cuaraccon, and I hold her son against her good behaviour. The same applies to you. You will never inherit the Holding, don't lose what little respect you still hold in Shehaios by destroying it."

"Threaten my son and I will destroy you!" snarled Jagus. The sword rasped from his scabbard, but before it was fully drawn, he became aware that Caras had anticipated him. Four Arhaien men descended on him, two pinioning each arm. Others turned on Jagus's supporters. A dozen hand-to-hand fights broke out in the hall, as Jagus's companions rallied to his support and found themselves against a wall of Arhaien defenders.

Caras wrested the sword from Jagus's grasp.

"I will not let you do this, Jagus. Fighting among ourselves wins us nothing, defends nothing, achieves nothing."

"What of honour? Or courage?" spat Jagus, struggling unsuccessfully against his captors. "You cowardly wretch – you seize me when I come here to negotiate in good faith – you set your men on me, you won't fight me yourself."

"I have more important things to do with my life than lay it before your sword," retorted Caras. "I told you, Arhaios is not bound to answer the challenge of one foolish man."

"One foolish man who speaks the truth!" cried Jagus. "Rainur has sold you, Caras, you and every Holding in Shehaios. He has sold you for a place in the Imperial family, he has the Emperor's pretty daughter, the Emperor's favour and any number of the Emperor's trinkets, he brings into the Haven an army to protect his position. His ambition lies in the gold and the games of the Imperial City. I know, I've been there, I've tasted temptation!"

"You speak from your own weakness," said Caras in disgust. "And prove to me again why you will never be a Holder. Take him away."

Shouting and protesting, he was dragged away. There was still a scrappy, hand-to-hand brawl going on in the hall, but Jagus's men were unnerved by his abrupt and unceremonious capture. They had not expected to have to fight. One by one, those who remained retreated towards the doorway.

"Let them go," commanded Caras, over the noise. "Let them return to their camp and to the Lady of Riskeld and tell them Arhaios will enforce its authority with those who have no valid dispute!" He hesitated, scanning the chaos in the hall, seeing one, then two men down, one cursing and sobbing with pain, the other still and silent. It was not a sight he had ever wanted to see in the hall of his Holding. All very well to agree in cold blood that it was better to spill some blood now than much later on, but the men lying on the ground were his own people, Oreathans. It hurt him to look at them.

He wrenched open the Meeting House door and shouted for Elani, and Arhaios's healer. He would not let Jagus's words wound him. Everyone knew Jagus was much more noise than substance. Everyone knew that.

When the healers were at work with the injured, and Jagus's followers had fled the hall, Caras peremptorily called a dozen or so of his people together. They saddled up and rode straight to the camp outside Arhaios's boundaries, to arrive, mounted and impressive, hard on the heels of the retreating deputation with their story of Jagus's capture.

The impetus of their sudden arrival carried them into the camp without a fight. Caras dismounted and strode into the hide tent where he knew he would find the Lady of Riskeld. She was listening with alarm to the news of Jagus's downfall when the cause of it walked into her tent.

She turned on him with fury and outrage in her face, reaching for the scabbard already buckled across her hips.

"Before you draw it, hear me out," said Caras before she could speak. "Once declared the dispute may be hard to heal, and I have no quarrel with your people."

Iareth regarded him steadily with a burning anger in her eyes. She was a small, sturdy woman, not immediately striking to look at but bearing herself with a fierce, contained pride which brought the beauty of strength to her weathered face. The effect on her skin of the salt winds of her homeland made her look much older than Caras, although she was only a few years his senior.

Caras and Iareth had exchanged many words over the past months, without drawing any closer to each other. Caras always felt compelled to monitor his every move with Iareth, to be sure he gave her no grounds for complaint.

Until he pulled the ground from beneath Jagus's feet, he had tied himself in knots trying to conciliate her.

He could see how startled she was by the sudden reversal, the swift and resolute meeting of violence with violence. But even now, she was not prepared to give way.

"I have heard you, Lord Caras," she said coldly. "And what I have heard is a man who doesn't understand what he is asking us to accept. Perhaps Lord Rainur doesn't, though I find that hard to believe, since he must know the Empire at least as well as Lord Jagus does. If you knew it that well, I'm not sure you'd ask. But since you do ask … we have a dispute, Lord Caras, and gagging Lord Jagus will not settle it."

Caras studied her reflectively for a few minutes.

"Very well. We have a dispute," he acknowledged. "But I won't fight you over it. Go back to Riskeld, and look to your own defences. Be strong. Hold Riskeld for your people. Don't waste their blood fighting mine."

"If Caiivorians come to our Holding we will fight them, whether they come in the King's name or yours," she warned.

"When that day comes, we will talk again," replied Caras. "Until then, a truce. We disagree. We do not need to fight." He paused. "Do I have your word?"

"If I choose not to give it?"

"Arhaios does not seek a fight. But if the fight is brought to us, we will defend ourselves. I ask you not to take it that far."

She hesitated.

"What of Lord Jagus?"

"Lord Jagus is a different matter, and not your concern." Caras hesitated. "Of those two brothers, it is not Lord Rainur who suffers from frustrated ambitions, my lady."

There was a brief silence.

"I need your answer, Iareth," prompted Caras. "The longer this camp stays here, the greater the likelihood of conflict with my people. Not all those here are your people or even Jagus's, and I very much doubt their concern with the welfare of anyone except themselves. I wish them gone from my Holding."

"I will consider your offer."

"Until the morning."

It was a cordial ultimatum, but it was an ultimatum nevertheless. Images of solidity always tended to feature in descriptions of Caras ti' Leath, and the lady of Riskeld knew an immovable object when she saw one.

"You will have your answer in the morning," she conceded.

He nodded to her courteously, and left the tent. He was fairly sure that she was face-saving by delaying. In the morning, she would be gone.

And with luck, by the time he was called on to enforce any part of the Imperial agreement throughout his domain, he would have dreamed up a politically acceptable way of doing it. He suspected there was something in the deal with the Empire that Rainur had not yet told them, and he suspected it had something to do with gold. It was the one issue, he realised afterwards, Rainur had managed to avoid at Dornas. Their discussions had only been concerned with persuading Shaihens to accept the arrival of the Imperial troops, not with the cost of persuading the Imperial troops to protect Shehaios.

He hoped the price was one they could afford.

Chapter 17
Iareth's Challenge

It was still dark beneath the eaves of the Holder's House when Elani woke him. Caras could smell the sharp cold air as he emerged from the cocoon of thick Shaihen fleece that covered him.

He opened his eyes and screwed them up against the bright glow of the lamp in Elani's hand. She was fully dressed and looked as if she had been up for hours.

"It's dawn," she said, softly. "She's coming."

Caras sat up, the cold striking a wakeful blow against his skin as the fleece slipped off his naked shoulders. When he lay down with Elani last night, content with a successful day's work, there had been no need of fleece and wool to keep them warm.

"Who's coming?"

"Iareth of Riskeld."

Caras frowned uncomprehendingly, his mind thick with sleep.

"No. She's going."

Elani shook her head.

"She wouldn't attack without Jagus!" Caras continued in growing alarm.

"Oh, I think she would, Caras," said Elani, gently. "I thought when you told me that you'd underestimated her. So did Leath."

Caras cursed, hurled the skins off him and began to pull his clothes on.

"Why?" he demanded. "Why is she doing this?"

"She was raped by an Imperial general, my love. That takes a lot of forgiving."

"That was fifteen years ago," snapped Caras.

"And she was fifteen years old."

Caras didn't answer. In his mind was a memory of a young Merveccian girl clinging to him while she sobbed like he had never heard anyone sob before. *"Oh, Lord Caras, you don't know what's happened to us."* He didn't know what had happened to her. He assumed she was dead now, along with all her kin, when vengeance fell on Prassan.

He snatched up a boot and rammed his foot into it.

"The Holder should look to the needs of her people, not her own feelings."

"Riskeld have already invited the Imperial army in once," said Elani. "It's really not surprising they don't want to do it again. They offered shelter to stranded men. They guided the soldiers' ships to safety in Riskeld through the offshore shoals. They paid a heavy price for their goodwill."

Caras paused and ran his hands across his face and through his thick grey hair.

"I never actually asked you," he realised. He looked at his wife. "Do you think Rainur's doing the right thing? Do you think I'm doing the right thing?"

Elani came over and sat down beside him.

"You'd have known if I thought you were wrong, love."

He put his hands on her shoulders and looked into her face. "But … ?"

"I'm afraid," admitted Elani. "We're all afraid. But I'm lucky. Not everyone has your strength to draw on."

"I'm not—," began Caras.

"Don't be modest," Elani interrupted, embracing him firmly. "You know I only married you for your body."

Caras smiled, returning the hug.

"Is that your way of telling me I'm a complete idiot?"

"Of course it isn't." Elani paused, her arms still around him. "Be careful, Caras. Iareth is a bitter and frightened woman. She hates the Empire, but I don't think she's too keen on men in general."

"Then what the hell was she doing with Jagus?"

"Keeping a careful distance from him, I think," replied Elani, getting to her feet. "I'll go and see if Leath goes with you or not."

"She's not well. Tell her to let me do it. I got us into this, I'd better deal with the consequences."

"She'll make up her own mind, Caras, she always does. I'll find out what she says."

Caras did not wait for her return. As soon as he was dressed he went down from the sleeping platform below the thick thatch and through the house to the narrow room behind the Holder's dining hall. Confined in the gloom, the armoury of Arhaios had spent most of the last century or more gathering dust there.

It was one of the minor duties of Arhaios's Horsemaster to maintain the arms of the Holding, and when Caras went in he found a lamp already lit. Its yellow glow fell on the young face of Kierce's half-sister, Madred.

She turned as Caras came in.

"Tuli's getting the horses," she explained. "He'll go with you."

"Will you?" said Caras, bluntly. There was no woman in Arhaios, old or young, more proud of their own ability, strength and independence than Madred. It was already clear that the skill and intuition her father had passed to Kierce had skipped her full brother Tuli and surfaced again in her. Caras was almost tempted to call her Madred ti' Kierce, but Tuli was touchy on the subject and Caras was ever careful not to offend his people unnecessarily. Tuli was a competent trainer of horses. It was up to the family to sort the matter out.

"Would you like me to?" asked Madred.

"Yes," said Caras. "I think I would." He crossed the room and reached for the sword he had carried with him to the Haven. He paused. On a rack beside it lay the weapon he had taken from Jagus the day before.

He released the sword of Arhaios and picked up the Imperial blade Jagus had brought back with him from the south. It was a superior weapon, refined over generations of use when Shaihen swords saw the light of day mainly for ceremony and sport.

Madred watched him in concern as he picked up Jagus's sword and strapped it on.

"If the Lady Iareth brings a dispute— ," she began.

"She will fight with this sword, and Arhaios with hers," finished Caras. He smiled at Madred's anxiety. "I know, Maddi. I still hope there won't be any fighting."

When he left the yard behind the Holder's House, he found himself joined by Leath, borne on a litter by half a dozen willing volunteers from the Holding. He knew she shouldn't be there. He could see the unhealthy pallor on her skin, the tremor in her hand, and the effort it took her to keep the pain from showing on her face, but he knew better than to try and argue with her. She wouldn't be there unless she felt Oreath needed her to be there.

"I'm sorry, Leath," said Caras heavily. "I had hoped we wouldn't come to this."

"So did I. But Iareth's people have suffered. It's uphill work combating facts with promises, Caras, no matter how golden they are."

He rode slowly down to the bridge, keeping pace with Leath's bearers. Tuli was among them, just the sort of sturdy, fit young man the job required.

The people of Arhaios had been watching the river crossing throughout the night, as they had been watching it, night and day, since Jagus established the camp on the other side of the river. When Caras and Leath arrived, they stopped behind an armed block of Arhaiens on the west bank of the river facing a dozen armed men and women of Riskeld on the east bank. Iareth stood among her people as if carved there in stone.

Leath glanced at Caras. He rode forwards to the first planks of the bridge.

"I thought you would be gone by now, Lady Iareth," he called. "I thought we reached an agreement yesterday."

"I promised you only an answer by this morning," replied Iareth. She drew her sword. "Here it is. If you will let me cross the bridge, I will deliver it. If not, come across and receive it."

Caras hesitated.

"I'll let you cross the bridge," he said. "But only so that I don't have to shout at you. There's really no need for this, Lady Iareth—."

"That, in part, is what's disputed," responded Iareth. She started across the bridge, with only two of her attendants following.

"Let them through," said Leath.

Caras dismounted and stood beside Leath, awaiting Iareth's arrival. She strode up to them both and laid the sword down without another word.

"Riskeld knows what the rule of Empire means," she said. "The soldiers who came to our Holding did what they did because they did not recognise the authority that governed us. Imperial Commander Volun laughed in my mother's face when she tried to assert the Holder's authority. When she persisted, he struck her down. When she continued to protest about the treatment of her people, he told his men to lay hands on her daughter. They held her down while he forced himself on her. They cheered. I still hear them sometimes, Lord Caras, and I know that it was done – it was all done – to demonstrate the emptiness of the power my mother believed she held. The hurt he did me was nothing to what he inflicted on my mother. She was Holder then and I am Holder now and I will not allow my people to suffer as she was forced to let them suffer."

"The behaviour of the Imperial soldiers was inexcusable," acknowledged Leath, quietly. "No-one disputes that. But the responsibility for it stopped with that Imperial Commander. He acted outside the authority of the Empire, as I was at pains to point out to him. Commander Volun could accept a woman's authority when he had to, Iareth. He was ready enough to accept mine. Though I did take the precaution of bringing a thousand armed Oreathans and the best of Arhaios's horsemen with me to assert it."

"Too late," responded Iareth, bitterly.

"You suffered," said Leath sharply. "You didn't lose your Holding." She paused. "The strength of Oreath gave Volun food for thought. But what sent him packing from your Holding was something else I drew his attention to. Vordeith writes down what it agrees. Emperor Zelt had agreed, in writing – if my memory serves me – something along the lines of "… allowing free trade and traffic with Shehaios, giving all due account to its people and customs as befitting the rights of a friendly territory." Commander Volun made a serious error of judgement at Riskeld, and if he didn't understand it when he landed there, he had plenty of time to reflect on it later." She paused to steady her breathing. The beads of perspiration on her forehead showed the effort this argument took.

"It happened, Lady Leath," insisted Iareth, stiffly. "And an inconvenience to his career is hardly comparable to what Commander Volun inflicted on us. Allow the Empire's authority into Shehaios and it will happen again."

"Iareth, my dear, it will happen again somewhere, sometime, whatever we do. Human beings will always commit evil acts – we invented the game. This fight is not about good and evil. It's about survival, and there are some men you have to learn to trust. Lord Jagus is not one of them. His brother is. My grandson is another. Take up your sword, and go home, and trust him. If the spirit of Volun comes to your Holding again, he will have gone through the Chief of Oreath and the Lord High Magician first. In which case, you will need your sword for yourself, because there will be nothing else you can do."

Iareth glared at her, almost as pale as the sick old woman was.

"I will not be beholden to any man!" she blurted out.

Leath sighed wearily.

"Well, I think that's the problem," she admitted. There was a brief pause, and then she looked at Caras. "I am tired of this. Pick up the sword for me, Caras."

Caras hesitated. By picking up the sword, he was accepting Iareth's challenge.

"Pick up the sword for me, Caras," repeated Leath, quietly.

Reluctantly, Caras bent to accept the blade of Riskeld.

"Do you name a champion?" Leath asked the challenger.

"I name Lord Jagus," retorted Iareth.

"Lord Jagus is otherwise engaged," Caras answered. "But he offers you his sword."

He drew the Imperial sword from its scabbard and handed it to Iareth.

"I don't want to do this, Iareth," he said. "But if we are to do it, then it will be at the cost of no more than two lives. I accept the challenge for Arhaios. Who do you choose to fight for Riskeld, and when do you want to meet?"

"I will fight for Riskeld," said Iareth. "And I choose to meet here. Now." She raised Jagus's sword. "Fight me," she asserted.

Caras looked at her, slightly startled.

"Personally? Now?"

Iareth brought the sword slashing down towards his face. Caras swayed back hastily and the blade caught him a glancing blow on the cheek. He put his hand to the blood flowing from the cut, conscious of his audience. Leath, watching from a face gaunt with pain, Elani pale with horror, Tuli gawping open-mouthed and Madred watching him with her half-brother's dark eyes.

He raised Riskeld's sword. Iareth attacked again, and this time he turned the blow aside, but he did not respond. Iareth paused, and settled into a fighting stance. Her next attack came fast and furious, blow after blow, driving him back and eventually leaving blood on his shoulder before he drove her off, panting, to recoup.

Caras was a middling competent swordsman, but he had never developed a passion for it. The opening round showed him, to his dismay, that Iareth was more skilful than he was. If he continued just to try and defend himself he would be driven back until he was cut to pieces. Iareth was not playing. Given half a chance, she would kill him. He was a man, and beneath her contempt.

He was a man with the authority of Arhaios on his sword. He could not let her defeat him.

His mind closed out the people gathered watching him and concentrated on the woman in front of him, on the Imperial blade that threatened him. He let her come to him again, but when he parried the attack this time, he drove it home, using his strength. Iareth resisted, blocking and turning his advance, Jagus's sword flashing back at him over and over again with deadly speed and an even deadlier edge. For several minutes the fight raged backwards and forwards between them, the advantage going first one way and then the other, but then the pace, and the heavier weight of the Imperial sword, began to tell. Iareth began to give ground.

Caras sensed her tiring, but he did not ease up. Now she was defending rather than attacking; now she was trying desperately to anticipate each blow, and it was only a matter of time until he found his opening. He lunged towards her. She deflected the blow heading for her body awkwardly, at the last minute, and they closed together in a brief battle of strength.

It was not a contest. Caras forced her sword hand down, swept the weapon from her grasp and hurled her to the ground.

"I fought you!" he snapped, breathlessly, his own sword at her throat. "Now yield."

"Bear witness, Lady Leath," shouted Iareth. "This is the choice the Empire leaves me. Yield or die. I was forced to yield once before, Lord Caras. I will not do it again!"

Caras paused with fury raging through his blood. She had forced him into physical combat and now she accused him of taking advantage of his strength. She had trapped him into an impossible situation.

"And I will not kill you, Lady Iareth," he grated. He turned aside abruptly and brought the sword down viciously against a large boulder.

It happened to hit a fissure in the rock. It sank in and wedged deep in the cleft. He wrenched at it with a curse, and the sword broke in half in his hand. He hurled the hilt at Iareth's feet.

"Take that back to Riskeld. See how well you can defend your people with it. But don't look to Oreath for protection when your real enemies come."

He turned and flung himself onto his horse and rode back up the hill to Arhaios.

Part II

Chapter 18
The Arrival of the Imperial Army

The Emperor's general and his personal envoy had passed through the Gate to Shehaios, and were on their way through the mountains towards the Haven. With them, the glory and wealth of Imperial power shining from their armour and the brave colours of their cloaks and banners, marched an army of thousands. The Imperial lion was no longer a guest at the wedding, nor even a presence to be taken into account. He was here, in all his strength, as he was always going to be.

Such a spectacle had never been seen before in Shehaios. There was a vast crowd of Shaihens gathered on the hillside above the road to the Gate, awaiting their arrival. Kierce was among them, but he saw the Army of the Sacred Union long before the rest of the crowd did, watching through the eyes of a hawk circling high above them.

Prepared for them as he was, the actual sight of them in all their glory still had the power to arouse a sense of wonder.

There could be no doubt that what he looked at was an army, not a rabble of warlike individuals. They were flanked by a mounted escort, but most of them were on foot, marching in step as the advance guard had done, each footfall like one massive footfall. Kierce could see the units that made up the whole as he could not yet see the individuals who made up the units. He could see the pattern of colours, denoting some significance of seniority or speciality. He could see the cohesive quality which lent this mass of men a unity quite unlike the unity of Shehaios.

Kierce understood the power of Shehaios. Only now, however, did he begin to understand the power of the Sacred Union. This single, mighty force could be directed and manipulated without any reference to the will of the individuals who formed it. A Warrior of the Sacred Union obeyed orders. He did not have a choice in the matter.

Kierce had watched with fascination the rapid construction of the advance camp, the impressive organisation of men and measurement following a pre-ordained plan. He watched ditches and foundations, buildings and defences begin to appear quicker than a Shaihen group of similar size could have decided what to build and where, and he was impressed. He had spent some time with the men of the army's advance guard trying to gain some insight into the Caiivorian mind, so far without much success. He couldn't even find his way into their shoes, let alone walk a mile in them. The efficiency and the ignorance of the Empire's people seemed to him to be in conflict.

The soldiers themselves reminded him of nothing so much as a bachelor herd, gathering together for company and protection, ready to lash out if anything hit the appropriate trigger. The inherent aggression did not surprise him – they were after all soldiers, and it was no different to what he would expect from a group of Shaihen men. He regarded it as more to do with being male than being human.

What he found alien was the way they all seemed to live their lives in half light, watching without seeing, hearing without listening, doing without even his kinsmens' level of understanding. A deep-seated belief in a hierarchy that always had a human figure at the head, whether he be captain, emperor or god, blunted the senses Shaihens took for granted, and caused Kierce to distance himself from their thinking with discomfort. He had never thought of the world in that way, and its implications disturbed him. He realised that even with his insight, it was not always going to be possible for a Shaihen to tell what these people would do.

At this moment, he was solely intent on admiring the Imperial army's arrival from a distance.

The bird was becoming increasingly interested in the baggage train. As it focussed on the scraps of rubbish discarded by the passing throng of humanity, its view of the Imperial Army became distinctly less impressive. Kierce reverted to the world through his own eyes.

He became aware that a small number of the cavalry accompanying the troops were not down on the road with their comrades, but making their way – a little precariously for horses which were plainly not mountain-bred – along a sheep track above the watching crowds. Kierce watched them, puzzling over their role. He was sitting a little above the main throng, and they should have passed between him and the rest of the onlookers. But as they approached, the leading horsemen swung off the narrow track and turned up the hill towards him.

"You there!"

His accent was strong, stronger than the advance guard, placing him in the far south of the Empire. He waved peremptorily in a downward direction.

"Get back with the others."

"I prefer the view from here," remarked Kierce, blandly.

"Just get back down with the others."

"Why?"

Kierce asked the question while he dug around for the answer, and understood without the curt soldier's conscious input. They feared an attack from this huge crowd gathered above them. The horsemen riding along the hillside either side of the road were there to plunge down into the Shaihens at the first sign of any trouble and stop it before it got out of hand. They did not want anyone on the hill above them.

"Do as you're told," snapped the soldier.

Kierce, prepared to pander to the visitors' fears, had been about to do so. The direct order, issued with such ignorance, irked him. He said nothing, but got to his feet and moved obediently down the hill to the back of the crowd below.

The soldier followed him down, and then turned to continue on his way. Or at least, he attempted to. His horse continued to follow Kierce down the hill.

The soldier cursed and wrenched on the reins, but the horse – trained to Imperial standards though he was – suddenly became immensely stubborn. Kierce turned as if in surprise that the soldier was following him.

"I wouldn't bring a horse down here if I were you," he advised, sagely. "It's very steep. You wouldn't want him to lose his footing."

As if on cue, the horse's front hoof slid on the rock and he lurched to regain his balance. The soldier drew him sharply to a halt. The rest of the troop was beginning to follow his precarious descent. They all stopped in various stages of disarray.

"Foolish as this might sound to you," said Kierce, "I'll tell you now your horses won't pass behind me."

"You just shut up," snarled the cavalryman. "Get down there with the others."

He turned the horse's head uphill, dug in his spurs and simultaneously whacked its rump with the flat of his sword. The horse jumped and snorted, but would not move forwards.

Quietly, Kierce made his way back up the hill. Immediately he had passed them the soldiers' horses started calmly up and onto the track once again, docile and obedient. The leader of the troop checked and turned back, watching Kierce, as his followers moved on.

Kierce gave a slight bow, and descended once more to the back of the crowd. With a scowl on his face, the soldier swung his horse and rode on.

Kierce deliberately absented himself from the welcoming committee that greeted the leaders of the Imperial forces. He shared with his predecessor a dislike of formal occasions. The level of pretence present at such events placed an immense strain on the patience and tact of the Magician, and Kierce's sense of humour was likely to become dangerous under such circumstances.

After the show was all over and he had recovered his horse from its wanderings on the hill behind him, he was making his way down to join the masses on the road back to the Haven when he spotted a familiar figure among the throng.

Caras rode with an escort of a dozen or so, keeping themselves a distinct unit from the pressing crowd. A bound captive rode in the centre of their party.

Kierce made his way over to join them.

"Enjoy the journey?" he enquired.

Caras turned.

"Oh, it's you, Kierce. I wondered if you were here."

"Everybody's here." Kierce studied the scar on Caras's face curiously. "Perhaps you didn't."

"What?"

"Enjoy the journey. It wasn't your prisoner who gave you that, though, was it?"

"Iareth," said Caras, sourly.

Kierce winced.

"You do pick your enemies, Caras."

"I didn't pick them."

"Tell me you won?"

"It was unwinnable. She's gone back to Riskeld, and I've placed Riskeld outside the boundaries of Oreath's protection. It won't make any difference. Riskeld's neighbours will still trade with them, the minstrels will still take the news to them. If it comes to it, we'll still have to protect them. It was all a complete waste of bloody time and effort. Stupid woman."

"She did hurt you, didn't she?" said Kierce wryly. "Still, if you've clipped Jagus's wings and tamed Aunt Brethil, two out of three isn't bad."

"I can talk to Brethil. She listens to reason. Iareth can't see past … past what happened to her fifteen years ago."

"Perhaps I should try speaking to her?"

Caras gave him a cynical look.

"You're the wrong sex, Kierce. I don't think even your seduction technique will be good enough. It needs to last longer than one night to keep Iareth under your spell."

Kierce sighed.

"I don't do that any more," he admitted, regretfully.

Caras raised an eyebrow. "Really?"

"Really." Kierce paused. "I did learn something from Turloch." He met Caras's eyes briefly, and looked away. "When the Magician uses his power to destroy, it destroys something of himself. Take enough small cuts in the same place and you can fell an oak. If I can't control myself … Well. I don't need to tell you. I hate it when you're right, Caras. It makes me wonder why I bother."

Caras studied Kierce covertly as they rode on for a while in companionable silence. He didn't seem any different. He had never looked like the wild man of the plains. He always dressed well, wore his hair tied back from his face and his beard trimmed. The black cloak that hung from his shoulders had weight and quality but it was nothing particularly remarkable. There was nothing about him that would say to those soldiers pouring in to the camp behind them, this is the Lord High Magician of Shehaios.

"I don't want to say it to them," said Kierce with a smile.

Caras started slightly. He forgot Kierce no longer had to pretend any need to wait until he had spoken. Caras supposed every word he had said had been superfluous.

"No," said Kierce. "What you choose to say aloud tells me as much as what you're thinking. I choose not to say what I am to the soldiers of the Sacred Union."

"Why not?"

"They don't understand what it means. They want me to cast spells on their enemies and cure boils. Tell them their future from the entrails of a chicken. That sort of thing. I really can't be doing with all that. I'd rather they just assumed I was a charlatan, which is what most of the officers think – their gods being, of course, infinitely superior to anyone else's."

"We don't have any gods," said Caras, puzzled.

"That, Caras, is a concept beyond the grasp of any Caiivorian I've met so far," said Kierce, drily. "They have gods, they have devils, they have demons. They have guardian spirits and evil spirits, they have spirits of places, plants, animals and the undead. They have ghosts and goblins and witches and sorcerers and things that are half man and half beast." He smiled at the bemused expression on Caras's face. "Exactly. Show me a man who is not an animal and I'll show you something more wonderful than all their gods."

Caras shook his head.

"They are strange people." He hesitated. "Still, shouldn't you be there? Welcoming the chiefs of their party? Or something?"

"I decided Rainur can do it without me. I had no part in the making of this alliance, remember. I wanted to make the point that they shouldn't assume I support everything Turloch stood for."

Caras regarded him with some concern.

"But surely … you do? The Lord High Magician is the Lord High Magician. It's … well, you kind of … know everything. The decisions you make are those of the Magician, whether it's you or Turloch?"

Kierce gave him an ironic look.

"Are you Leath?"

"No, but that's different!"

"Not as different as you think." He turned the subject. "So, what are you going to do with Jagus?"

Caras let out a weary groan. "I've no idea. I can't banish him, there'll be uproar if I execute him and if I turn him loose he'll be like a spark on dry grassland. I thought I'd try the problem on Rainur, he's his brother."

"He's not at the Haven. He's at the Imperial camp."

"Well, I'm not taking Jagus there. I'll wait for his return."

Kierce paused, considering the matter.

"It's a fire that might be directed, you know. Maybe there's no point my talking to Iareth, but I could have a go at Jagus. Fool that he is, he's still a Shaihen."

Caras looked at him suspiciously.

"Depends what you're going to say to him."

"I was thinking more of what he'd say to me. If Rainur is working for the benefit of Shehaios, opposition to Rainur is treachery that could well attract the wrath of the Lord High Magician." He leaned conspiratorially towards Caras. "D'you think I could do a good line in wrath?"

Caras smiled.

"Sloth, possibly."

"Oh, would that I could," sighed Kierce. "Those days are behind me, I'm afraid. You see why I didn't want to take this on? I have to be sober, hard-working and chaste. Life is hardly worth living. No wonder Turloch was such a miserable sod. Tell me if I get like him."

"I can't imagine it," replied Caras. He glanced at Kierce, wondering how far Rainur could trust him. "Entirely chaste?"

"The Queen and I are very formal. Though it would help if Rainur would stop trying to persuade us to get to know each other." Kierce met his gaze wryly. "Rainur thinks I keep away from her because I don't like her. What can I do?"

"Resist the temptation," said Caras sharply. "She's carrying his child."

"Oh, consider it resisted," replied Kierce amiably.

Rainur did not know what to do with Jagus, either. He confined him to guest quarters within the Palace, and sought Kierce's opinion on the matter. Kierce agreed to talk to the King's wayward brother. He doubted he could summon Turloch's authority, but then Turloch had not been successful in appeasing Jagus's bitterness either.

Jagus's son, Sheldo, the King's nephew, had been among Caras's party and remained in the Haven with Rainur when Caras left. He was just leaving his father as Kierce turned into the passageway which led to Jagus's room. From the uncharacteristically troubled look on his open and usually cheerful face, the visit to his father had not been an easy one.

The room Kierce entered was dim and rather bleak. The one small window was shuttered, and the furnishing sparse. These rooms were intended as little more than sleeping quarters. They were a poor place in which to spend hours on end and Jagus was taking his confinement badly. There was something close to despair in his eyes. Kierce could read his resentment that Caras appeared at the moment to have more influence with his son than he did. When he heard the door open, Kierce knew he was hoping Sheldo had returned.

"I'm sorry if I disappoint you, Lord Jagus."

"Don't apologise. It was I who neglected my son, I suppose." Jagus spoke brusquely, eradicating any emotion from his voice.

"Not the only obligation you neglected, Jagus," observed Kierce. "You should welcome Caras's influence with the boy. Perhaps at least there's a chance the Holding of Cuaraccon will stay in your family."

He strolled across the room and tested the shutter, disliking the claustrophobic feel of the room. It was barred on the outside.

Jagus glared at him.

"I don't need lecturing, Lord Kierce. Your censure would be better directed at that autocratic pup usurping the authority of Arhaios. If Turloch were alive, he would have something to say about a man's freedom being taken from him like this!"

"Turloch is not alive," said Kierce. He turned and fixed his gaze firmly on Jagus. "I am."

Jagus met his eyes briefly, then turned away and sat down.

"What do you want, Lord High Magician?"

"What do you want, Jagus?"

Jagus gave a short, scornful laugh.

"You're supposed to know."

"I can only know if you know. There are some things you want you know you're not going to get. Accept that and there may be a way out of here."

Kierce knew he'd struck home, though no-one but the Magician would have detected the flare of hope which leapt in Jagus at that suggestion.

"I am kept captive unjustly," he insisted. "Caras had no right to do what he did."

"You didn't leave him any choice. Are you interested in defending Shehaios, Jagus, or when it comes down to it, is it all just a wrestling match with your brother?"

"If you're really Turloch's heir, you'd know the answer to that."

Kierce smiled.

"No. I can only read your mind. That doesn't answer my question. Do you understand where the power of Shehaios comes from?"

Jagus frowned at him.

"Where does my power come from?" prompted Kierce. "Why do you accept me as the Magician even though you would prefer to scrape me off the bottom of your shoe?"

Jagus had the grace to look faintly embarrassed at the accusation.

"I mean no disrespect to you, Kierce."

Kierce's smile broadened to a grin.

"There's no point in flattering me, Jagus. Why is there no point in flattering me?"

He was well aware that Jagus regarded the man who now held the Lord High Magician's title as a half-wild creature with no sense of pride or propriety. Jagus's half-hearted attempt to moderate his contempt foundered on Kierce's open amusement.

"Because you can read my mind," he snapped. "You know what I'm thinking."

"Exactly. I know. Every power I have at my command has its origins in the knowledge and understanding of *haios,* the whole and the connections. We're governed by the need to maintain the *wholeness* of the land where we live. Is fighting Caras contributing to the maintenance of the wholeness? Is fighting Rainur?"

"Rainur and Caras are giving away our land to the foreigners. How are the connections with the bit of Shehaios that has an Imperial camp on it?"

"So far so good. It's early days yet. Where does the power of the Empire come from?"

"Comes from its damn great army," said Jagus, sourly. "Paid for mostly by a lot of stolen and otherwise ill-gotten wealth from the Imperial City." He gave Kierce a scornful look. "You've never been south of the Gate, have you, Kierce?"

"I've been talking to a lot of people who have. Armies do not get inside your head, Jagus, unless your head is already in an army. The Empire is like a snake, it swallows its prey whole and digests it internally. When it comes to digest Shehaios, it will find we have spread through its body and taken it over."

"I envy your confidence."

Kierce shrugged.

"I'm a gambler, Lord Jagus."

"Turloch wasn't."

"No. That's why he wouldn't stay to see it through. But even he knew it was a gamble that had to be taken." He paused. "You know something of Caiivorian ways, Jagus. There is a role for you in the defence of Shehaios if we can trust you to fulfil it."

Jagus frowned at him.

"Explaining Shehaios to the Caiivorians?"

Kierce smiled.

"I don't think that would be the best use of your talents. I'm sweating here trying to explain it to you. There are armies outside the Sacred Union. Less organised but no less deadly. If I gave you a sword, Jagus, could you kill me with it?"

Jagus looked slightly startled.

"I regard myself as a son of the Spirit, Kierce, whatever you think."

"I didn't mean to suggest you weren't. I was talking hypothetically. Leave aside whether you'd actually want to or not – would you be *able* to kill me?"

"Well, I … I doubt it. I wouldn't try it. It's not a fair fight, you'd see me coming."

"So how would you do it?"

Jagus frowned at him cautiously and considered his answer.

"I wouldn't do it alone," he said, quietly.

"Exactly. If you struck me hard enough, often enough, you would exceed my power to heal myself. You could kill me. I'm mortal. And I can't stand beside every Holder, every man, woman and child in Shehaios. I can't heal every one who is hit. They need the Imperial protection, and they need to have fighting skills that give them a chance against Caiivorian attackers. And that's something you know more about than probably anyone else in the land."

Jagus paused, thinking it over. Kierce gave him a little time to reflect.

"You want me to teach Shaihens to fight?" said Jagus, eventually.

"For the crown and the unity of Shehaios and not against it. You're only one man, but you could make a difference, and this need is urgent. The real threat comes from the blind rabble of landless warriors coming at us from the mountains and the eastern ocean. They won't swallow us whole, they'll just wipe us out. Hinds to their spears, as Brynnen so aptly put it. The wholeness of Shehaios includes her people, and if we surrender our land to a people with no understanding—." He checked abruptly. "Well. That's what it is we're defending. I could use your help if you're willing to give it."

He watched Jagus turn it over in his mind, genuinely touched by love for his heritage, but not immune to the thought that Kierce was actually offering him the chance to train his own army. He was aware, even as it occurred to him, that it was an aspect of the plan Kierce was also sensible to. He looked up at the Magician thoughtfully.

"Rainur wouldn't accept it. Caras wouldn't accept it."

"Both Rainur and Caras will accept the judgement of the Lord High Magician. You won't ever be a Holder, Jagus. But you could be a general."

"Of our own army?"

"Of a Shaihen army."

Jagus got to his feet and walked across the room, deep in thought. Kierce let him think, kept his distance and made no comment on what Jagus chose not to say.

"I can train men how I choose? I will have my freedom?"

"As long as you remain loyal to Shehaios."

Jagus watched him narrowly. "Loyal to you?"

Kierce shrugged. "If you choose to see it that way."

"I don't forgive Caras for taking my liberty. I don't forgive Rainur for abandoning Loia."

"Neither of those things are my concern," replied Kierce steadily. He met Jagus's eyes. "Don't make them my concern. Just remember, Jagus. I play to win."

Chapter 19
Kierce Makes an Entry

Cathva smiled at the expression on her husband's face as he looked around the transformed Holder's Hall.

It was laid out for a feast in honour of the Imperial representatives. Rainur wanted Envoy Davitis and Commander Hiren to feel they were coming to a land no less civilised than an Imperial province, and he knew how such things were done in Vordeith. He had been anxious to impress them.

Cathva surveyed the fruits of her efforts with quiet pride. It had been something of a heroic struggle to get past the fixed ideas of the Palace staff, and her own sense of achievement was as much reward as Rainur's pleasure. Musicians played. Imported Imperial wine, to be served in imported Imperial glassware, awaited the guests. Dishes of silver, bronze and finely crafted pottery sat piled with a tastefully chosen mixture of southern delicacies and the best of the rich land's produce. She could have been in a guest salon of the Imperial Palace, except for the occasional quaint reminder that she was in Shehaios. Rainur, mediating between two servants arguing furiously about how to handle the wine. Jugs of mead and ale and even – more unusually still to the rest of the Empire – clear, wholesome water, set among the flagons. The food still laid out on low tables around the room so that the guests could sit where they chose and move around during the meal.

She was waiting for Rainur's compliment, but she became aware that he had stopped admiring the arrangements, and was scanning the guests milling about in the hall. There were only Shaihens there so far, investigating some of the strange items on offer with interest.

"Well, I think even Davitis will have to invent his complaints," she said. "He's bound to have some. Don't you think it's amusing of my father to send him here as Envoy?"

"Amusing?"

"Davitis the Hopeless, conqueror of the people who offered no resistance and welcomed him with open arms. Such a victory for him to take back to Vordeith."

Rainur smiled, but he still seemed distracted.

"I gathered he was unlikely to distinguish himself in any other way. I suppose this was a convenient place for your father to get rid of him where he couldn't do any harm. I'm more worried about the Commander."

"Oh, you don't need to be. Hiren's what they call a soldier's soldier, I wouldn't be surprised if he forgets to use the plates. At least Davitis will appreciate the gesture. He won't be very pleased, but if you're going to start trying to please Davitis …"

Her hand fluttered affectionately on Rainur's arm, drawing his attention to the door. *Talk of the devil.*

A slender young Vordeithan nobleman entered the hall and stood looking around him, his chin tilted in an attitude evidently intended to look commanding, which actually made him look short-sighted. He was clad in a short tunic of sky-blue silk, extravagantly embroidered in silver thread, which exposed a considerable amount of smooth, oiled thigh. A swatch of darker blue material was draped across his shoulder and bracelets gilded both forearms from wrist to elbow. His small head, with its close-shaven down of black hair, poked up rather like a chicken's above more bands of gold encircling his neck.

He did have good legs, though. Cathva almost envied him his legs.

A little behind him, but not pausing to remain in his company, came a grizzled, middle-aged man in the white tunic and scarlet dress-cloak of an Imperial Commander. She saw the Palace's brewer step up to him as he strode into the hall. She momentarily held her breath at the breach of Imperial etiquette, but Hiren appeared to take it in his stride. Within minutes he was deep in easy conversation with the artisan.

"Where's Kierce?" said Rainur. "He said he would be here this time."

"He may yet come," said Cathva, hoping he didn't.

"I hope so. I don't know what more I can do to convince Kierce to show them it's the Lord High Magician they must respect, as well as Turloch's memory. Turloch had a personal reputation in Vordeith's Halls of Learning, Kierce doesn't. Your father won't even know we've lost Turloch, yet."

Cathva shivered slightly.

"No, I don't suppose he will," she admitted, by which she meant she had not told him. She was very relieved at Kierce's apparent decision to distance himself from the Imperial presence. It made it all the easier for her to avoid him, and that was as far as her strategy for dealing with the memory of the Temple of the Spring went. If she denied it often enough, perhaps she could convince herself it never happened.

They made their way across the hall to welcome their guests.

"I'll tell them to announce Kierce if he arrives," said Rainur. "If he's not already here, perhaps it'll help if he makes an entrance when he gets here."

The reception was well under way and buzzing with conversation when Cathva saw the steward enter the room, and prepare to make the announcement. She fixed her gaze on Davitis, grateful for the man's facility for talking non-stop garbage.

"Kierce ti' Turloch, Lord High Magician of Shehaios."

The momentary panic that flashed through her head did not break through the polite smile on her face, and it didn't matter that she didn't hear what Davitis said. She hadn't been listening anyway.

A sudden hush fell on the hall.

The Envoy stopped in mid-sentence, leaving his unnaturally red lips slightly parted. His kohl-rimmed eyes widened as he gazed past her shoulder towards the door of the hall. Rainur appeared silently by her side; Cathva turned to him enquiringly and he nodded towards the doorway.

"He's making an entrance. I should have known better."

Cathva turned reluctantly to look at what everyone else was staring at.

A shimmering white unicorn, three times life-size, stood where she expected to see Kierce. On its back was a man similarly larger than life, clad in white with a silver helmet and a cloak of gold. In his outstretched hand he held aloft the Magician's staff, glowing with all its subtle shades of wood, the ages of many trees contained within one human artefact.

Cathva grasped Rainur's arm tightly. He laid a reassuring hand over hers.

"It's an illusion," he said. "That's part of what the Magician does. Creates illusions. Only Turloch tended not to be so … vulgar about it."

The unreal white of the unicorn's coat was dazzling. She saw Davitis raise a hand to shield his eyes as if he was warding off evil. Commander Hiren fingered the war-god's icon around his neck and gazed critically at the unreal figure before him. It did look a remarkably solid creature. She felt she could have reached out and touched it. She looked up at the mighty rider on its back, but he was anonymous behind a masked Imperial helmet.

"Shehaios welcomes the Sacred Union of the Empire," said Kierce's voice.

The vision faded and all that remained was the small, dark figure of the Magician standing in the doorway. He bowed gracefully to the company, sauntered into the hall and began to chat to one of the grinning Palace staff, who seemed to fully appreciate his joke.

Cathva was very conscious that Davitis did not.

"A little touch of theatre, Citizen Davitis," she said, calmly. "Please don't be alarmed."

She saw Rainur glance at her gratefully. She knew he was baffled by her antipathy towards Kierce; he was constantly telling her what entertaining company he could be if she gave him a chance. Cathva declined to tell him just how entertaining Kierce could be.

"I am not at all alarmed, Majesty," said Davitis, stiffly. "But concerned. Such tricks smack of necromancy."

Cathva laughed gaily, and steered him towards the food, leaving Rainur free to tackle Kierce.

Kierce was investigating some extraordinary gastronomic offering of leaves and goats' innards when Rainur came up to him.

"How was that for an entrance, then?"

"Not quite what I had in mind," said Rainur, tersely. "But I suppose, at least, you're here."

"More than Turloch would have been."

"Turloch would not have antagonised one of our distinguished guests and raised awkward questions in the mind of the other. If I know what they're thinking, Kierce, why don't you?"

"I do." Kierce glanced at the two Imperial representatives, the slim, bronzed figure of the young envoy, his skin and hair shining with oils and his face painted as Cathva's was, and the stocky, hard-bitten Commander. "An interesting combination. Not much of a sacred union there, is there?"

"They represent the Emperor. The Commander is the only one we need concern ourselves with. I have no authority over his army. He seems personable enough, though I really only know him by reputation. A very successful general, not a politician."

"That surprises me. Tell me about Davitis."

He saw Rainur try to curb the automatic dismissal which came into his head.

"He's a member of the Imperial Royal family."

"Which wife?"

"None of them. His father was one of Zelt's advisors. Admission to the family was a reward for services rendered."

"I don't think I dare enquire what services."

Rainur shifted uncomfortably. The unspoken trust Kierce's predecessor had shared with the King was beyond the reach of either of them. Kierce knew Rainur missed Turloch's dispassionate wisdom, and the arid wit of which he appeared to have been the sole beneficiary. Rainur could not resist a continual temptation to tell Kierce what to do, and Kierce's coldness towards the Emperor's representatives – towards Cathva in particular –annoyed the King intensely.

"You're Zelt's mouthpiece, Rainur," said Kierce. "Hiren's his sword. What's Davitis for?"

"Appearances. Since I would not openly exchange sovereignty for the title of Imperial Governor, the Emperor had to be seen to send someone. Davitis has the right connections, and he's failed at everything else." Rainur hesitated anxiously. "You are aware, I hope, that it was necessary for the Emperor to present the occupation of Shehaios to his own people as a conquest?"

"It's a standing joke among the soldiers," replied Kierce. "Yes, I knew that, Rainur. So Davitis holds no real authority at all. Good."

The Envoy was still with Cathva, but Kierce could feel his censorious gaze. It was difficult to miss the wave of animosity washing across the hall towards him. He viewed it with a touch of relish. His new responsibilities severely curtailed his opportunities to enjoy himself.

Rainur saw him glance across the hall.

"Be careful, Kierce. He's a dedicated disciple of Tay-Aien. He shares the Emperor's god."

"The Emperor has many gods."

"The Emperor is his own god. He wishes to be an omnipotent, omniscient one. Which is what Tay-Aien's god is. I'm sure you understand Zelt's attraction to such a cult."

"Tay-Aien," echoed Kierce, thoughtfully.

'*God in the world.*' Cathva's god.

He saw Davitis turn determinedly towards him. Cathva followed him, and despite the undisturbed surface of the hostess's poise, he sensed her steeling herself to approach him.

He moved forwards to greet them.

"Citizen Davitis. Lord Rainur has just been recounting your achievements."

He saw Davitis's dark eyes narrow in suspicion, but Cathva intervened before he could say anything.

"Lord Kierce," she said. "Our Lord High Magician."

"I know who he is," said Davitis, coldly. "I am surprised to find your King permits a shaman a free hand to practice his deceits. I give you due warning, Lord Kierce, that it is not customary practice in the Empire of the Sacred Union to allow such liberties. My lady the Queen was quite disturbed by your foolishness."

"I offer my sincere apologies to my lady the Queen for any offence I may have caused her," said Kierce, with a fleeting glance at Cathva. He knew without even thinking about it that Cathva shared Rainur's scornful opinion of Davitis. He couldn't resist following the empathy through.

He sensed a huge, light-filled room, cold and magnificent. Cathva was entirely at ease in it, surrounded by a perfumed crowd of bright, masked faces. He heard echoes of laughter, knew that Davitis was the butt of it, and then the image suddenly blurred. He was aware of a sudden, sharp pain that was not in his head, and the mind he was sharing losing focus rapidly.

He broke contact abruptly and caught Cathva's arm as she staggered, her face deathly pale. He moved in and out of minds all the time, and no-one was ever aware of him doing it.

"Forgive me," she murmured – to Davitis, not to him. "A moment of weakness."

Tilsey was suddenly beside them to take Cathva's weight from him. She steered her heavily pregnant mistress to a seat, with Davitis accompanying them, effusive with polite concern. Kierce saw Rainur throw him a curious and slightly suspicious glance before hurrying to her side.

He stayed where he was and let Cathva's crowd of concerned attendants fuss over her. He hadn't tried to get close to her since the Temple. He was surprised how quickly and clearly he had got into her memories, but he had merely looked, not asked her to do or think anything. He was startled by the effect he appeared to have on her. It could not go on. Somehow, he had to make amends for the wrong he had done her, and put an end to this nonsense Turloch had persuaded him into.

But now was perhaps not the time. He found Davitis heading back towards him, the envoy's mind forming a lecture on the dangers the dark arts of a Shaihen witch-doctor presented to a delicate woman of Imperial breeding. Kierce prepared himself to meet the diatribe.

There were almost as many gods within the Empire as there were soldiers in its army, and most of the Caiivorians Kierce had met worshipped more than one of them, suiting the homage to the occasion which prompted it. He listened patiently to what felt like the shortcomings of all them. Words flowed without the hindrance of meaning from Davitis's mouth and fluttered around Kierce like a banner flapping in the wind, just too close to his head to be anything other than irritating.

The writings of Tay-Aien were among the multiplicity of works Turloch particularly enjoined him to study and he had, in fact, been doing so. After suffering in polite silence for some time, Kierce picked up a jug from the low table in front of him. He did not interrupt Davitis, but made sure the envoy's eyes followed his hand as he tilted the jug and poured clear water into his glass.

"More wine, envoy?" he enquired, underneath the Caiivorian's discourse.

"Thank you," responded Davitis, barely missing a beat.

From the same jug, Kierce filled Davitis's glass with red wine.

The envoy paused and blinked. Kierce regarded him with an air of courteous enquiry.

"Do go on," he invited. "This is quite fascinating."

Davitis glanced around the room to see if anyone else was watching. Kierce knew he was doubting his own eyes. He didn't want to make a fool of himself. He sipped cautiously at the wine.

"A good vintage," he stammered. "Will you not have some, Lord Kierce?"

"Not a taste I've acquired," admitted Kierce. "Our climate is hardly suited to grapes. No doubt it's one of the benefits the Empire will bring us. Along with the writings of Tay-Aien, of course."

Davitis regarded his deadpan expression warily, aware of the amusement in his eyes.

"One's spiritual welfare is more than a matter of charlatan trickery, Lord Kierce," he stated with some surliness.

"Absolutely," agreed Kierce. "I really couldn't agree more. No charlatan trickery in the words of Tay-Aien I'm sure."

"They are holy writings—," began Davitis.

"You know, I will try the wine," interrupted Kierce. "It has a fine scent – you have a word for the scent don't you? I really think I may be missing something here."

He reached for his glass. The vessel into which he had poured water was full almost to the brim with a dark red wine.

Kierce wasted too much time on Davitis. He knew very well it was Commander Hiren he needed to talk to, and he saw Davitis deliver some short words to the general just before the affronted Envoy left.

He knew what was said, but he didn't feel particularly disturbed by the slander. He already knew Hiren's faith in his own belligerent gods was not easily shaken, and the Commander's reaction to Kierce's grand entrance was simply to wonder how he had done it. The solutions running through his mind were wide of the mark, but in principle, he was right. There had not been anything there. They had seen what Kierce had persuaded them to see.

He apologised to the Commander for his dilatory introduction.

"Think nothing of it, Lord Kierce," said Hiren. "You are such a frequent visitor to our camp, I feel as though I know you quite well already."

Kierce gave him a guarded look. One of Hiren's eyes was half-closed by a deep scar that ran right across his face, but Kierce felt he saw more through his one and a half eyes than many men did through two perfectly good ones. It was quite true that most of Kierce's exploration of Caiivorian culture so far had been among the soldiers of the Sacred Union rather than their leaders.

"You've discovered my secret, Commander."

"Hardly that," said Hiren with a smile. "Didn't you realise your activities among my men are the cause of my colleague's concerns?"

"I'm not aware I conducted any activities among your people."

Kierce's confusion was genuine. He had made no apparitions appear to Hiren's soldiers. All he had done was talk to them.

"You sought their opinions, I believe, Lord Kierce. A highly extraordinary activity for a priest."

Kierce laughed outwardly and cursed inwardly.

"I see I've transgressed your laws already, Commander. I hope you might excuse me on grounds of ignorance."

"Oh, more extraordinary activity for a priest," said Hiren. "*Ignorance*, Lord Kierce?"

"Of your people, yes. Our contact with the Army of the Sacred Union has been limited and not always happy." Kierce hesitated, judging his man, but he was already aware that politically acceptable lies were almost as redundant in speaking with Hiren as they were in speaking to Kierce himself. The mind he was tentatively touching had no clutter of fears to distract him; Hiren's gods were glorious and warlike deities who knew their place. What Kierce could see was an intelligent man unafraid to face either the hard decision or his own death. "Don't be fooled by the smiling crowds, Commander. Not every Shaihen welcomes you wholeheartedly to our land."

"I'd be a little concerned for someone's sanity if they did." Hiren paused, and Kierce knew he was doing exactly what Kierce had just done – assessing the measure of the man he was speaking to. "The Lord High Magician of Shehaios is adept in the manipulation of images, it seems. Would you be willing to tell me about the sting in the tail of the warm welcome any more than you would be willing to explain how you made a warrior on a unicorn appear in King Rainur's feast hall?" He left another marginal pause before adding, "Or turned Citizen Davitis's water into wine?"

Davitis had not told him that.

"Oh, I'd hazard a guess you'll be able to work out the sting in the tail for yourself, Commander," replied Kierce drily. "Given a little time."

"I think I'll look on that as a challenge," said Hiren. "And will I be able to work out the other?"

Kierce hesitated.

"It's not impossible," he acknowledged.

"Now I really am intrigued," confessed Hiren. "I don't think I've ever met a wizard quite like you, Lord Kierce, though I gather your predecessor held some renown amongst the learned men of Vordeith."

"I'm not sure you're quite what I was expecting of an Imperial Commander," said Kierce. He hesitated. The only other Imperial Commander he had any knowledge of was the man who had abused the hospitality of Riskeld all those years ago. Caras's problems were not far from the front of his mind and he wondered what reaction the name would provoke from a fellow-soldier.

It provoked a very searching look.

"Interesting that one of the first Imperial names to pass your lips is that of a traitor, Lord Kierce," commented Hiren.

"Another measure of my ignorance, Commander Hiren, not my duplicity," admitted Kierce. "I wasn't aware that Volun was regarded as a traitor by the Empire."

"Why do you ask about him?"

"One of our Holdings has some … history with Commander Volun and his men. They are not among those celebrating your arrival."

"I think I can appreciate why. Volun made his name subduing the tribes of Western Aranth. He has never taken much trouble to distinguish friend from foe. He was a good man in the field, but he has always suffered from too great a sense of his own importance. It will be his downfall. There is only one Great Man in Vordeith, may he live for ever." The accolade ran off his tongue without any feeling, a phrase recited by rote. He referred of course to his supreme commander, His Greatness, Emperor Zelt an' Korsos.

"This is sufficient to make him a traitor?" suggested Kierce tentatively. "Too great a sense of his own importance?"

"Volun is back among the Western Tribes he was sent to subdue." Hiren went on. "But he is no longer campaigning to restore their loyalty to the Empire. Instead, the fool sets himself up as a rival to His Greatness and seeks to bind the loyalty of the Western tribes to himself. He calls himself King of the West, and until some over-bold Western Tribesman – or more likely some loyal Imperial soldier – cuts his head off, I suppose that's the crown he wears, for what it's worth. That is what makes him a traitor. There remains only one Great Man in the Empire of the Sacred Union."

"Oh, may he live for ever," finished Kierce. "So Volun is across the sea off our western coast, calling himself King, and nursing a grudge against the Empire."

"He is," said Hiren. "So now you know why we're here, Lord Kierce."

Kierce smiled. He felt he had at last found his way into a pair of Imperial boots.

Chapter 20
The Sword of Arhaios

Within months of its arrival, the Army of the Sacred Union was a presence the inhabitants of the southern half of Shehaios could not remain unaware of. Two days ride south of Arhaios was one of a series of watch-towers being carved out of the forest all across Shehaios, from the east coast to the west. The Imperial Army were certainly industrious in their construction work – towers and garrisons were appearing everywhere. What they seemed less assiduous about was fighting any Caiivorian raiders.

No Holdings within a certain radius of the garrisons suffered as Mervecc had, but raids on the poorest and most distant Holdings, high in the mountains, escalated rather than abated. As far as Caras could see, the Imperial Army was neither doing anything about it nor remotely interested in doing anything about it.

There were tears in his eyes as he listened yet again to a lament for the rape and desecration of a Shaihen mountain holding. There had been too many such songs this summer, and now, for the second time, he was hearing the horror brought home. Brynnen the minstrel was describing an attack on an Oreathan Holding. The people who died, the slaves who disappeared into the maw of the Caiivorian Empire, were Caras's people.

Before the men and women gathered in the Arhaien Meeting House began to discuss the news Brynnen had brought, Caras got up and left. He had heard every argument a dozen times. He was sick to death of argument.

He saw Elani half rise to her feet in surprise at his abrupt departure but Leath laid a restraining hand on her shoulder. It was his grandmother who followed him outside.

He heard her racking cough behind him. The evening air struck chill after the crowded warmth of the Meeting House.

"Go back, Leath," he said. "One of us ought to be making soothing noises."

"You seem to need more soothing than they do," said Leath. "Slow down, son, I don't move as fast as I used to."

Caras paused briefly to allow her to catch him up.

"None of us are moving fast enough," he said, morosely. "Except me, backwards." He hesitated and looked at Leath. "Why has it taken me this long to see it? Why didn't you give me a good kick when we heard the first song, when the first of our people fled here from the mountains?"

"I quite often feel like giving you a good kick, Caras. What have you done to deserve it this time?"

"It's not what I've done. It's what I haven't done. Those are our people Brynnen was singing about. We have to do something about it."

"It's my responsibility to decide when it's in Oreath's best interests to raise arms."

"It's a responsibility you've already passed to me, and it's time I acted like it. Go back to the hall, I'll send the word out tomorrow. I need a night to think it through."

Leath regarded him warily.

"More than a night, Caras. Where is this coming from?"

"Where do you think it's coming from? Our people are being attacked!"

"You decided to accept Rainur's solution. We are under the protection of the Army of the Sacred Union."

"We might be. The people Brynnen was singing about aren't."

Leath said nothing for a few minutes.

"You know what happened to Mervecc. Besides, these people are in the mountains, Caras. It's a very difficult place to pick a fight."

"The raiders seem to manage."

"They target Holdings. Going up there and flushing the raiders themselves out is a very different matter. If it was easy Rainur wouldn't have invited the Imperial army in to defend us."

"I think the Imperial Army invited themselves," retorted Caras. "They seem content simply to have got here. I'm not sure any longer if they've come to defend Shehaios against Caiivorian raiders or to protect the Caiivorian Empire from us. They don't seem to do anything except erect buildings all over our land."

"I understand how you feel, Caras. If I was fifty years younger, I'd probably feel the same. But it's not a matter of leading a short sortie and punishing a few Caiivorian raiders – that will achieve very little, at immense risk. Oreath can't spare you, Caras. It certainly can't afford to lose you. I'm not getting any better. You'll be chief soon."

"What kind of chief? One who only fights women? One who won't defend his people?

"One Jagus called a coward?"

Caras checked and turned on her angrily.

"That has nothing to do with it!"

Leath met his eyes.

"Doesn't it? There are times when a Holder needs his pride, Caras. But it isn't immediately before a fall."

"You have so little faith in me you assume that if I go to fight these savages who attack undefended people in their homes, I'll lose?"

"No. But why do you think the Imperial Army aren't doing it?"

"It's not their people who are suffering."

"It takes more planning than one sleepless night!"

"Fine. I'll give it two."

"You will not, Caras. You will stay here. You are not a warrior."

They came to a halt in the middle of the Holding, face to face, steel-grey eyes meeting steel-blue. Caras knew he was challenging her authority as he had never done before. He waited resolutely. Leath's expression tightened with anger.

"You're going to do it whatever I say, aren't you?"

Caras said nothing. He didn't need to.

"You stubborn bastard."

"It takes one to know one, grandmother," said Caras, quietly. "I don't think I'm fit to be your heir if I don't do this, Leath."

"You won't be my heir if you get yourself killed on a fool's errand," snapped Leath.

"I have no intention of getting myself killed. Nor am I going to spend years up there hunting the bastards. I simply want the opportunity to show them that we can strike back. We are not hinds to their spears. An injury to one is an injury to all, and will not go unpunished."

"Talk to Kierce first." she began.

"Kierce!" exploded Caras. "Now I can't go anywhere without Kierce to defend me? By the Spirit, Leath, are you trying to castrate me?"

"Kierce is the Lord High Magician—".

"Kierce is Kierce," snapped Caras. "Did he listen when you told him not to hunt the bear that attacked Gaeroch? No. So I know what he thinks. I've just consulted Kierce!" He paused. "I will send the call out to Oreath tomorrow."

Leath glared at him, her laboured breath rattling in her throat.

"Don't you dare lose your life over this, Caras. Don't you dare!"

When Caras first approached the unfamiliar structure on the borders of Mervecc and Oreath, it told him more surely than anything else had done that there were strangers within his borders. It commanded a high point within this landscape of height and scale, a creation of straight lines and solidarity, cut like a wound from the forest around it. Trees had been felled both to provide timber for the buildings within the earthen ramparts and to clear the line of sight from the watch tower rising in the south west corner of the fort.

The guard camps were manned by one Unit, the smallest component groups of the Imperial Army, and Caras approached it with his five-hundred strong band of farmers and craftsmen determined to seek a realisation of the alliance with the Empire. He had hoped for a larger Shaihen force, but the sentiments that had worked in his favour when Jagus was campaigning for Oreath to rise in opposition to him now worked against him. He had just told his people that they did not need to fight if they accepted the protection of the Imperial forces, and the preference of men with families and stock to feed and care for was to stay right where they were. Those who rallied to his call were predominantly young, unattached and male.

Messages had flown backwards and forwards from Arhaios to the Haven and thence to the Imperial guard-posts at the same time as they had been flying around Oreath raising volunteers. Caras was hoping to ride with the support of the Imperial Army, and he knew Unit Commander Scaiien at Fessan, on the border between Oreath and Mervecc, should be expecting him.

He did not anticipate being met half a mile from the guard camp by an armed group of Imperial soldiers. They surrounded him, very efficiently separating Caras from his straggling followers, took his sword from him and escorted him into the fortress.

Caras stormed into the presence of the Unit Commander beside himself with rage, and demanded the restoration of his sword and the release of his followers.

Unit Commander Scaiien was if anything a little younger than Caras himself, a professional soldier out to impress his superiors. He made it quite evident that he did not welcome the arrival of a bunch of unruly natives in his territory.

"My orders, Lord Caras," he said, the harshness of his tone emphasised by the North Caiivorian accent that Caras associated with Orlii, with the very raiders they were here to fight, "are to establish the army's presence in these mountains. To whoever needs to know it."

"This is my land," grated Caras. "You are here with my permission."

Scaiien smiled cynically. He picked up the sword lying on the table in front of him.

"Take it, Lord Caras. But it can do no good up here. Go home and keep it for your ceremonies. I'm not here to chase phantoms."

"The people who lost their Holdings don't see them as phantoms, Unit Commander," retorted Caras, sheathing the sword resentfully. "And neither do I. These people are invading my land!"

"Start trying to find them in these hills, and you'll find they are phantoms," replied Scaiien. "Lord Caras, I've talked to some of your people already – I have your peasants worrying my heels all the time with the same request. But when it comes down to it, they can't even show me where their Holdings are."

Caras frowned at him.

"What do you mean, they can't show you where their Holdings are? Of course they know where their Holdings are."

Scaiien got to his feet and crossed the small room. It was on the end of the newly constructed barracks, and the whole building smelled of fresh cut wood. It was an empty, chilly, functional place about as welcoming as Scaiien's attitude.

The Unit Commander reached onto a shelf where several rolls of vellum were stored, lifted one down and unrolled it on the table in front of Caras.

Caras looked at the document blankly. He was very conscious that Scaiien knew full well he had no idea what he was looking at. He could see the amusement on the Commander's face as he watched him.

"It's a map of the world around you," explained Scaiien. "It's what I start from. You will see there is little on it, because we haven't been here long enough to chart it, but it's not our business to get involved in local squabbles over ownership, Lord Caras. Show me proof of these Holdings, and the right of your people to hold them, and perhaps I can act. But unless it's written down," Scaiien allowed the parchment to roll up again, and replaced it on its shelf. "It doesn't exist."

"That's ridiculous!"

"Going off into the mountains to fight seasoned warriors with no idea of how you're going to do it – that's ridiculous, Lord Caras."

"Which is why we came here first," said Caras coldly. "I thought you might be willing to help us. I thought that's why you were here."

"We're here to establish the Army's presence," repeated Scaiien implacably, looking directly at Caras as he spoke. "Go back to your farm, Lord Caras."

Caras, of course, did not. He led the warriors of Oreath on into the mountains, turning their backs on Fessan in disgust. This was the support Leath had worn herself out persuading her people to accept, the support he had fought Iareth for. A destruction of trees and a fortification to defend the Imperial presence itself. What use was that to hungry people driven from their Holdings? What use to Gascon's devastated market place?

Unit Commander Scaiien watched them pass along the road south of Fessan, below the gaze of the Imperial watch-tower. A motley collection of men and women, all of them in the bright colours of Shehaios, milling around their brave and forthright leader in no particular order or discipline. Caras looked big among his people, a strong, handsome man fired by faith in his cause. Scaiien could see the confidence he inspired among those who followed him. Scaiien had seen such men before.

He turned to his Second Commander as the Shaihens headed up into the hills. He unhooked a coin from the money belt around his waist and tossed it to his lieutenant.

"Will you take a wager, Second Commander?" he suggested with a wry smile.

The lieutenant caught the coin.

"What are you betting, sir? They win or they lose?"

"That's not a wager, it's a foregone conclusion," replied Scaiien cynically. "I'm betting on less than half of them making it back here alive. Do I have a taker?"

The Second Commander smiled.

"I'll take you on, sir. Will you give me odds on Lord Caras's life?"

Scaiien grimaced.

"That's harder to call. They'll guard him with their lives. Safer to gamble that he'll be the only one left."

Chapter 21
Under Attack

Caras looked down from the mountainside onto a modest cluster of yellow-stone buildings. Most of them were long, turf-roofed dwellings, some with open workshops at one end, nearly all with animal byres attached. There was one small Meeting House, and he was looking at the Holding over the unfamiliar barrier of a sturdy paling fence.

He could see big, plaid-clad men watching the barely-discernible track which led from the Holding down into the forest, and from time to time a group of them sauntered around the outside of the perimeter fence, their upper bodies bulked by leather armour, weapons hung from their belts. Their arrogance stirred a fury in Caras's blood. They guarded the place as if they owned it.

Unfortunately, at the moment, they did. He had established that these Caiivorians were using Nassun as their base to wreak havoc on the surrounding countryside, gathering stock and slaves together there, presumably until they felt they had enough to drive back through the perilous passes to the markets of Caiivor. It was a pattern Shaihens had come to recognise over recent months.

"The question is," he said eventually, after studying the scene in silence for some considerable time. "Can we do it without destroying Nassun?"

It was not going to be easy. The village itself took up the whole of the flat platform on which it sat. Below it, terraces cut into the hillside grew Nassun's crops, and all around it were the steep slopes of mountain pasture. He realised, as Unit Commander Scaiien could have told him if he'd asked, that his horses were not going to be much use to him here.

Eskin, one of the local Holders acting as his guide, looked at him doubtfully.

"Can we?" he asked.

Caras sat down on the hillside and turned away from the view of Nassun towards Eskin.

"I don't know. Is it worth rebuilding the place after we've destroyed the menace that's there now?"

"The place we can rebuild, Lord Caras," agreed Eskin. "But watch the terraces, and you will see our women harvesting food for the Caiivorians. Inside the Meeting House, they hold captives from Nassun and all the surrounding Holdings. If we destroy Nassun … "

Caras closed his eyes.

"We destroy them." He paused. "So our first task is to rescue our people. By the Spirit, how are we going to do that?"

"They are formidable fighters." said Eskin doubtfully.

"Maybe we can be more formidable." He turned back to study the Holding. "I suspect the numbers are in our favour. None of these bands of raiders are very big and once we release the prisoners, they will fight with us. We must watch and learn. See where the women go, how we can separate them from the men who hold them captive. Then work out how to attack, where to come from."

"You think we can do it, Lord Caras?" said Eskin.

"I know we can do it, Eskin."

He settled down to watch with renewed resolve. Kierce might be the inspired twelve stones player, but Caras felt he could play a good solid game with the hand he was dealt.

They had approached Nassun from the forest below, keeping their strength hidden in its crowding gloom. Most of his forces remained camped there, away from the eyes of the guards at Nassun. The men with him scouting his intended target were mostly refugees from smaller abandoned Holdings he had passed on the way, local people who knew the land intimately. He spent two days studying Nassun, until he thought he had a plan worked out in his mind, and then made his way back down into the forest to rejoin the bulk of his men. He travelled on foot, the conspicuous horses left with his army at the forest encampment.

They had made most of the journey from Fessan in autumn sunshine, but it began to rain steadily as they descended from the hills above Nassun, turning the grass slippery with mud. A boisterous gale was blowing in from the Western Ocean, a foretaste of winter to warn Caras that he did not have much time to achieve his victory in the mountains. But his leather cape was proof against wind and rain and his confidence proof against the strength of his enemy. Taking back Nassun would send just the message he sought to send. It would restore hope to those whose kin he rescued and give the Caiivorians due warning that they had Oreath to contend with, never mind the Imperial army.

Caras's local guides took him by a tortuous path through the forest back to the track. They were still descending towards their camp when they heard the sound of hoofbeats behind them. Caras was slightly mystified. To the best of his knowledge, the Caiivorians in Nassun were not horsemen. Horses could not traverse the routes they took into Shehaios. Nevertheless, he was taking no chances; he and his companions scattered to hide in the undergrowth around the track as the noise of the horses approached. Soon, however, he could hear voices too. Shaihen voices. Speaking Arhaien dialect.

He emerged from the trees almost under the nose of Tuli's scatterbrained chestnut mare. It crossed his mind, even as he did so, that he could never have crept up on Kierce like this. Or on Gaeroch, come to that.

The mare reared up in alarm at Caras's appearance, bringing the chattering band of Oreathan horsemen to a ragged halt. Tuli calmed his prancing horse and turned towards Caras with a grin.

"Lord Caras! We bring you a victory!" he shouted.

"What are you doing here?" demanded Caras, grimly.

"We got tired of waiting. We went down to Crescogh's Holding. Ten Caiivorians, Lord Caras! We killed them all!"

"I told you to wait here," cut in Caras. "I left you to guard the camp. Who is keeping watch?"

"They're keeping a watch," said Tuli, carelessly. "You should have seen the Caiivorians' faces when we rode down on them, Caras, you'd think they'd never seen a mounted warrior before!"

"Tuli, shut up," rasped Caras. "I left those who follow the Horsemaster's calling on guard because you're used to watching and listening for danger beyond the Holding. I didn't ask you to go off and start your own fights!"

"Nevertheless, we did," retorted Tuli, unabashed. "And we won. Crescogh has his Holding back, and he has men with him to keep it, too."

"And does he have food? Does he have stock?"

"Those things are in Nassun," said Tuli. "We killed ten Caiivorians, we can kill a hundred. Just take us there, Lord Caras."

"I think it's going to be a bit more complicated than that, Tuli," said Caras sourly. He patted the mare's sweat-streaked neck grudgingly and sighed. "Still, I suppose I should congratulate you. You won back Crescogh's Holding."

He started back along the track, with Tuli riding beside him.

"Ten Caiivorians, Lord Caras!" repeated Tuli, bursting with pride. "I killed one myself."

Caras looked at the unmitigated triumph in his face, and recalled the sense of nausea that had overcome him when he looked at the Caiivorian robber he had killed in these forests. Not for the first time, he wondered how Tuli and Kierce could share the same father.

"Well done, Tuli," he repeated without much conviction.

They heard the noise before they reached their camp. Shouts and screams and the clash of iron.

With a curse, Caras turned and heaved Tuli off his horse, leapt into the saddle in his place and took off for the camp. The chestnut mare was an appalling creature to ride. Riding Kierce's Red Sky was always a pleasure, the horse doing half the rider's thinking for him, but Tuli preferred to show off his abilities by riding creatures no-one else could manage. The mare knew Caras was not Tuli, and fought him every step of the way. He had to force her to go where she did not want to go.

The men and women who had followed Tuli to Crescogh's Holding galloped with him, some of them overtaking him as they approached the place where they had left their companions.

He burst out of the woodland into the site of the Shaihen camp and onto a scene of desolation. The fight was almost over. Most of those he had left in the camp lay dead or dying around it, clearly taken by surprise, cut down before they could even draw a weapon to defend themselves. Those that remained formed a desperate circle in the centre, fighting back to back against the overwhelming strength of their Caiivorian assailants.

Caras rode straight in to the fight, hacking at the Caiivorians from the rear. The rest of his men did the same, and then came those who followed him on foot. One by one they hurled themselves in fury against the Caiivorians. One by one the Caiivorians turned and cut them down.

Caras found himself fighting against three Caiivorians and his horse, which twisted and plunged beneath him, trying to flee. As he brought his sword down against one of his opponents, the mare reared up, curling her body away from the combat. His sword slashed into his enemy, almost severing the Caiivorian's arm just below his shoulder. It was a fateful blow for both of them. The pull of the sword in his enemy's flesh combined with the horse's movement was enough to bring Caras down. He toppled awkwardly on top of his enemy, struck his head and fell face down in the mud with the Caiivorian's blood spilling over him. The fight surged on over his body, but that was the last Caras saw of it.

He came round with the sensation of waking from a dream of falling. As he came to his senses, he realised it was because someone had just thrown him down onto a rock-hard floor. He raised his head cautiously and a leather-clad heel kicked him in the face. He lay still. The foot that had struck him, and its partner, passed before his eyes, forwards and then back again.

"I'm told you're a chief, little man," said a harsh Caiivorian voice somewhere above him. "Give me a name and I'll see what price it might fetch."

Caras said nothing.

"A silent Shaihen!" exclaimed the Caiivorian. "That's worth something in itself." He nudged Caras's head with his toe. "Get up, little man."

Caras rolled over awkwardly, unbalanced by the hands tied securely behind his back. He tried to still the shivering in his body. Everything of value had been taken from him, from his cloak and boots and leather jerkin to his weapons and the rings on his fingers. Even the small jewelled rings in his ears had been ripped out. He could feel the blood still sticky along his neck from the wounds left in his earlobes though he couldn't distinguish that particular hurt from the sea of pain that was washing through his head. He rose to his knees.

"Far enough," rasped the Caiivorian.

Caras checked. Behind the broad figure of his captor, a squat, grey-haired, middle-aged man in the garments of a North Caiivorian warrior, he could see a lattice of wooden bars erected across the width and height of what looked, otherwise, like a small Meeting House. Behind the bars Shaihen faces stared at him. He saw Madred among them, watching him helplessly with the hurt of a wounded animal in her dark eyes. At least she still lived.

He looked up at the Caiivorian.

"My name is Caras ti' Leath," he said, with as much dignity as he could muster. "This is my land."

A ripple of laughter spread through the Caiivorians around him.

"This is my land," repeated Caras. "Kill me and you will have the King of Shehaios and the Imperial Army to fight. That is the price of my name."

He didn't know that it was. He had not sought Rainur's approval for this act of folly, and the Imperial Army had specifically declined to support him in it. But his pride was all he had left.

The Caiivorian hit Caras carelessly across the face with a fist full of heavy, studded rings. Caras's head reeled, and the man's voice reached him distantly as he turned to address his followers.

"Now you see why I never sell a Shaihen slave until I've cut out its tongue. If it's not casting spells it's boasting of its superiority." He looked back at Caras as the prisoner pulled himself upright again. "Be careful what you say, Shaihen, or I will silence you. Girstan son of Cromed does not fear your magic."

"He should," said Caras.

"He doesn't." Another of the Caiivorians spoke, a huge swarthy man wearing a plain brown robe beneath his breastplate of untanned leather. He carried a mark on his forehead like a stylised flame. It looked as if it had been burned into his skin. Caras had never seen such a mark before, and he only realised as he noticed it that Girstan and the rest of his followers did not wear tattoos on their faces like the men at Prassan or the robber he had killed in the forest.

The swarthy man with the brand mark leered over him.

"Look on Tay-Aien's priest and be afraid yourself, Shaihen. Lord Girstan fights under the protection of a greater god than yours!"

"If I'm not mistaken," Girstan went on "Leath is the Chief of Oreath's name. So maybe you are worth something. But only to Oreath. I'm really not sure you're worth my trouble. Perhaps after all it's just as easy to cut out your tongue and sell you on the slave market."

"Send your demand to the Haven," said Caras. "And I can promise you the reward due to you."

If Kierce did rescue him, he would never let him forget it. But he might also deliver the reward Caras felt Girstan deserved, even if it was not the one Girstan was thinking of.

Girstan regarded him suspiciously.

"Put him in the stock pens," he directed eventually. "I don't trust him near the others. No telling what evil these creatures will devise."

Caras was hauled to his feet and manhandled out of the Meeting House. He twisted in his captor's grasp towards the barred area where the remnant of his army was huddled.

"How many?" he shouted desperately.

"Thirty one," Madred answered. "Tuli escaped. Maybe with twenty more—."

She broke off as the guard's fist shot through the bars to silence her. Caras shut his eyes before the blow connected and turned away. The Caiivorians hustled him out of the hall.

Maybe twenty with Tuli. Thirty here. Some with Crescogh at his Holding. Sixty at most, probably less, and half of those destined for slavery in Caiivor. His head pounded like the inside of a beaten drum. His face was numb with pain and he felt barely strong enough to stand.

He could hardly have got it more wrong if he had tried.

Above the Caiivorian palisade around Nassun, Tuli watched the Meeting House door with single-minded devotion. He knew they must be in the Meeting House. That was where the Caiivorians took their prisoners.

He was not as high up as Caras had been when he spied on Nassun, so he was lying flat on the open hillside, daubed in mud and dust to disguise him from the Caiivorian guards. He hadn't been quick enough to stop Madred hurling herself over Caras's body and screaming promises of reward at the Caiivorians if they spared the life of a Shaihen chieftain. He was never as quick as Madred, never even in the same contest as Kierce. He knew he wasn't, and he never would be. Most of the time he was quite glad of it. Kierce and Maddi's heads, like their father's, seemed full of things that seemed to Tuli singularly unimportant.

Caras's life was important. Every Arhaien knew that.

He was very relieved to see Caras emerge from the hall almost on his own feet, even though he stumbled at the rough handling of his escort. Tuli was startled to see how small his future chief looked between his Caiivorian guards.

Tuli raised himself cautiously from the ground, crouching to load his sling. He stood up carefully, and paused, choosing his target. Caras had to see it. He had to understand it. Tuli could not be sure that he would, just as he was never entirely sure whether the charms his brother gave him were real or simply Kierce's esoteric sense of humour at work. He hoped this one was real. It was the only thing he could think of.

He swung the sling slowly, working it to speed, feeling the rhythm and the aim of it. At the right moment, he turned and loosed Kierce's parting shot in a high arc over the palisade into Nassun.

Caras saw the small object fly into Nassun Holding; he saw it land several paces away from him, shattering as it hit the rocky ground. The Caiivorians were taking him towards it, and he saw as he approached that it was – or had been until it hit the ground – a small earthenware bottle, like those the healers used to store drops of precious essences and distillations. There were dozens around his house, a reflection of Elani's interest in the healers' arts, but the small shards lying on the ground in front of him did not remind him of Elani. They reminded him of Kierce, carefully squeezing the scent of a female dragon into just such a bottle.

As he approached it, he stopped, resisting the attempts of his guards to jostle him forwards. He drew in a deep breath. He could only just detect the faint sickly smell carried on the breeze, but then he wasn't a male dragon.

The guards seized hold of him and tried to drag him forwards; he dug in his heels and fought every step.

He thought he caught a glimpse of a familiar figure on the slope above the Holding, though perhaps it was wishful thinking. Perhaps he imagined Kierce had come to rescue him, just as he imagined that a broken herb bottle contained the power to summon dragons to his assistance.

Then he heard a voice drifting to him from beyond the fence. Someone was singing, in Arhaien dialect. The subject matter could have been Kierce, but the tone was far too strident.

It was Tuli. He seemed to be singing a vaguely bawdy ballad about riding a dragon.

"Move, damn you!"

The Caiivorian guard punched his shoulder, and he staggered forwards a pace, then hurled himself backwards and wrenched himself free of their grasp. He began to pick up on Tuli's song, singing in as broad an Arhaien accent as he could muster. He had learned something about the Caiivorian view of Shaihen magic this year. Whatever Girstan and his priest said, the mere fact that they had mentioned it gave him hope that these Caiivorians feared it no less than any other. The more incomprehensible his song the more significant he thought it might seem to them. He didn't know how long he had to play this for. For all he knew, he could sing it for ever to no purpose.

He lurched clumsily away from his guards, taunting them with their inability to keep a firm hold of him. He dodged, and sang, and teased them for several minutes before he saw the Tay-Aien priest burst out of one of the nearby houses and stride across the Holding towards him.

"Silence him!" he shouted. "Don't you realise what he's doing? Silence him!"

Caras sensed the priest's intervention marking the end of his game. He turned away from the man, and tried to run. Something heavy thudded into his back, jolting him instead into the arms of his guards.

Blows rained down on his head. His hands were still tied behind him, he was powerless to protect himself. His senses swam, and the song became utter nonsense, but he shouted out snatches when he could.

His legs were kicked from under him. His voice faltered as he fell, but then he heard the song carried on by many voices, from the direction of the Meeting House. They could not have had the first idea why they were singing it. They were simply following his lead. He was amazed that they could hear him.

Once they had him down, the Caiivorian guards were intent on making sure he stayed there. A welter of punches and kicks laid into him; he thought it was the branded priest who was using some kind of implement to lend weight to his wrath. He heard bone crack as it slammed across his body, and pain soared through him with renewed intensity. There was nothing he could do, no escape and no defence. He lay on the ground, while the beating continued, and began to wonder which release would come first, death or the possibly non-existent dragons. After a while, he ceased to care. Whatever made it stop.

He didn't know how long it was before he felt the earth shake beneath him. The low, bone-rattling, teeth-jarring roar he and Kierce had experienced facing the dragon across the deer carcasses in the forests of Mervecc resonated through him once more, but this time it did not die back again. It rose like a swelling wave of deafening, head-splitting sound. Several shingles from a nearby roof shook loose and came tumbling down. A clay wall cracked suddenly from top to bottom. The blows thudding into Caras's body checked abruptly.

The stench of dragon's breath settled like a choking cloud over Nassun, breath after breath feeding into its foulness with every wave of sound.

Caras's guards began to cough and shout at each other. The Tay-Aien priest began to chant something.

"Cut him loose," shouted one of the Caiivorians with a note of panic in his voice. "Let them have him!"

They seized hold of Caras, cut the ropes around his wrists and hauled him to his feet. There was the same terror-struck look in their eyes as Caras had seen in Orlii.

"All of them," said Caras. His voice came out barely above a whisper, and he had to force himself to say it louder. "All of them! Every Shaihen prisoner you hold or—".

The palisade fence around the Holding shuddered. A rending of splintering wood pitched in to the almost inaudible bass song of the dragons' voices. The fence split apart like kindling as a thirty-foot long male dragon broke through with the Holding reflected in his face and the mountains in his tail.

Caras was still not entirely sure whether he was in a dream or in reality, but if it was reality, he didn't have long to turn this into a rescue instead of a different way of dying. The roaring was subsiding as the dragons neared the source of their pursuit.

"All of them!" he repeated with all the strength he could muster. "Release every Shaihen captive you hold, or I will summon more!"

He hardly needed to issue the demand. A mighty cheer erupted from the Meeting House as the bars shaken loose by the dragons' voices fell before the combined weight of the prisoners held behind them.

There was more splintering of wood to his left. Another, somewhat smaller, male broke through.

Caras began to back away from his dumbstruck captors, snatching breath in the small spaces between the agony in his body. He threw a glance towards the Meeting House where the former prisoners were spilling out and scattering across the Holding, some to the gates and some to the breaches made by the dragons. A third breach appeared as he looked, a third dragon. How many were there?

He couldn't run. Only will-power and desperation kept him on his feet at all. He dragged himself towards the gap left by the first dragon, who was lumbering with lowered head and grim determination towards the second one.

A familiar short, stocky figure appeared in the gap, bizarrely reflecting the mountainside on his skin just like a dragon. Tuli scrambled through the broken fence and ran towards him. Caras heard the clash of the dragons' meeting as he fell into Tuli's arms, and the young Horsemaster half carried him away from the doomed Holding. Caras looked round to see a large chunk of a wall demolished by a lashing tail and he realised he had been right about one thing. They hadn't been able to do it without destroying Nassun.

It went into the Shaihen histories as the battle of Tuli's dragon, and into Unit Commander Scaiien's money-belt as a wager well made.

It lived ever after in Caras's heart as the loss of four hundred and twenty three young men and women of Oreath.

Chapter 22
The Price

"You've done *what*?"

Kierce's laconic statement propelled Caras abruptly, and unwisely, onto his feet. Pain from his fractured ribs momentarily stole his ability to breathe. With the hand that was not strapped across his chest he grasped the arm of Leath's worn, leatherbound chair, and lowered himself carefully back down.

"Sorry," said Kierce. "I felt that."

"You've let Jagus go?" Caras spoke carefully, focussing on his breathing through the stars studding his gaze. He had not long been back in Arhaios, and it had been a difficult, painful journey. Madred had tied him to the horse for the first few days, so that he didn't fall off when he passed out.

"I felt it the first time, too," added Kierce. He gave Caras a very direct look. "You know Leath was right. It was a bloody stupid thing to do, Caras. It wouldn't take much to make Jagus Leath's successor."

"Restoring his liberty to him, for instance?" suggested Caras.

"The rightful heir getting butchered by mountain bandits. That would do it. Leath's dying, and there's nothing I can do about it."

"You're supposed to be able to heal people."

"Not when they're less than totally committed to the idea of being healed. Life is a fatal disease, it always ends in death."

Caras had returned to find Leath on her sick bed, barely able to speak to him. The look of horror she cast over him when she recognised the extent of his injuries hurt more than the infliction of them had done. He had seen Kierce's arrival as her lifeline. He thought that's why he'd come.

"Are you trying to tell me Leath wants to die?"

"Not exactly. I'm telling you I can't heal her. And I'm not going to heal you, you deserve to suffer."

"I'm not asking you to heal me," retorted Caras. "But I did think I could rely on you not to stab me in the back. Jagus swore to kill me, Kierce, he drew a sword in my Meeting House!"

"And you taught him a lesson. It was well done, Caras, I'm not arguing with you. I'm only letting him go on his oath to use his freedom in the service of Shehaios. Not in the service of his personal vendettas."

"And you think you can trust him?"

"Certainly I can trust him. I know just how much he's lying. What do you think Jagus wants, Caras?"

"He wants to hear his own voice," snapped Caras.

"Well, he wants his own voice heard. He's a Shaihen." He paused. "We're not going to keep Caiivorian raiders from taking the land and the lives of our people the way you tried to do it, Caras. We're going to do it Rainur's way.

And since this isn't a game to be risked on one play, we'll keep Jagus's way in reserve."

"Rainur's way isn't working," said Caras, "And I dread to think what Jagus's way is."

"We haven't started doing it Rainur's way yet," said Kierce, quietly. "The Emperor has kept faith with his side of the bargain. His daughter is married to Rainur and she's carrying his heir. We have soldiers guarding our borders."

"After a fashion," snorted Caras.

"Certainly, after their own fashion. Therein lies the price, Caras. The bit Rainur hasn't told you about yet."

Caras looked at him with foreboding. He didn't like it when Kierce's voice went quiet and level like that. It meant he knew Caras was not going to be pleased by what he was going to say.

"Can I afford it?"

"I don't think you can afford to do anything else. Especially now. If you ever had a choice, you lost it at Nassun. It's not gold the Emperor wants from Shehaios. It's men."

"Men?"

"For every ten men in a Holding, Shehaios must send one a year to serve in the Army of the Sacred Union. The first levy is to be raised on the anniversary of the King's marriage. You have some work to do, Caras, you've just slaughtered four hundred of the most likely candidates."

Caras stared at him.

"Tell me this is a joke, Kierce."

"This time, I'm afraid I can't. This is the deal."

Caras received this in stunned silence. This was not a twist he had dreamed of. He saw again the bodies lying in the mud below Nassun. He mentally ran through the boys and young men he knew, and his blood ran cold at the thought of choosing between them. He looked at Kierce, lounging in Leath's comfortable lair. None of this seemed to touch him.

"How long have you known about this?" he queried, stonily.

"I learned it from Turloch."

"And you approve? *Turloch* approved?"

"It's not a question of approving, Caras, you said as much yourself. It's the road we travel."

"Yes, but we look to the Magician to guide us on that road," retorted Caras. "Not to sell our children to the enemy! What kind of protection is that?"

"Define enemy," said Kierce, quietly. "You saw the army arrive."

"Oh, I saw them arrive. And I see them doing nothing to protect our Holders. They don't even accept that this is our land – now you're telling me they're going to take our young men to fight the Empire's battles? This is not an alliance. This is an army of occupation!"

"Well spotted, Caras," said Kierce. "It is. It could never have been anything else. We are part of the Empire. The heir to the throne will trace one side of his inheritance from the Imperial family. But this is no more than you agreed to. The Empire sends soldiers north. We send recruits south. The boundaries are no more. Our enemies are the Empire's enemies, and the Empire's enemies are ours. That's what it was all about."

Caras glared at him, struggling to contain his fury at the obligation that had been kept from him.

"So you approve of the Empire teaching our young men to fight? I don't remember you admiring the quality in Jagus."

"On the contrary. It's the one admirable quality he has. As for teaching our young men to fight – well, I thought I was going to have to argue that one with you. But you got there before me. Not the way I would have chosen to prove how much we need to learn from the Imperial army, but it served the purpose."

Caras got to his feet, clenching his teeth in savage pleasure at the jarring pain of the movement.

Kierce also stood up, and moved a pace towards him.

"Which is why you should use Jagus, not Jagus's weapon."

"What does that mean?"

"Think about Jagus for a while."

"Do I have to?"

"Yes, you do," replied Kierce. "You can't force the men of Oreath into the Imperial Army, you have to rely on volunteers. As a young man, Jagus would have looked on a chance to train with the Imperial Army as a gift. He's always sought to be something other than the King's younger brother. He would have jumped at the chance to learn the skills to defend his homeland. The skills you lacked." He paused, and Caras was conscious of him studying the effect of his words. He couldn't feel anything, but his scalp crawled at the idea of what Kierce was doing. It was so much easier when Turloch was Lord High Magician, and you never even knew he was there.

"It's a longer game, Caras. They don't go for ever. The obligation is to serve for five years. They'll come back stronger, with a knowledge of the Empire that you don't have and even I can never experience. And Jagus will be waiting for them."

"Jagus?" Caras turned towards him with some alarm. "Where is Jagus?"

Kierce's answer did nothing to reassure him.

"I've persuaded Rainur to send him to Hieath."

"*Hieath?*" exploded Caras, and cursed at the agony which shot through him. "Are you mad? Ered's a rebellion waiting to break out as it is !"

"No he isn't," said Kierce, scathingly. "Ered's an old woman, he just likes to complain about everything and self-righteously do nothing himself so he can't be blamed. But he's got his people talking up a storm about striking back against the Caiivorian raiders. You should have gone there for your army. You could have got a lot of Hieathens killed as well."

"So what are you going to do?" retorted Caras angrily. "Get them killed in Caiivor instead?"

"Give them a hope in hell," returned Kierce. "Let Jagus show them what the Imperial Army can teach them and there'll be no holding them back. Ered won't have any say in it. Face it, it's the only way we'd get Hieath to meet their obligation to the Imperial treaty. I could talk at Ered until I was blue in the face and I wouldn't shift him. Ered's more of a rock than you are." He smiled ruefully. "You did say you didn't know what to do with Jagus."

"Well, I'd never have thought of that!"

"Think of it. Think of this Imperial draft like a boy on the brink of manhood instead of like a Holder who has just lost four hundred of his people. Tell this the right way, and you'll have boys fighting each other for the privilege of being chosen to go."

"I am a Holder who has just lost four hundred of my people."

"And it is a privilege. Most occupied territories provide slaves, not soldiers."

"Well, forgive me if I'm not impressed. The boys may fight each other, but I'll have their mothers fighting me. I can already see Elani laying a sword at my feet if I propose sending our son to fight in the Imperial army for five years. How can I ask my people to do what I don't know I could bring myself to do?" He gazed accusingly at Kierce. "How about your family, Kierce? Do you see any of them going?"

Kierce's smile broadened.

"Seems to me a wonderful opportunity to get rid of Dragon-master Tuli and let Maddi have the title she deserves," he replied wryly.

"Get rid of him! Kierce, he's your brother!"

"And I'm very fond of him," protested Kierce, mildly. "Tuli has many excellent qualities. Some of them saved your life, for which I'm also extremely grateful. But it has to be said that when it comes to training horses he has all the skill and sensitivity of a falling rock. My personable clod of a brother would be much happier trying to persuade the Imperial cavalry that a horse that is not in pain will serve them so much better than one that is. You should see what they use for harness, Caras. I can taste blood in my mouth every time I look at what they call a bridle. In that company, Tuli's abilities will shine instead of being always overshadowed by me and his sister. As long as he doesn't crack his head against Imperial discipline, I strongly suspect he'll rapidly become a man of some consequence. Getting him back out of the Imperial cavalry could be a problem." He paused. "I can't offer anyone else. Apart from Tuli, I have nothing but sisters and Caiivorian women don't fight."

"So Iareth was right," said Caras sourly. "Strength is to be our only authority from now on."

172

"Hardly," replied Kierce, "Strength is the authority you met at Nassun. I'm asking you to accept the authority of the Keeper of the Gate." He hesitated. "And the Lord High Magician."

"So why is there no Holders' Council to discuss it? Since when has the Lord High Magician been the King's messenger?"

"Since the Army of the Sacred Union arrived. Rainur can't afford another drawn sword in his hall, Caras. Cathva's bodyguard were alarmed enough by the last one. I rather think Commander Hiren would not stand for it, and I really don't want to see you seized by the Imperial Army as a traitor. It would complicate the game no end."

Caras regarded him resentfully. He should be able to trust the Lord High Magician implicitly. But face to face with his old friend, he wasn't sure where Kierce stopped and Shaihen magic began.

He still didn't understand his refusal to heal Leath, nor his incredible faith in Jagus, and considering his reluctance to enter it, Kierce looked very well on the Magician's life. He had left the cloak of his office in the outer hall, but Caras had noticed how comfortably it seemed to suit him, and how completely it could envelope him.

"You're enjoying this, aren't you?" he suggested acidly.

"Has more of an edge than twelve stones."

"They're not stones you're playing with!"

"*I* know that," said Kierce, pointedly. He regarded Caras with some sympathy. "Don't worry too much about what the Caiivorians will teach us. We have so much to teach them it's difficult to know where to start. Have trust in your own people, Caras. This fight belongs to all of us. If our own people haven't learned the histories of Shehaios then it hardly matters what the Empire teaches them."

Caras reflected in silence for some moments.

"Will it teach them to die?"

"Shehaios is teaching them that. It nearly taught you. Pompous ass."

Chapter 23
The Faces of the Magician

When Kierce left the Holder's house at Arhaios for the company of his family, he was most complimentary to Tuli. He knew exactly how close to disaster Caras had come, and he also knew how little he could have done to prevent it. He had never felt such a debt of gratitude to his half-brother in his life. Giving him the dragon scent had been a careless gesture, a parting joke at the expense of Tuli's ability to look after himself in the mountains.

It was unusually gratifying for Tuli to find himself the object of his elder brother's favour. He related the killing of his Caiivorian warrior with pride, and in return listened eagerly to the opportunities the Imperial army might afford a skilful and courageous horseman. He was so overwhelmed that Kierce had found something he really believed Tuli would be good at he was struck with immediate enthusiasm.

Tuli being a sociable and loquacious young man and something of the hero at the moment, his excitement at this new opportunity opening up for him was quickly spread among his contemporaries. Arhaios took the decision out of the hands of its Holder. The fashion began before Caras made the announcement.

Kierce went with Tuli to the Meeting House at Arhaios when he spread the news, the first time he had been there since Turloch died. He retreated to a quieter corner of the hall, leaving Tuli to his animated group of young friends as he had left the unfortunate Orlii to the enthusiastic mercies of his stepmother and youngest sister.

He was well aware that the people of Arhaios responded differently to him now. This had always been his home ground, a place where he was so well known he had nothing to prove. It was strange to be back, and not known any longer. He had seen it in Verril's muted reproach for the scant concern he had shown for Orlii's welfare. He had seen it in Tuli's unwontedly fulsome respect no less than in Caras's mistrust. Even Madred had been a little shy of him, less willing to trade insults. Shaihens did not go in for reverence, but they nevertheless treated the Magician with respect and a certain wariness. A man from whom you could hold no secrets was an uncomfortable companion.

He saw one of the girls who used to welcome him home from the hills in conversation with her friends across the other side of the hall. He had said a fond enough farewell to Roa when he left. He had asked no promises of her, and she had wanted none from him. They both knew perfectly well what the relationship had been based on.

He saw her look across at him, and knew she had felt his eyes on her. He smiled. Roa had featured in his thoughts more than once since he left Arhaios, and his division from Cathva deepened the deprivation his office imposed on him. She smiled back at him, but the sense of trepidation that lay behind it turned him cold. It was on a par with Caras's suspicion of him. None of them trusted him now they knew his power, though it had been that power which drew the girl at least to him in the first place.

He turned away from her. Abstaining from adultery with Rainur's queen did not mean he ever had any intention of leading a celibate life. But it was different now they knew. Any woman he let his eye rest on tended to fear he would do what he had, in fact, been in the habit of doing; using his power to impose his will on theirs. They had no idea that he was actually less likely to do it now than he had been for some years past. All, so far, had seen the Magician, and none the man. Kierce was already beginning to wonder if he still existed, or whether he had turned into the monster Cathva saw when she looked at him. Cathva was worrying him. Her fears about her child's parentage were beginning to sap her strength and health, causing Kierce and Rainur concern for her ability to deliver the baby successfully. There was little Kierce could do, except keep as far away from her as possible.

He was no longer looking at the girls in the Meeting House, but he was still listening. He knew they were talking about him, teasing Roa. He heard the whispers turn to giggling speculation on what it might be like to lie with the Lord High Magician.

Try it.

A sudden well of silence dropped on the girls. They looked at each other, unsure whether they had heard what they had heard. Whether the others had heard it. Gradually they realised that they were all aware of the response, and all aware that Kierce was eavesdropping. A tremor of shock ran through all of them in varying degrees. This was not behaviour expected of the Lord High Magician.

Kierce focussed on Roa. Still he did not look at her. But in her mind she felt him touch her, kiss her. She heard him whisper in her ear, caress her as if she was in his arms. The touching became more intimate. She tried to pretend nothing was happening, but it was too real, too powerful, far stronger than her own imagination unaided. She gave a low whimper, then got up, red-faced and shot out of the Meeting House. The fascinated amusement of her companions followed her out of the door.

So, more slowly, did Kierce.

She was walking rapidly away from the Meeting House, and she turned as she heard him come after her.

"Stop it, Kierce. Please – leave me alone."

Kierce backed off mentally as he drew closer physically.

"Come on, Roa, I was only teasing … "

"Don't. Please – don't. It's not right. You shouldn't do that."

He caught up with her. She stopped reluctantly as he put his arm around her waist.

"You didn't used to mind. You used to like it."

"I used to like you doing it for real. But that was before … it's different now. Especially when you do things like that. You … you frighten me."

The tension in her body confirmed her words. She would not yield to his embrace.

"It's still me, Roa. I haven't changed."

She looked at him doubtfully.

"You must have done."

"Why must I? The only difference is that you know who I am. I'm the same."

"You're not the same to me."

There was an awkward silence. All he could find in her mind was a desire to extricate herself from this situation without angering him. He could find no trace of what she had once felt for him.

"I'm sorry, Kierce, but … I know you're the Magician. I just can't think of you as anything else any more. I … I blush when I think what we used to do, what I used to say to you."

"Then stop bloody thinking."

He pulled her firmly towards him and kissed her soundly. She didn't resist him, but he couldn't get past the barrier in her head. She was obeying the wishes of the Magician, not enjoying herself with a man who excited her. Kierce was used to playing both sides, and he found the missing section intensely frustrating, the more so because he could not understand it. He had always been infinitely subtle with Roa. He had never needed to be anything else.

He drew back and frowned at her. He was getting no spark of either affection or desire from her. She was still anxious only to be free of him. He touched her face tenderly, his hand stroking the soft curve of her cheek and jaw.

"Does it burn you, Roa?" he asked gently. "It used to light a fire or two. Why not now? Have I grown two heads? I'm the Lord High Magician, I'm supposed to understand everything. Look at me. I don't even understand you." He paused, watching vainly for a response. "It's a title, Roa. That's all. Same as Horsemaster was. It's just another name. I am still what I am, and what I always was – why do you think we had such a good time together?"

"You mean, you … you always did … ?"

"I always knew what you were thinking and what you wanted. Until now, that is. Now, I don't know what you want. Only that it's not what I want." He let go of her with a sigh. "Well, have it your way. I am the Magician. All it means is that I'm not free to do what I'd like to do. It constrains me, Roa, not you." He studied her with regret. "Foolish of me to think there was anything of me that attracted you. Why would it?"

He turned and walked away from her. She watched him go dumbly, with no attempt to stop him and only relief in her heart. She had never known who he was.

176

There was nothing to keep him in Arhaios.

Elani smiled at the character assassination of Kierce that Caras brought into the east room of the Holder's House the evening after the Magician's departure for Hieath. She was sitting by the hearth, using the firelight to sew by. The autumn was drawing towards winter, and the daylight through the translucent window faded early. The boys, Caras's son Taegen and his ward Sheldo, were still outside, but Alsareth was sitting below the window absorbed in some esoteric game with the collection of autumn leaves scattered around her.

Caras had heard the talk in the Meeting House. He understood that he had been outplayed yet again. He had never won a game against Kierce since they were boys.

"You know why, don't you?" commented Elani, critically.

"No. Why?"

"You always take him at face value. And it's always the face he wants you to see." She glanced at Caras. "He has others."

"I know he does," retorted Caras cynically. "That's why I don't trust him."

Elani looked at him covertly as he gazed truculently into the fire. Caras had no idea how many times she had looked at him like that since he returned, grateful for his solid presence in the room. She knew how close she had come to losing him. She knew it was part of the price for marrying the heir to Oreath, but it didn't make it any easier to live with. Part of the reason she had not joined her voice to Leath's to attempt to stop him going in the first place was because she knew her reasons for doing so were entirely selfish, and Caras was married to Oreath before he was married to her. Oreath had first call on his loyalty. That would always be the case. That was how Shehaios was.

"Don't be too hard on him," she continued. "He trained for fifteen years as Gaeroch's heir. How long did he have as apprentice Magician?"

"Partly his own fault," replied Caras. "Turloch might have taught him more if he hadn't always been such an arrogant and selfish bastard. Could hardly contain his scorn at my blundering failures, could he?"

Elani paused.

"If I didn't know you better, my darling," she admitted "I'd suspect you of being jealous."

"Jealous?" exclaimed Caras. "What of?"

"Kierce. You've always been the senior partner, the heir to the Holding. Suddenly, you've switched roles. He's the ultimate authority and you're still just heir to the Holding."

"That's sheer nonsense," muttered Caras, nudging a log precariously back into the fire with his foot. "It's not jealousy – for Spirit's sake, he's just empowered Jagus to raise an army. You do realise that Jagus's last words to me when I left him in the Haven were a solemn promise to kill me?" The half-burned log fell into the flames, flinging a shower of sparks and ash across his leg. He moved back abruptly. "I thought Kierce was my friend."

"He is," said Elani, calmly. "I'm sure he knows what he's doing."

"Oh, I'm sure he does, too. I just don't think any of the rest of us have worked it out yet."

"You worried him too, Caras," she said, quietly. "And for once, I think he felt as helpless as the rest of us. Have some sympathy for those you leave behind to worry about you."

Caras looked up with chagrin in his eyes. He came over to her and rested his left hand on her shoulder.

"I'm sorry."

Elani smiled.

"So you've said. And as I've told you, all the time you come back you don't need to be sorry." She hesitated. "But it seems a little unfair to apologise to me and resent Kierce for loving you as well."

Caras shook his head with a rueful smile.

"Even you fall for it, Elani. Believe me, Kierce does not go in for love. And what he uses the word for, I'm fairly sure he only does with women."

Elani did not answer immediately.

"He told me a little about Mervecc," she said eventually. "When he was there with Turloch, trying heal what had been torn apart."

She spoke with her eyes on the wounds on her husband's body, but Caras looked at her sharply.

"You spoke to him? When?"

"Just before he left for Hieath."

"I didn't know."

"Why should you?"

"So what did he say?"

Elani paused.

"He's not as tough as he likes to make out he is, Caras. He just needed someone to talk to."

"Then why wouldn't he talk to me?"

"Maybe because you're continually accusing him of being an arrogant and selfish bastard," suggested Elani, calmly. "Whereas in fact, my darling … "

She left the sentence hanging, but Caras merely muttered to himself about the injustice of the remark rather than finishing it.

"Kierce needed a bit of female company," she continued serenely. "Roa ran away from him and I gather the love of his life is forbidden to him."

"What?" interrupted Caras in alarm. "What love of his life?"

Elani met his eyes.

"You must know. My lips are sealed, so if you don't you'll just have to guess."

"You don't mean - ? You can't mean - ?" He turned away dismissively. "Kierce has never loved anyone. You know what he's like."

"Oh, I know very well what he's like," said Elani coyly. "And Roa is an empty-headed little fool. She doesn't know what she's missing."

There was a long silence.

"You're teasing me," Caras accused her quietly. He returned to her side, and put his arm around her, forcing her to lay aside the sewing.

"Of course I am. Would I dare suggest to a jealous husband I was flirting with his best friend? Trust him, Caras. You don't need to go off and fight battles to prove you're stronger than he is. You have different strengths."

"And you don't know him as well as you think you do. None of us do." He leaned over and kissed her with a deep and tender passion. "It's you I trust, Elani. With everything I love."

Chapter 24
Midwinter Birth

Winter brought a welcome respite from southern incursions. It was a hard one, and the mountains were impassable. Even the route through the Gate was closed down for several weeks. A sense of relief fell over the mountain lands together with the blanket of snow, though every Holder, especially those supporting Imperial protectors and those whose Holdings were swollen by refugees from the south, took stock of their resources. Many, like Caras, wondered how many winters and how many more mouths they would have to provide for.

As the the last days of the year slipped away, so did the life of Leath, Chief of Oreath.

Her final judgement of Caras's ill-fated expedition to the border was in the end much less harsh than his own. She was content to remind him that the fight was about survival, not about right and wrong.

"I wanted nothing more than to die in this place and to leave it in good hands," she confided to him, as he kept vigil by her bedside. She smiled faintly as Caras closed both her hands in his and raised them gently to his lips.

"Those are good hands. But they can't hold it alone," she opened her eyes and looked into Caras's face. "Have faith in the Lord High Magician, Caras. Your belief is the source of his power, and Shehaios can't survive without it. Kierce won't always call it right, but you must be careful not to get so close to the man you can't see the Magician. And don't be so dazzled by the Magician you can't see the man."

"I will try," promised Caras.

Leath closed her eyes, content to be issuing instructions to the end. She spoke little more after that.

Caras stayed with her. Some time during that period, he was conscious of Kierce's presence, although he did not see him. It was not something he had ever experienced before, but in the room where life and death came together, it didn't seem extraordinary. It was a room he left as Holder of Arhaios and Chief of Oreath.

For a death, there was a birth. As Kierce had feared, it was not an easy one. Cathva, no less than Kierce, was convinced now that her baby had been conceived in the Temple of the Spring on the night before her wedding, and the child the rest of the Palace anticipated so joyfully had become a burden to her. She grew pale instead of rosy. The patience of the Palace staff became stretched to breaking point by her ill-tempered whims, but the zest with which she had once commanded miracles was missing from her eyes and her voice.

Kierce paced the passageway adjacent to the private quarters of the Shaihen King and his family with restless anxiety. A light snow drifted through the open arches between him and the Palace courtyard, landing on the gold stone flags beneath his feet. He could have been in the room where Cathva finally lay in labour, many days past her due date. Rainur, fearing he was about to lose his Imperial wife or his heir, or both, had sought his help days ago. He knew Rainur had taken his refusal as overt hostility, given the importance of this child.

But he could not risk the child's safety by frightening her as he knew his mere presence could frighten her. He wished he had found an opportunity over the last few weeks to allay her fears, but he had found it impossible to talk to her alone. Cathva avoided him, and after the incident at the feast, Rainur tended to protect her from him rather than continuing to encourage their association. Davitis protected her from him. Even Tilsey protected her from him. He could only have gained her company by using the powers that terrified her and that, he suspected, would make matters worse.

He turned and paced back to the other end of the passageway where Orlii watched him silently. He knew the boy was more than a little frightened by his restless energy. Orlii didn't understand why he wouldn't help the Queen. He didn't know what Kierce was going to do.

Kierce didn't know what he was going to do. These last weeks had been a nightmare. Cathva's fears had worn her out when she needed her strength and with every hour that passed since her labour began, Kierce was more and more aware of the odds piling up against a successful birth. He knew what should be happening. He knew it wasn't. Of all the possible consequences to their fateful encounter in the Spring, he had not expected this one. To lose both of them.

He sent Orlii away. He couldn't stand the boy's uncomprehending anxiety. Orlii slunk off wordlessly, looking as if he had been sent on his way with a sound thrashing.

The day passed, into night. It was bitterly cold in the unshuttered corridor, but Kierce barely noticed. When he saw the first light of dawn began to break into the courtyard, he could stand it no longer.

He sat down outside the door, and took himself beyond it to see in detail what was going on.

He chose Tilsey. She was kneeling by Cathva's bed, holding her hand, whispering helpless platitudes. Cathva lay exhausted, her bloodless face glistening with sweat, tears of fear, pain and failure in her eyes. He sensed the distress of the baby as he sensed Rainur leave her side and turn towards the door. He sank his head into his hands and came back to himself as Rainur emerged. He knew what Rainur was going to ask him.

"Kierce—," began Rainur.

"You don't know what it is you're asking," said Kierce, heavily.

"I can't afford to lose either one of them, let alone both. This is not just my child, this is the Imperial heir. Whatever your feelings for her, you have to help us, Kierce."

Kierce got slowly to his feet and regarded Rainur solemnly.

"Just remember exactly what you said there, Rainur. Even though you've no idea what it meant."

He brushed past the king and went through to the room where Cathva lay. Her anxious attendants drew back to let the Magician pass. He took Tilsey's place physically this time, and gently transferred Cathva's hand to his own grasp. She opened her eyes at the unfamiliar touch.

Kierce tensed, ready to counter her horrified reaction with all the reassurance he could muster.

She smiled at him.

Hardly a smile. He felt rather than saw it, she was barely conscious. With an overwhelming sense of relief, he realised she was too delirious to conjure the monster she had made him into. She looked at him, and saw only Kierce himself, man and magician.

For the first time, Kierce understood what had happened at the Temple. He hadn't needed to create the man of her dreams for her. She'd seen him, naked in front of her, playing at god.

"You came back," she whispered.

"Of course I did. We conceived him together. We're going to give birth to him together."

Cathva gave a slight, distracted shake of her head.

"I can't do it."

"Yes, you can. Just relax, breathe and go with me. I'll do it with you."

The distance was so slight, he had joined with her almost before he realised it, feeding his strength into her drained body. The heaving sobs of her breathing steadied gradually, until her lungs filled and emptied in tune with his.

Both felt the contractions start again. The sudden ferocity of the sensation brought a gasp from both of them; as it subsided, Kierce realised he was crushing her hand no less than she was crushing his. He relaxed his grip, and smiled at her. The next wave washed over them before he could speak. Cathva cried out and he calmed her urgently. There was no stopping now, the child would not survive another delay.

"Push, push." shouted the midwife at the business end.

Relax, breathe, push, and this time Kierce was roaring with her.

"I can see the head." reported the midwife, excitedly.

Relax, breathe, push. There were tears in Kierce's eyes now, as well. He had no idea it would take so much effort.

Relax, breathe, push. The baby's head was out. Two more, and the child was in the midwife's hands, his thin cry music to the ears of all those in the room.

Panting in relief, Kierce and Cathva gazed at each other in shared triumph. He caught her up in his arms, hugging her tear-stained face to his chest.

"We did it. By the Spirit, we bloody did it!"

For that moment, he completely forgot that it was not officially his child and she was not officially his woman. He forgot everything except the overwhelming instincts and emotions that had brought this child into the world. He pulled her close and kissed her, not as a magician, or a spirit, but simply as a man in love with the mother of his son. Cathva responded instinctively. To the man, and not the magician.

It lasted a long time, and for Kierce it could have lasted for ever. But gradually, he began to be aware of the midwife waiting, somewhat startled, to place the baby in his mother's arms. Of the embarrassed tension in the room, Tilsey gazing at them in astonishment, and Rainur standing by the door looking thunderstruck.

Kierce moved back to let Cathva take her son. As the midwife placed the mewling scrap of humanity at his mother's breast, Kierce gently stroked the soft down on his head, marvelling at him. He had been present at births before, but not human ones, let alone that of his own flesh and blood. So ordinary a thing to be so miraculous.

Nevertheless, he was well aware that the betrayal of his feelings had created a whole host of other problems and if he didn't address some of them now, he never would. He planted a delicate kiss on the forehead of infant and mother, then stood slowly on cramped legs.

"May I?" he enquired of Cathva.

"You have to ask me?"

He took the baby carefully. The child began to cry and cast around for the warmth of his mother's breast. Kierce hushed him softly. For a few precious minutes, he held his son. Then he turned and carried him across the room to where Rainur still stood with a face set like granite. Without a word, he laid the child in Rainur's arms.

Rainur glared at him.

"What kind of a Lord High Magician are you?" he snarled.

Kierce met his eyes.

"What kind of a Lord High Magician do you expect me to be? You asked me to help whatever my feelings for Cathva."

"Yes, but I—".

"We've delivered you a healthy son and heir. Be grateful."

He left them to it. Before he changed his mind.

Chapter 25
The Feast of Disorder

Orlii saw Kierce leave the Palace. He was riding Red Sky without a saddle, and the skin of the bear that killed his father was wrapped around him.

The air was thick with snow, and within moments of spotting him, heading east into the empty wilderness between the Haven and the coast, Orlii had lost sight of him again.

The boy checked in the middle of the road, a hundred or more paces behind the last blurred sight of Sky's black tail. Kierce had not given him a backward glance. It was as if he did not exist.

He shivered uncontrollably. He wasn't dressed to be outdoors in the harsh midwinter. He couldn't possibly follow. He turned reluctantly back towards the warmth of the Palace.

He didn't understand what had happened here. News of the Shaihen prince's birth was on the tongue of every member of the royal household within minutes of its occurrence, registering a collective sigh of relief after the fraught waiting of the last few weeks. Preparations for the midwinter feast went on with renewed enthusiasm, freed at last of the fear that there would be little to celebrate. But Orlii didn't understand why no-one wanted to acknowledge the Lord High Magician's contribution. He had been at Mervecc with Kierce when he learned about healing; he knew Rainur's child owed its life to the Magician's intervention. He would have expected the Shaihens to be toasting Kierce in malt barley spirit, and Kierce to be participating with gusto. Not taking off silently into nowhere as if he was never coming back.

He could only hope that Kierce was intending to come back, but hope had not been much of a friend to Orlii in his short life. The alternative, that his service to the Magician was at an end, was too miserable to contemplate. Serving the Lord High Magician of Shehaios was a strange and unnerving destiny for a Caiivorian slave to have found, but when Kierce came down from the mountain above the Haven wearing the Magician's cloak, Orlii saw the change in him and vowed he would never serve another master. He treasured the offhand affection Kierce occasionally chose to show him as if it was a father's love.

Orlii lived daily with small proofs of the reality of Shaihen magic, he had no need to believe or disbelieve. It was a constant source of surprise to him that Kierce made such sparing use of the power Orlii knew he had. Sometimes, nightmares of the tyrannical malevolence he had feared when Kierce and Caras first captured him still haunted him. Other times, he imagined serving a master who dwelt in splendid temples surrounded by votive gifts from humbled suppliants. Like Cathva, he recognised the power

Kierce held. Like Cathva, he yearned for a share of it. And like Cathva, he both feared it and fundamentally failed to understand it.

One of Cathva's guards accosted him as he came through the Meeting House, pressing a slim wooden chitty into his hand.

"As soon as you can, Orlii," murmured the young man. "I must see her tonight, I'm back at camp tomorrow." He grinned and winked at the boy. "And I had a promise."

Orlii nodded silently, tucked the message inside his shirt and moved away.

"Soon as you can, Orlii," the soldier called after him.

"I'll go right away, my lord."

"Oh, and Captain Bascal asks if we're going to see your Master in camp before the Feast of Disorder. He owes him a game."

An ache of emptiness lurched inside Orlii's chest.

"I don't know, my lord," he muttered.

"Well, tell him Bascal's good for another couple of hundred any time. Bastard's always boasting about the family wealth. Kierce is generous when he wins."

"Yes, lord."

Orlii all but fled from the hall, clutching the soldier's love-letter like a talisman. He had learned long ago not to shed tears at the blows life dealt him.

He ran the soldier's errand, as he had run innumerable such errands since Kierce began to divide his time between the Haven and the Imperial camp. He knew how to make himself valuable to Caiivorians. The life he had carved for himself with them, the one the Shaihens had snatched him from, had been tolerable, even privileged. If he had only succeeded in telling his masters where to find the remnant of Prassan's resistance, and the two noblemen who had suddenly appeared to support them, he would have won himself considerable merit. Dedicated as he was to Kierce, serving the Magician was not easy. The arrival of the Imperial army had at last given him the chance to make himself useful to a few people who understood how to reward him.

He spent a lot of time riding from the camp to Mervecc and the more scattered Holdings around it, and never returned to the Haven without a clutch of wooden chitties like the one he had just delivered. The tokens which went back the other way were varied and often immodest, but they seldom stirred Orlii. He couldn't see what the fascination of women was. Shaihen women frightened him more than a little.

It was some time before he discovered how the story of the young prince's birth had twisted in the telling.

Orlii heard it first from the lips of a woman who all but pounced on him as he was returning through the Haven from an outlying farm. He recognised the need to run instantly, but he had got out of the habit of dodging. He wasn't quick enough. She cornered him.

185

He didn't know what she was going on about at first. It took him some time to recall that she had a daughter one of his clients had held some correspondence with.

The messages she gave him for the faithless soldier would have filled more than a small chit of wood. Most of it, he couldn't have delivered anyway. It was liberally scattered with wild and exotic Shaihen words he didn't understand. They sounded very much like curses.

Orlii just listened, and nodded, and agreed emphatically. The man was a bastard. He should be strung up and castrated. Whatever. Can I go, now, my lady?

"You can go, boy, and tell that man I hope he dies of his diseased manhood. And while you're about it you can tell the Magician who consorts with the Caiivorian filth he's a disgrace to the name. We know just what he is now."

"Yes, my lady," said Orlii in relief. Nevertheless, something made him pause. None of what she'd said made much sense to him, and the last comment made less sense than the rest, but he detected a slur against his master in there somewhere. "If your daughter is sick, my lady, I could ask Lord Kierce—."

"Get away with you, you think I'd let that fiend near my daughter now I know?"

"No, I meant Lord Kierce, my lady, the Lord High Magician."

"I know who you meant, boy." She looked cynically at his startled face. "Didn't you know the story's out? Did he think it would stay a secret, what he forced that poor girl to endure even as he was tearing Rainur's child from her body?"

"He … did what?" exclaimed Orlii in astonishment.

"Has he fled the Haven? He should. If I were Rainur - ".

"He hasn't fled!" For the first time in his life, Orlii answered back. "Lord Kierce fears no-one, lady, and he does as he chooses. If there was any justice in this stupid place you wouldn't dare say a word against him!"

"I'll say what I like about whoever I like, Caiivorian. And I won't be the only one, you mark my words!"

Covered in their virgin white, the Shaihen hills looked pure and peaceful. The days following the snowstorm were sharp and clear, the stars dusting the sky as frost dusted the ground beneath.

Surviving amid such harsh beauty was hard work. That was why Kierce took himself off into it; he had no wish to die, and the necessity to hunt, to guard the fire and the shelter that kept him alive, occupied his body and at least part of his mind. He foraged for hours with Red Sky, prizing traces of nourishment from the frozen landscape.

But he also sat for hours gazing into the fire while the frost formed on his furs and on his beard, wondering if he could go back.

When he laid the baby in Rainur's arms, he felt as if he had given away his life. He could not see the future. What had been a duty, a game he was obliged to play, was now his son's life – everything. He relived again and again the joyous moment of birth, the magic of the child in his arms, and the falling of the barrier between himself and Cathva. Sometimes he imagined hurling the Magician's cloak into the fire, taking Cathva and their son and riding off with them to work the horses. The idyll brought a wry and slightly bitter smile to his face. He really couldn't see Cathva living in the hills, carrying her baby in a sling, preparing their meals from a fresh kill. He couldn't even see her learning to track a wild horse, nurturing the patience and the inner peace it took to win its trust.

He could imagine hurling the Magician's cloak into the fire. He had all but done that, he realised, in the Temple of the Spring. What happened between him and Cathva couldn't stay hidden. It could never have stayed hidden. It wasn't only that he had given in to temptation, it was the fact that the temptation was there, so powerfully there. For both of them.

He could live with her hating him from a distance. He wasn't sure he could live with her loving him from the same distance.

Kierce could not so easily give up being the Magician. He could not close himself off from his land and his people. As the days passed, he became aware of the stories circulating in the Haven. He thought he recognised Cathva's signature on them. Rainur was furious, no doubt of that, but Kierce thought it was beyond Rainur's imagination to invent such tales.

It made sense, in a cold-blooded Caiivorian way, for Cathva to ensure that any accusations of disloyalty attached to him alone. It meant she had decided her position was more important to her than her feelings.

Kierce sighed, and deposited his hard-sought batch of firewood on the ground beside the vigorous flames of his fire. He could hear a wolf calling, that long, lonely sound, echoing across the cold wastes. He had seen it, several times, an injured male. It belonged with no pack. He was surprised it had survived this long into the winter.

Turloch had forced the same decision on him, trusting his protection to the secrecy Turloch always trusted to. No-one had ever thought he was the wise and venerable fount of knowledge his predecessor had been. They trusted him against their better judgement. So what was left now?

Should he celebrate the midwinter feast – the passing of the shortest day and the beginning of a new year – among his people? Or go back to the life that made no judgement on him, and distance himself from the pain of watching the child he gave birth to raised as another man's son.

He stood, watching himself through the eyes of the wolf, sharing its desperate hunger. He shouldn't feed it. It was only prolonging the agony.

Eventually, he crawled into his snow shelter and dug out a haunch of the deer he had killed and butchered a few days earlier. It was frozen. He dragged it onto the fire.

The wolf crept nearer, flat to the ground, believing itself invisible.

"You'll have to wait for it to thaw out, lad," said Kierce, for the sake of hearing a human voice. "Get impatient and tackle me, and it'll be the end of you."

The wolf yowled in surprise and dismay, understanding its cover was blown, too tired and dispirited to run. It lay watching him, giving its life into his hands.

There was, he realised, another choice. He had an outstanding invitation from Hiren to join the Imperial troops for the festival of one of the Caiivorian gods, a celebration held a few days earlier than the Shaihen one and known as the Feast of Disorder. He had not intended to accept. It promised to be an occasion fraught with opportunities for foolhardiness.

He decided, in the end, to join the wake for the old year before he decided how to meet the new one.

The Imperial army had acted with their customary efficiency in establishing their presence a short day's ride south of the Haven. A vast wooden barrack hall already stood on the site of their encampment, a big barn of a place with a fire in the centre. It looked not unlike a Shaihen Meeting House, and it had never felt more like one to Kierce as Commander Hiren escorted him inside, guest of honour to the feast.

The Shaihen midwinter feast was an occasion for gluttony and indulgence, but the declared object of the Feast of Disorder was to sate every bodily appetite as much as opportunity allowed. It was the one point in the Caiivorian year when anarchy ruled, even in the Imperial camp.

Since Shaihens observed no framework of laws, there was little thrill in breaking them; Kierce did not fully appreciate the difference a history of deprivation and circumscription could make to the removing of the boundaries until he was in the middle of it.

He always felt at ease in Hiren's camp, relaxing in company that no longer expected him to be anything other than he was, and it did not escape him that at this special time in the Shaihen calendar, he felt more at home among the Caiivorians than among his own people. With Kierce's encouragement, Hiren's officers followed their commander's lead and more or less disregarded the Magician's title. He was a Shaihen wizard, but they didn't believe in his magic and he was not offended by their disbelief. They exchanged jokes and stories, boasts and ridicule with him as with one of their own.

The difference at the Feast of Disorder was the tangible absence of authority. The only restriction on what was said, what was done, or how much was consumed, seemed to be the individual's awareness of the consequences. If the night passed without any outbreak of violence, Kierce felt he would be very surprised.

The presence of women in the hall reminded Kierce, with momentary guilt, of Orlii's existence. He really should get out of this habit of abandoning the boy. Though when he asked – and when he thought about how all those girls had got their invitations – he realised Orlii had been kept busy while he was away.

Kierce saw the service Orlii provided for the soldiers as an inevitable consequence of locating a bachelor herd – whether or not all of them were in fact bachelors – next to a mixed one. No-one forced Shaihen women to be charmed by the glamour of Imperial colours. He had reached a tentative understanding with Hiren of the balance of power between them; Hiren turned a blind eye to the fraternising, but where uglier incidents had occurred – as inevitably they had – the perpetrators had been left in no doubt of their transgression. He understood that the Shaihen people, young and old, male and female, were to be treated with respect.

Kierce confined his attention to his drinking companions. Sexual politics had got him into enough trouble already; diving with abandon into a Caiivorian orgy where the men already significantly outnumbered the women was asking for disaster. Some of the couples separating themselves out from the company were becoming more intimate as the evening wore on. Some sought privacy. Others, in the true spirit of the Feast of Disorder, sought the opposite. It wasn't easy to ignore it.

He could wish that he could stop thinking of Cathva. Sometimes, he imagined he caught a glimpse of her somewhere through the sea of bodies and the increasing haze of alcohol, though he knew she wasn't there.

Kierce's capacity to drink was significant, but it wasn't limitless.

As the stories grew more lewd and the conversation began to plumb drunken depths, he began to entertain his companions with a little illustration. The images he conjured for them drew shouts of appreciation and laughter from a crowd who were all too drunk themselves to wonder at his ability to do it. He made the figures dance and gyrate enticingly, just out of reach, insubstantial perfection that disappeared if you tried to touch it.

They were all thoroughly absorbed in the entertainment when Davitis appeared among them. Part of the celebration was the pretence of those who normally occupied positions of authority that they were among equals.

Davitis was far from sober, but he was nothing like as drunk as Kierce and his companions.

"What's so amusing over here?" he enquired.

His enquiry was met by gales of laughter. Kierce was focussed on the group of men around him; only they could see the images he was creating. He was vaguely aware that to Davitis, they were laughing at thin air. He was only vaguely aware of anything.

He was aware of the sneer behind the Envoy's patronising jocularity. It seemed to demand that he remove it.

He hauled himself to his feet, fell back, and tried again. The dancing figure flickered in and out of existence as his head swam, but he steadied himself and the image steadied with him. He and the image both moved towards Davitis. To the eyes of his observers, they merged, so that the naked girl approached the Envoy. Catcalls and whoops of hilarity followed her.

Davitis frowned in bemusement.

"I would appreciate it if someone explained the joke," he protested.

Kierce turned a coquettish pirouette in front of him. His audience rocked with laughter.

"What the hell are you doing, Kierce?" demanded Davitis in astonishment.

Kierce flashed the image the others were seeing across his mind. The figure shifted and shimmered between the girl and the Magician in a blur of flesh and desire.

"What the hell are you doing?" repeated Davitis with more alarm. He turned to keep his eyes on Kierce as the bewildering confusion of images began to circle him. "Stop this. I command you to stop!"

The whistles and shouts of the soldiers commanded him to continue.

"You won't tempt him like that, Kierce," shouted one of them.

"You want me to give him what he wants?" queried Kierce. He shrugged slightly, and the girl's shape shifted to a young boy's.

"Stop it!" cried Davitis in rising panic. "This is not funny, Kierce!"

"Oh it is," replied Kierce. "It is hilariously funny. The holy writings haven't reached your prick then Davitis? It still knows what it likes!"

"The Emperor will know what devil inhabits the Spirit of Shehaios," vowed Davitis furiously, his eyes still locked on the naked boy in front of him. "I'll see you punished for this, Kierce!"

He was not allowed to say more. Kierce flung himself at him and kissed him full on the mouth.

An uproarious cheer arose from their audience.

Davitis thrust him away. Kierce staggered, tripped and fell sprawling on his back, shaking with laughter.

Hiren stepped quietly up to Davitis and steered him away from the unruly crowd.

"He's very, very drunk, Davitis," said the Commander, quietly. "Until the moment he fell over, he was drunker than I've ever seen a man who was still standing. You will have an apology in the morning, but tonight is the feast of disorder and he is my guest. Let it go, please."

"Choose your guests with more care," snarled Davitis. "The Magician of Shehaios is an evil I will have rooted out of this place."

"Perhaps," said Hiren. "But not tonight."

Chapter 26
Resolutions

Kierce surfaced to the sound of shouting and the crash of iron on wood.

For a few moments, he thought the cacophony was inside him, but when he forced his eyes open, he realised it was external. The thumping ache in his head was not.

He raised a stiff arm to rub the sleep from his eyes. Without the fire, now a mere a glow of ash and embers, and the mass of bodies that had occupied it last night, the hall was cold. His breath formed a cloud in the air.

He coughed on the stale smoke that hung in a pall half way up the walls of the hall, and raised himself up awkwardly. He had never in his life got so paralytic before and he was conscious that he had not been a wise magician. Quite what folly he had committed he didn't recall. But he had a feeling that Turloch's ashes might be whirling themselves into a dust-storm of retribution somewhere.

He went outside to investigate the noise, swinging his arms to waken and warm his chilled body. Outside, he found a troop of Imperial soldiers marshalled on the packed earth parade ground outside the barrack hall, the one area swept clear of the surrounding snow. The shouting was of their commander issuing orders, the crashing the sound of sword on shield.

Kierce saw Hiren watching the drilling from outside his own quarters. He appeared to be merely observing, not taking part. Kierce went over to join him.

"I'm afraid this is a little vengeance being wrought," said Hiren, as he approached. "They were on duty last night."

"They didn't get to party?" Kierce commented in broader Arhaien dialect than he usually used speaking to Caras, and Hiren looked at him uncomprehendingly. Kierce gave a wan smile. "They were unable to join the Feast of Disorder?"

"They were forbidden the celebrations. So they see no reason why the wicked should rest in peace." He regarded Kierce in amusement. The Commander himself looked none the worse for the excesses of the festival but Kierce caught a brief glimpse of the grey and haggard face he was looking at. "I see Shaihen wizards can suffer from hangovers."

"Mine and everyone else's, I think," admitted Kierce. "This can't be all my headache."

"Oh, I assure you, there are plenty about this morning. From which I will assume that the feast of disorder was much enjoyed, as always."

"I assume so. I really couldn't tell you. I don't remember."

"Ah," said Hiren. He paused, watching the soldiers. "You don't remember kissing the Imperial envoy, then?"

Kierce groaned and covered his eyes with his hand.

"I didn't actually do that, did I?"

"I'm afraid you did. I had to promise him a fulsome apology when you were sober."

"Shit," muttered Kierce beneath his breath. "I suppose I'd better give him one, then."

"I think you better had," agreed Hiren. "He took some calming down." He paused. "If you will forgive my presumption – I would advise you to be a little circumspect in your dealings with the envoy, Shaihen wizard. He follows the cult of Tay-Aien because His Greatness favours it, and Davitis ever strives to win favour with His Greatness. But Tay-Aien's god is a jealous god, and he doesn't tolerate rivals." He glanced at Kierce. "I'm sure you understand me."

Kierce met his scarred companion's gaze. "Thank you."

Hiren shrugged. "You were my guest."

"Should I offer you an apology, too?"

"No need. It was an enlightening evening. My gods are not jealous, and I find much to be said for the Shaihen religion."

"It's not—," Kierce broke off. It was really too much effort to get into a meaningful discussion on why he was not a representative of a religious order. "It was a Caiivorian celebration."

"Nevertheless, the entertainment you provided was most intriguing."

"What entertainment?" asked Kierce, guardedly.

"The dancers. The girl."

"Oh, did I make her up? That's a shame. I was hoping she'd been real, she was just my type."

"I imagine she would be. Though I understand from those with a better view that she had something of the look of Queen Cathva about her."

Hiren shot him an inquisitorial glance. Considering the condition of his head, Kierce covered rapidly.

"I shouldn't be surprised. Queen Cathva is a very beautiful woman."

It took a heroic effort this morning just to process his own thoughts, but he nevertheless summoned the strength for a quick glimpse into Hiren's mind. It confirmed that the rumours had indeed reached the Imperial camp.

He became aware that Hiren was now looking at him a little curiously, and realised his skill perhaps lacked its usual subtlety. Cathva was the only person he had ever known to be aware of his presence when he read their minds. Hiren was unaware even that he was really able to do it, but he had evidently felt something then. Perhaps, reflected Kierce, the echo of his hangover. He needed to get rid of it.

"You seem to be very free with your favours to the Imperial royal family, Lord Kierce," commented Hiren drily. "I must admit, I've always found the combination of sex, politics and religion a little too rich for my constitution." He slapped Kierce on the back. "May your gods go with you, Shaihen wizard.

Come on, let me see if my aide or your Orlii can find you a cure for that head."

"Thank you," said Kierce. "But I need to find Orlii and I need to get this poison out of my body. I have the means, thank you. I'll take a ride to get some air into my lungs, and then I might feel up to making an apology to Davitis."

He didn't find Orlii. He didn't look all that hard, and in fact the boy came and found him after he returned from an invigorating ride on Red Sky which did much to refresh his spirits. He was attending to the horse when Orlii appeared.

"Should I do that, Master?" he asked.

"Not much to do," replied Kierce, cheerfully. His ability to heal himself could cleanse alcohol from his bloodstream as easily as any other poison, and he was no longer suffering. He was enjoying the brisk, rhythmic work of rubbing the sweat from Red Sky's thick winter coat. He glanced at Orlii. He sensed something changed about the boy, a certain uncharacteristic cockiness, maybe even the hint of a swagger. There was a Caiivorian tradition concerning virgins and the feast of disorder.

"Did you enjoy your Feast of Disorder, Orlii?"

A small and secret smile twitched at Orlii's lips. Kierce paused in his labours and turned to look at him.

"You crafty bugger," he grinned. "How come you got a woman and I didn't?"

Orlii cast his eyes down and scuffed a pointless path through the snow at his feet. Kierce looked a little closer. It was not a woman Orlii had spent the night with. A slight shock ran through the Magician.

"Spirit save us," he exclaimed. "*Davitis*!"

Orlii looked at him with unusual animation in his customarily solemn and watchful eyes.

"You showed me what he wanted."

"Yes, but you didn't have to give it to him!"

Of course he did. The only way Orlii knew how to win power over anyone was to anticipate what they wanted and give it to them. Why he should want to win power over Davitis, Kierce did not clearly understand, but he could see that he did and was proud of his achievement. Kierce gazed at him in concern. He hadn't even realised Orlii was in the hall last night, let alone witness to his drunken exploits. It was possible that just as he had inadvertently given the image of the girl Cathva's form, he had modelled the boy who kissed Davitis on Orlii.

"I ... I thought you would be pleased," said Orlii, nervously.

"Orlii ... "

Kierce sighed and cursed all Caiivorian insecurities to the devil they credited most of them to.

"You don't give your body to please me, or Davitis, or anyone but yourself. The one thing Turloch taught me if he taught me nothing else. Your body, your soul, yourself – it belongs to you, Orlii and no-one else."

"You are angry," said Orlii, in dismay. "I didn't mean to make you angry."

"Give me strength," muttered Kierce. "Look, let me start again. Did you enjoy your Feast of Disorder, Orlii?"

Orlii looked at him uncertainly, and nodded.

"Yes, Lord Kierce."

"Then that's all that matters," Kierce turned back to the horse. "You were only ever my servant in your own mind. You're free to go with whoever, wherever you like, whenever you like. So go."

He became aware of an abyss of despair opening up behind him and leaned against the horse with a groan.

"I am not dismissing you. If you want to stay with me, stay with me. If you want to go with Davitis … you're a very strange boy. But go with him if you wish."

He looked back at Orlii and saw the relief rush into the serious dark eyes.

"I don't want to go with him, I just … it was … "

"Fun?"

Orlii looked a little shamefaced. Kierce shrugged.

"Then enjoy it. Just don't confuse fun with love."

Even as the words left his mouth, he realised the crassness of saying such a thing to a boy who had grown up as someone's property. He didn't know what the word meant, any more than he knew what freedom meant.

Kierce felt a rare moment of genuine compassion for this lost soul who had fetched up so incongruously under his wing. He was a boy yet, in that no-man's land between childhood and manhood. He didn't really know what he wanted; he had hardly grasped the fact that he had the right to want anything.

Kierce abruptly grasped Orlii's shoulders, and then put his arms around the thin body and embraced him.

"Serve me if it makes you happy, you foolish boy. After all, what would I do without you?"

It was a lie, but when he read the gratitude and affection which rolled over the bewilderment of Orlii's immediate reaction he felt a little humbled. He really hadn't given the boy much cause to love him. Orlii came a long way down the list of creatures who demanded his attention. Somewhere considerably below Red Sky.

Orlii already towered over the small Shaihen; he lowered his head briefly to rest it on Kierce's shoulder.

Suddenly, Kierce felt him tense. He drew back.

"Master—," he said.

Kierce looked round. Davitis had just come through a small stand of trees behind them, and was standing watching them.

Kierce and Orlii exchanged a smile. For the first time, they shared a joke that both of them understood. Both of them could read Davitis's small and suspicious mind.

"I have an apology to make," said Kierce. He squeezed Orlii's arm. "You don't. Make yourself scarce."

He picked up the cloak he had shed while working on the horse and made his way over to Davitis as Orlii attended to Red Sky.

"Citizen Davitis," Kierce greeted him. "I believe the feast of disorder was a little more disorderly than you bargained for. I'm sorry if my behaviour offended you."

Davitis glared at him with an undiluted hatred that sent a shiver down Kierce's spine.

"Your very existence offends me," he rasped. "You enquire where no man should enquire, and uncover what should remain hidden." He considered Kierce balefully. The Magician was still a little hollow-eyed, but he no longer looked like a man who had drunk himself insensible a few hours earlier.

Davitis took a step closer to Kierce and glowered down at him. His perfume clogged in Kierce's nose. The aftermath of his taste hung in his memory. He met the Envoy's gaze with equanimity.

"I know what you did," hissed Davitis, "you bewitched me. You won't get away with it. The Emperor will know of it."

"You sure you want the Emperor to know of it?" enquired Kierce drily. "Bit fond of Tay-Aien's strictures about such things, the way I hear it."

Davitis glared at him.

"You have no understanding of the powers you play with." He raised his voice. "No understanding at all. And what's more you seem to have no desire to rectify your ignorance. I ask you to curb your influence on my men and you flaunt it. You are invited to take part in our celebrations and you distort and disgrace them. The writings of Tay-Aien speak of the demons in this world who tempt men from the ways of virtue and the more I look the more I find the mark of that demon on you, Lord Kierce!"

Davitis became aware that he had an audience. A couple of passing soldiers stopped and turned to look curiously at the confrontation. Thinking it was his oratory that had detained them, Davitis continued with renewed strength and enthusiastic vitriol. He enlarged upon the nature of good and evil, the teachings of Tay-Aien and the necessity for absolute obedience. It was not permitted to glance either side of the true path, nor to question it. The law was written, and that was an end of it. He abused every aspect of Shaihen magic in general and Kierce's character in particular.

He spoke, uninterrupted, for several minutes. Kierce remained silent. In fact he remained motionless, his eyes on Davitis with every appearance of giving the matter his complete, grave and chastened attention.

Gradually, it began to dawn on Davitis that far from being impressed with his sermon, there was considerable hilarity breaking out among his audience.

He glanced round at them. There were some dozen soldiers gathered watching the envoy and the magician, smiling and laughing. Davitis looked hard at Kierce. He remained Kierce, a small, dark-haired, bearded man wearing a jacket of scarlet buckskin beneath a black cloak.

"Have you finished, Citizen Davitis?" enquired the Magician, quietly.

"What have you done?" demanded Davitis.

"I've stood here very politely and listened to you insult me," replied Kierce. "I offered you my apologies if I had offended you. If you choose not to accept them, that's your privilege. If you choose not to apologise to me that, also, is your privilege. All I would like to add is *'Seek the truth wherever you find it and hold it firm though it pierce your hand with thorns like nails.'*"

He quoted the writings of Tay-Aien in the writer's native language, and Davitis' jaw dropped slightly. Kierce smiled.

"Oh, it's a good book, in its way. I specially liked the twist at the end, though unlike you, I saw it coming a mile off."

He inclined his head in a modest bow, and disappeared. Davitis started, and found himself staring at a tree, which he assumed Kierce must have been standing in front of.

He muttered a curse under his breath at the capriciousness of evil, and stalked off as determined as ever to uncover this vileness to the Emperor at the earliest opportunity. There was in truth little Kierce could have said or done that would have deterred him, a fact which Kierce himself was well aware of.

Which was why the onlookers had been entertained by the sight of Davitis discoursing on the fundamentals of good and evil to a tree.

Midwinter feast or not, Rainur had spies out for Kierce's return to the Haven.

As he rode towards the town, he was met by one of the Palace staff with a polite but formal request for the Lord High Magician to attend the King immediately on his arrival.

Kierce paused for some moments. He could simply turn his back on the royal household and ride away. There was no compulsion for the King and the Magician to work together, and the Shaihen histories were full of tales of their differences.

But he had already made the decision to come back. What ruled both of them was the defence of the Whole Land, the Fair Land, the Home of the Free, and there were enough threats facing Shehaios as it was.

He swung himself off the black stallion's back.

"Take Sky," he instructed Orlii. "And the other one when it gets here."

Orlii gave him a blank look, blinked and found himself staring at a startled grey gelding standing where Kierce had stood. The horse stamped and snorted in annoyance at being snatched from its peaceful rumination in the Palace stable.

The creatures Kierce communed with were simply lumps of unfeeling meat to Orlii, you either dominated them or ran away from them. He couldn't begin to understand how Kierce did it, but it was not the first time he had employed his powers to change places with a creature who already happened to be where he wanted to go. He had done it to Orlii himself before now, an unpleasant and nauseatingly disorienting experience.

Resignedly, the Magician's servant unhooked the spare lead rope from his saddle, and dismounted to set about calming the king's affronted horse.

Kierce unbolted the stable door and let himself out. The Haven's Horsemaster was outside in the yard investigating another animal's feet. He looked round in astonishment as Kierce emerged.

"Don't worry," said Kierce. "Orlii will bring the grey back with him."

"I wish you wouldn't bloody do that, Kierce," complained the Horsemaster, irascibly. "They have the fidgets for days when you displace them like that. You of all people…."

"All our needs must give way to those of the King," cut in Kierce over his shoulder, striding towards the Palace.

"Bollocks," muttered the Horsemaster. "You're showing off again. Flash bastard." He raised his voice with the comment he knew would provoke a reaction. "Turloch didn't behave like this!"

"Turloch's dead."

He knew precisely where Rainur was, and the fact that he was currently in deep discussions with the Master of the Treasury did not deter him. Rainur wanted to see him immediately; Rainur would see him immediately.

"Lock up your women, Rainur, it's the Lord High Magician," he proclaimed, sweeping into the room.

Rainur turned to him in annoyance and astonishment.

"What are you talking about?"

Kierce confronted him, raiding the King's mind ruthlessly. His confusion was genuine. Not only had he not started the rumours, he appeared to be unaware of them.

"Not you, then," commented Kierce, a touch bitterly. "So it was Cathva. I suspected as much."

Rainur glanced at the Master of the Treasury, made a hasty apology and got rid of the man.

"Kierce, you read minds, I don't," said Rainur curtly, once they were alone. "I have no idea what you're talking about."

Kierce flung himself down on a settle beneath the light from a pane of golden Shaihen slate.

"No, you're right, you haven't. And you've no idea what you've married, either."

There was a frosty silence.

"Perhaps I should have asked you this the first day you appeared wearing Turloch's cloak," said the King, with quiet reserve. "I rather assumed you'd have told me, but I'm beginning to understand I can't assume anything where you're concerned. Do me the courtesy of a straight answer, Kierce. Do you have a problem with the Imperial presence in Shehaios?"

"We all have a problem with the Imperial presence in Shehaios," retorted Kierce. "But you and Turloch made those decisions while I was chasing horses in Oreath. I do know we can't go backwards from where we are. You throw the stones and play the hand that falls to you."

"I thought you played with more skill," said Rainur, coldly.

Kierce glared at him.

"First Cathva and now Davitis," continued Rainur. "Can you spell diplomacy, Kierce?"

"This isn't about bloody Davitis!"

"Bloody Davitis is the Imperial Envoy. He reports to the Emperor. He's a fool. You know that, I know that, and the Emperor knows that, but he's still the Imperial Envoy!"

There was another charged pause.

"All right," conceded Kierce, grudgingly. "Davitis was a mistake." He paused. "I was drunk."

"And you think it was wise to get drunk in the company of Imperial soldiers at the Feast of Disorder?"

"The Lord High Magician has knowledge. He isn't always wise," said Kierce sourly. "If you want to know all the things we shouldn't do, read Davitis's book. The other thing's called life, Rainur. Turloch no longer had one. I do." He hesitated. "I apologised to the idiot."

"And took the opportunity to make mock of him again!"

"Well," Kierce turned towards the window with a wry smile. "He does ask for it."

"Kierce, you're the Lord High Magician!" exclaimed Rainur in exasperation. "Nothing you do happens in isolation. The Emperor may take what Davitis says with a pinch of salt, but I can assure you he listens with more respect to what his daughter tells him. She is not a fool, and he well knows it. If he gets the same story from both of them he's going to start asking some questions I'm going to find it hard to answer." He paused. "Why is Cathva afraid of you, Kierce?"

"She's like Davitis. A bloody Caiivorian. She doesn't understand me. She's afraid of the power I hold."

"I'm not sure it isn't us gullible Shaihens who don't understand you. I'm afraid Cathva's problem is not failing to understand you but knowing you a little too well." Rainur paused. "Did you force yourself on Cathva?"

Kierce got to his feet angrily and looked the King in the eye.

"I have never forced anything on Cathva."

"But you do desire her?"

Kierce smiled without humour.

"If you're going to take issue with every man in Shehaios who desires her, you're going to have your work cut out, Rainur. She's a most desirable woman."

"Not every man in Shehaios is the Lord High Magician," replied Rainur. "The Caiivorians should respect you, Kierce. In the absence of any better model they should think of you in the way they think of their own gods. Yet here you are pursuing Cathva, ridiculing Davitis, drinking and gambling with Hiren. Do you know what you're doing? Because I surely don't!"

"I am not a god, I am not a priest," returned Kierce angrily. "I am the Lord High Magician, I know … I need to know people. Turloch did it from a distance, I do it from the inside. I get close. Sometimes I get too close. That's the way I am and I'm damned if I'm going to spend my life apologising for it. I gave birth to your son, Rainur – I couldn't have done that from a distance."

"Nevertheless," said Rainur, coolly. "Distance is required."

He turned his back on Kierce and walked away, a physical indication of the gap between them. Kierce could see, without even looking at the King's mind, how dearly he wished he could simply unleash the anger he felt and banish the Magician for ever from his Haven. But if the Vordeithan court had taught Rainur anything, it had taught him how to overcome his feelings.

"Do you intend to remain here?"

"I see no good reason to be anywhere else. Is he well?"

"Who?"

"Your son," said Kierce, ironically. "I haven't seen him since he was born, Rainur. You haven't even told me his name. Let alone thanked me."

"His name is Sartin," acknowledged Rainur with only marginally less hostility. It was a name that meant "the Lord's son", by implication "the chosen one". "He is well, and I thank you for that." He paused. "It seems to me the Lord High Magician should have a residence of his own in the Haven. I don't mean Turloch's derelict old place. Somewhere more befitting your status."

Somewhere you won't be under the same roof as Cathva, read Kierce, almost as if Rainur had actually said it. He made no comment.

"Shaihens don't need any display to understand what the Lord High Magician is any more than they need a display to understand what the Keeper of the Gate or the Holder of their land is," continued Rainur. "Caiivorians do. They attach much importance to display and ritual, and give less respect to a power that doesn't have it." He glanced at Kierce. "Especially when the holder of that power does not court respect."

"I can't do that, Rainur," said Kierce. "I really can't. Life is too short."

"Then at least construct a residence that does it for you. You cannot remain here."

"Well, that's the heart of the matter," stated Kierce. "You can't keep me from the child I brought into the world, Rainur. Not once you asked me to do it. Whatever my feelings for Cathva, you said."

"Because I thought you disliked her," snapped Rainur.

Kierce shrugged.

"Now you know I don't."

Rainur hesitated.

"Of course you are not excluded from the Palace," he said stiffly. "But as far as Prince Sartin is concerned, I leave the matter in Cathva's hands. If she does not want you to see the child, I ask you to respect her wishes. You've shown her little enough respect so far."

Kierce walked back over to the opaque window and contemplated the surreal lines of the Haven revealed through it. He knew Rainur was talking about the kind of building associated with many of the Caiivorian religions, rather than a homestead. The temples and supplicants Orlii dreamed of were a source of ridicule to him. He didn't understand the point of them any more than he understood the point of Cathva's face painting and constricting clothes or Davitis's devotion to a written word he didn't understand. He liked colour and decoration – he was quite partial to red dye for his own garments – but it didn't matter to him any more than Red Sky's colour mattered when choosing a name. He lived one level down from the surface and sometimes forgot there was anywhere else to be.

"It would please Orlii, I suppose," he reflected. There were possibilities in the idea. "A tower, perhaps. Something tall and phallic."

He could physically feel the look Rainur directed at him. He smiled.

"I will respect Cathva's wishes," he promised. He turned towards the King. "We'll keep it symbolic, shall we?"

Chapter 27
Cathva and the Magician

In most of the matters surrounding the birth of her baby, Cathva had been granted her own way. But there was one issue on which she had been forced to concede to the Shaihens. She was scandalised by the idea that she should feed her own infant; they were no less scandalised by the idea that any other woman should. A wet nurse would not be provided.

She resisted it. She was aghast that they could demand that of her, after the exhausting   hours of labour. The first few days had been a complete nightmare, but now she had recovered her strength and got used to the idea, she was surprised to find she was enjoying it. It came as a pleasant shock to her how much she adored the incontinent scrap of life that had caused her such pain.

When Kierce arrived, she was suckling the baby.

She looked round, and knew she had not heard him come in. He must already have been in the room for several minutes. She hastily detached the sated infant and covered herself.

"I'm not sure my husband has given permission for you to be here, Lord Kierce."

"I didn't seek it," replied Kierce.

She handed the baby to Tilsey as Kierce approached her, but he simply changed tack and went up to the servant. Tilsey gave him the child without hesitation. Cathva watched the unselfconscious competence with which he took the baby, studied him admiringly, then put him on his shoulder as the tiny face screwed up with windy discomfort. She could almost have believed he was just a man taking delight in his baby son.

Kierce glanced at her with the smile still on his face.

"I do have some experience, Lady Cathva," he said. "I was eleven when my youngest sister was born. My stepmother was delighted by my ability to tell her what her daughter was yelling for."

Cathva said nothing. She found it as hard to imagine Kierce as an eleven-year-old boy as she did to think of him as part of a family, helping his stepmother with a new baby.

"It all seemed very unfamiliar to you, Lady Cathva."

"A princess of the Imperial Household does not spend her time on childcare."

"Oh, yes. I heard about the wet nurse," grinned Kierce. He tilted his head to peer at the small one snuffling about on his shoulder. "Well, I could help give birth to you, young man, but I can't feed you. Your mother will have to continue to put up with that indignity. She has a hard life of it."

"Lord Kierce, I really don't think Lord Rainur would like your being here …" Cathva tried again. He showed no sign of wishing to hand the child back, and she was getting increasingly nervous. He had swept in and taken control of the child's birth, not to mention her own emotions, and she feared his intentions now. She didn't understand what he wanted here, what his real interest in the baby was.

"Lord Rainur leaves such matters to your judgement, Lady Cathva," replied Kierce. He turned towards her. "You know why I wish to be here."

She looked at him across the baby in his arms and a knot of fear twisted inside her. Until the moment of his birth, Cathva's child had been to her a symbolic thing that belonged either to Rainur or to Kierce. When she held him in her arms, she knew he belonged to her, and through her to the Imperial Family. She was startled by the jealous rush of love that enveloped and empowered her despite the weakness of her exhausted body.

At the triumphant conclusion of her long and arduous labour, she had seen in Kierce's euphoric embrace the man she met in the Temple of Life and understood, for a moment, what she felt for him. But then he gave the baby to Rainur. She heard Rainur call him the Lord High Magician and she realised he had been in her mind, in her body, and the emotion of his reaction to the birth could simply have been her own. There may not have been anything of Kierce actually there, and seeing her precious son in his arms she ached to snatch the prince away from him to safety.

Kierce contemplated her across the gulf of mistrust.

"You still don't understand, do you, Cathva?" he sighed. Reluctantly, he handed the baby back to Tilsey. "Would you leave us alone, please, there are things I must discuss with Queen Cathva."

"No!" exclaimed Cathva in alarm. "I forbid you to leave the room!"

Kierce exchanged a confidential smile with her Shaihen companion.

"It's time I sorted this out, Tilsey."

"I quite agree, Lord Kierce," said Tilsey, shortly. "It's long since time you did." She gave him a sharp glance as she took Sartin from him. "Just be careful how you sort it out. I don't know where those things she said about you came from, but they don't belong in the Shehaios I grew up in."

"Tilsey !" exclaimed Cathva, outraged at this breach of confidence.

"I'm leaving, my lady," said Tilsey obediently.

"You are not. You're not to leave me with—".

"With the Lord High Magician? I think I have to, my lady."

She gathered up the prince and his necessities, and left the room. Kierce turned towards the anxious queen.

"You know he wouldn't have survived if I hadn't helped you through his birth. I doubt you'd have survived it yourself. How can you still believe that I mean you any harm?"

Cathva regarded him warily. Her heart was racing. She had no idea what he was going to do, only that she could not stop him.

"What do you want, Lord Kierce?"

He met her eyes. She shrank from him, and he reached out a hand towards her as if it was an instinctive reaction. She did not take it. She sat down, trembling.

"I need you to trust me, Lady Cathva," he said quietly. "Look at me."

She remained still, gazing at her feet.

"Look at me," repeated Kierce, insistently.

Slowly and reluctantly, she looked up, into his face, just below his eye-line. The memory of Sartin's birth was like an unreal dream; the memory of facing him through the falling waters of the Haven's Spring was much stronger. She still wondered how she had found the courage to do that, still less to give herself up to the thrilling, fearful sensuality of what followed it.

He touched the perfectly groomed and bound tresses of her hair gently. Cathva closed her eyes.

"You want me, Lord Kierce?"

"All the time. But you are Rainur's Queen. And I am your devoted servant."

She opened her eyes and looked at him in astonishment.

"Servant?"

"And now you will look at me," said Kierce, with amused triumph.

She gazed at him in bemusement.

"That night … in the temple … ?"

"Oh, I certainly wanted you then!" He paused, and added more soberly. "I was testing newly acquired powers. I got … carried away. I should not have let it happen."

"Let it happen?" echoed Cathva. "You *made* it happen!"

"I enticed you into the spring," admitted Kierce. "If you hadn't been such a temptress, it wouldn't have gone so far." He hesitated. "I'm sorry I made you fear me. I'm not sorry I made love to you. And neither are you."

She started.

"Do you—?"

"Know what you're thinking? Of course I do." He paused. "It was just me, Cathva. No spirits, no gods. Nothing you need teach my son—". He checked at the slip of the tongue and corrected himself. "Your son to fear."

"But the power you hold!" whispered Cathva. "If you know … you must know how I've dreaded being alone with you. How I dreaded … dreaded …"

"What your child would be. Yes, I knew. It nearly killed him. You're the mother of a fine, healthy boy, Cathva, that's all. Though I think a remarkably handsome one, don't you?"

"What … what do you want, Lord Kierce?" The question was asked this time with more than a little anticipation. Cathva was astute enough to understand that he had not called himself her servant by accident. That was precisely where the argument had started.

"I want – I need – to be part of Sartin's life," replied Kierce. "You gave birth to him. I shared it with you. Can you imagine how that makes me feel about him?"

"You could make another claim to him?" suggested Cathva.

"Of course I could. Where do you think he gets those good looks from?" Kierce smiled. "But I won't do that. Rainur needs an heir, he doesn't need to know it was you and I who gave him one." He paused. "So let's have no more talk of tearing children from your body and forcing my carnal desires on you, shall we?"

Cathva blushed demurely.

"Forgive me. I … I feared Lord Rainur's anger. I have never seen my lord lose his temper before, but he was beside himself when you left the birth-room. He knew something had passed between us." She put everything she could into the melting blue eyes she turned towards him. "I had to tell him something."

Kierce frowned slightly at her. Her heart beat a little faster. Of course he knew she was massaging the truth. A host of suspicions tormented Rainur in the days following the birth, but she knew very well the worst of them had now subsided. Something Kierce had said to him reassured him. She was disappointed by the proof that Rainur could be as gullible a fool as most of his people.

"So what did you tell him?"

"What could I tell him?" Cathva's limpid gaze was as innocent as she knew how to make it. She knew when he touched her mind, and he was not doing it. "If it was a moment that wrought your emotions, Lord Kierce, pity my distress, I beg of you! I hardly knew myself what you had done – or why you had embraced me. I only knew you held a power I could not resist. I only knew I had to obey your will. What else could I do?"

"You didn't tell Rainur that?" exclaimed Kierce.

"It's the truth, isn't it?"

"I didn't force you, Cathva. I didn't take your will away from you."

She lowered her eyes again.

"Forgive me, Lord High Magician, if I do not understand how you choose to exercise your power. I am still learning the ways of Shehaios."

"It had nothing to do with Shehaios," retorted Kierce. "It was to do with you and me, Cathva, and you know that perfectly well. It shouldn't have happened, and the consequences if Rainur knew that it had are something I don't want to have to deal with. He chooses not to look too hard. Don't force him to."

"As you wish, Lord Kierce," said Cathva, demurely.

"Cathva!"

She kept her eyes lowered, letting his frustration wash over her. This was a novel and heady sensation. Was the Lord High Magician indeed her servant?

"In the temple," she said eventually, "I asked you … Does the King of Shehaios not serve you?"

"I don't serve him," replied Kierce.

She looked at him steadily, beginning to revel in the thrill of her own courage. She knew the reality of the power he held. She had felt it touch her. That was why she had feared him. But she had turned to him in the spring out of a desire to touch and hold that power for herself and she could dare to imagine now that it might be within her grasp.

"That isn't what I asked you."

"All Shaihens serve only the Spirit of Shehaios. The whole and the connections, past, present and future."

"Even those who have the power of a god?"

"Oh, especially those," replied Kierce, carelessly. "I said I'm your servant, Lady Cathva, because that's a word you understand. I will be bound by your wishes. I promised Rainur as much."

"But the man I met in the Temple did not need to be bound by anything. He could have had anything he wanted." She looked at him critically, the contained energy in his wiry body, the well-defined, mobile face. The eyes that saw straight through to her deepest desire. "I've met men who believed they were gods before, but never a god who claims he's a man. You can't deny the power you hold, Lord Kierce. It's not a matter of ritual and trickery. There is magic in Shehaios."

"You are talking to the Lord High Magician, Cathva. Do you think I don't know that?"

"Then why do you not … use it? I should be afraid of you. We should all be afraid of you."

"You fear power, Lady Cathva? Why?"

She gave a slightly incredulous laugh, and spread her arms helplessly. It was a question too ridiculous for her to frame an answer to. Power was His Greatness Emperor Zelt an' Korsos, a huge and indomitable will that ruled the known world. It was inconceivable to Cathva that her father would choose not to take something he wanted. It seemed ludicrous that it should even cross his mind to concern himself with the wishes of those affected by his choice, unless they were among the elite, powerful men themselves whose favour even the Emperor would be wise not to lose. No such elite could threaten Kierce. His power was unassailable.

She sensed him reaching out to understand her. She relaxed her guard and let him see it all, the wealth and power she desired. If he could make this dream come true, he could have every last fibre of her being.

"That's not my way, Cathva," he said softly.

"You said you would obey my wishes, Lord Kierce."

"Your wishes regarding your son."

"Oh, I see."

He was separate from her again, and she gave him a slightly arch look, reprisal for his disappointing lack of courage. It seemed there was no Shaihen born who knew how to hold power.

"What am I to tell Lord Rainur? That you wish to see Sartin because Sartin is your son?"

"I don't think we'd better tell him that," admitted Kierce, cautiously. "Even Rainur might find it a bit hard to be diplomatic about that. We don't need to tell him anything, Lady Cathva. He leaves the decision in your hands."

Cathva raised a delicate hand to her face as if overcome by modesty.

"My goodness. I hold the happiness of the Lord High Magician in my hands, then."

Kierce watched her steadily. She knew he was not deceived by the act for a moment, but there was very little he could do about it. While both Rainur and Kierce believed without question that Sartin was their son, he was Cathva's most powerful weapon. What was beyond any doubt was that he was her son, a child of the Imperial family, heir to this outpost of her father's domains. If it came to a choice, she held the key to which of the two representatives of Shaihen power His Greatness chose to bestow his friendship on.

She smiled at him.

"I am happy to grant your wish, Lord Kierce. I hope you may one day feel able to grant mine."

Kierce bowed to her with slightly mocking reverence.

"I have never been able to do anything else, Lady Cathva."

Part III

Chapter 28
The Enemies of the Empire

The Emperor was getting dressed.

It took some time. Zelt an' Korsos was never less than magnificent when he appeared in public.

He did, however, have a habit of receiving embassies from his ministers while the layers of fine cloth were draped reverently around him. It amused him to keep the ambassadors guessing whether he was listening, or admiring the detail of an embroidered collar. There were bearers of unwelcome news who heard their death sentence in terms of a pulled thread.

For a moment, Zelt toyed with the idea of numbering High Commander Moricen among them, but he knew it would not do. The crisis was sufficiently real for him to have need of all his commanders. Moricen wasn't Hiren, but he was all Vordeith had right now. Zelt spared a moment of regret that the nearest he could get to his most reliable warhorse was the exuberant, rambling letter from his daughter, the reading of which the High Commander's entry had interrupted.

"Perhaps we should look to our ship-builders for some answers," observed the Emperor. "How was it Volun was permitted to build up a fleet capable of threatening us like this?"

"The Aranthans are pirates, Your Greatness. They have stolen many vessels, and built more of their own."

"Are you telling me our fleet ran from a rabble of exiled barbarians in a collection of leaking hulks and cockleshells?"

"Volun has a formidable fleet, Your Greatness. There was no lack of courage from the Warriors of the Sacred Union."

"Then the lack must have been in those who commanded them."

For years, exiles from Imperial order had eked out a life of piracy from bases in the flat salt marshes of the western continent, a constant thorn in the Empire's side. Western Aranth was the graveyard of many an Imperial Commander ambitious to make his reputation by taming the tribes who had settled amid its treacherous, shifting channels. Volun had been the most successful.

Appropriate, reflected the Emperor. The man was a brawling, uncultured fool. Self-declared King of a rabble of pirates and barbarians was about what he was fit for. Then again, he had always been an ambitious, brawling, uncultured fool.

The most easterly point of Aranth lay off the west coast of Shehaios; all intelligence had suggested that if Volun had the audacity to strike at all, it would be at the weak point of the Empire. Not at its armoured heart. Yet his fleet was sailing ever closer to the Imperial City, and according to Moricen it had just wiped out most of the ships which formed Vordeith's first line of defence.

Nevertheless, Volun had a long way to go yet to occupy Zelt's throne, and if he was expecting to find the connections he could once command still waiting for him in Vordeith, he would be disappointed. The estates, family, friends and supporters of a man declared a traitor to the Sacred Union were the first to suffer, and Zelt had systematically rooted out every vestige of the faction associated with Volun. He was too well connected for anything less than ruthless measures. There was only one Great Man in Vordeith.

Zelt curled an arm across the bulk of his stomach and examined his sleeve critically.

"I said blue."

His dressers divested him of the robe without a murmur and brought him another in a marginally different shade of blue.

"We were outmanoeuvred, Greatness," Moricen was saying. "Our ships—".

"Volun stole his, did he not?"

"Yes, Greatness."

"Well, who did he steal them from?"

Moricen said nothing.

"Do you have any good news for me, Moricen?"

"Not from the West, Your Greatness."

"Then come back when you can bring me some." He turned and smiled at his Commander. "We will have Games. There will be no whisper of Volun until he is whipped through the streets to die the death of all traitors. I will keep the people from panic, Moricen, you make sure they do not find themselves watching Volun sail up the river to Vordeith."

"Greatness ... "

Win or die, Moricen, don't trouble me with the details.

It took Moricen a moment to read the look in the Emperor's eye. He was not the brightest spark in the fire.

The Commander lowered his gaze and bowed in silent acceptance of his fate.

"Now," continued Zelt, comfortably. "Tell me what you make of my good friend Hiren's exploits in the barbaric north? I receive the most intriguing communications from my daughter."

"I hear reports of a successful campaign against the King of Qivor. Raiders will no longer be troubling the east coast of She-eye-os."

Zelt frowned slightly as Moricen tripped over the awkward and unfamiliar name.

"Oh, *Shehaios*!" he said. "Well, well. I hope Shehaios is grateful. What's the man's name?"

"King Rainur, Greatness," supplied one of his attendants.

"*Ry – i – n'oor*," he corrected his aide's excruciating pronunciation with relish. He was proud of his smattering of Shaihen. He liked words. They were like garments, a cultured man could clothe himself in their richness. *Rai – nur*. Bright Hope of the Morning. King Bright Hope of the Holy Land. Words. Wonderful words.

Zelt liked to think of himself as a cultured man. Of course, there had to be the Games. One could not expect the masses to appreciate fine ideas and after all … one had to be able to relax. But he wished to be remembered as the patron of priests and poets, his long reign as one under which Academia flourished. There were even Shaihen minstrels in his Palace, though fewer than there had been. Shaihen minstrels did not always seem to know when to be silent.

Zelt the Fair, Champion of the Free, Emperor of the Whole World. He frowned slightly. That was not quite right.

Zelt the Fair, Holy Emperor of the Free World.

As long as Volun did not sail up the river to Vordeith. It was a distinct possibility.

He had let the words seduce him. His most experienced field general was messing about protecting fishermen at the edges of the Empire while the defence of his throne hung in the balance off the coast west of Vordeith.

Moricen was not going to speak in defence of a rival. Not when he'd been proved right and Hiren wrong.

"You have an enemy to engage, Moricen," said Zelt, shortly.

Moricen knelt briefly in a sign of obeisance and left the chamber.

Zelt had already dismissed him from mind as he ripped the sleeve off the delicate garment.

"I said, blue!"

He sighed as his minions scurried to find him another robe.

"God defend the Sacred Union when my generals mistake my enemies, and my tailors mistake the colour of the sky. Send me the Brother-Master of the House of Tay-Aien. I feel a need to pray."

Somewhat against the odds, by the time Rainur's first wedding anniversary came round, Shehaios had mustered sufficient recruits for the Imperial army. They didn't quite meet the target, but they were close enough for the difference to be glossed over.

Kierce's alliance with Hiren went from strength to strength. It was in the Spring following Sartin's birth, shortly after the first Shaihen draft headed south for their first taste of Caiivorian military training, that Hiren took action against the raiders tormenting the people of Ccheven's coastal Holdings. He did not march east. He went south, into North Caiivor.

The raiders came mostly from a petty kingdom on the east coast of Caiivor. It was a place that paid its dues to Imperial rule, but Hiren knew perfectly well that the raiders were operating with the full backing of their king. His coffers were swelling with the proceeds, his court was graced with Shaihen slaves.

Hiren swept through the kingdom, cutting down everything in his way. He razed villages that opposed him, destroyed the spring planting, slaughtered the stock, spared none of the people for the transgressions of their King. The disloyal monarch was killed in his lair, and one of his rivals instated as Imperial governor with whatever title he chose to take.

Hiren returned to Shehaios, and informed Rainur that he could promise Colis a peaceful year.

In the Empire's northernmost kingdom, the Lord High Magician felt entitled to celebrate the peaceful year which followed. The Caiivorians who were there remained firmly entrenched, but few more came. Hiren's lesson was salutary. An attack on Shehaios was an attack on the Empire.

> *My land is laid waste and with it my heart*
> *Sacred the Union that broke us apart*
> *If my child stole wealth from the rich and the free*
> *Sing for the glory, the gods' victory*
> *Why is it his corpse looks so small in the grave?*
> *All hail to the glorious, the sacred, the brave*
> *Our memories lie buried in this tormented ground*
> *Your foes are all vanquished, your honour redounds*
> *When we starve it is only our ghosts who live on*
> *Sing loudly, oh victors, you are singing our song.*

The skill with which Brynnen sang it, Caras hardly noticed that the song was composed in two different languages.

He suspected the soldiers who heard it in the Haven noticed. He suspected, also, that they only heard the rousing praise for their valour. The rest was just a melodic jumble of archaic Shaihen words.

If they understood the rest, he was surprised Brynnen was still singing it.

He understood the message it brought him. This was not a song of *caii* raiders, but a song of *our people*, the ones on whom the punishment was inflicted. Grateful though he was for the relief Hiren brought his neighbour's east coast Holdings, he resolved to spend the year schooling himself and his people in the use of Jagus's weapon.

It occasioned another major argument between himself and a significant minority of his people, though by the very nature of it, it did not result in anyone drawing a sword on him. The division did not manifest itself entirely by gender – one of his most effective lieutenants was Madred, master of the Arhaien horse since Tuli left with the first draft of Imperial recruits – but there was no getting away from the fact that there were more men than women in the volunteer army that he set to training in the discipline of the fight. A number of Oreath's women accused him openly of being seduced by the image of the plumed Imperial troops who had arrived with such panache and remained such a powerful and dominant presence in the Haven.

Elani did not go that far, but he was conscious of her disapproval. His foray against Girstan had changed the relationship between them; she intimated strongly that she would not let him go as easily another time. They seemed to spend more time in bed arguing with each other than doing anything else, at the moment.

"Perhaps that's because you spend more time out organising the defences of Oreath than you do in Arhaios," suggested Elani.

"I do what I need to do."

"I thought it's what you fought Iareth about."

"It's what she fought me about. I won because I was physically stronger than her." He leaned over and kissed her in the hope that a little reminder of his physical presence would bring the argument to an end, at least for tonight.

Elani moved restlessly away from him.

"That doesn't make you right."

He sighed.

"No, of course it doesn't. I mean, I was right, but that's not why I won the fight. I wasn't even a better swordsman than her. That was her point. Forget justice, forget skill, if you go into a straightforward test of muscle, the strongest wins. That's not an argument against making yourself as strong as possible. After all, the only boy in the Holding who used to be able to beat me in a wrestling bout was half my size."

"You mean Kierce. That's not fair—."

"It is. He didn't beat me by not fighting. He fought smarter. He always knew precisely where to strike and he was always one move ahead of me. He always bloody is."

"It was a game. It was a competition. You weren't trying to kill each other. Shehaios wasn't born out of competition, I just don't see how it can be the way to defend it. It's precisely Jagus's argument – all that nonsense about channelling the Spirit of Life through a sword."

"Kierce let Jagus go. He asked him to raise an army. You and Leath have always told me not to argue with Kierce."

"Kierce is working with the alliance."

She didn't elaborate. All Oreath had heard the rumours about the amount of time the Magician spent in the Imperial camp. About the trysts Orlii brokered. And something about the Caiivorian Queen which Caras strove resolutely not to believe. Kierce had given him a solemn assurance.

"Elani, the alliance with the Sacred Union depends on one man. It's Rainur's diplomatic skill and his personal commitment to the Imperial Family that really holds it together. The independence of Shehaios cannot depend on one man. Why else did Kierce empower Jagus? Jagus understands the value of getting the Sacred Union to train our own people – without him, Hieath would never have hit the quota this Spring."

"Exactly," said Elani. "Kierce gave the job to Jagus. Not to you. Not to our Holders and craftsmen and healers and … and even minstrels, for Spirit's sake!"

"You think I'll be safer trusting my life to a man who's sworn to kill me, Elani? I'm trusting Shehaios to have a greater hold over Jagus than his thirst for vengeance. I'm trusting Kierce. I have every reason not to trust Jagus. If Rainur loses his game with the Emperor… It's a fight for all of us and I want our people to be able to enter that fight as well prepared for it as I can make them."

She did not look convinced.

"Elani, come on, what else can I do? What did you marry, a mouse or a lion?"

He made a more determined attempt to beguile her into less solemn intercourse.

Elani didn't so much repel him as freeze out his attentions.

"You use Kierce. You always have."

"What?" He propped himself on one elbow and looked down at her in astonishment. "I use Kierce?"

"Of course you do. Can't you imagine for one second what it's like to feel the fears and passions of everyone around you? He can't fool himself they want what makes him feel good."

"He fools them!"

"Individually, perhaps." She met his eyes with exasperation. "But of course, you don't need to know what everyone else's fears and passions are. You're always too full of answers to listen to the questions."

He turned away from her and flopped on his back by her side.

"I have to have answers. I'm Chief of Oreath."

"Then be content to be Chief of Oreath, and don't expect the world to look the same to those of us who aren't," retorted Elani.

He lay for a moment in disconsolate silence. To his surprise, and pleasure, Elani's hand touched his thigh gently.

"You are a clay clod, Caras. You really are."

He turned back towards her and took her in his arms.

"I'm frightened," said Elani. "I'm frightened I'm going to lose you, too."

"Rocks are damned hard to lose," growled Caras.

He had other things on his mind, or it might have occurred to him at the time to wonder who else she thought she had already lost.

Chapter 29
Allies

"To His Greatness Zelt an' Korsos, Twenty-Third Emperor of the Sacred Union

Greetings from your most dutiful and obedient daughter Cathva, Queen of Shehaios.

Tomorrow is the second anniversary of my marriage, and my happiness pales only in comparison to the overwhelming happiness of all your people for Your Greatness's glorious victory over the traitor, Volun.

I thank god for the invincible might of Your Greatness's warriors, and rejoice that the immortals show once more their eternal love for our Great Emperor. "

Cathva paused, gazing out of the open window while her inexpert scribe caught up. She would probably have to get the letter copied again in a fair hand before she sent it, but it didn't matter. Nor did it matter that the cost of the wasted parchment would probably have fed the boy for a week before he came to the Haven. Orlii was surprisingly quick to learn, but the lessons were not her prime reason for enjoying his company.

Cathva did not like ugliness around her – she was pleased the malodorous *caii* child had cleaned up so well. It was almost a shame that Kierce had gifted the tall, handsome youth to Davitis, though she could understand why he had done it.

The courtyard outside was a sea of delicate, early season colours. In the middle of it, Sartin pressed his small, chubby hands against the trunk of a slim fruit tree, laden with tight-curled buds of blossom. He was steadying himself against it as he dodged from side to side, giggling with delight. His movements were very small, little more than a shift of weight from one foot to the other – standing upright was still a novelty to him. The other side of the tree, the Lord High Magician darted back and forth, grabbing at the air as if he was trying with all his might to catch the child and failing spectacularly.

Cathva watched him with slightly patronising amusement. She was surprised Hiren ever took him seriously enough to listen to what he had to tell him – the fact that he did greatly increased her respect for a soldier she knew her father held in high regard.

According to Kierce, it was the winds alone that had saved His Greatness. The winds that fifteen years earlier had sealed Riskeld's fate shifted back into their usual pattern, forsook Volun's headlong rush for the Imperial City, and blew him unrelentingly north. By the time he could beat back to Vordeith, his chance was gone.

Offical news of the threat to Vordeith had been a lot longer reaching Shehaios than Kierce's sources. Evidence, if more were needed, of how serious it had been. And it was not necessarily over. Volun retreated; he was not defeated. He was in Aranth, plotting his next move.

"You are ever in my prayers, father, for without your protection, I fear for this pleasant land which has made your daughter so happy. The rejoicing at the victories of your good servant, Hiren an' Driezi—"

"My lady…"

Her scribe's voice was timorous and troubled.

"I speak too fast, Orlii," she said, pleasantly. "I'm sorry, you should stop me sooner."

"It's not that, my lady … the Commander's name, my lady?"

"an' Driezi. His family name."

"Yes, my lady, but … the symbols?"

"Of course. I'll show you."

She crossed the small, sunlit room and wrote Hiren's name on the parchment in front of Orlii.

She had barely noticed the scrawny barbarian boy who arrived with Kierce, but once she realised Kierce had a personal servant, it hadn't taken her long to recognise his value. She had learned much more about the Lord High Magician during these little writing tutorials than she had from Kierce's own lips.

Kierce just played the fool.

Since Rainur began to put various petty obstacles in the way of him visiting either Cathva or her son, Kierce had taken to changing places with various domestic animals to take him straight to Cathva's presence. She would walk into a room where a cat lay supine on a cushion – not a sight she particularly welcomed – and the next minute she would look round and Kierce would be there.

The first time he did it, she almost fainted from the shock. She had felt him touch her mind, she had seen him create illusions; she had not seen him physically move into the space of another creature.

But he didn't frighten her now. It wasn't long before she got so used to it she was in the habit of giving every animal she passed a long hard look, just in case.

Kierce could never resist embroidering a successful trick. As well as taking the place of the creature, he began to take on its form as well. He would be a dog walking by her side through the Haven. A bird outside her window. The cat, laid out on her bed.

It took her a while to realise what he was doing, and she was never quite sure she always saw him, though when she did recognise him she was always right. She found it highly amusing, especially when he did it while she was with Rainur. She couldn't help feeling delighted and flattered that he took such trouble to enjoy her company, even though she knew it was Sartin he really came to see.

Kierce might behave like a lovestruck adolescent, but the love was not for her.

She looked back out of the window. She had never seen a man who so artlessly adored his son. Most of the men she knew who cared a fig for their offspring had their sons' lives planned out for them before birth, but with Sartin, Kierce became a child. She watched him now, enjoying his reward in Sartin's smile, Sartin's joyous giggle, Sartin's bursting pride at watching Kierce fall over while he dodged and kept his feet under him, and thought how much other men's relationships with their children were fraught with their own hopes and ambitions.

And yet, Kierce's ambition for Sartin was greater than any other man's. He wanted Sartin raised as Rainur's son. He wanted him to be heir to the Shaihen throne, the embodiment of the joining of his people to the Empire of the Sacred Union.

She smiled as the great strategist made a theatrical dive and rolled on the grass with howls of frustration. Sartin stumped over to him on his unsteady legs and fell on his chest. Kierce caught him up, and lifted him to arm's length above him. She could hear Sartin's squeals of delight from where she stood.

Sartin was dutifully affectionate to the man he was learning to call his father, but his face never lit up for Rainur the way it did when he saw Kierce. Cathva could entirely understand why. Her own heart jumped a little, no matter what she said to it. The problem was, she didn't know whether what she saw in Kierce was his love for Sartin, or a reflection of Sartin's love for him. She still wasn't sure whether a creature so subject to the feelings of those around him had any feelings of his own. He had desires, but he had made no attempt to fulfil them, despite the fact that he could read in her mind how little there was to stop him.

She sighed a little. She must do what she could to ensure her father did not recall Hiren. Shehaios had enjoyed a year of peace, and Kierce had spent little time in the Haven. The year to come looked more ominous, and she suspected he would be spending a lot of time on the wing over Oreath, looking west across the sea to Aranth.

Caras recognised the name of the Emperor's enemy, and he knew the news that reached him of the battle at Vordeith was incomplete. He didn't know what was missing until the spring of Prince Sartin's second year, when a familiar pattern of raids began to hit Oreath's coastline.

The nature of Oreath's coastline, a mass of shoals and currents, offered some protection, but for two centuries the Imperial navy's command of the Western Ocean had been its main defence against the North Caiivorian exiles who had settled at the edge of the western continent. Volun's decimation of the Imperial fleet emboldened them to venture across the strip of ocean between them and Shehaios to attack Caras's west coast ports just as Qivor had attacked Ccheven in the east until Hiren put a stop to their raiding.

When the raiders came this time, they did not meet the peaceful, unprepared villagers their eastern counterparts had preyed upon. The Chief of Oreath had seen to it that Ccheven's bitter experience and that of his own mountain Holders was not wasted. Every settlement kept a watch night and day from the best available local vantage point. Every fisherman and villager kept their eye on the birds and the fish for any signs of approaching ships. A system of beacons alerted neighbouring Holdings to rally all available strength in the event of an attack, and when an attack came, Oreath fell on the raiders with all the strength the locality could muster.

With knowledge of the ground on which they fought, and an element of surprise in their favour, the people of Oreath were no longer hinds before the spears of their enemy. The minstrels became busy with songs of triumph.

Caras was once more the hero of his people, and whatever reservations Elani still felt she kept to herself. She smiled at him over the growing swell of his latest offspring, and told him Leath would have been proud of him. If she also asked him once too often what he thought Kierce's view of Oreath's militancy would be, it was an irritant he could dismiss. He knew Kierce's mind on this. It was virtually Kierce's idea.

Nevertheless, he felt the lack of Kierce's advice. He knew he struggled to see things that Kierce would have alerted him to in a second, usually with a joke. He heard far more news of the Empire now than he had ever heard, and he had the evidence of Shehaios's growing involvement with it.

Caras had not been to the Haven since Rainur's wedding. He had not bothered to attend the emasculated Holders' Council the previous autumn, and there had been no word of one since. Caras decided it was time Oreath consulted both the King and the Lord High Magician.

The first thing he saw as he approached the Haven from the west was the site of a major construction being erected on the hillside above the town, somewhere near where Turloch's cottage had stood. The enormous baulks of timber he could see, and the size of some of the counter-balances designed to lift them, were of an Imperial scale. Yet this was not being built in the Imperial camp which lay just south of the Haven. This was in the Haven itself, a structure that would dominate it once completed.

Caras turned aside to take a closer look. As he approached the site, he saw a tall young man and an older one in animated discussion, gesticulating towards the space where the building would be. The young man he recognised with a shock as Orlii. Which lessened his shock a little when he discovered that the man overseeing the whole organised chaos of mud and timber around him was Kierce.

It was, he gathered, Rainur's idea to build what was becoming known as the Magician's Tower, but he could see that it had fired Kierce's imagination. Caras had some difficulty interpreting the drawing Kierce showed him, but if he read it correctly, the final design for the edifice teetered on a knife-edge between the sublime and the ridiculous.

"If it's going to be done," said Kierce, cheerfully. "It's going to be done gloriously."

"I'm sure it will be." It was not lost on Caras that Kierce had recorded his vision on parchment, and that there were a number of Imperial Army engineers among the construction team. "But I don't understand why you need a ... well, it's a Palace really, isn't it? Turloch seemed content to live in Rainur's."

Kierce smiled.

"These days, Shehaios has an audience. We have to make our presence visible. Rainur tells me I have to make my presence visible. Well," he glanced back at the building site, "it won't come much more visible than that." He put his arm around Caras's shoulder. "I will be asked to cure boils. I can see it coming."

Caras laughed, relieved to find the familiar Kierce still present.

"It's good to see you, Caras. I was beginning to wonder if you were still speaking to me after our slight difference of opinion over whether Jagus deserved an army or an execution."

"I understand why you did that."

Kierce gave him a quizzical look.

"So you do," he commented in surprise. He shook his head. "You go all the way along the river valley, but you get to the spring in the mountains in the end, don't you Caras?" He paused. "I'm glad to see you're in one piece this time."

"I'm learning," acknowledged Caras, shortly. "The trouble with going all the way along the river valley is that you can find you've walked straight into a bog."

"I should find time to come back to Arhaios," said Kierce. "It's possible to forget that the Haven is not Shehaios."

"We may need you back there sooner than you think."

"The threat has shifted westwards," agreed Kierce. "How much have you worked out?"

"Not enough. Tell me about Volun. Is he the monster Iareth fears? Does it matter to us? His fight is with the Empire."

"But he knows that Shehaios exists," finished Kierce. "And he may well make use of that knowledge. It's not me you need to talk to, Caras. It's Hiren."

Caras paused reflectively. The rumoured friendship between the Magician and the general of the Imperial army worried him almost as much as the other rumours.

"Talk to one Imperial Commander about another?" he queried cautiously.

"And don't say that to him," said Kierce in amusement. "Volun is not an Imperial Commander. He's a traitor to Hiren's army and to Hiren's Empire. Hiren detests him possibly as much as Iareth detests him. They were colleagues, comrades in arms. Hiren feels violated too."

"But will he do anything?" asked Caras, with memories of Unit Commander Scaiien.

"Oh, Hiren will do something," promised Kierce. "Your arrival is timely, Caras. I was wondering how I was going to persuade you to let the Imperial Army take up residence at Arhaios."

There were changes at the Royal Palace, too. The formal Imperial guard was no longer in evidence. Caiivorian soldiers mingled among the comings and goings of the Palace, usually unarmed. Caras saw Shaihen girls with tall Caiivorian escorts, mixed groups huddled over a twelve-stones grid in the Meeting House. Most emphatically, he saw the difference when he was invited to meet Commander Hiren at Rainur's table on the evening of his arrival at the Haven.

Caras regularly entertained people from his Holding in his own dining hall. The meals Elani presided over were loud and generally cheerful occasions, well lubricated with ale and little moderated by the mixture of sexes and status around the table.

It was a tradition of Shaihen society that the woman of the household presided over the meal, but Elani was rarely the only one of her sex present at Arhaien gatherings. When Cathva greeted him that evening, just as beautiful and delicate as he remembered her, it did not take him long to realise that she was the only woman among them. Moreover, the rest were all men who held positions of power within Shehaios, unlike his own guests who were as likely to include the potter's apprentice as the principal Holders of the region.

As well as Hiren, Davitis the Imperial Envoy was present and Gascon of Mervecc, apparently a frequent visitor to the Haven. Kierce, Rainur and Caras himself made up the party. Orlii was also there, but he did not eat with them. He exchanged a few words with the guests as he moved around filling glasses with Imperial wine, fetching and carrying the various dishes. He looked relaxed and happy, as he had discussing the Magician's tower with its builders, but his presence still made Caras uneasy. Leath had warned Kierce he could not afford to own a slave. Orlii was no longer the terrified child they had taken from Prassan, but whether or not he was a free man, Caras couldn't tell.

He was supposed to be taking the opportunity to talk to Hiren, but Hiren was deep in discussion with Gascon and Rainur, and Caras was left with Davitis. He was half-listening to what Davitis was saying, but he was watching Kierce.

Kierce was talking to Cathva. There was nothing distant or formal about the body language of either of them. Caras was conscious that Rainur also was only half attending to the conversation around him. He could almost touch the hostility between King and Magician.

It gradually began to get through to him that Davitis, following his gaze, was talking about Kierce and Cathva as well. Davitis was very anxious that Caras should know every last word of gossip that was circulating the Haven and the Imperial Camp concerning the Magician and the Queen. He seemed to be saying something about Kierce's ability to cast spells, and having suffered such an assault himself. Caras couldn't make a lot of sense out of it, but he could see for himself how Cathva's wonderful blue eyes fixed on Kierce when he spoke. He could see the way Kierce smiled at her, the little exchanges of touch and gesture.

It was not something he had expected. It came as a slight shock to see Kierce asserting his position as quite so overtly – Caras tended to assume that Turloch's retiring habits were the seemly way for the Lord High Magician to behave – and he had trusted Kierce's word. He had never suspected that Rainur was reluctant to call the Holders' Council not so much because the plain speaking traditional to the gathering might lead to a confrontation with Ered of Hieath but because it might lead him to a confrontation with the Lord High Magician.

With matters as they were in Shehaios, what Kierce was doing was utter madness, and Caras lost no time after the gathering dispersed in telling him so.

"I can't stop what hasn't started," replied Kierce, calmly. "There is nothing going on between me and Cathva, Caras."

"Do you think I'm blind as well as stupid?" retorted Caras.

"I think you're seeing things that don't exist. It's much more appropriate for the Lord High Magician to be on friendly terms with the Queen than for her to be terrified by the sight of him, Caras."

"I thought you read minds. I can read Rainur's!"

"Not surprising. He thinks the way you do on this." Kierce looked at him. "Do I need to mention Elani?"

"You may regret it," said Caras ominously.

"I merely meant as evidence of my facility for virtue. You know I will always be deeply in love with Elani, but I would never come between the two of you."

"I've never known you to be deeply in love with anyone but yourself," returned Caras. "Elani wouldn't have you. She's too much sense. I'm not sure Cathva has."

"I was talking to Cathva about her son," said Kierce, patiently. "She had a difficult time with him, and we gave birth to him together. I have a bond with Sartin that Rainur can't have. He resents it. Rainur is jealous of my relationship with his son, Caras, not with his wife." He smiled at Caras. "As I said, he thinks like you in these matters. Two possessive men dedicated to a selfless ideal. It makes you both great Shaihen leaders. It makes you a pain in the ass to live with sometimes."

"You have the nerve to accuse Rainur of being difficult to live with!" exclaimed Caras.

"Oh, I'm just an idle, selfish bastard. You know that. You were supposed to be discussing the defences of Oreath with Hiren at that dinner, not guarding my morals. Did you do what you came here to do?"

Caras had barely exchanged a greeting with Commander Hiren. Kierce knew that without asking.

"No," he admitted curtly. He couldn't play games of bluff against Kierce. He had never been able to. He could never tell when he was lying and when he was joking.

"Then do it now. Volun is the threat to Shehaios. He knows there's a route to the Imperial City down through the Gate. For the Spirit's sake, talk to Hiren!"

Rainur was prowling restlessly around the garden where Kierce played with Sartin at the end of what he had found to be a trying day. His head was full of Hiren's arrangements for extending the Imperial Army's occupation of Shehaios. Kierce strolled beside him, the King's disquiet breaking against his mind like storm-whipped surf dispersing across a beach.

"A garrison at the Haven, and watch-towers along the southern border," said Rainur. "That was all it was supposed to be."

"You can hardly deny them Ccheven," said Kierce, mildly. "Given what Hiren's already done to protect them. All our borders need defending."

"But Oreath? Arhaios?"

"Oreath has a coastline as well."

He measured Rainur's strides idly, overwhelmingly reminded of Caras. Same restless pacing. Same torn loyalties. Same conflict between dream and reality. Rainur dreamed of the harmony and beauty of Shehaios. He had fallen in love with the grandeur and comfort of Vordeith.

"I'm astonished that Caras has agreed to it." He turned and looked speculatively at Kierce. "Well, no. Perhaps I'm not."

Kierce shrugged.

"Not my doing. Caras worked it out for himself." He smiled. "He does that. I always enjoy watching him."

Rainur scowled. Kierce could see he was thinking less of the Magician's influence with Caras than of the scurrilous authority Kierce exercised in the Imperial camp. It appeared to Rainur that Kierce spent most of his time gambling, or brokering correspondence between Shaihen women and Imperial soldiers. It was not entirely true. It was not entirely untrue, either, though Orlii did most of the message-carrying.

"They're honest with me," said Kierce, quietly. "They trust me. I play a straight game and I keep my word."

When have you ever done either?

"I sometimes wonder who's side you're on."

"That's your mistake, Rainur. You're still thinking in terms of sides." He paused. "You conceived this child. You have to nurture it."

220

"And that's another thing," muttered Rainur.

Kierce wasn't sure, in fact, that Rainur had conceived the Imperial alliance. His heart did not seem to be in this great work of his reign, but if he was building someone else's dream he was unaware of it.

"You left the matter of Sartin to the Queen," said Kierce. "I have never seen him without her permission."

"I should never have left you the liberty," retorted Rainur. "I should have known you'd abuse it."

"Abuse it?"

"You expect me to believe Cathva willingly allows you into her quarters? Allows you free access to her son?" Rainur glowered at him. "You manipulate thoughts, Kierce. I know you do."

Kierce smiled.

"And Turloch didn't?"

He met Rainur's outraged glare with equanimity.

"Turloch didn't." said Rainur, icily.

"You didn't see Turloch doing it." Kierce paused. "Think about it, Rainur. How often did you argue with Turloch?"

"I never had occasion to argue with Turloch."

Kierce shrugged.

"Doesn't that tell you something?"

"It tells me you don't share the same vision of Shehaios," said Rainur, bluntly. "That's why I didn't argue with Turloch. We were going in the same direction. Working for the same thing."

"I just want to do what pleases me, Rainur, I don't want to make everyone's choices for them. It pleases me to enjoy the company of your son, and, for that matter, the company of your wife."

"She was terrified of you."

"A small misunderstanding."

"You're easily misunderstood!"

In fact, I can't believe a word you say.

"If I'd wanted to challenge you, I'd have done it with Oreath's sword, not Hiren's," said Kierce, quietly. "If I'd been interested in power, I could have had Caras. He would never have noticed. He'd have grown up doing exactly what I wanted him to do. Well," he checked, growing tired of the continual need to defend himself, "I suppose he did, in a way. I wanted him to be Caras. I let you take the sword away from him, I'm happy for you to be Rainur." He smiled. "Do me the courtesy of allowing me to be Kierce. Not Turloch."

Chapter 30
Riskeld

The sight of a small fleet of Imperial ships off the coast of Riskeld brought back uncomfortable memories to its inhabitants.

Iareth watched them from the heart of her Holding, a low hill rising amid a wilderness of river and marsh. As so many West Coast Holdings were, Riskeld was an island the world around it constantly threatened to overwhelm.

The ships changed course slightly, heading for the navigable channel along the main river estuary. It was a clear demonstration not only that they were heading for Riskeld, but that they did so with local knowledge. They had been sent with Oreath's blessing.

Iareth knew the threat Shehaios faced across the Western Ocean. The minstrels still came to Riskeld. She knew perfectly well that the Western tribes brought a danger to Oreath that swept aside her differences with her chieftain. She knew Caras's preparations for fighting the invaders, she knew he intended to do it with the support of the Imperial Army. She suspected it was not strictly necessary for Imperial troops to land in Riskeld, but she was not surprised that Caras had taken advantage of the situation to regain the authority and assuage the pride he had lost in the fight at Arhaios.

Iareth thought back to the last time she had stood on the hill watching ships of the Imperial navy approaching the harbour at Riskeld. She remembered the young girl laughing with her friend in excited anticipation of handsome Imperial soldiers, ornaments and gold pieces, gifts for a pretty girl from far off lands. That laughing girl seemed to belong to another self, another lifetime. A dream of a world that had never been.

She turned to make her way down to the harbour. Her people were rallying in alarm at the sight which approached their shores, uncertain whether or not to take up arms against the unwelcome visitors. But Caras, she conceded, had won the fight. They stood together or they died one by one, until the dream of the world that had never been died with them, a song with no voice left to sing it.

The Imperial ships dropped anchor in the harbour. Their boats were lowered and their men disembarked into them under the watchful eyes of most of Riskeld's population, silent, resentful, but resigned to their Holder's judgement. Iareth could see in the foremost boat the figure in a scarlet cloak that marked his status as Imperial commander. She shuddered slightly at the sight. He had his back to the shore so she couldn't see his face, but he was the same build as the hated Volun, tall and spare. She recalled the muscles like knotted ropes that held her like a plaything. She cut the memory off abruptly. She could not afford to dwell on that.

The boat grounded on the beach, and Iareth walked down across the wet sand to greet her visitors as the Imperial Commander swung himself out of the boat and into the surf. He turned and splashed ashore through the lapping waters, his men following him closely.

Iareth stopped dead. The blood drained from her face.

The man in the Imperial Commander's cloak paused on the shoreline above the gently breaking surf, and smiled at the small woman in front of him. He was over fifty now, his dark hair grey at the temples and thin on top. The hollows of his gaunt face were deeper, but the outline of his features and the cruel dark eyes were an image etched for ever in Iareth's memory.

"Lady Iareth, I believe," said Volun. "I'm so glad you've come to welcome me back."

Iareth did not say a word. She snatched out the knife at her side and hurled herself at the King of the West.

Three of his men stepped in front of him, weapons drawn, blocking her attack. Three blades stabbed into her without hesitation. She slumped against one of the soldiers; he thrust her aside and she fell lifeless onto the shore, her blood seeping into the water which swirled at Volun's heels.

Chapter 31
Storms from the West

Kierce's attention was focussed further west than Riskeld, on the activity across the sea among the marshes of Aranth. The prospect of an attack on his own people preoccupied him to such an extent he didn't see it when it happened.

The size of the threat confronting them daunted him, and he found himself looking more and more to the sound practical advice of the Imperial Commander in Chief. Whatever Hiren needed, Kierce felt Shehaios was – for the time being – obliged to provide. The rapidly growing extent of the Imperial influence that so concerned Rainur he put to one side. He'd deal with that later.

The Imperial Army arrived at Arhaios in mid-summer, and by the spring of the following year the forest had felt the impact of their presence.

The smell of the new wooden building reminded Caras forcibly of the frontier watchtower below Nassun as Hiren unrolled the map of Oreath's coastline in front of him, but Hiren was not Scaiien. Caras had to confess himself impressed by Hiren, even if, like his people, he had been less than impressed by the presence of the Imperial Army.

There had been some difficult incidents to test Caras's authority over the past months, and he had reason to be grateful for the way Hiren had dealt with some of them. Kierce's presence for much of the time had actually made matters worse. He – or at least, Orlii – had been too closely involved in some of the incidents, and there were too many people in Arhaios who had known Kierce before he acquired the title. Caras found himself having to ask Kierce to send Orlii back to the Haven, not a conversation either of them had enjoyed having.

In some ways, it would be a relief if the ships Kierce had seen massing in the marshy, inhospitable lowlands across the western sea were the invasion fleet they feared. It would distract them all from their differences and focus attention on the mutual enemy.

Even as the thought crossed his mind, Caras was appalled to catch himself wishing an attack on his people. He frowned in concentration at Hiren's map.

At least he understood what he was looking at this time, though he still had difficulty relating his knowledge of his land to the lines on the paper. They didn't seem nearly enough for the purpose. They told so little of the story.

They weren't right, either. Kierce had seen that coastline with a bird's eye, he had been less than complimentary about the accuracy of Hiren's map. Nevertheless, he was looking at it keenly now, his hand hovering over the broken outline of Aranth.

"Your sailors don't actually try and use this thing to go anywhere, do they?" he asked, a little irritably. "It's almost worse than useless."

"Who needs to know the coastline of Aranth?" said Hiren. "Apart from the pirates who live there?"

"I doubt they need pictures drawn for them," said Kierce.

"I doubt it too. That's been our problem. Where do you think they are?"

"Well, as I said. It's hard to show you on this." He indicated an area below a bulge of land sticking out into the sea. "There's actually a passable harbour there, though I suspect the approach is pretty shallow. That's where they were gathering." His finger tracked north east across the empty space marked simply "Western Ocean". "And this is the direction they're heading in."

"If that's true, it doesn't leave much doubt."

"None at all. It's Oreath they're heading for this time."

Caras glanced at the doubtful cast to Hiren's damaged face. He found the Commander's relationship with Kierce a source of some fascination. It was quite evident that Hiren had no idea how Kierce came by some of his information, and if Caras had told him Kierce saw it through the eyes of a seabird wheeling over the heads of their enemies, he would not have believed him.

"Where in Oreath? Where do you put your money, Lord Caras?"

Caras studied the soulless representation of his ancestors' lands. Very few of his Holdings were marked on it.

He found the one that was. The one that would be marked on any mariner's map.

It lay behind a long spit of sand built up over the years by the sea, pushing its river mouth steadily further north. Toshan was effectively some distance inland now, on a small hummock amid the flat, wet wastes of its meandering river.

The river flowed from the heart of Oreath. Once past Toshan, an enemy with boats designed for shallow waters could be at his door.

"How navigable is that river?"

"It's Toshan's lifeblood," said Caras. "They keep the lower stretches navigable. The people of my west coast all have to work to keep their land prosperous, Commander."

"The Aranthans have been raiding the Holdings," added Kierce. "They know their strengths and their weaknesses."

"They know they're not undefended," said Caras.

"Defended against raiders. None of our Holdings can muster enough strength to withstand the kind of numbers heading our way across that sea." Kierce looked at Hiren. "We need to get it right, Hiren. We won't get a second chance."

"Then we must stop them where they land," said Hiren. "And we must force them to land where we want them. Tell me about Toshan's defences, Lord Caras."

Caras turned back to the plan, slightly gratified by Hiren's unquestioning assumption that he had anticipated the dangers.

Caras heard something about fighting at Riskeld, but Riskeld was outside the Oreathan defence network and details were hard to come by. When some of Riskeld's neighbours rode to find out how they fared, the people of Riskeld would not let them past their borders. They said they needed no assistance, and Caras did not pursue the matter. His attention was preoccupied elsewhere.

Kierce saw the little cluster of Imperial ships, but he thought nothing of them. The Empire's forces were still present in Aranth, waging their interminable fight against the Western Tribes, and Imperial ships still risked the pirates, carrying men and supplies. He was looking for the vessels of the Aranthan pirates, small, light, shallow-draughted craft quite unlike the ponderous troop carriers of the Empire's navy.

The ones that were heading inexorably for Toshan.

The Chief of Oreath and the Lord High Magician watched from the dunes that ranged the coast north and east of Toshan as the enemy ships dropped sail at the mouth of the estuary.

The invading force began the long row upstream to the settlement, a tricky approach that could not be negotiated by a square-sailed ship. Vessel after vessel, each crammed with warriors, was driven apace across the water by ranks of powerful oarsmen.

Kierce wondered whether they would row right around the curve of the land below Toshan before they realised that the river no longer ran inland from that mouth. Toshan had cut the flow of their lifeblood at the start of the sandspit, sending the river tumbling over it into the sea two miles down the coast from where the Aranthan ships had entered it.

The dam wouldn't last more than one high tide. They had to take this force while it waited for the way ahead to clear.

He did not need to look to know the fear in Caras's mind as they watched in silence. It was in his own. This was the nightmare come true. The force that faced them was mighty, even mightier than it had looked from a distance.

"How many warriors on each ship?" asked Caras.

"Upwards of two hundred. This lot … the way they're crammed to the gunwhales, more like three."

"I've counted thirty-nine ships," said Caras. "This isn't a fleet that suffered a defeat by the Imperial navy a year ago."

"Of course it isn't. It's a fleet that won a significant victory over the Imperial navy a year ago. If the winds had stayed in Volun's favour, he'd have been in Vordeith now. Zelt got out of that by the skin of his teeth."

"So why haven't they gone back to Vordeith?"

"I doubt you'd catch Zelt an' Korsos with the same trick twice. No father of the Lady Cathva is going to be a fool."

He saw Caras considering the connection.

"You made a promise about Cathva."

"I did indeed." Kierce glanced at him. "You want Hiren here though, don't you?"

"I don't know that I want to be here at all," replied Caras.

Kierce's misgivings redoubled. Caras's nerves were affecting him; the rock so seldom showed any. He relied on Caras to be his simple, unchanging anchor point, but he knew there was nothing very simple about the passions that surged beneath Caras's even-tempered exterior. His civilised ability to control them was deceptive; it was not rational good-sense that had brought him to Toshan. It was a burning desire to defend his land. Light the tinder, and that fire could burn just as fierce as anything Jagus ignited.

Their plans and preparations, that had seemed so sound when they drew them up with Hiren, seemed to Kierce suddenly full of holes. Beyond the mound of rising land behind them on which Toshan stood, the land was an impassable expanse of river and marsh. On top of it, the only trackway out of Toshan followed its solidity north-east; the road was stopped now by a deep trench running across the hillside. The earth excavated from it reared in a second barrier, designed to force the invading forces north along the coast, where the full might of Hiren's army waited to fall on them. But Volun was a former Imperial general. Once he saw that ditch, he would know someone was lying in wait for him. It was up to Caras to convince him that it was Oreath alone who came to confront him, before he looked hard enough to discern the real enemy he had to deal with. Like a forest of strange and deadly trees, the great stone-hurling engines and catapults of the Imperial artillery stood ready to cut down the invaders, but unless the Aranthans could be enticed below their fire, they were useless.

Kierce knew how industriously Caras had been studying his new role of warlord, but he doubted how well his recently acquired skills would compare to Hiren's unsentimental competence. The Oreathans were still ordinary Shaihens, taken from their farms and crafts and trades to spend a few months learning the art of warfare from the Imperial army. The drumbeats and shouts marking the oarsmen's rhythm across the water seemed to speak of a power and savagery the Magician's own people could barely imagine and he could only wonder how their courage would hold under such an onslaught.

Kierce couldn't help turning over in his mind Cathva's insistence, often repeated, that he failed to realise the power he held. It was the guiding principal of Shaihen magic, known to every child born in the Fair Land, that the Magician's strength was to heal, not to destroy, and he knew why. He had spent some of his time in the Haven delving into the matter, horrifying himself with the forces of destruction that lay awaiting a magician sufficiently evil to conjure them.

Or sufficiently desperate.

If the armies amassed here were not forces of destruction, he didn't know what else to call them. He had warned them of the threat. Turloch had engineered the presence of the Imperial army. The use of the magician's strength was entirely at the magician's discretion.

He turned as Hiren came up quietly behind them, keeping out of sight of the approaching fleet. He surveyed the scene with a grim satisfaction, as if he could already see himself returning to the Imperial City with the crowning victory of his career under his belt.

"Keep control of your men – and your bloody women – Caras, and we'll take the bastards. They're rowing right into our hands."

"There's a lot of them," said Caras.

"Not so many," said Hiren. "The rowers are slaves. They don't fight. The ones who do fight are slash and thieve barbarians, whatever Volun likes to call them. Lure them out, make them think they've only got your rabble of barbarians to deal with and they won't know what's hit them."

Kierce wished he could share Hiren's confidence. He found it vaguely worrying that he could not distinguish Volun among the approaching hordes.

"We could do it another way."

"Not the time to change tactics now, Kierce," said Hiren brusquely. "Besides, I see no reason for it. As I said, they're rowing right into our hands."

"I wasn't exactly thinking of a change of tactics," admitted Kierce. "More of the fact that I am the Lord High Magician."

Caras turned a look of astonishment on him, but Hiren spoke before the Shaihen could find words to express his horror.

"You keep your bloody trickery to yourself, wizard. This day belongs to the Empire." He glanced at the man he should, technically, regard as his superior. In line with the terms of the alliance, Caras was overall commander of the joint force gathered at Toshan. In practice, neither Hiren nor Caras behaved as if that were the case.

Caras made no comment. Kierce could see he was still slightly stunned that the Magician could take such a cavalier attitude to the guiding principles of Shaihen magic. Though since Kierce had never followed an abstract principle in his life, he didn't know why it came as such a shock to Caras now. The code of survival was his morality. Always had been.

"Knew we should have left you in the Haven," muttered Hiren. "You stay here and pray to your Spirit, Kierce. The gods of war ride on my spear. Draw up your horsemen and sing your songs, Lord Caras. Let them think they've got it easy."

Hiren received the signal that Caras's forces were in place and wondered whether, out of courtesy, he should tell Kierce. Hiren had to concede that everything Kierce had told him had been borne out by facts, but he didn't trust the Magician's sources of information when he had other, more reliable ones, available. The gods gave the victory, but in Hiren's experience the gods favoured a good general and Hiren's gods were in the ascendant today. Shehaios had little knowledge of the realities of war.

He strolled towards Kierce, who was standing on the hillside a little apart from the Imperial army command post. He was gazing in the direction of Toshan, but he wouldn't have been able to see anything from where he was.

"Lord Caras is in position," said the Commander.

Kierce smiled.

"When you have known Lord Caras as long as I have, Hiren, you would never doubt he was where you expect him to be. I wish I was as confident about Volun's whereabouts."

"He's in Toshan," said Hiren. He paused. He had seldom seen Kierce look less sure of himself. "Lord Caras is a personal friend of yours, I believe?"

"More than that," said Kierce. "My better half, you could say—".

He broke off abruptly, whipping round like an animal suddenly scenting danger. His eyes gazed unseeingly past Hiren's shoulder into the middle distance.

Hiren studied him, intrigued. He was not a fanciful man, but there was something about Kierce's sudden and absolute stillness that brought a chill touch to his flesh. The small man who watched so intently with senses other than eyesight did not seem the same creature as the one who clowned around in the Imperial camp.

Hiren shrugged off his imaginings and turned back towards his command post.

"Come on, wizard," he said. "Down here where we can keep an eye on you."

He heard a small rush of air behind him and looked round. Kierce had gone.

I'll be back! Hiren heard.

"For god's sake, Kierce!"

There was no-one there to hear him.

Hiren swung round to his nearest aides. There were poor odds on him bringing the Chief of Oreath back with him from this day's work. Losing the Lord High Magician as well was an act of political ineptness Hiren could not afford.

"Get after him," he rasped. "Half a dozen men and your fastest horses. Guard the silly bugger with your lives."

"Yes sir." The aide turned smartly to obey but then hesitated. "Where did he go, sir?"

Hiren cast about him. It was a matter of seconds ago that Kierce had been standing on the hill beside him, but now there was no sign of him. Hiren cursed comprehensively under his breath.

"Order rescinded," he acknowledged, sourly. "I knew we should have left him in the Haven. If you see him, tell me. Otherwise, may his own bloody Spirit protect him."

Kierce and Red Sky came to a halt several miles inland from Toshan, both breathing hard from the exertion. Red Sky was standing fetlock deep in brackish water, and shifting uneasily to keep his feet from sinking further. A breast high forest of reeds surrounded them on all sides.

Less than half a mile away, a mud and log causeway raised a road a modest height above the fen. On the causeway were two thousand Imperial soldiers, marching towards Toshan.

Kierce watched for some moments at a loss. He couldn't make sense of what he saw. They wore the helmets and armour of Hiren's men, they carried the shields and swords Hiren's men carried. But there was something different about them that he couldn't quite pin down, and he knew for a fact that they were not Hiren's men.

The danger inherent in their presence impressed itself on him without the need to understand it precisely. He reached for the polished redwood hilt hung from his belt, and drew the shaft of intricately carved wood, inlaid with subtle shades from a multitude of different trees. Both the cloak and the staff of the Magician took on whatever shape the current incumbent of the office found most convenient, and worn like this the staff was much easier to carry on horseback.

He grasped it firmly and gazed intently at the Imperial troops. He had no idea if he could communicate across this distance to a Caiivorian mind, let alone one as prosaic as Hiren's, but Hiren was the man who could make sense of this. Even as he concentrated on the message, it began to make sense to him, too.

Hiren was preparing to move his men forward when an image suddenly came into his head of a band of marching soldiers. He paused, checking his preparations, thinking he must have forgotten something, before he properly recognised the irrelevance of the picture in his mind. He shook his head in annoyance. He could do without being distracted by tricks of his own imagination. He began to wonder if perhaps it was time to retire.

The image refused to go away. He knew it was not real, and yet it seemed to have an existence more solid than a figment of his imagination. The soldiers had the untouchable almost-reality of the unicorn that had welcomed him to King Rainur's hall.

The thought gave him pause. Kierce was not there, and Hiren had no idea why he should create such an image at such a time even if he was, but still … there was a but.

Hiren narrowed his eyes to look more closely at that which wasn't there. He saw the causeway, and the surrounding fen, the mass of men approaching, marching to an Imperial army step but not in Imperial army order.

He closed down the image abruptly, pulling out the map Kierce had drawn them of the area surrounding Toshan. He saw the causeway almost immediately. He knew it. They had crossed it themselves on the way there.

There wasn't time to dither. He needed to be moving the army forward to be in position to support Caras. He let the map roll itself and swiftly returned it to its protective scrip as he turned to summon one of his aides. He relayed a message to one of his cavalry commanders to take a unit of mounted men and scout the road inland, adding a caveat to take care on the treacherously soft ground. If he lost a cavalry troop in the bog on this fool's errand, he really would have to retire.

The aide disappeared with the obedience an Imperial commander would expect of his staff. Hiren was very glad there was no-one there who required him to justify that order. He was almost entirely convinced he had just depleted his battle strength by one unit of horse for no reason at all.

Chapter 32
Toshan

The wind was blowing steadily off the sea as Caras waited, his cavalry massed behind him. He screwed up his eyes against the grains of sand it carried and the bright, pale light of a sun with a thousand reflections. This place was all water; water and a land so flat and treacherous it was hardly land at all. In front of him stretched an expanse of packed sand, bound together by grass tough enough to cut unprotected skin. Heavy going, for a horse at full gallop. He must not let them break too soon.

The horse shifted restlessly under him, aware of the tension in its rider.

This was the first time any of these people, any of these horses, had been tested in battle like this. They had practised manoeuvres, learned techniques, played at it. He didn't know if any of that would be any use now. He could still feel the overwhelming helplessness of Nassun, the heaving mass of Caiivorians around him, his sword pulling him down into a sea of mud…

He couldn't see Toshan from here, the shoulder of the hill below which it nestled hid it from him. He strained his eyes towards the outline of the rise, waiting for the first signs of the men whose boats he had seen skimming so powerfully towards the little port. Were they coming? Did he want them to?

He became aware that Madred's horse, standing beside him, was as still as a rock. He steadied his own mount and took a hold of himself. No point losing the battle before he'd drawn a sword in anger. They'd done everything they could. They didn't need to win anything, they just needed to draw the invaders out of Toshan towards Hiren.

Waiting was always difficult. Especially when they were waiting for the enemy to see how easily they could be defeated. They were over a thousand horsemen. Volun's ships carried six times their number.

"The ashes of our ancestors nurture the soil of this land. We are the people of Shehaios, the Whole Land. We are the people of the Spirit, the children of life, but to live through this day we ride into the face of death."

His own words. Spoken to the people who waited at his back, looking death in the face.

"Our enemies come to desecrate and destroy this land; they carry death on their swords. Go with courage, go with a song of victory, for today death is life. As long as one of our people still wields a sword, the enemy shall not hold one inch of this land!"

He saw them. Spilling down the side of the hill where the trench Hiren's men had dug stopped their progress inland. As they saw the brave line of the Shaihen defence, they swung towards him, a ragged black mass like a swarm of bees.

He could hear them now. The nearest of them broke into a run, long spears lowered. They were not warriors of the Sacred Union; they came in a loose mob of yelling fury. Hiren said it made them vulnerable.

They didn't look very vulnerable.

The sands were black with them, and still they came, pouring over the low rise that hid Toshan from his sight. The light soil hung in a growing cloud over them, dimming the brilliant light into a sickly yellow.

He drew his sword and raised it above his head. Not too soon. The horses should be going full tilt when they hit, they needed to have plenty of wind left.

Hold, Oreath.

He could feel them behind him, straining to break, not just stand here in the path of that deadly mass of shrieking bloodlust. So many of them. So very many of them.

He let the sword drop.

"She-haios!" he cried and sent the horse forwards.

With the echoing roar of *The Holy Land* on their lips, his people followed.

The impact of their charge took a swathe out of their foe, but the line of his enemy tightened in front of him as he rode through them, and the coherence of his own troops disintegrated. Within moments, his horsemen were either impaled on enemy spears or surrounded by them, each man engulfed in the overwhelming odds, fighting for his own life.

Having led the charge, Caras was in the thick of it for longer than he could afford to be. He wielded his weapon as hard and as fast as he could, desperately watching for threats that came from all sides. He noticed the blows that caught him no more than he felt the revulsion leisure would have allowed him at the feel of his blade biting into human flesh and human bone.

He fought with the experience of Nassun at the back of his mind. Beyond the instinctive immediacy of his own defence, he struggled to keep focus on the tactics of the battle. *In and out*, Hiren said. *It's a feint, not an attack. Just fight long enough to convince them.*

He didn't add, *otherwise they'll slaughter you.* How long was long enough? As he struggled desperately to keep his head above the drowning wave of mayhem around him, Caras wondered if he should have taken Hiren's full advice, and stayed back from the charge. Kept a distance.

Caras spared a brief glance at Madred. She was fighting furiously by his side, her sword working and her horse twisting and dancing like an extension to her armoured body. It was her role to look after him, but Caras wasn't sure when it came down to it which of them was the more anxious to protect the other. He wasn't sure he could face Madred's half-brother if he returned from the battle without the Magician's favourite sister.

He launched himself at an enemy about to ram a spear through the chest of Madred's horse. The man saw him coming and swung the weapon round towards him; Caras wrenched his horse aside and slid alongside the spear, his sword falling with all his weight on the man's unprotected head. It split through hair and bone in a foul gout of blood and brains.

He barely saw it. He was too busy making sure he yanked the sword out and swung to face the next enemy. Madred had got separated from him; the fray had swept her back towards the dunes. He remembered seeing blood on the shoulder of her grey horse.

Nothing he could do about that. How much longer now? How many had he lost? Were they still going forwards?

Madred shouted something, a wild sort of grin on her face. He couldn't hear what she said.

Too late, he saw a man rear up from the ground beneath him and lunge for the belly of his horse. He felt the animal stagger beneath him. The world lurched as it went down on its knees.

The horse sank down and he half leaped and half fell clear of it as it rolled kicking against the death which was rapidly overtaking it. For a very dangerous split second, the world stood still while Caras watched it. Like every man and woman and a significant number of the other beasts on this bloody field, he knew the horse personally. Kierce had trained it for him.

He spun round as heard his name carried faintly through the din. He saw a sword blade slash towards him and swung wildly at it. He deflected the blow, but even with its energy almost spent it bit through the leather of his sleeve and into his forearm. The sword fell out of his hand, and he staggered back. His weapon was only lying at his feet, but his muscles would not respond quickly enough. He saw his enemy's blade sweep purposefully up, ready to strike again.

Madred was coming towards him, riding her own grey and leading a chestnut with an empty saddle. He found himself insanely trying to calculate in cold blood which of them would reach him first; Madred or the man trying to kill him. He threw himself aside as the blow came down towards his head, and then Madred's horse slammed into the Aranthan, knocking him flying. She rode over him, and Caras was close enough to hear the sickening sigh of his death as his chest caved in beneath the horse's hooves.

He rolled to his feet, and swept his arm back towards the dunes.

"Go!" he bellowed. "Enough! Retreat!"

"Mount, Caras!" Madred's scream reached him raggedly. "Get on the fucking horse!"

He vaulted onto the chestnut and they turned, shoulder to shoulder, to lead the rout. He heard his messenger, the one Caiivorian among their party, sound the retreat on the war horn of the Imperial army, and suddenly understood the voice of the braying instrument. You could hear the damn thing.

All around him, horsemen struggled to extricate themselves from the fight. It all seemed hideously chaotic, completely unrelated to the efficient-seeming plans he had pored over with Hiren. He looked from one side to the other, and estimated he had gathered some fifty riders to his retreat.

Fifty?

He steered his horse towards the rising land on his right, and as it surged up the slope, he sat back and hauled with all his strength. Once set running, the horse's flight instinct was hard to stop, but Caras was not about to be over-ruled by his horse. It slowed to a plunging, agitated standstill, and the rest of his people came to something approaching a halt in a disparate circle around him.

He raised his hand to enforce the order to stand, searching the heaving sea of bodies that was the continuing fight. There were more breaking out now. Some didn't see him, or couldn't stop, and hurtled flat out along the plain in the line of least resistance. Most saw him on the hillside, and raced towards him.

His fifty became a couple of hundred, but the enemy were beginning to follow now. At least one big group of Oreathans were pinned down in an island of defiance, with waves of Western tribesmen slashing at them from all sides.

He pointed towards them, and swept a look around his shattered followers. To a man, and woman, they gathered themselves and their sweating horses, formed themselves into ranks and followed him back down the hill.

They held closer this time, more aware of the dangers. They swept through the scatter of men chasing them and ploughed through the rest towards their companions, carving open a line of retreat. All Caras could think of now was the plan in his head. *Cut the enemy down, keep fighting, don't stop for a minute, and whatever you do, don't stand still.* In and out. Clear the way, and get them out.

There was a moment of confusion as the tight-grouped defenders broke their formation and spilled out past them, then they were all turning, as if in one mind, the trumpets bellowing, Caras yelling, the screams of dying men and dying horses drowning his senses in cacophony so hideous it was unreal. He was steeped in the stench of blood – some of it, he realised vaguely, was probably his; his arm was a slippery vermilion mess, the fingers clenched tight around the hilt of his sword numb and cold. His head thumped and danced like a ball being kicked around a yard, but he felt no real pain. He felt nothing real at all.

They fled across the dragging ground, tired legs straining to serve the desperate desire for flight of both horse and rider.

He did not turn aside for the safety of the hill, but took his troops straight towards the rising impenetrability of the dunes. With wild shrieks of triumph rising above the cries of the fallen, their enemy streamed after them in anticipation of slaughter.

Past the finger of higher ground hiding Hiren's troops from their view he led them. Not far. Not far now.

He heard the screaming as the full might of the Imperial artillery smashed into his enemy. He couldn't see, there was a solid mass of his own people behind him, though it was a chillingly smaller mass than the one which had waited on the floodplain with him a lifetime ago.

Caras risked a glance towards the hill running parallel to their flight on his right. He expected to see Hiren's troops pouring down it. He saw nothing but the artillery reloading.

The dunes were looming before him. If the enemy were still on his tail when he reached them, he would be at their mercy. The dunes were a sea of sand and bog, a horse could barely pick its way through, let alone gallop. He tried frantically to remember how far, how long they had to run. He glanced back again. Still no sign. Where in the Spirit's name was Hiren? Where was the army that could throw back this mob at his heels?

The artillery cut another swathe through the enemy, but there were so many, it wasn't going to be enough to stop them. Only the massed ranks of Hiren's infantry could get between him and his pursuers to stop them, and Hiren's infantry were not there.

Caras struggled to turn his horse towards the hill. He was not going to lead his people to flounder to their deaths in the dunes. But now the horse was exhausted beyond any listening; it was just going to run until it dropped. In a straight line.

Madred still rode at his shoulder and she saw what he was trying to do. She drove her own horse forwards with a heroic spurt of effort and began to cut across him, forcing his horse to turn the way he wanted to go. He sent her a prayer of thanks in the hope that she might have Kierce's telepathic sense as well as his equestrian skills.

Some of Caras's men managed to follow him; others ran on out of control, scattered by the hunters behind. And then, at last, he heard Imperial trumpets and the full formidable might of Hiren's footsoldiers burst over the brow of the rise and down onto the enemy.

Caras only caught glimpses as his horse plunged up the slope of the low hill, but he could see that it was not clear yet that Hiren's arrival had come in time to save the Oreathan forces. He could see Shaihen warriors caught by the pursuing Aranthans, fighting for their lives. Some of his horsemen were already floundering into soft sand. In a short space of time, they too would be trapped and slaughtered. Fury burned through him; after all they had given, after all they had endured, it was the one who doubted their ability to do it who had failed them. This disaster was down to Hiren. He couldn't imagine what could have delayed the Imperial commander so catastrophically.

His horse staggered to a halt at the top of the rise and stood trembling, its body lathered in sweat. Only now did he see the savage gash on its upper foreleg. He slid out of the saddle, and was surprised how difficult it was to stand. His head spun, and somehow it was difficult to plant his feet steadily on the ground.

He looked back down on the battle below. Once set in motion, the Imperial troops began to roll like a blanket of iron over everything in their path. The enemy that had seemed so daunting began to look like so many ants, running in all directions while the serried ranks of armoured soldiers advanced inexorably – through them, over them, in spite of them, trampling on a field of dead enemies.

He saw a pall of smoke rising in a heat haze behind the hill where Toshan lay. If everything else had gone according to plan, that was the sight of the Aranthans' boats burning. Literally. The people of Toshan had been hidden in the southern marshes, waiting for the invaders to pass through their Holding.

The Imperial champions had taken their time coming to the rescue but they had, eventually, done it. All that was left now was the complete destruction of Volun's army; no mercy, no escape, for rebels against the Sacred Union of Empire.

His part in this battle was over.

His arm was beginning to register an agony of pain. Caras took a firm hold of his swimming head, and left the Sacred Union to get on with it while he rounded up his surviving heroes and counted the cost of baiting the Imperial trap.

Chapter 33
The Magician's Fight

Kierce was up to his waist in fen, a consequence of changing places with a water fowl.

Wet feet, however, were not his chief concern. He stood in the brackish water half a mile ahead of the King of the West's approaching soldiers, his hands resting on the causeway. Gradually, the earth bank on which it was built began to crumble. Mud slid away, turning the water around him brown and glutinous. The collapse gained momentum, feeding from itself as water rushed in where the soil had fallen away. Logs rotted and parted from each other, decay that should have taken years destroying them in seconds. Some rolled into the mire, others sank down where they were to be lost beneath the enfolding earth.

In terms of historical time, a causeway made of mud and log was by its nature a temporary structure. Kierce did not reckon hastening its disintegration really counted as destroying anything. The waters were not deep enough to drown anyone, so it would not even directly cause the death of the soldiers currently marching along it. Though it would, he trusted, leave them sitting ducks to the attentions of the men he fervently hoped Hiren had sent in this direction.

All the time he worked at the causeway he could see Volun's men approaching across the flat wetlands. By the time the last five hundred paces of the causeway were heaving and bubbling in the marsh around him, they were getting close enough to worry him. But even as he glanced north towards the point where the road moved onto solid ground and led through the low hills to Toshan, he saw Hiren's men appear. Not just cavalry, but two whole troops, over twelve hundred men, horse, foot and light artillery. Hiren's scouts had seen at a glance what they were facing and Hiren reacted accordingly to their news. This was as great a threat as the thronging hordes in Toshan itself, the more so because they had very nearly been unaware of its presence.

Seeing the Imperial troops coming on apace to meet the army of the West, Kierce decided he had done enough. It was getting increasingly difficult to move in a medium that was now more mud than water. He launched himself towards the northern edge of the fen. Both the speed of his journey to spy out the forces he now recognised as Volun's and the effort of pulling apart the causeway had drained his energies, and it was as much as he could do to force himself through the clinging mire. May their gods help the soldiers of the West trying to get through that five hundred paces under the assault of their enemies, he reflected grimly.

His thoughts turned to Caras and Madred riding into battle at this very moment. He had avoided dwelling too much on the reality of the battle plans.

He knew the odds as well as Hiren did. He had a little more faith in Caras than the Imperial commander did, but he wondered how much of that was simply a refusal to face the possibility of losing his friend, or his sister, or both.

Suddenly, Kierce gave a cry of agony. His body arced back in pain, and he fell clumsily, the bog reaching out a greedy grasp pull him into its heart.

The torment of life being wrenched from whole and vigorous people – the Magician's view of the first clash of Caras's cavalry and their enemy – hammered down on his senses like a hailstorm of small darts. Dying was a part of living and one of the many extraordinary sensations he had learned to be at ease with but this was something different. The pain was real, unending, remorseless. It caught him completely by surprise. He had felt the suffering of Mervecc, he had felt Caras's defeat at Nassun, but nothing prepared him for this. He had no defence against it. He had never been so close to a battle before, a battle fought by his own people, even his own family, mounted on horses he had trained.

The Lord High Magician, the heart of Shaihen power, was helpless as the fight raged through his body. He floundered in the half-land, half-sea of the road he had destroyed. His strength was draining from him. The mire he had intended to trap the enemy was slowly but surely sucking him down.

Once Caras had accounted for all his men and brought the survivors back into the safety of the dunes he sought out Hiren, watching the progress of the battle from the ridge. Keeping a distance, thought Caras, wearily.

"I'm glad to welcome you back, Lord Caras," Hiren greeted him. "What are your losses?"

With a heavy heart, Caras told him. They seemed enormous to him, but Hiren did not seem surprised.

"May I offer the Chief of Oreath my congratulations on a job well done."

"It could have been done better," said Caras, sourly.

"Always the case. It's a wise commander who recognises it and a foolish one who dwells on it." He glanced at Caras, taking in the blood on his arm and face. "You don't make a bad warrior for a farmer, Lord Caras. If you had run earlier … it could have been a little tricky, to be honest."

Caras regarded him resentfully. His vision was misted red, and he could not stop his body trembling.

"And if you had been there a little earlier, many of my people would still be alive. What kept you?"

"A little local difficulty," replied Hiren with a smile. "We have a prize, Lord Caras. When this is all over, I'll show you. The victory we claim here today is as great as either of us could have dreamed. First of course," he looked back down onto the field of battle, "we have to secure the victory." He paused, watching. "I could use your cavalry in support of the left flank – may I have your permission to deploy them?"

"I think we've done enough," snapped Caras.

"It's your battle, Lord Caras," replied Hiren.

Caras sighed. Hiren was right. It was Shaihen soil they were defending. The words of his own speech mocked him in memory. It was the sort of thing the Chief of Oreath had to say before a battle. He found it left a sour taste in the mouth afterwards.

"All right. I'll tell them."

"Tell them to report to the Troop Commander. And then get that wound on your arm seen to. No point you surviving all that and dying from loss of blood, my lord."

Like Hiren himself, Caras had a tendency to forget that orders from the Commander were supposed to be couched as requests. Shaihen hierarchies were infinitely flexible, placing power at the bottom and responsibility at the top and it made perfect sense to him to bow to the authority of Hiren's experience.

He turned to do Hiren's bidding, then paused.

"Where's Kierce?" he asked.

"I have no idea," said Hiren. "Lord Kierce, as you know, is a law unto himself."

When the focus of the battle of Toshan shifted to the Imperial troops, the intensity of the empathic pain battering the Lord High Magician subsided. He surfaced with a sense of relief that he still lived.

He didn't remember getting out of the swamp. He lay on firm ground that sloped slightly towards his feet. Warm breath wafted across his head and he looked up at Red Sky standing over him, head lowered, blowing a little anxiously into his hair.

He became aware that there were other men present, too. Imperial soldiers. They were less caked in mud than he was, but even so they were splashed with it from head to foot, their legs as grimy as he was. Some lay near where he lay. One sat, helmetless, his head bound in a bloody bandage which covered one eye.

He looked round as Kierce moved, and Kierce recognised one of the officers from the company he had entertained at the Feast of Disorder. Kierce sat up slowly. He was still conscious of the slaughter going on the other side of the hill, but it was less immediate. He paused a moment to get control over the sensations that still assailed him.

"I can only assume you pulled me out," he said. "Thank you."

The officer gave him a slight smile. His own injuries were sufficiently disabling to keep him from the fight down in the river meadow.

"Not me personally. Whoever was nearest. Couldn't let you drown, Lord High Magician, what would we do for entertainment next feast day?"

"Well, thanks to all of you then. The Lord High Magician shouldn't be overcome by his own land. If I'd died like that I'd never have lived it down."

"Our thanks to you," replied the officer. "I don't know how you wrecked that causeway but it was a stroke of genius. Made our job easy."

Kierce looked questioningly at the horrific wound on the soldier's head. The officer shrugged.

"Comparatively."

"You defeated them?" He looked towards the marsh. It was a scene of utter desolation. Among the wreckage of the causeway lay a wreckage of men and horses, unreal in their covering of the all-pervading mud. Kierce shuddered, all too conscious of the similar scene being created the other side of the hill on the river meadow outside Toshan.

"I take it that's the remains of the Army of the West."

"Those who didn't run or surrender, yes. Commander Hiren will be granted a triumph for bringing Volun to the Imperial City, that's for sure. They should grant you one really, Lord Kierce. You made it happen."

"You caught Volun? He was with them?"

"The King of the West, sir," said the officer drily. "Is almost as muddy as you are."

Kierce smiled.

"Yes. Fond though I am of Shehaios, I don't usually like getting this close to it. I'm surprised you saw me."

"Those of us with eyesight recognised you. Though there were some who claimed there was a swamp beast plunging around in there." He paused. "Do you mind my asking how you did do it, sir?"

"The causeway? I am the Lord High Magician of Shehaios."

He still felt dazed with weariness and sick with the echoes of pain and death which continued to resound through his body. But it was time, he felt, to use his powers for what they were intended for.

He knelt beside the wounded soldier nearest to him. The man lay staring silently up at the sky, bathed in sweat, teeth gritted, waiting for aid to come. A gaping wound yawned on his right thigh. Kierce pulled away the clothing stuck to the man's skin around the injury, evoking a moan of anguish.

"Lord Kierce – what are you doing?" asked the officer with the head wound, anxiously.

"I'm doing what I'm supposed to do," replied Kierce. He laid his hands on the man's leg and closed his eyes.

The officer watched him in alarm. He made a strange figure, plastered in mud, shaking slightly from the weakness of the wounds no-one else could see. As the astonished Caiivorian watched, Kierce seemed to grow. An overwhelming sense of searching, driving passion washed over the soldier's mind, a spinning confusion of time, experiment and discovery.

He looked in amazement as Kierce gave a slight sigh of relief and sat back on his heels. His injured companion lay sleeping, a fresh, healthy pink scar running across his right leg. Kierce looked round wearily.

"Only three of you?" he queried. "Is that all the injuries you took?"

"We … we lost two, sir," stammered the officer. "Lord Kierce—."

Kierce got to his feet and moved over to the next patient. The officer rose as well and laid a hand on his arm.

"Lord Kierce, I can't allow this," he exclaimed. "This is … this is witchcraft!"

"It's magic, you fool," replied Kierce. "What else would the Lord High Magician do?"

"But this is not trickery, or illusion, it's … real. It's ungodly. Unnatural."

"Is it natural then for a man to have a hole carved by a iron blade in his leg? Or in his head? We forge the swords, we work out how to heal the wounds they make, that's mankind's gift." He smiled at the troubled officer. "The gift of magic is just to make it happen a little quicker."

The officer did not move.

"I can't let you do it."

"That man was bleeding to death. You'd rather I'd let him suffer? Let him die?" Kierce frowned. "By the Spirit, you would, too. You'll let me make naked girls dance for you, you'll let me tear the earth apart, but you won't let me heal your own people. What fools your gods make of you!"

The world lurched slightly sideways. Kierce realised just how near to exhaustion he was. He wasn't sure he had the strength to do any more anyway. He certainly didn't have the strength to argue about it. He turned away.

"Well, I'll go heal my own people then. If I have the energy to do anything. Thank you for the service you did me. I'm sorry you won't allow me to return the favour." He hesitated and looked back at the soldier's injured face. "You sure you won't allow me to? It's going to ruin your chances with the women."

The officer grasped the hilt of his sword.

"With all due respect, Lord Kierce, you're not touching me."

Kierce shrugged.

"Well, I suppose it hasn't done Hiren too much harm. Farewell, Captain."

He reached Red Sky, and paused. The energy required to climb onto his back seemed immense.

The horse lowered itself to the ground. Kierce gratefully grasped the saddle and swung himself into it as Red Sky surged back onto his feet. He patted the stallion's neck.

"Thanks, old boy. Now what bloody unicorn would have done that, eh?"

Turloch, of course, would not be in this position. He would not be close enough to a battlefield for it to invade his senses and cripple him like this. He would not have almost drowned and be even now covered in mud, because he would not have pulled down any causeway. And he would not have tried to heal a god-fearing Imperial soldier.

Kierce felt he was beginning to understand why Turloch had become such a dried up husk of a human being.

Caras would have been less surprised to find Kierce at the field hospital behind the Imperial command post than he had been to find healers among the normal camp followers of the Imperial army in the first place. Though as Hiren said, if a few herbs can save a man's life, why lose a good soldier for the sake of having the right plants. Their medicine was crude compared to the skills of Shaihen healers, and they could be ruthless in deciding who was worth trying to treat and who should be despatched where they lay to find glory by death on the field of battle. Nevertheless, the mere existence of a hospital was welcome.

Kierce was not there however, and the Arhaien healer who bound Caras's arm had not seen him.

His tasks completed, Caras made his way with Madred back to join Hiren. On the way, Madred paused and drew Caras's attention to a solitary figure on horseback moving slowly east through the dunes, away from Toshan. He dipped down out of sight and Caras waited until he reappeared.

"Is that Red Sky?" he asked uncertainly.

"Oh, it's Red Sky," said Madred. She frowned. "It's just ..."

"What?"

"Well, it must be Kierce riding him, but ... I don't know. I've never seen Kierce ride so clumsily."

Caras looked again. It seemed to be all the figure on the horse could do to stay upright in the saddle. He rode like a man half-conscious.

Caras called out to him. He had to shout three times before Kierce looked up. He checked and then turned towards them. Caras and Madred made their way across the dunes towards him. Caras could see the exhaustion in his face. He looked worse than some of those who had gone through the battle with him.

"Kierce!" he hailed him. "What happened?"

Kierce glanced at the bandage on Caras's arm.

"I felt that," he commented. "You lost your horse, too, didn't you? And nearly your head. Idiot."

He met the concern in Caras's eyes with immeasurable weariness.

"I was there, Caras." He closed his eyes suddenly with a grimace of pain. "Still am. Any idea how long this is going on for?"

"You need to ask Hiren. A while yet, I think."

Kierce cursed softly.

"I don't think I can take much more of this. I'm no use here. I might as well head back to Arhaios."

"You can't go alone – not in the condition you're in." Caras did not understand what was wrong with him, but that there was something very wrong was obvious. Normally he would not have doubted Kierce's ability to look after himself.

"If I stay here my 'condition' won't improve," replied Kierce. "I shouldn't be here. In fact Hiren was right, I should have stayed in the Haven." He paused and looked from Caras to Madred. "I'm glad you both came through it. Sorry I didn't say so. I already knew."

"I'll go with him," offered Madred.

Caras hesitated. It didn't seem enough, but he didn't know who else he could spare. Not right now. He couldn't possibly leave himself, and all the Oreathan horsemen who were still fit were in the fight. He wished Orlii at least was there, but Orlii had returned to the Haven.

"I'll see if Hiren can spare a couple of men," he said. He hesitated. "What happened, Kierce?"

He had to wait while Kierce recovered from another shaft of pain.

"You fought a battle, Caras," said Kierce, breathlessly. "That's all. I'm too close to a Shaihen battle on Shaihen soil. It hurts. Another little twist Turloch didn't tell me about." He paused, breathing heavily. "I would like … to get out of here. Are you coming, Madred?"

Madred looked at Caras. He nodded.

"Go with him. I'll talk to Hiren."

By the time the day ended, all that was left for the Imperial troops to do was a mopping up operation. The day belonged to Oreath and the Empire.

Hiren was like a sated lion with his paws on his kill, and Caras was beginning to feel a little euphoric in the aftermath. His losses had not been quite as catastrophic as he had feared, and in the context of the victory they had won, they seemed bearable. The threat had been utterly defeated. They had won a famous victory. He was aware of the subtle difference in Hiren's attitude towards them and deeply gratified to have earned it. They had proved themselves equal partners to their Imperial allies, not frightened sheep dependent on the guard-dogs protection. He was immensely proud of his people and in retrospect not dissatisfied with himself. He felt the ghost of Nassun had been laid.

As final proof of their triumph, Hiren allowed him a glimpse of their prize captive, heavily guarded in their base camp inland of the site of the battle. Hiren had exhaustively stripped the renegade commander of every vestige of Imperial army accoutrements. He was wearing only the coarse tunic of his erstwhile subjects and the chains of his captivity, a tall, gaunt, ageing man still bearing traces of the swamp that had proved his downfall.

"So that's the famous Volun," commented Caras regarding the prisoner from the doorway of the tent. "How did he come to be here? How come Kierce didn't see him until it was almost too late?"

Hiren let the tent flap close and they turned to make their way back to their own quarters.

"I don't entirely understand how Lord Kierce gathers his intelligence," admitted Hiren. "But I suspect he didn't see Volun because he wasn't looking for him. Volun was masquerading as an Imperial soldier. From a distance, that's what he would have looked like."

Caras slowed his pace.

"When he attacked the Imperial navy last year – did he capture any of their ships?"

"Captured a significant number of them," acknowledged Hiren. "Not that we announced the fact, of course. After all, the fight at Vordeith was an Imperial victory." He made the claim with wry humour, knowing full well that Caras knew the truth of the matter.

Caras halted.

"Where did Volun come from?"

"Western Aranth."

"No, I mean he was here. He was in Shehaios. He marched on Toshan from inland, he had landed here already—."

Caras broke off, turned abruptly and headed back to the tent that contained the prisoner. He swept past Volun's guards and went straight up to the deposed King of the West.

Volun rose to his feet at the intrusion and faced Caras with cold reserve. He glanced briefly over Caras's head at Hiren's familiar figure with a faintly disparaging air of enquiry. Caras was tall for a Shaihen. Volun was tall for a Caiivorian. He made Caras look small.

"Where did you come ashore?" rasped Caras. "Which of my people have you already attacked?"

Volun looked at him disdainfully.

"You must be the old woman's successor," he said. "A doughty old witch if ever there was one—".

Caras hit him in the face.

"Where did you come ashore?" He seized Volun by the front of his tunic. Volun's hands were bound; he could not defend himself.

The Imperial guard glanced uncertainly at Hiren who shook his head. He stood watching the exchange with arms folded and a slight smile on his face.

"Was it Riskeld? Have you been in Riskeld?"

"I heard you'd crossed swords with the Lady Iareth yourself, Lord Caras," replied Volun. "But you didn't have the stomach to finish it. That's always a mistake, you know—".

Caras hurled him back against the low pallet bed on which he had been sitting. Volun tripped against it and staggered; Caras hit him again, and drew his sword as Volun fell to the ground.

Hiren moved forwards swiftly and seized Caras's wrist.

"I can't let you do that, I'm afraid," he said. "That's the Emperor's privilege."

"Iareth," hissed Caras. Hatred consumed him, fed by guilt. He had failed her. Leath had promised Volun would have to go through the Chief of Oreath and the Lord High Magician to return to Riskeld. He had gone through both. "Does she live?"

"I did what I should have done last time," replied Volun coldly, picking himself up off the floor. "The Holder of Riskeld, as she called herself, is dead. And so is all her family. Riskeld is in the hands of my men." He glanced again at Hiren. "You haven't got me to Vordeith yet, Hiren."

With a low and vicious oath, Caras hurled himself from Hiren's grasp, lunged forwards and drove the sword through Volun's heart.

"Caras!" shouted Hiren in dismay.

Volun stared at Caras in astonishment. He reached out towards the hilt of the sword. He fell back as the strength drained from him and his hand closed over Caras's, hugging the sword blade to his body. A faint smile of triumph touched his face before his eyes glazed and he collapsed clumsily, hitting the bed before he crumpled to the ground.

Caras wrenched the sword free, snatching his hand from Volun's death grasp.

Hiren pushed past him and bent over Volun's body.

"Damn you, Caras, I thought you were a man of peace – hadn't you done enough killing today to leave this one to me?

"Why did he smile?" Caras found himself more unnerved by Volun's dying than any of the slaughter he had seen and committed on the battlefield. "Why did he smile at me like that?"

Hiren sighed wearily.

"You gave him what he wanted," he explained, sourly. "He survived the battle. The best he could hope for was a quick, clean death. You shouldn't have done it, Caras. His Greatness will not be pleased."

Caras cleaned the blood from his sword slowly. It wasn't the prospect of the Emperor's wrath that made his vengeance feel hollow and unpleasant. It was its inability to bring back the Oreathan Holder Volun had attacked.

"He was going to die anyway."

"In Vordeith. Slowly. Publicly humiliated. A high profile execution is always good entertainment, and we'd have put on a magnificent show for this wretch. Now I've got to take a damn corpse back to Vordeith, just to prove the bastard's dead."

Chapter 34
Aftermath

Hiren sent an escort after Kierce and Madred, but it never found them.

Kierce did not intend it to. He had had his fill of Imperial company for the time being.

They rode on a long way from Toshan, until after dusk. Both horses and riders were dropping with weariness, and eventually Madred rebelled.

"This," she decreed, stopping in a forest clearing, "is far enough."

Kierce stirred himself, realising he was half asleep. Small wonder Madred did not trust him to keep them safe. But he couldn't stop yet.

"No. It's not far enough."

"Kierce, how far is going to be 'far enough'? Far enough that we ride blind over a cliff? Or into a pack of hungry wolves?"

"No wolves here."

"Do you know? Can you still see anything?" She slid off the horse. "This is far enough."

"It's not."

"Well, I think it is." She patted the neck of her grey mare. "Whisper thinks it is. Red Sky thinks it is. You're outnumbered, Kierce, give in."

Kierce gazed wistfully east.

"I would have liked to get further."

"I would like to eat!" exclaimed Madred. She leaned against the grey mare's saddle, studying Kierce across the horse's back. "It must be over now. Surely you can't still feel it?"

"Not sure I can tell any more."

There was a pause. Kierce still sat on Red Sky, still reluctant to give up the journey.

"I was there too, you know," said Madred quietly.

Kierce looked round at her. Of his three half-siblings, Madred was most like him, both of them taking after their father. Her long dark hair, which she had worn in one long plait down her back as long as he could remember, had been cut off, the better to accommodate a helmet. But the face was the same, strong rather than pretty, drawing you to the steady brown eyes that saw more than the reflection of light through a lens.

"You may have felt it when Caras's horse went down," she went on. "I saw it. I saw the Lord of Arhaios fall, and I couldn't do anything about it. I saw him sit grieving for the loss of our horse while a sword bore down on his head. I thought … " She swallowed the emotion that rose in her throat. "I thought he was going to die, Kierce. I thought I was watching him be killed. We all of us went through … I think the Caiivorians must have invented the place because they fight so much. Hell. All of us. Not just you."

She dropped her forehead against the saddle so that he could not see her face. Not that he needed to see it to know she was crying, release from the day that had overwhelmed both of them.

Kierce dismounted slowly, and set about relieving Red Sky of the sweaty burden of his saddle and bridle.

"We shouldn't have been there. Neither of us should have been there."

Madred raised her head, sniffing.

"If we hadn't, Caras would be dead."

"So we train our horses to become killers too." He came round Red Sky and put the tack down on the ground. "Are you going to unsaddle that horse?"

Madred brushed the tears away with the back of her hand and turned from him, tight-lipped, to unsaddle Whisper.

"If you can't take the heat, that's your business," she retorted. "Don't speak for me."

"I'm inclined to think the Caiivorians have a point. Women don't belong on the battlefield."

Madred turned on him angrily.

"You've been spending too much time with Imperial soldiers. How dare you say that? Were you at Nassun? Were you riding beside Caras today?"

"Would you do it again?" said Kierce, quietly.

She hesitated. He saw her shrink from the prospect, but she swallowed hard and replied,

"If I needed to. If Caras needed me to. Does he belong on the battlefield any more than you or I do? He doesn't do it for fun."

"Not yet, no." He smiled slightly at Madred's uncomprehending frown. "We're all men, Maddi, we all like to fight and we all like to win. Shall I tell you what Caras is doing, at this precise moment?"

Madred shook her head. He hardly needed the powers of the Magician, to see the feelings she harboured for Caras; it was enough to be her brother.

"He's celebrating victory. He's drinking. He's going to carry on drinking, because he has a great deal to forget. If I were Caras I would be feeling just as pleased with myself as he is right now. At the first opportunity I'd get roaring drunk and sing and dance until the dead complained and my memory of the battle was all of the exhilaration of victory."

"I know what you'd do, Kierce – Caras is different. Are you telling me what you see, or making it up?"

Kierce shrugged.

"Same difference." He summoned his mind to focus on the familiar, reassuring presence of his friend. "There's a dark-haired girl from Toshan who's not unlike you to look at. Slimmer. Pretty. She's gazing at Caras as if he's a hero from the histories and Caras … Caras is expanding. Everything about him is swelling. His head, his pride, his sense of self-justification, his guilt, his heart, his—".

"Now you are making it up," snapped Madred, as his hand traced the description, and she saw where it was going.

"All that separates Caras and Hiren is their place of birth, neither of them feel this the way I felt it." He paused. "Nor even the way you felt it."

"I thought you were supposed to know people," retorted Madred, presenting her back again as she gave her attention to Whisper.

"I do."

"You don't know me."

Kierce's smile twisted ruefully.

"Oh, I do, Maddi. You I know better than anyone."

"Then if you know how tired, and how hungry and how—."

She broke off. This time, he came over to her and attempted to put his arms around her. She rejected him resentfully.

"If you'd let Hiren's men find us we could both have got some sleep."

"You can sleep," replied Kierce.

"You're asleep already," retorted Madred. She paused. "Your body's been listening to your mind all day, Kierce. Turn it around and listen to your body." She looked at him through the tears and summoned a smile. "Honestly, you should see yourself. If there was anyone around I'd be ashamed to be seen with you."

Kierce looked down at the generous covering of dried mud which most of him still carried.

"Madred, do you know how much you sounded like your mother then?"

"Mother would throw up her hands in horror and shriek at the sight of you."

Madred met his eyes. An unspoken apology passed between them. She raised her hands and gave a theatrical squeal, and then pointed down through the trees.

"Stream! Water!"

Kierce pointed up at the sky.

"Dark. Fire."

"You do water, I'll do fire. If you see any fish, they're supper. Otherwise its barley broth."

"You know I only like barley distilled," replied Kierce, heading towards the stream.

"Then catch a fish," Madred shouted after him.

It took them many weary days' riding to reach Arhaios, and the minstrels were not long behind them with the official songs of the victory at Toshan. Kierce largely left it to them to tell the tale, and felt even more disinclined to carry it back to the Haven. He remained in Arhaios, taking some time to remember the Holding that had bred him.

He was still there when Caras returned in all his triumphant glory. Oreath turned out in force to welcome the warriors home. Men, women and children from Holdings all across Caras's land lined the way up from the river crossing to the Halls of Learning and crowded outside the Meeting House. They cheered the heroes of Toshan all the way home.

Kierce joined the family waiting outside the Holder's house. Elani smiled a welcome to him, and he could see the relief in her eyes. Her man was returning. Kierce was aware of those whose loved ones were not, as he had been aware of every Shaihen's death in the battle. He felt the grief of the bereaved and the euphoria of the cheering, garland-waving crowds competing for his spirit.

Caras's eldest son, Taegen, hurled himself into Kierce's arms, reckless with excitement. Kierce caught him and swung him up onto his shoulders. Alsa stood with Madred, Sheldo beside them striving for dignity while his eyes glowed with the thrill of the victors' return. Kierce knew these images would make a deep and lasting impression on all the children who witnessed them, especially those this close to the hero of the hour.

When Caras finally reached them, he was allowed one brief embrace from his wife before their son and daughter broke free of their minders and hurled themselves on their father.

Madred glanced at Kierce.

And if we hadn't been there ...

Kierce smiled, but made no comment.

When the celebrations were over and the visitors had dispersed from Arhaios, Kierce was able to reflect with Caras on the battle's impact beyond his land. They met in the homely comfort of the Holder's House, surrounded by memories of the world they had grown up in.

"Hiren's asked me to go to Vordeith with him," said Caras. "Maybe just because he doesn't want to have to explain why the City will be denied the entertainment of Volun's execution, but he did invite me to share in the triumph."

"Only because you're no threat to his laurels," observed Kierce, laconically. "Only Imperial officers can be awarded Imperial victories."

"I don't want an Imperial victory," said Caras. "And not only do I not want to go to Vordeith, I can't. I've still got raiders plaguing the southern border, Jagus is still in Hieath building his own army – Spirit knows what he'll do with it. Or maybe you do, since you let him do it."

"He won't—." began Kierce. But Caras was not listening.

"And I still have a dispute with Riskeld. I couldn't make one of Iareth's kin Holder, Volun left none of them alive. Whoever I chose would have been resented, and I'm sure many of Iareth's people think they're still living under an occupying force, whatever I say."

Kierce shrugged. "So don't go to Vordeith. I doubt it will lessen Hiren's enjoyment of his Triumph."

"If Hiren goes alone, he will present Toshan as entirely an Imperial victory. Won't he?"

"He doesn't really have the liberty to present it any other way, Caras. Inviting you to go too is as far as he can go in acknowledging your part in it. There aren't many Caiivorians who would have done as much."

Caras got to his feet and strode across the warm, low-beamed room. He poured mead from a jug on the side and handed a cup to Kierce. Kierce knew what it was in his mind to say, but he was going to wait for Caras to say it.

"I can't go. But the Emperor should know the truth."

"Then send a minstrel to Vordeith."

"The minstrels will do their own sending, but I don't think the Emperor listens to anyone but generals and kings."

"Rules me out on both counts then. I am neither, Caras."

"No. You're the Lord High Magician. You more than anyone are the head and the symbol of Shaihen power. Take that to the Imperial City."

Kierce paused reflectively. Visiting Vordeith was not something that had crossed his mind until he read it in Caras's; the prospect alarmed him. He was still wrestling with the idea of returning to the Haven and he had seen glimpses of the Imperial City in the minds of Rainur and Cathva. He had some sense of its size and splendour, its duplicity and squalor; he had seen the haze of taverns and homes and streets jumbled in the minds of a thousand Imperial soldiers. He recoiled from the very idea of such a place.

"You won the bloody battle, Caras."

"We both know I've neither won the battle nor finished it, yet," said Caras, quietly. "I can't afford to leave Shehaios."

"Neither can I."

"You can get back a lot quicker," replied Caras, with a smile. "Anyway … well, you're the Magician, you know better than I do how it works. But you never really leave at all. Do you?"

Kierce didn't answer.

"Turloch used to do it all the time," added Caras. "He always went with Rainur. And he always kept his eye on what was going on here."

"There are a lot of things Turloch used to do that I can't do. I say that with humility, Caras. I can't keep the distance he kept. I don't know how he did it."

"Surely travelling to the Imperial City doesn't take much skill? The former Horsemaster of Arhaios can still ride a horse, I think."

"It's not the journey, you fool, it's … being among Caiivorians. In Caiivor."

Caras frowned uncomprehendingly.

"I thought you liked Caiivorians."

"I get on with Hiren. So do you."

"You spend half your life in the Imperial Camp," replied Caras. *And the other half with the Caiivorian queen*, he added but did not say aloud.

"The Imperial Camp runs to Hiren's command. It reflects his personality. It's an efficient, secure, calm little world – everyone knows the rules, everyone knows their place. It's an easy place to be." Kierce knew he was losing Caras. His companion had no idea what he was talking about. "Caiivorians live in fear. The soldiers don't – at least, not until they're formed up in battle order, and then they know who their enemy is and how to deal with him. In their Holdings, in their towns – it's bound to be different. And after Toshan, I don't know …" He hesitated. Even to Caras, he didn't know how to say, 'I'm afraid of what it will feel like.'

"I really don't see how anything you felt at Toshan compares to what those of us who fought it experienced," interrupted Caras, impatiently. "We're all of us having to face up to doing things we don't like. That's what having responsibility means. I thought you'd discovered that."

"Caras, please don't start trying to teach me about power and responsibility."

"Sorry. Old habits die hard." Caras smiled at him and shook his head. "Men don't change, and you always were an idle, self-centred bastard. Used to be quite proud of it, in fact. The cloak doesn't fool me, Kierce. I know it's still you wearing it. Why don't you want to go to Vordeith? Too long away from Cathva?"

"You're on dangerous ground, Caras."

"Oh, I think I'm developing quite a taste for dangerous ground," said Caras, comfortably.

Kierce's eyes followed him as he crossed the room and sat down again.

"This is the man who slew the King of the West speaking, is it?" he suggested sarcastically.

"You know I'm not proud of that," replied Caras without looking up. "But neither would I have been particularly proud of humiliating him in the streets of Vordeith."

"And you think I would?" retorted Kierce. "What do you want me to do, Caras? Go on a spying mission? Today Toshan, tomorrow Vordeith?"

"Don't be ridiculous," said Caras. "But if Hiren takes the news, it won't even be known that our people were there. I think there are times in the game when you have to let your opponent know what pieces you hold." He met Kierce's eyes. "Aren't there?"

"I'll think about it," he conceded.

Curiously enough, within hours of his arrival back in the Haven, Kierce got the same invitation from Hiren, couched in terms that were more difficult to refuse.

Chapter 35
Winning the Peace

Davitis greeted the news from Toshan as if he were the Emperor himself issuing plaudits to his loyal and valiant soldiers. He then calmly announced that as Imperial envoy and de facto governor of Shehaios, it was his duty to report these triumphs to the Emperor personally. He thus rather neatly managed to enrage and offend both Hiren and Rainur in the same sentence.

He was, of course, going to get his way less over Volun's dead body than over Hiren's. Not that Hiren needed to go that far to establish that it was going to take more than Davitis to steal his victory. Merely point out quietly to the envoy that he was at liberty to go to Vordeith whenever he liked, but he would travel the lawless roads through North Caiivor without any escort unless he could call upon his loyal Shaihen subjects to provide protection for their beloved governor.

It was the last straw for Davitis. He had been at odds with Shaihen culture since his exchange with Kierce at the feast of welcome and he bitterly resented Hiren's close relationship with their hosts. He raged ineffectually for a while, and then sat long into the night scratching away with his pen. He compiled a passionate and exhaustive report on the true seditious nature of Shehaios, and the trickery they cloaked with the name of magic. He elaborated at great length on the malign influence it exercised over Commander Hiren, to the point where an uninformed reader would have envisaged the unfortunate Commander ranting completely bereft of his reason.

Davitis found out how Volun had died, and made much of Shaihen abrogation of Imperial justice. Shaihen weakness had allowed Volun to land on Imperial soil. The Shaihen King's brother was mustering forces in the heart of the country ready to rise against the Sacred Union. The Haven was infested with godless immorality and the Emperor's authority was mocked on all sides.

"... Your Greatness, the powers you vested in King Rainur are sadly abused. I am now the sole representative of Imperial order in this place, and live daily in fear for my life and my soul. I apply urgently for your good offices in bringing this unruly province to account."

He sealed and sent the missive at first light, before Hiren was aware of what he had done.

Kierce was rather surprised to see Hiren approaching him at the site of the Magician's Tower. Hiren usually did not enter the Haven without either an invitation or a formal appointment – a rule of his own making, not his hosts', but one he followed scrupulously. He looked out of place turning up in the streets of the Haven alone. Though Kierce did have some idea why he might be there.

They turned to walk together into the hills to the west of the tower. Well away from the ears of others, Hiren paused to look out across the vista of mountain and stream which rolled before them.

"I like this place," he admitted, savouring the view of the Haven's valley winding its green ribbon across the hillside. His eyes scanned across the dense forest falling away northwards, as if he was imprinting the full view on his memory. "I thought I'd pretty much seen everything in my life until I came here, but I hadn't seen Shehaios. Once I return to Vordeith, I doubt I shall come back. In fact, I hope not to. This is one victory more than I'd dreamed of and my career may not be as near its end as I'd thought. I think you've made me believe in the Sacred Union again, wizard."

"I'll be happy to think that you're at the heart of the Empire somewhere, Hiren. If that's what you want, I wish you success. We couldn't have done it all without you."

"Ah, but if I hadn't been here, would you have needed to do it?"

Kierce shrugged.

"That we will never know. I played the hand that fell to me."

Hiren turned abruptly towards him.

"Kierce, Volun has changed Shehaios's fortunes, not just mine. The Emperor noticed Shehaios largely because Rainur made him notice it. He understood the strategic argument, but he didn't attach that much significance to it. Sometimes His Greatness believes that everyone really does wish him to live for ever. He didn't think Volun was a real threat. He humoured me in sending me here with an army of fresh-faced boys, it was as much a training exercise as anything."

"You trained them well."

"They made me proud of them," acknowledged Hiren. "But the battle we fought at Toshan was not a training exercise, and it's bound to change the Emperor's view of the threat. Volun's shattered his complacency and sent him looking for enemies. He'll look North, and Davitis has just sent him a long report about the evils of Shaihen magic and the general state of anarchy and untrustworthy lack of morality that exists under the current regime in Shehaios. I believe these things may be of concern to you, Lord High Magician, and I tell you them in the firm belief that you either do, or shortly will, know them anyway." He paused. "You are no ordinary man, Lord Kierce."

"No," agreed Kierce, easily. "I'm the Lord High Magician. And I thank you for the Imperial overview. It certainly is of concern to me."

"There are magicians and soothsayers, wizards, shamans, priests and sorcerers all across the Empire. Some are mere charlatans, some have knowledge and skills, some are holy men. Some speak with the gods. You have no gods, Lord Kierce."

Kierce shrugged.

"I'm Shaihen."

Hiren wasn't going to let him get away with such answers.

"So tell me what it means, then. To be a Shaihen."

Kierce hesitated. Hiren was a respected Imperial general about to return in triumph to the Imperial City with the head of the Emperor's enemy. He had admitted himself that his sights were now set higher than the honourable retirement he had been looking forward to. Now was a time for Kierce to remember how to spell diplomacy.

"It really just means we are a people who love our land," he answered. "*She* – land; *haios* – holy."

Hiren smiled drily.

"I'm very fond of my home, too. I don't think it makes me a Shaihen."

"It's a start," replied Kierce. "Shaihens ... don't normally try and translate 'haios'. There is no word for it in your language. It doesn't only mean holy, it means whole – it means we are part of our land, and it is a part of us. We don't own our land as you own yours. If anything, it owns us. We seek to understand it, to know why our crops grow and the rivers run. Why the rains fall and the winds blow. What place each creature holds and what place we ourselves hold, individually and collectively." He smiled at Hiren. "Good husbandry. Very prosaic, I'm afraid. Not at all the powers of darkness you were dreaming of."

"How do you know what I dream of?"

No, Hiren was not going to let him get away with easy answers.

"The Lord High Magician ... has a gift. He shows the people of Shehaios where they might go. I'm a creator of illusions, Hiren, a dreamer of dreams."

"No, you're not," said Hiren, quietly. "You're a man who knows what I think before I say it. You're a man who disappears in the blink of an eye. You're a man who pulls down five hundred strides of solid roadway in the length of time it takes Lord Caras to make a speech."

"Ah, well," said Kierce, modestly. "Caras always did like the sound of his own voice..."

"And you are a creature of power, Lord Kierce. I hesitate to call you a man any longer."

"Nevertheless, it's what I am. All these things are possible. Though admittedly not quite the way I do them. Image-makers must be allowed a little licence with reality."

Hiren regarded him thoughtfully, but Kierce was giving no more. There were points at which he allowed himself to be reached, and fathomless depths where he did not.

"You knew the news I came to tell you," said Hiren.

Kierce smiled and reached inside the buckskin jerkin beneath his cloak. He drew out a parchment fastened with the Imperial seal.

"I think this is the letter that worries you, Commander."

Hiren laughed in relief.

"You never cease to amaze me, Kierce."

"As a matter of fact, you have Orlii to thank for this," replied Kierce. "He's been cultivating his lover all the time we've been in Oreath."

"If you come with me to Vordeith, be careful of saying such things," warned Hiren. "We don't have people who read minds, but we do have any number who twist words. I'm told you're familiar with the writings of Tay-Aien, and if I remind you the Emperor is a devotee, you'll appreciate what I'm saying."

"I do," said Kierce. "But I wasn't aware I was coming to Vordeith with you."

Hiren hesitated.

"What do you intend to do with Davitis's letter?"

Kierce turned it over in his hands.

"To be honest, I don't know. Not really the Magician's role to destroy information, even misinformation, but it does read a little like my death warrant."

Hiren paused.

"Can you remove and replace the seal without leaving any evidence?"

Kierce gave him a slightly condescending look.

"Can I draw my own breath?"

"Will you entrust it to me?" said Hiren. "I know Davitis's style, and I know how an Imperial report is written. I will replace Davitis's slander with something … well, something less like your death warrant, at least. It'll keep Davitis quiet in the belief that he's made his case to the Emperor, and by the time he discovers that all is not as he expected it to be … you can be in the Imperial City making your case direct to the Emperor himself. You won't find it difficult. Quote Tay-Aien to him and he'll be eating out of your hand."

"Do I need to?" said Kierce, reluctantly.

There was a brief silence before Hiren answered.

"I think so. I can't just keep quiet about what you are, Kierce. In the service of the Empire, you are a magnificent ally. But Shehaios must remain in the service of the Empire. I wouldn't be doing my duty if I allowed it scope to turn against us. I need to know, no less than the Emperor does, that you are a servant of the Sacred Union."

Kierce gazed out across the view that was so similar to the one from the Magician's cottage behind and slightly above them.

"You're a very clever man, Hiren," he admitted. "You're wasted on the army."

"The army taught me all I know. If I die in its service, I die content. This is not my land, Kierce, it's yours. I don't understand it and I doubt I'll ever come back here, but still … it deserves to survive. And unless I read it wrong, it's your responsibility to make sure it does."

"I will go and study the writings of the great Tay-Aien," conceded Kierce, with a sigh. "Oh, by the Spirit, if the man weren't so tedious it would be less of a trial."

"The Emperor sets great store by the learned and wise."

"Learned *and* wise?" protested Kierce.

Hiren smiled.

"No drinking and no jokes!"

Kierce smiled back.

"You're a hard man, Commander."

Chapter 36
Vordeith

The cushion by Cathva's side was getting steadily more sodden as the oxen hauled her ponderous conveyance southwards. The wind was driving the incessant rain through the tightly-shuttered window in the carriage door. Inside, the smell of stale perfume accentuated, rather than hid, the reek of damp fabric and tired bodies.

Cathva gazed moodily at Tilsey. She had been so eager to seize the opportunity Hiren's escort afforded her to visit her father, she had forgotten quite how far it was from Shehaios to Vordeith, and quite how bad the roads were south of the Gate.

She had thought the company would make the journey pass quicker, but Kierce travelled on horseback. Of course. What else would he do? Cathva had never sat on a horse in her life, and had no intention of ever doing so. A lady of the Imperial royal family travelled always by carriage or chair, she did not expose herself to the smell and filth of a beast of burden.

Whether Rainur knew, when he agreed to her going, that Kierce would be in the party, Cathva neither knew nor cared. She had watched the fight to possess the victory at Toshan unfold with keen personal interest, well aware of the impact the news would have in Vordeith. It was more than ever clear to her that Rainur was not the key to the relationship between Shehaios and the Emperor. That was why this journey had to be made.

Kierce shared the wagon with her briefly, while they were still in Shehaios, but she could tell how intensely he disliked it. He talked to her about her father, but his eyes strayed constantly to the little window, open then in the brighter weather they had left behind in the Fair Land. She was fascinated how much he reminded her of a caged bird. How strange, she thought, as she tried to entertain him with the idiosyncrasies of the Great Emperor, the things that could torment a Shaihen Magician.

He didn't repeat the experience.

The journey through Northern Caiivor, of necessity, was from town to town, stopping overnight under the protection of the local land-owners. Cathva had anticipated sharing the hospitality of the Caiivorian nobles with Kierce. She thought she would have plenty of opportunities to talk to him about her plans for them in Vordeith.

It was not to be. Kierce rode with Hiren during the day, and when the party sought the protection of a castle overnight, they left the Magician outside the walls of the town.

She hadn't even had a chance to ask him why. In these lawless territories, no man slept outside the protection of someone's walls or someone's guards, and she knew Hiren feared for Kierce's safety as much as she did. She noticed he had not brought Orlii with him, and she wondered how well protected he really was.

Cathva stared at the blank sides of the wagon and gave a slight sigh. With the weather so foul, she couldn't even see glimpses of the passing landscape through the tiny square window in the carriage door. This was going to be a very, very tedious journey.

She lay back against the cushioned seat and closed her eyes, pretending she could sleep through the jolting ruts of the road.

Kierce seldom read Cathva's thoughts. It took him too close, and he was well aware of the dangers in the game they were playing. All the time they were in the Haven, Sartin was in the middle. He and Cathva only touched each other through the child.

Away from the Haven, it could be more difficult to keep that distance. Kierce felt he was going to have a tough enough time convincing the Emperor he was a devoted follower of the high moral laws of Tay-Aien as it was, without having to do it while conducting an adulterous affair with the Emperor's daughter.

Even if he had felt at liberty to enjoy it, however, the temptation of her company would not have been strong enough to overcome his revulsion at the appearance of the places where his Caiivorian companions lodged. He did see the landscape through which they travelled. He saw what generations of warfare had done to it.

There were remains and ruins everywhere of holdings reminiscent of Shaihen Holdings, scattered small farms and rambling country mansions, but none still inhabited. The people of Caiivor crowded together within high walls, with towers looking out across the countryside and huge gates, which closed to keep out the terrors of the night. Some of these edifices were compact, and lowered over scattered villages and fields; most sprawled their grim sheild around the whole local population. Immediately inside the walls, a huddle of mean huts and cottages typically propped each other up, and even the more substantial houses further in were built cheek by jowl. The last stronghold of every sizeable settlement was a fortified building in the centre, and it was always this solid heart that Hiren was heading for, guest of the local lord.

Kierce could not bring himself to submit to the cold embrace of so much cut stone any more than he could bring himself to travel in Cathva's jolting, reeking carriage.

The further they got from Shehaios, the greater his fear of reaching his destination grew. He could not stay outside the Imperial City. Hiren expected him to meet the Emperor, and Kierce hardly felt able to tell him he was afraid of walls. There were walls in Shehaios; the central column of the Magician's Tower was built of stone. But none of it crushed him as he felt the castles of Caiivor threatened to crush him.

Fearful man, he confided to Red Sky, as he lay gazing at the clouds in the night sky. *Instinctively frightened of an unknown society.*

Red Sky snorted gently, his mind full of the sweet grass gripped in his teeth.

Kierce found himself thinking of Cathva, hesitantly stripping off layers of disguise in the Temple. It was a nice image to replay, but he found himself replaying also the thoughts running through her head as she did it, her apprehensive fascination with the gods of the strange land. Arrogance, or courage? Two faces of the same stone, he concluded, but the lion of Empire lived in her heart. Sharp-clawed and sleek, a feline predator.

He closed his eyes. No more dreaming of Cathva, he told himself.

Even though he knew she was dreaming of him.

She would be surprised how much he disliked the image of Zelt an' Korsos she had given him. Her unquestioning admiration for the Great Man shone through every word she said about him. There was, in fact, something in the reverence of her love for him that Kierce didn't like to explore too deeply. The parallel between the powerful figure of the Emperor and the powerful figure of the Magician, certainly the Magician she had met in the temple of life, hardly needed drawing.

He dozed, his senses locked to the life around him, subconsciously attuned to any hint of danger. Turloch might undertake to protect the King in the heart of the Empire. Kierce barely trusted himself for his own protection.

As they progressed further south and west, Kierce noticed a change in the surroundings with the gradual change in the climate. This was a soft fertile land of vines and sun-ripened fruit, still largely protected by the Empire. He began to see recognisable Holdings, walled with watch-towers where the Hall of Learning should have been but nevertheless displaying the richness and grace of an Arhaios or a Cuaraccon. The towns were no less crowded and stank worse than ever in the balmy heat but there was a vibrancy about them, which contrasted with the grimness of the north. It was a wealthy land, speaking to him of generations of cultivation, and ingenuity, channelling water to nurture delicacies favoured by the Empire's aristocracy. It was a country not without its seductive quality, and for odd moments he could allow himself to be seduced.

He was riding alongside Hiren one day when the Commander pointed out a distant town across the rolling landscape. That, he said with a smile, was his *she-haios*, his holy land, the place of his birth. Kierce shared the joke with him, but as Hiren had not been home for nearly twenty years, Kierce knew it was not true. Hiren's heart belonged exclusively to his gods of power and glory and the army he served them with.

Nevertheless, Kierce felt more at ease in the heart of the Empire than on its fringes. Here, the utter dominance of the warriors was lessened as the threat that caused it lessened, the fear of those they ruled was reduced, and he began to feel he could move among the local people without suffocating.

He began to address his mind to the strategy of his forthcoming meeting with the Emperor. He knew it would take some self-discipline. He had to take seriously a man who wished to be addressed as Your Greatness. He had to smile, and be polite and deferential to a man who taught his daughter that love and fear were the same thing.

He was not at all sure he was equal to the task.

Kierce had seen the image of Vordeith in the minds of others, but he was nevertheless unprepared for the sheer scale of the real thing.

He approached it along a broad avenue, passing through miles of wealthy estates, each like a small Holding in themselves except that they centred around one vast house where the estate owner lived like a minor king. Along the last few miles, on a parched strip of land between the walls of the estates and the broad paved way itself, the Empire displayed its fallen enemies to the contempt and ridicule of those about to enter the ruling city. It was a reminder of its power, and a warning to any who came to the city to dispute it.

Kierce passed by the Imperial outcasts with his eyes averted, trying to shut his mind to the suffering that assailed his senses, but he still heard them. Some of the evil he glimpsed almost warranted the punishment its perpetrators were suffering; in the minds of others, he could identify nothing he would have called a crime at all. Shackled to stakes alongside each other were former kings, bandit leaders and common thieves, and some whose only offence was to lose favour with the powerful men of Vordeith. Some were there for a short, salutary period of humiliation, others were mutilated in symbolic retribution for their transgressions. A few were left to die a slow horrific death from thirst and starvation. Attempting to give succour to those who lined the road to Vordeith was, he was told, a short way of ending up tied to a stake alongside them.

He passed gratefully from the gruesome parade through the foetid shanty town that huddled beneath the city walls and into the City of Kings itself. Vordeith was a city shaped by the genius of a previous Emperor, a vision of order built in stone and undermined by its inhabitants. The network of streets and alleys, which all led back to the broad river at the heart of the city, were crowded with tradesmen's booths and lowly dwellings of plaster and wood filling what any aesthetic sense would have left as space. The only space was to be found around the grand houses of the elite, and even there it was at a premium. Where roads met in broad squares, stalls and street vendors spilled their goods over the statues to Imperial victories and Imperial heroes erected there, not a few of them raised in praise of His Greatness Emperor Zelt an' Korsos. The river itself, when he reached it, was no less hectic. People lived on boats, traded from boats, served food and drink from boats. Barges from the west coast harbour brought goods from all over the Caiivorian Empire up the river to trade in the streets of the capital.

Despite the vigour of its people, despite the dazzling wealth of its temples and the soaring architecture of its grand buildings, every step Kierce took into the city of Vordeith seemed heavier. A coldness closed around his heart, as if he was approaching a prison cell and not the centre of the most glorious city in his world. The noise of the multitude who dwelt there, their hopes, their fears, their schemes and perversions lapped at his senses like a building tidal wave about to break over him. The gold adorning temple roofs, the brilliant painted frescoes around the buildings of the wealthy, overwhelmed him as if he had gorged on foods too rich for his digestion.

The Emperor's residence occupied an extensive enclave on the east side of the city, built upon a huge platform of dressed stone slabs. It reared on its forest of pillars, an expanse of polished stone surmounted by ornate carving, a residence of giants with ceilings soaring high overhead and statues half as big again as the men they commemorated.

The approach took the Emperor's supplicants up two flights of steps, one to the platform, and another to the mighty doors of the palace itself, passing between two towering statues of the bull-headed lion of the warrior god. Inside, Hiren escorted Kierce through a hall which looked as if it could have encompassed most of Arhaios Holding within its walls, and along an interminable corridor, lit with mysterious light from windows the height of many men above their heads. They paused finally at another great doorway, guarded by Imperial sentries in a red and gold livery Kierce believed denoted the Emperor's personal guard. He did not ask. Hiren had not spoken a word since they entered the Palace. The tension he sensed in the Commander did nothing to allay his own unease. This was a fundamentally alien world to a Shaihen mind.

They waited, in silence, until the Imperial guard allowed them through into the presence of His Greatness, the 23rd Emperor of the Sacred Union.

Kierce met the Emperor Zelt an' Korsos long before he came face to face with him in his pillared marble palace.

He met his wealth in the broad streets of magnificent architecture, which invited the light of the brilliant southern skies into the city of Vordeith. He saw his inequity in the contrast between those glories of scale and balance and the mean hovels crowded against the city walls where those excluded from the citizenry of Vordeith scratched an existence. He saw Zelt's depravity in the scenes of lust and violence acted out on street corners and spilling from beyond taverns and brothels. He saw his hypocrisy in the multitude of richly decorated temples and his vanity in the statues of Imperial heroes and sculptures to Imperial triumphs. Most of all he saw his power in the mind of every human being in Vordeith. The will of His Greatness the Emperor governed every aspect of his peoples' lives; if they lived to serve him, they lived happily. If they did not … they did not live.

To Kierce's mind, Emperor Zelt an' Korsos of Caiivor, Cathva's adored father, was an embodiment of evil. Freedom was anathema to him.

How Turloch and Rainur had negotiated anything with him, Kierce had difficulty understanding. It showed him Turloch in a new light, if his predecessor had successfully and repeatedly had dealings with this gross mind that spread like an infection into everything and everyone around him.

The small black eyes that raked Kierce as he halted before the sumptuously upholstered throne almost bounced the Magician's own deep gaze back on himself. It pulled him up short. No fool held onto power in the political hothouse of this city for nearly thirty years. He knew instantly that he did not dare put a foot wrong with this man. This was a serious match for his skill.

"Lord Kierce." The Emperor turned his attention from Hiren's introduction to greet him. Even his voice was ravaged by indulgence. It resonated from somewhere deep within the monstrous body. Like his power, the Emperor's physical presence had expanded into an amorphous mass. "You stand before me. There are many who kneel, and some who abase themselves."

"You rule the proud as well as the humble, Greatness. That is your glory."

The Emperor smiled, a facial expression that involved many folds. Kierce was sure of his ground here. Hiren had primed him on the Emperor's preferences, and he was reading the right reactions in the mind in front of him, though he did it through gritted teeth at the rest of the garbage that floated around the Emperor's consciousness.

"I like a man of courage. Pride in what he is. Where the hell are you from?" He turned to one of his flock of hovering attendants. "Where the hell is he from?"

"Shehaios," said Kierce. "The site of Commander Hiren's recent victory, your Greatness."

"Oh, that bloody unpronounceable place in the north," said the Emperor. "Where my daughter went. Do you know my daughter, Lord Kierce?"

"I have the great honour to know your daughter very well, Your Greatness," said Kierce with perfect composure.

"H'mph," grunted the Emperor, "I said to her, why the hell do you want to go somewhere you can't bloody say? Still, she seems to like it there."

"We're very happy to have such a wise and beautiful queen in Shehaios," said Kierce.

"Wise?" said the Emperor whimsically. "She's a woman, for god's sake. Get your flattery right, Lord Kierce."

"My apologies, Your Greatness," said Kierce, trying not to smile.

"Mind you, Cathva is smarter than your average whore, I grant you that." He paused, his eyes resting on Kierce's bowed head. Kierce did not dare look up. The Emperor did not like people to laugh at his jokes. He made them entirely for his own amusement. "Well, Commander Hiren seems to have found it a conducive place to be as well. He tells me your barbarians fought loyally for him. I suppose you're here for a reward?"

"Our reward was the defeat of the enemies of the Sacred Union, your Greatness."

"And your own enemies."

"And our own enemies. We are honoured by this happy alliance, Your Greatness, and seek nothing more than your continued friendship."

There was a long pause from Zelt. He did not much like the word friendship, it hinted too much of equality. Kierce watched him carefully, though not with his eyes. He found he could concentrate better if he did not have to look at Zelt's hard black gaze, and he had to concentrate. Zelt's mind fizzed with possibilities and threats, he was constantly weighing one against the other, watching everything, picking up every nuance. It gave him an unnerving ability to spring surprises, to go where even Kierce least expected him to go.

"I would prefer it then if you delivered my enemies to me rather than executing justice yourselves," said Zelt. "Such enthusiasm belongs within the harness of the army. Outside that harness, it disturbs me."

Kierce greeted this change of tack with a slight sense of alarm.

"I can only assure you that it need not do so, Your Greatness."

"Really? I am disappointed that my dear son Rainur did not come to pay his respects to his father."

Kierce glanced up briefly, startled by the image of Rainur in the Emperor's mind. Zelt liked Rainur, but he didn't trust him. Rainur was a proud man. Now he was a proud man with an army.

"Lord Rainur shows his loyalty by remaining to guard our lands from Your Greatness's enemies," said Kierce. "He sends you assurances of his greatest respect and loyalty."

"I'm sure he does." Zelt smiled at Kierce's evident discomfort."And you may convey the same to him, Lord Kierce. Commander Hiren tells me the chief of your warriors is like all other Shaihens, and more concerned with the mud of his farm than the glory of battle."

"Commander Hiren speaks the truth, Your Greatness."

"Then he may find his reward of little value. But poor thing though it is, you may take Caras ti' Leath the sword of an Imperial Commander in recognition of his valour. I understand you are some kinsman of his, Lord Kierce. Will he like his reward, do you think?"

"I think he will be … overwhelmed," admitted Kierce. He understood only too well the double edge of the sword Zelt offered Caras. It bound the general of the victorious Shaihen forces to the Empire rather than to Rainur. The Chief of Oreath was free to grant his loyalty where he chose. If Imperial Commander Caras ever raised arms against the Empire, he would, like Volun, become a traitor to it.

Kierce found himself immensely grateful that Caras had not accepted Hiren's invitation to come to Vordeith. He could just see Caras kneeling before His Grossness to exchange his freedom for the warrior's laurels he did not want.

"Commander Hiren has been telling me about you, Lord Kierce," continued the Emperor. "So has my daughter, though not what I once thought she might be going to tell me. She now seems to be of the same opinion as Commander Hiren, that I should take note of the Shaihen wisdom you bring me. But she's a woman and he's just delivered me the head of my enemy and may think he can take liberties with me. What do you think, Lord Kierce?"

Kierce mastered his expression and raised his head.

"I wouldn't presume to anticipate your judgement on that matter, Your Greatness. I await your pleasure as to how you would like to decide it. I am equally happy to discuss philosophy or play you at twelve stones."

"You fancy yourself a player of the stones?" The Emperor leaned towards Kierce and lowered his voice. "And would you see to it you lost that game, Lord Kierce?"

Kierce hesitated fractionally. It was impossible to pre-judge that answer. The Emperor could jump either way. In that situation, all Kierce could do was go for the truth and trust his instincts. He knew the worst thing he could do was prevaricate.

"I always play to win, Your Greatness."

The Emperor regarded him thoughtfully and Kierce waited apprehensively.

"Now is that courage, or is it foolhardiness?" mused the Emperor. He sat back and gestured towards an empty chair on his right hand. "All right. I accept your opening gambit, Lord High Magician of Shehaios." He pronounced the name faultlessly. "Talk to me. Tell me whether Hiren's been feeding me pearls of wisdom or a heap of garbage."

It was an exhausting and nerve-wracking debate, and at the end of it Kierce still wasn't sure whether he'd been discussing philosophy or playing twelve stones. He seemed to have been doing both, and never had he faced a tougher opponent.

He was fairly sure he'd won. The Emperor's interest in Tay-Aien was not about morality, it was about control. Tay-Aien's teachings were very easy to structure and impose hierarchically; it offered him a mechanism from the bottom upwards which would get some control over these unruly tribal loyalties that divided his Empire at every turn. Kierce better understood Hiren's joke about his own *she-haios* now. To every displaced tribesman, his own land and culture were as sacred as the Shaihens was to them. It fuelled every battle the Empire faced. And there he was, Lord High Magician of Shehaios, sitting at the Emperor's feet discussing how best to control this urge for freedom.

He left the Emperor's presence without any sense of victory, feeling very much like Caras reporting his losses to Hiren at the battle of Toshan. The whole business left a similarly sour taste in his mouth. The Emperor was an astute and erudite man, and he wielded his power wisely. He chose his favourites shrewdly and discarded them ruthlessly if they got above themselves. The justice he despatched might be arbitrary, but it was swift, clear and unsentimental and he understood the fundamental basis of his power. Like his daughter, the people of Vordeith both feared and worshipped him. The prosperity of the city depended on his strength and his strength depended on the prosperity of the city. He was a creation of his own Empire and the power it gave him.

Kierce found his own way back to Hiren's residence, his host having been dismissed from the debate. He was conscious of the curiosity that followed him along the streets. There was no particular hostility in it, but his hair, his clothes, the stocky, shaggy little horse he rode all distinguished him as a foreign visitor and an object of some interest.

He did not seek Hiren's company when he arrived at the house, making straight for the guest room he had been given. He dismissed with terseness bordering on violence the multiplicity of servants who hovered around awaiting his pleasure. He hated the feel of their presence, the matching reverse-side monstrosity to the one he had just left.

He sat down and drank a draught of wine and closed his eyes. There was a tightness in his chest, and he was conscious of his own breathing. If he stayed too long in this place, in this world, he suspected he could quite literally suffocate. He had Hiren's Triumph to get through yet, and tomorrow the Emperor had invited him to attend the Games. Which would prove the worse experience, he couldn't tell.

If he got through this, he promised himself, and he ever got back to Shehaios, he would wash this filth from himself in the Haven's spring and spend a month in the hills of Arhaios. And the wild horses he tracked would not drag him back here. Ever.

Assuming Caras did not murder him first for accepting the title of Imperial Commander on his behalf. He could still see the look on Caras's face when he offered him the silver icon of the bull-headed lion he had taken from a Caiivorian robber in the forests of Oreath.

He became aware of someone approaching his quarters. He contemplated making himself invisible, until he saw the cause of the impending intrusion into his solitude.

Queen Cathva was at the household, enquiring after him.

From the moment they entered the City and the heaviness began to settle around Kierce's heart, Cathva's spirits had soared. He had never seen her so animated nor so beautiful. That she too loved the home of her birth he couldn't doubt, and he could even understand why. The City resonated with life as much as, to Kierce, it resonated with horrors. It was a wonderful place for those who liked human creations.

Any enjoyment he derived from Vordeith, he suspected he was going to feel in Cathva's company. Her vivacity was infectious. When he was with her, he could breathe.

He anticipated the messenger, and went down to meet her.

She turned to greet him with a glorious smile and held out her hands towards him.

"I knew I only had to get you here!" she exclaimed, with an air of mischief. "And now you've done your duty and charmed the old man, I can show you what you miss by shutting yourself away in your cold eyrie up north." She paused, holding his hands and gazing into his face. "This is my Haven, Kierce. You don't need to become a beast. You can walk beside me here as a man. What more proper than the Queen of Shehaios showing an honoured guest from her new home the delights and treasures of her old one?"

Kierce smiled at her.

"Right now?"

"There's a lot to see!"

She folded her hand around his arm and led him outside. What appeared to Kierce to be a small army of guards and attendants formed up behind them. He began to realise she was showing him off to the city as much as she was showing the city off to him, from which he guessed that the reports of his debate with the Emperor were in his favour.

"What do you mean," he said conversationally, as they left Hiren's house. "You only had to get me here?"

He was glad she had chosen to walk. Since she wouldn't ride, the only other transport available in the city, apart from the river, was to be carried in a litter by slaves. Kierce had difficulty with the way Caiivorians harnessed their horses; he had still more difficulty with the idea of harnessing men.

"I knew my father would see it in you. I knew you could show him. He never knew about Turloch, Turloch and Rainur designed it that way." She smiled at him. "This is the beginning, Lord Kierce."

"The beginning of what?"

Kierce began to try and find out, but Cathva's mind was side-tracked onto the guided tour and all he could see was the triumph of Imperial battles past, carved in stone.

He let it drop, and allowed the sights of the city and Cathva's cheerful enthusiasm wash over him. It was her company that he took pleasure in; he dutifully admired what he was shown, but none of it really touched him until they were on their way back. They were passing a large, imposing pillared building on their right opposite a square fronting an ornate temple to their left. Cathva was waxing lyrical about the riches of the temple, but Kierce's attention was arrested by the larger, plainer building she had ignored. He paused and turned towards it. There was something in there that drew him as none of the temples had done.

"What's that place?"

Cathva looked round.

"Academia," she said, dismissively. She saw his interest and sought for a translation. "Library. Halls of Learning." She paused as Kierce continued to study the building, deep in reflection. "Turloch spent all his time in Vordeith in there. I don't think he ever came out." She squeezed Kierce's arm. "*Please* don't turn into Turloch, whatever you do. Repulsive little man." She gave a slight shudder and then rallied defensively against Kierce's questioning smile. "Well, he was, wasn't he?"

She checked. Just for a moment, he knew she remembered looking across the spring of life into his face and Turloch's eyes.

She took her hand from his arm and moved away towards the square.

"Did the Emperor actually meet Turloch?" asked Kierce. "I mean, were they introduced, formally?"

"He was there when Rainur met him. I think he was probably presented, when they first came. As Rainur's chief advisor. My father never really took much notice of him."

"And he spent all his time in Academia," murmured Kierce. So that was how Turloch did it. That was how he survived in this place. He didn't. He opted out and lost himself in the accumulated knowledge of the Imperial City's intellectuals. "And Rainur?"

"Oh, Rainur was frequently given an audience. He was an expert. Engaging without being ingratiating, modest without being servile, appreciative of everything yet full of his own dreams. He didn't kneel before His Greatness either." She gave a slight sigh. "Rainur charmed us all. I could have married him ten times over."

There was a pregnant pause.

"Rainur is a good man," said Kierce.

"He is," said Cathva. She turned an arch look on him. "You, Lord Kierce, are not."

"Cathva—." He moved forwards beside her. He wanted to touch her, but he was aware of the retinue waiting at their discreet distance. "Cathva, I didn't come here to be with you. I came because … because Hiren left me no choice. I don't belong here. I don't—," He hesitated, "I don't belong with you."

"It was Davitis who forced Hiren's hand," said Cathva, dreamily.

"Yes, but—."

"And who do you think goaded Davitis into writing that letter?" She turned the deep blue eyes full of mischief towards him. Kierce started. He'd never even thought to look.

"Actually, it was Orlii," said Cathva. "On my instructions. Your servant can twist that foolish man around his little finger. It was a stroke of genius, giving Davitis Orlii. "

"I didn't give him Orlii!" rasped Kierce. "And I think I'm less of a genius than a dumb fool! Orlii persuaded Davitis to write that letter, convinced

Hiren it had gone to the Emperor and then stole it back and gave it to me? Is that what you're telling me?"

"It made sure Hiren had to tell the Emperor what he knew about you," said Cathva. "Don't worry, Kierce. If Hiren hadn't invited you to Vordeith, I would have done. The whole point was to get you here, not to let Davitis get his vindictive little way. Come on!" She chided the dark anger on Kierce's face. "You know Davitis was going to crack sooner or later. Orlii had been keeping the lid on his paranoia for months."

"I know he would have confirmed what you'd already hinted at," said Kierce grimly. "I'm still working out why, Cathva. Am I here as a sacrifice? Or just to indulge your thirst for a fight? Emperor and Magician, bright ideas beaten into swords!"

"You wouldn't be so foolish, Kierce. I know that now. You're here to meet the Emperor, Priest of Tay-Aien. So that he knows who you are. So that he trusts you."

So that you will be safe when Rainur is gone.

The thought he read in her mind, so calm and matter of fact, turned him cold. He turned and walked away from her. He knew that was what they had planned. He knew that was the warning Hiren had delivered. He thought he had headed it off.

In fact, he may have just made it possible.

Kierce knew about the Games of the Imperial City. Everyone knew about the Games of the Imperial City. They were the pinnacle of entertainment no visitor to Vordeith could miss.

He spent most of the display concentrating on preventing his body from shaking. He felt it not as the sharp pain of Toshan, but more as an enervating fever that he struggled to keep secret. He could not afford to let the Emperor see how it affected him.

Kierce killed animals. He ate meat. He wore skins. He enjoyed tracking and killing his prey. He did not enjoy watching animals trapped and goaded into fighting each other. Men using their weapons against creatures who killed in defence, or hunger, or desperation. There was nothing of the skill of the hunt in this and nothing of the necessity of the farm either. It was killing for the thrill of killing and fighting for the pleasure of fighting, a celebration of man's power over the life around him and the absolute antithesis of Shaihen magic.

He wanted to escape, but if he left, he would offend his host, and the entire journey, the lies and the dissembling, would have been for nothing.

Offending the Emperor was a capital offence. It was not impossible he could end up in the arena, one of the performing animals. The amazing Magician of Shehaios. How many would it take to kill him? How many, to be quick enough to strike hard enough, often enough, to exceed his power to heal himself?

He could not understand how these people, so civilised in so many ways, failed to make the connection between the cruelty they inflicted and the cruelty they suffered. Why did they not strive to free themselves of both? He began to have some sympathy for poor old Tay-Aien, striving to impose some sanity on this wilful passion for destruction.

Beside him, Cathva applauded her chosen champions with animation, too absorbed in her own pleasure to be aware of Kierce's silent pain. Finally, the combats and the bloodshed were over. There was a pause while slaves swept the arena and scattered sawdust to cover the blood. Some of the crowd began to leave. Kierce glanced at the Emperor, still reclining comfortably on his seat. The hypocritical old tyrant seemed to embody all the foulness Kierce had just witnessed. Never had a corpulent body looked more in need of a sharp blade thrust deep into its flesh. It really was just as well Caras hadn't come. He'd have been quite likely to do it.

Cathva leaned slightly towards him.

"The dancers are His Greatness's favourite."

"Do they kill anybody?" asked Kierce, sourly.

"Of course not. They dance. Watch." She leaned a little closer and rested her hand briefly on his thigh. "I think you'll like this."

The dancers were a large troupe, filling the arena. They were all exceptionally beautiful young men and women and their clothing decorated their nakedness rather than covered it. Their musicians stood in a group in the centre and began to beat a rhythm. Wild, strident music arose around it, setting the dancers in motion across the freshly dried blood of the killing ground beneath their feet.

Kierce sat up and stopped trying to shrink through the floor of the Emperor's pavilion. No wonder the illusion he had created at the Feast of Disorder had gone down so well with the soldiers, he reflected. He was showing them a memory of the arena – despite the fact that it was a memory he did not have.

As the dance unfolded, erotic, enticing and enchanting, he began at last to enjoy what was being displayed for his enjoyment. Cathva turned to him in amusement as the dance ended.

"I told you you'd like that," she said.

But Kierce was still studying the arena. He took Cathva's gaze down with him, dimming the sunlight around the edges of the arena and sending a shaft of light onto two dancers in the middle, a man and a woman. Cathva watched, fascinated.

A collective gasp arose from the crowd, a massed orgasmic sigh. It escaped Cathva too. She half rose from her seat, clutching her face with her hands, and turned an appalled stare on Kierce.

"How *dare* you!" she exclaimed.

Kierce chuckled. "Oh, Cathva! What did you see?"

The last was a dance of his own making, an illusion the dancers below were ignorant of. Every man and woman in the audience had seen briefly before their own eyes a glimpse of their most secret, most desired sexual fantasy.

He met Cathva's eyes, and knew what she had seen. It was something that could be denied no longer.

Chapter 37
Return from Vordeith

The Magician's Tower arose with impressive speed to dominate the western side of the Haven. It was completed less than four years after its conception, and Kierce was using it long before the interior was finished.

At its centre was a narrow stone tower, topped by a conical roof of golden slates cut from Shaihen rock, thicker than the window glazing but with the same golden sheen. Below the roof, a ring of arches encircled the tower, letting light flood down through the interior. Apart from structural cross-beams, the stone tower was hollow, one soaring space from the inlaid stone floor to the gold-filtered sky above.

Around the outside, four floors of stone and wood encircled the central tower, each floor divided into three rooms and each room richly decorated. The decoration and adornment, in fact, was never completed – it was Kierce's intention that future generations should add to the treasures of the Magician's Tower. Each level was dedicated to one of the elements that made up the Shaihen view of life. The first level, dedicated to water and to life itself, depicted riotous images of fertility. The second showed the fruits of earthly life, and was full of wonderful objects of artistry and craftsmanship and images of natural beauty. Above that were the winds of the music which carried the continuity of Shaihen life and at the top, the narrowest of the levels, the fire of the phoenix, a celebration of those things which transcended death and most embodied the Spirit of Shehaios.

Beyond the tower, almost completely obscured by its grandeur, the small earthen cottage with the turf roof survived. It had a new roof and a new door, and Kierce took up residence there before the Tower was more than a hole in the ground, from the moment his relations with Rainur began to decline.

Once he returned from Vordeith, his visits to the Palace grew even less frequent. He went there solely to see Sartin. After their visit to Vordeith, Cathva came to him.

When he made love to Cathva in Vordeith there was none of the violence that had accompanied their first steamy coupling. She knew when he was in her mind. She responded to him. Physical union was not an expression of what bound them together, it *was* what bound them together. The satisfaction of her desires was the only thing Cathva felt deeply, the only point at which they met, but it was a profound meeting. When they were joined, physically and mentally, it was so complete, it was like a small death to part again.

Kierce had intended to restrict the affair to a brief indulgence of passion in the Imperial City, where he felt it belonged. He had not intended to bring it back to Shehaios with him, but by the time he returned he was forced to accept that it was something he had never had control over. He might be the magician, but he was well caught in Cathva's spell. It was not something either of them was strong enough to give up.

They remained discreet. The Lord High Magician returned from the Imperial City charged by the Emperor with promulgating the very teachings he had mocked Davitis for and it made Davitis a rather more dangerous enemy. Cathva was careful never to appear to go to the Tower alone and patiently endured interminable discussions with Davitis to impress upon Rainur the purity of her purpose in visiting it.

Cathva's father himself assisted her in her deception, though he was singularly unaware of it.

Shortly after Kierce left Vordeith, the Emperor fell ill. It was a debilitating rather than life-threatening sickness, that laid him low for the best part of a year and severely dampened his enthusiasm for instituting any major changes he might otherwise have contemplated.

Had Kierce still been in the city, Hiren might have interrogated him about it. As it was, Hiren held his counsel and no-one else dreamed of making any connection between the Emperor's sudden inexplicable illness and the strange little northern priest who had, apparently, delivered them from the King of the West and been a five-minute wonder to the city.

As the Emperor recovered, he did notice that the recurrence of his problem seemed to coincide with his visits to the arena, and he gradually lost his taste for the games.

It was not long after her return to the Haven that Cathva began to receive letters from her father's sickbed. Less letters, in fact, than diktats beseeching his offspring to attend to the teachings of Tay-Aien. Most of the content was plainly despatched wholesale to all his many children, but for his favourite daughter in the wild northern reaches of his Empire there were personalised sections.

"My dearest Cathva. I commend you to the worthy Lord Kierce, learned in the words of the wise. I advise you most urgently to study under this man, and obey his instructions in all things."

Cathva broke off in a fit of giggles as Kierce took the advice literally, tumbling her down beneath him onto the silks of the couch that filled one alcove of the room. They were on the Tower's first floor, surrounded by celebrations of fertility.

She held the letter aloft while she attended to the instructions of his lips. The low murmur of a small fountain filled the background, bubbling its depiction of the Haven's spring into a shallow pool of yellow Shaihen stone, polished until it shone gold beneath the water.

Her father's words fluttered from her hand as Kierce pulled her gown over her head.

"Oh, gods, what have you done to me, that I should dare laugh at him?" she said, gazing up into Kierce's face. His deft fingers worked at the lacing of her undergarments. "This is blasphemy of the worst kind, Kierce, you do understand that?"

"Every pompous ass deserves to be laughed at," said Kierce, punctuating the words with kisses. "Anyway," he paused and looked down at her. "This is a temple dedicated to life. We are worshipping the act of procreation. What's blasphemous about that?"

"I meant, we are laughing at my father. He really sounds quite serious about it."

Kierce grinned.

"I'm sure he is. What do you think he wanted to talk to me about?"

"Organising the Tay-Aien brotherhood?"

Kierce shook his head.

"The power behind it. What people believe, what they fear. What they dream of. Oh, you give me some very, very nice dreams, Cathva,"

He buried his face in her breasts, and worked his way down her body.

"I'm sure you're a wicked man, Kierce," sighed Cathva. "I don't know how you fooled my father you were a priest."

"Gambler's bluff," murmured Kierce, indistinctly. "Stop talking, woman."

Kierce was not surprised by Zelt's sudden interest in spiritual matters; it was a concern that often affected powerful men faced with their own mortality. Nor, of course, was he surprised by the illness that was causing Zelt to face his own mortality. On balance, he felt he'd probably done the old monster a favour by undermining his health – shedding a little of the grossness he carried around with him would add years to the Emperor's life expectancy.

His intention, however, had simply been to buy Shaihen independence a little more time, and he succeeded in doing so. Apart from the new military commander who escorted them back to the Haven, the Imperial representation in the Haven remained unchanged. Rainur remained King and as far as Zelt was concerned, Kierce remained a priest of Tay-Aien's god.

It was shortly after Sartin's third birthday that the decree Kierce had long been expecting finally issued from Vordeith. The only officially recognised temples within the Empire would henceforth be those dedicated to the god of Tay-Aien. All Imperial officials, kings and governors would be required to declare their adherence to the creed.

On a glorious spring day when it was very tempting to be elsewhere than within the walls of the Palace, Kierce answered a summons from Rainur to discuss the Emperor's ultimatum. Sartin saw him coming and ambushed him on the way with pleas to be taken riding, which Kierce delayed rather than refused. This should not take long. There was only ever one answer you could give to the Emperor.

Rainur rarely spoke to Kierce now, except in the presence of others. He watched Kierce's relationship with Cathva as much for signs of intimidation as signs of intimacy. His suspicion and enmity were fixed on the Magician; he refused to believe his Queen was anything other than pure and beautiful and above suspicion.

He sat and read, and re-read, the Emperor's decree. The connection between the title Kierce had returned from Vordeith with, Cathva's sudden religiosity, and this unacceptable imposition on Shaihen freedom began to work its way slowly into his mind, to reveal to him what he did not want revealed.

There could be no division between the King and Magician. Shehaios was the Whole Land. How could it be the Whole Land, split in two halves?

How could he split himself into two halves, and deny the half he had wedded to Cathva? He thought of her with Kierce. Kierce, stripping away the elegant Imperial refinement which sheltered her beauty from his crude humour. Kierce's infuriating, untouchable arrogance. The narrow face with its frame of well-groomed black hair; the wicked grin that made his dark eyes glow like coals.

Rainur shook himself, conscious of his hatred twisting the image in his mind. He looked up a little guiltily as someone came into the room, but it was not Kierce. It was another deputation of worried Merveccians, after yet more protection from the *caii* raiders in the mountains.

He was still talking to them when Kierce did arrive, but he dismissed them peremptorily. There would be no witnesses to this conversation with the Lord High Magician.

"I'm not going anywhere, Rainur," said Kierce mildly as Gascon's men left the room far from satisfied. "You could have finished dealing with them."

"Every time Gascon sends to me he wants more and more," replied Rainur, shortly. "He has a substantial part of the Imperial army on his doorstep, he doesn't want Jagus charging in there wielding a sword, so what does he bloody want?"

"He has had a lot of raids to deal with. You're getting the same complaint from Caras, and it affects Mervecc's income more seriously than Oreath's. Merchants don't want to come through the Gate without an escort—."

"Don't teach me my business, Kierce," snapped Rainur. He snatched up the formal written decree from the Emperor. "Tell me what in confusion we're going to do about this!"

Kierce sat down and stretched lazily. "How about nothing? The whole of our agreement with the Empire is based on deception. The Imperial governor of Shehaios is the idiot Davitis, but you still hold power. They presented Hiren's arrival here as a conquest when we invited him to come and protect us. So as far as Tay-Aien's teachings go ... " he shrugged. "Well, you've already built the temple. All we have to do is dedicate it."

Rainur stared at him in amazement.

"To Tay-Aien?"

Kierce smiled.

"To Tay-Aien's priest. Follow the path of truth, follow the path of life? I can live with that."

There was a highly charged silence. Rainur looked at him, sprawled across the comfortably upholstered settle in Rainur's private study. The man who could read his mind seemed oblivious to the passionate thoughts churning around in it at the moment. He sat down before he gave way to a desire to lock his hands around Kierce's throat.

"You're not Tay-Aien's priest. That's just—."

"What I told the Emperor. Or rather, the construction the Emperor chose to put on what I did tell him. I said I was his servant." Kierce paused and his eyes met Rainur's briefly, awaking a passing image of embers. "Which I am, at present. One of the uncomfortable truths Turloch couldn't live with, I think. At no point did I ever say that I served any god. He just assumed that I did."

"Hiren knows you don't."

"Hiren is a much less complicated person than the Emperor. The Emperor has to believe in gods or he doesn't believe in himself. He can't conceive of a world in which there is no ultimate authority beyond death."

Rainur toyed with the Imperial parchment in his hands and tried to focus on Tay-Aien's teachings. All he could think of was that this man across the room was laughing at him. Cuckolded him. Took his beautiful, innocent Princess and made of her … what?

"Have you read Tay-Aien, Rainur?" asked Kierce.

"As much of it as I could stomach. It's full of bigotry and intolerance. You only have to watch the way Davitis tortures himself. It all seems solely concerned with measuring humanity against some unattainable perfection. What does that have to do with Shaihen magic?"

He looked up. *What do you have to do with Shaihen magic?* he wanted to ask.

Kierce smiled.

"You tell me, Rainur. I'm not much of an expert on unattainable perfection."And this time, his eyes held Rainur's, and Rainur knew he was fully aware of the emotions raging through him. Aware. Amused. Arrogant. Bastard. "Unlike Turloch," said Kierce, quietly. "Turloch was a great expert on unattainable perfection. I rarely create illusions, Rainur, people create enough of their own. This was never your dream you were building, was it? You don't really want to be a part of the Empire. You don't really want to be married to Cathva."

Rainur surged to his feet.

"How dare you!"

"Not the real Cathva. You wanted to make her into what you thought she should be, but you brought her to the home of freedom. It's her choice."

"Spirit defend me!" erupted Rainur, "Don't try and justify yourself, Kierce. It's not Cathva. It's you. You abuse the power you hold for your own entertainment." He hovered on the brink. If he said what was in his mind now it was irrevocable, and the split was wide open. Which side of it the Imperial alliance lay, he couldn't say.

Kierce got to his feet and turned casually away from him.

"Your marriage was part of a deal, Rainur, and there's no going back. Live with it."

"How do you live with yourself?" spat Rainur. "How do you live with Turloch's memory? You talk like the Lord High Magician, and you behave like—." He broke off. "You behave like the bloody Emperor."

Kierce winced and glanced back at him.

"Ouch. Well played, Rainur. I felt that." He turned to face the King, the small man with the power to command all Rainur's people. "The truth then, since you want it. Cathva's interpretation of love is ... different. But in no sense of the word did she ever love you. She chose instead to bestow her own crippled interpretation of the concept on me – chose is not the right word. The choice we have in such things is limited. As my own choice was." He met Rainur's eyes without apology. "I didn't intend to hurt or to undermine you, Rainur. I am not ... 'entertaining myself' with Cathva. I love her. Don't let it destroy Shehaios."

"You dare charge me with that!"

"You're living on borrowed time. The Emperor never intended to let you die in your bed as King of Shehaios. He barely needs an excuse to replace Davitis with a governor who will over-ride your authority. Don't give him one."

"I made the agreement with Emperor Zelt," said Rainur, curtly. "I retain an independent title."

"I know Zelt's mind. And Cathva has always known it. My advice is to discover the delights of Tay-Aien. You'll find the Tower an amenable place, it has aspects to suit all moods. You don't have to encounter me in every stone."

He paused, watching Rainur struggle.

"No-one who plays the Great Emperor wins. I believe I've held him to a draw so far but if you and I fight each other, I will lose too. And while you may very well want to see Kierce in the Arena, you don't want to see the Lord High Magician destroyed there. Do you?"

"Get out," hissed Rainur. "Get out of my sight, get out of my presence, and take your lies with you! You're a disgrace to the heritage you carry." He began to advance on Kierce. "You hide behind it because you know the trust I was born to is worth more to me than anything else – you cynical, manipulative, self-centred bastard!"

Kierce retreated diplomatically, aware how close Rainur was to losing control of his rage.

"I'll see what I can do for Gascon's problems," he said, mildly. "I'll be in Mervecc if you want me." He checked in the doorway. "The Shaihen woman Cathva brought with her from Vordeith – Tilsey. You may care to know that she worships the ground you tread on. Perhaps a source of some comfort to you?"

"Get out!" yelled Rainur.

Chapter 38
Davitis Recalled

Kierce disliked the rebuilt Mervecc with its strong fortifications. It bore too many of the hallmarks of the Caiivorian towns he had seen south of the Gate, and he was trying to devise a way of achieving the same level of protection without the grim side-effects suffered by the southerners.

Gascon was no uncouth warrior prince, but he was very fond of his Holding's wealth and prepared to sacrifice quite a lot to avoid losing it again.

"I must say, I've got some sympathy for Rainur," said Kierce, and smiled to himself at the misapprehension in Gascon's mind. Despite their attempts at discretion, he knew his affair with Cathva was a poorly kept secret. "I mean, you do have a substantial part of the Imperial Army on your doorstep, so if you don't want Jagus running amok, what do you want? Jagus did offer. He probably is capable of doing something effective, too, by now."

"Effective in terms of solving the problem, or just stirring things up?" asked Gascon.

"Difficult to tell," admitted Kierce. "They're an elusive enemy."

"Do you know where they are?"

Kierce strolled on a few paces without answering, studying the perimeter wall they were following around the Holding.

"Sometimes. I can't distinguish between the groups. And sometimes … somehow, I just don't see them. They're like ghosts. Nothing there."

Gascon swished away a fly with the cane he had taken to carrying. He had never completely recovered from the spear wound. Kierce could sympathise with his fondness for walls. A man who had suffered such a blow would go to some lengths to avoid repeating the experience.

"Well, Kierce, I don't know about you but I don't have much faith in Jagus's effectiveness against ghosts. I fear his attentions might cause them to multiply. I wonder if they're as strong as they are because Caras taught them they have nothing to fear from Shehaios."

Kierce did not comment. There was a particular group, and a particular leader, working to unite the scattered Caiivorian raiders into a cohesive force operating both sides of the Shaihen border. They called themselves *as-caii*, and their leader's name was reputed to be Girstan.

Rainur took considerable pains over the wording of his request to the Emperor that he should not be asked to do anything to compromise the long and peaceful history of personal liberty within his kingdom. The Emperor's response was ominous. It was not addressed to Rainur. It was for Davitis. It recalled him to Vordeith.

279

Kierce saw the Imperial messenger and the reply he carried as they passed through Mervecc. He did not return to the Haven. There was nothing to be done. Davitis reported directly to the Emperor, he could do no other than obey the summons he received. The real problem would be who replaced Davitis.

To his surprise, Davitis called in at Mervecc on his way through a few days later, pausing there overnight though he was barely a day's ride from the Gate. Kierce watched ironically as the vast baggage train of Davitis's belongings straggled into Mervecc. That had taken a while to pack. Davitis, he suspected, had been planning his return for some time. Davitis also knew the mind of the Emperor, though Kierce suspected he was hoping to be sent back with renewed powers to settle the scores he had been tallying up during his time in Shehaios. That, at least, Kierce felt was unlikely. Davitis had fulfilled his purpose.

Part of the reason for his visit to Mervecc seemed to become apparent later, when Orlii received a discreet message similar to many such messages he had received from Davitis since the first winter of the Imperial presence in Shehaios.

"Say goodbye from me," Kierce told him, as he left. "Tell him I'll miss him too."

Orlii grinned, and went on his way.

He returned unexpectedly late that night. He knocked tentatively on the door of the room where Kierce was staying, something he never normally did once Kierce had dismissed him.

"Are you sleeping, Master?" he whispered.

Kierce was not. He was going over and round the nascent confrontation between the Shaihen view of the Empire's authority and the Empire's own view of it, to no very great conclusion. With some surprise, he told Orlii to come in.

Orlii crept tentatively round the door. He was a big lad to creep anywhere now, eighteen years old, a tall, slim, handsome young Caiivorian man. The large, serious eyes watched from a round face that still had a boyish look to it, accentuated by the Imperial-style haircut.

"I am sorry to disturb you, Master," he said.

Kierce sighed and shifted stiffly, realising just how long he had been sitting lost in thought.

"I need disturbing, Orlii. Or at least, I need shifting. I'm disturbed enough already. What's the matter? Davitis?"

"Kind of." Orlii hesitated, looking at him apprehensively. "Davitis has invited me to go with him to the Imperial City."

"Do you want to go?"

"I am your servant, my lord."

"So you say. Do you want to go?" Kierce knew he did. He just thought it would be good for Orlii to actually say so out loud.

"I don't want to leave you, my lord."

"I've told you before. You're free to go wherever, with whomever, whenever you like. Tell me that you want to go."

Orlii looked at him with a tentative smile.

"I want to go, Lord Kierce."

Kierce smiled broadly back at him.

"Then go. You can keep an eye on the damn fool for me."

"I will come back," promised Orlii. "I know … I am still your servant, my lord."

"And you serve me best by doing what you want to do."

"I … did think that, my lord."

"You *thought*. Well, there's something I'd never have expected to hear from you when I first met you, Orlii. Maybe I've taught you something."

"You've taught me much, Master—," began Orlii, with feeling.

Kierce raised his hand.

"Don't get carried away. You're still a bloody Caiivorian with … well, with very few redeeming features. But you do have a few. When do you leave?"

"First thing tomorrow …" Orlii hesitated.

"Yes. Of course you can take the horse. I wouldn't inflict a journey in that ox cart on my worst enemy. And you aren't that, I trust, Orlii." He got to his feet, went over to the young man and embraced him. "Take care in Vordeith. Keep your wits about you. Though I suspect you'll get on with the place much better than I did."

"I will return," said Orlii again. "I will be what you want me to be."

Kierce frowned at him slightly.

"I don't want you to be anything but a free man, Orlii."

He watched Orlii lower his head and school his thoughts.

"Orlii," Kierce called him back as a vision of Davitis's baggage train came into his mind. "Be careful on the way as well. With all that stuff Davitis is carrying with him your party is going to look like a worm on a hook to the Caiivorian bandits. Keep watch as I've taught you to. Pay attention to your horse, she'll likely scent danger before you do. Remember, I won't be there to protect you this time."

"We have an Imperial army escort."

"Yes, but you're still a fat juicy Imperial prize. Be aware of it. Davitis won't be."

"Yes, Master."

As Kierce stood in the vecce at Mervecc waiting to see Orlii off the next morning, he began to think it was time he himself took the opposite road back to the Haven. He'd denied himself the pleasure of Cathva's company long enough; if Rainur's temper had not cooled by now, it was unlikely that it ever would.

Davitis was the last to arrive and everyone was waiting for him. When he saw Kierce there, he swung aside and came up to him. There was an insufferable smugness in his face.

"Farewell, Lord Kierce. Until we meet again," he said, meaningfully. "When the Emperor hears the truth about you, I suspect we may."

Kierce regarded him levelly.

"I wish you luck, Citizen Davitis. You'll need that and more to taint the reputation of the wise and learned Lord Kierce and the Emperor's favourite daughter. Tell him she studies under me. He'll be delighted."

"You're always so sure of yourself," sneered Davitis. "I really do look forward to seeing the evil flogged out of you before you're left to die by the road to Vordeith."

"Then I have to say I look forward to disappointing you," replied Kierce, drily. "If your dreams are that unpleasant, Davitis, I could recommend a herb …"

Davitis turned and walked away from him.

"Ah well," said Kierce to himself. "Maybe not, then."

Yet there was something in the vindictive triumph of the look Davitis turned on him as he left that made Kierce just wonder if he'd missed something.

He found out what it was when he returned to the Haven. When Cathva asked where Orlii was.

When he told her, she stared at him in disbelief. He was lying on the couch in the lavishly decorated room on the first level of the Tower, listening contentedly to the fountain. He was aware of her eyes fixing on him as he gazed down at the inlaid patterns of gold dancing beneath the waters. Depictions of fruits and flowers spread out from the fountain to become entangled with copulating animals and naked human dancers. It was an amazing piece of work, and it had taken the artist more than two solid years to do it. Kierce was pleased with the result. It wasn't quite what he had envisioned, but he was not the artist. The artist, quite evidently, had seen the Vordeithan Arena.

"You let him go? With Davitis?"

The horror in her voice surprised him, but it took a while to sink through his complacency. Cathva really was magnificent. He rolled over slightly so that he could see her dressing to return to the Palace. The pretence of marriage was over, but Rainur did not wish to jeopardise the inheritance of the boy he still unquestioningly believed to be his son by formally separating himself from his Imperial wife.

"He wanted to go and seek his fortune in the Imperial City. It wasn't my place to stop him."

Cathva paused with her gown still unlaced. Most unlike her, who hated untidiness.

"How could you be so stupid? Can you not read Davitis's mind?"

"Read it once. Didn't seem much to be gained by reading it again." Kierce frowned at her. "What? Davitis won't hurt Orlii. He's besotted with him."

"You think there aren't other boys in Vordeith? Kierce, I don't believe you could be this stupid! How can you not have seen it? You know Tay-Aien teaches that what Davitis does with Orlii is a sin."

"Vordeith is full of it, Cathva. It's full of everything. The people are obsessed with human appetites." He stretched a lazy hand towards her. "Look what it did to us."

Cathva moved impatiently out of his reach.

"That's irrelevant. You've read my father's letters. He's developed a passion for enforcing Tay-Aien's rules."

"If Davitis denounces Orlii he denounces himself. He's not going to cut his own throat."

"You've read Tay-Aien. All Davitis has to do is confess and do a penance and promise to try harder. He does it all the time. He can arrest Orlii and charge him with a capital offence!"

Kierce sat up, beginning to grasp the reason for her agitation. "But why would he?"

"Orlii is your servant. He knows everything about you. If he bears witness against you under torture, it will be known that he speaks the truth. Davitis knows you're not really a priest of Tay-Aien." She moved closer and stood over him, impatient and accusing. "Don't you understand anything, Magician? You deceived the Emperor. And you're about to be found out!"

Kierce digested this in shocked silence. He reached reluctantly for his own clothes.

"So that's why he was so bloody pleased with himself. I only see what I look for, Cathva. I only read the strategy when I know there's a game in progress. Orlii knew nothing of this."

"Of course he didn't. You think he would go willingly into captivity and torture? Do you know what they'll do to him?" She turned away in exasperation. "No, obviously not!"

He didn't, but Cathva did and he was beginning to.

"Less of a genius and more of a dumb fool," he reflected with quiet bitterness. "I will never understand how the Caiivorian mind works." He looked at the angry and frightened Caiivorian woman in front of him, who held him in such thrall. "I'll go after them."

"Blink! Be there!" commanded Cathva angrily.

Chapter 39
Murder on the Border

The bandits fell upon the Imperial party without warning.

They were camped on the plains south of the Gate to Shehaios. The Imperial soldiers kept watch, but the Caiivorian warriors knew the secret of moving silently through the darkness. The sentries' throats were cut before they knew anything was amiss.

Davitis and Orlii lay together in the envoy's tent. It was one of the reasons Davitis had not sought refuge at the nearest township. He wanted to delay the moment he had to give up Orlii as long as possible, and he wanted to keep his treasures safe from pilfering hands. Both his ambitions were doomed to an abrupt and violent end.

There was no time for them to do anything, even get dressed. Within seconds of the screams of their guards alerting them, the curtain protecting their privacy was ripped aside and half a dozen fully armed Caiivorian bandits stood looking at them.

Davitis was seized and dragged outside. Another of the attackers reached out to grab Orlii and haul him to his feet. Then the man paused, his eyes on the tattoo on Orlii's chest, the one remaining link to the people he had been born to. Orlii heard Davitis's cries of fear and protest turn rapidly to screams of agony and he gazed in terror at his captor.

"Girstan!" called the man, dragging Orlii over to one of the band's leaders. "Girstan, this is one of ours."

Orlii peered fearfully into the helmeted face in front of him. The bandits' leader was a thickset middle-aged man who looked as if he made a habit of slitting throats.

"You've been a long time away in bad company, boy," he said. He pulled his leather jerkin aside to reveal the same tattoo on his own chest. "*As-caii.* You know what it means?"

"Our ... our people," whispered Orlii. It was the only thing he could remember his mother ever telling him about his kin.

Girstan bared his teeth in a carnivorous smile.

"It means it's saved your life." He glanced at the man who held the trembling boy captive. "Watch him. We don't know what we're getting."

The man took Orlii outside, shivering in his nakedness. He saw Davitis lying curled on the ground in a pool of his own blood, abandoned to die, his last breaths drawn from him in sobs of pain.

He was taken to where the bandits' horses awaited them. His captor threw him to the ground, bound him hand and foot and told him to wait there. Orlii did not feel he had much choice. He had been a free man for a very short length of time.

Kierce knew he was too late by the time he approached the Imperial encampment. He kept a cautious distance from it until he could establish what had happened, but he quickly realised it was deserted. He rode down into it, steeling himself against the horror he knew he was going to find there.

He found Davitis, cold and dead, his life's blood in the ground around him. Unlike Orlii, Kierce saw the wound that had killed him. Davitis had been comprehensively castrated.

Kierce turned away from the enemy who could no longer harm him, and began to search for Orlii. He expected to find him similarly dealt with and was a little baffled when he found no trace of him.

He paused and contemplated the devastated camp, eerily silent in the light of a dull grey morning, its dead keeping the secrets of all except the bare facts of what had befallen it. He could leave it. The threat he had come to head off lay cold on the ground surrounded by his guards. He was reluctant to interrogate the site further, to go deeper into what had happened, but he could see the trail of the raiders led back towards Shehaios. He had seen on Davitis's mutilated body the symbol carved in blood on his chest, a flame inside a circle, the emblem of the *as-caii* and the tattoo mark on Orlii's breast. It didn't take a magician to work it out.

Kierce knew where they would go. They were among the first of the raiders to have settled across the border, and he had found their well-established, well-guarded encampment high in the mountains on the western border of Mervecc. It was in a small high valley almost completely enclosed by steep mountainside, accessible only along a stream bed on the east side. The peak that rose above it, also held and fortified by the *as-caii* settlers, commanded a view of the surrounding countryside for miles. It was difficult to find, and impossible to approach undetected.

Kierce was still reluctant to make himself known to the Caiivorian raiders – he could not foresee the consequences; he just suspected they would not be good. He took his time on the journey and it was some weeks after the attack on Davitis's party that he reached the Caiivorian warriors' encampment. He approached from the north, down one of the least steep sides enclosing the valley, picking his way carefully down the steep, south-facing slope. Red Sky kept him company nervously, snatching at the poor grazing and occasionally sniffing suspiciously at Kierce. Sky did not like him being a horse. It confused him. He generally didn't tolerate the company of other stallions, especially ones he couldn't boss around. He knew Kierce was still Kierce, and smelt like Kierce, but he had eyes as well and he liked his senses to agree with each other.

Dusk was falling as the two horses came down into the valley, and as Kierce had anticipated it was not long before men ventured out of the Caiivorian village and fanned out to surround these valuable-looking animals who had wandered so foolishly close to captivity. He had to hold on hard to Red Sky's flight instinct; the Caiivorians were less than skilful, and if they had really been wild horses, they would have been long gone before any man got a rope around them.

They were taken to a stockade in the centre of the village and tethered just outside it to keep them from the horses already contained inside. The other horses migrated uneasily to the opposite end of the enclosure, disturbed by the strange creature who had appeared in their midst. One brown mare alone broke from the herd and came trotting over to them whickering a greeting. Both Kierce and his horse recognised her as the one Orlii had taken with him.

When darkness fell and the horses were left unattended, Kierce ceased being one. He untethered both himself and Sky and cautiously began to explore the village, using all the senses he possessed.

It was a fairly humble place, a huddle of a dozen or so small drystone huts with two slightly grander buildings on the western side. Apart from the horses at the centre, there was little sign of any stock or any cultivation. It was a base, a place to rest and relax in between raids on the Holdings below, and a place to keep the goods, stock and people they stole until they migrated back south to trade them.

It did not take him long to find Orlii. He was sitting in one of the lowly huts, wearing the clothes of his captors, a worn fur cloak across his shoulders to keep out the draughts of the ill-made shelter. He was talking and laughing with half a dozen other young men around a smoky fire. Kierce watched him carefully, from all levels, but he neither thought nor behaved like a prisoner. In fact, for the first time, he thought almost like a free man.

Kierce moved away from the hut and waited in the shadow of a wood store. After a few minutes, Orlii emerged, frowning into the darkness. He looked around him, mystified, and was about to return to the hut when he suddenly saw Kierce. He started in astonishment.

"Lord Kierce!"

Kierce warned him to silence. "I don't want the reception Davitis enjoyed," he commented softly. He regarded Orlii critically. "I can only assume the mark on your chest protected you. Am I right?"

"They are my people," said Orlii, simply.

"Ah, they're your people! Well, I'm glad we've cleared that up. When I followed them here I was following the trail of a group of bandits who live by theft and murder."

Orlii hesitated. He was not used to arguing with Kierce.

"Many years ago," he began, humbly, "when I was a child, when I was taken into slavery… the people I belonged to lost everything. That's why they have no choice but to live as they do now. If they're bandits it's because they have no land. If they had land—".

"They'd be land-owning bandits," interrupted Kierce, harshly. "They'd still live by theft and murder. What do they want here, Orlii?"

Orlii did not answer.

"They want land?" suggested Kierce. He paused, subjecting Orlii to a hard, penetrating glare. "They want our land. Shehaios."

"They are *as-caii*," said Orlii unhappily. "My people. Lord Kierce, you promised me I was free."

Kierce sighed.

"I did. And you are."

He moved out of the shadow to make his way back to the horses. Orlii came after him.

"Lord Kierce – Master – we do not have to be enemies," he insisted. "My Lord Girstan would be willing to negotiate if Shehaios were willing to offer what he wanted."

"I'm not sure Shehaios can afford what Lord Girstan wants," retorted Kierce. He had seen Lord Girstan with Caras's eyes. He knew Orlii's people.

"He would be more humble if he understood how Shehaios is defended," argued Orlii. "He trusts his Tay-Aien priest, he doesn't know—."

He broke off as a sudden challenge rang out in the gloom. Both turned in alarm in the direction of the cry as four Caiivorians broke into a run towards them, two bearing spears, the others drawing swords as they ran.

Even as they watched, one raised his spear and launched it at Kierce. Orlii heard the Magician mutter a low and vicious oath, and was aware of something swishing past his ear. He looked round as Kierce's hand closed around the spear that had been flying towards his body.

"Get back," he directed Orlii, tersely. "You're one of them. It's me they're excited about."

Orlii backed away, glanced at the Caiivorian sentries and then fixed his gaze on Kierce.

"Show them," he whispered urgently. He fell to his knees in front of Kierce. "Show them what you are!"

Kierce hesitated for a split second. He had to do something. He could not just stand there, a small, unarmed Shaihen man in the middle of an enemy camp. If he simply disappeared, he could not rely on Orlii's badge of allegiance saving him from what would look to them like treachery.

He drew himself up and, just as he had when Shehaios first laid a claim on Orlii, he called his horse.

This time, the call echoed round the valley and resonated deep into the mountains. It seemed as if every creature around them paused and turned towards the Magician's summons. The human creatures felt it as well as heard it; Orlii knew what Kierce was doing, yet the powerful urge to obey the call still struck a chill into his heart.

The Caiivorian sentries slowed their pace. Others emerged from the huts with shouts and exclamations. Orlii remained on his knees, shaking slightly. He could see Red Sky's stocky form cantering towards them but for that moment Kierce still looked very small and very vulnerable, standing alone with half the Caiivorian village now raised in alarm.

Kierce drew the Magician's staff. Before Orlii's amazed eyes, the Enchanter of Caiivorian legend began to come to life. One moment Kierce stood before him with the small black Shaihen horse trotting to a halt beside him, and the next Orlii found himself cowering before an immense darkness against the night sky. The huge, looming shadow of a black-cloaked man on horseback was the very image of Orlii's half-forgotten childhood stories.

From the hills around them, the echoing response to Kierce's call began to sound, a distant symphony of wolf howls, bear growls and the yowling of wildcats intermingled with all the grunts and hoots and squeaks of everything from deer to mice. Underpinning it was the low, unmistakable rumble of a Shaihen dragon, and rising over the top a keening human cry of pain and defiance.

The mounted figure raised the staff above his head as the cacophony of sound died away, and the carved wooden thing of beauty became a long golden stave, glowing with power. It cast a strange, uncanny light over the startled Caiivorians. Others as well as Orlii fell to their knees. Some shielded their faces from the apparition before them. Others hung back, shouting and threatening, but unwilling to come closer, fearful of what had come among them.

A small group emerged now from the large hut at the western end of the village, the *as-caii*'s leaders. All were armed, and one wore the robes of a Tay-Aien priest. They passed rapidly through the wavering crowd without hesitation, haranguing their timorous warriors. The priest raised his spear as he emerged from the throng, and hurled it towards Kierce, together with a vitriolic incantation.

At the top of the spear's trajectory, just as it began to come down towards Kierce's body, it turned a somersault and broke apart into a cloud of dust. It drifted to the ground, the metal head plummeting with a dull thud onto the earth.

"I am the Lord High Magician," thundered Kierce. "You are within the land of *Haios* and you should beware of my power!"

He cracked a flash of lightning from the staff to the ground, raising a scream from some of the women cowering in the doorways of the huts and an awed roar from the men. The horses in the stockade behind him seethed in panic at the rails that confined them.

"Do you want to be my servant?"

Orlii heard the question in Kierce's normal voice. He looked up at the mighty figure in front of him and tried to believe it was the master he had served for five years. He knew Kierce would tell him it was an illusion. It looked terrifyingly real to him.

"Yes, my lord," he whispered.

"Respect this land!" the voice of the Magician boomed out again. "And respect the life of this man who serves me."

He pointed towards Orlii with the staff, letting the glow of golden light fall over him. Then he made Red Sky rear up, swung him round and set him at a gallop towards the narrow bank by the stream which was his only easy route out of that place.

The Caiivorians gave way before him, scattering from Red Sky's path.

It was with some satisfaction that Kierce saw the Tay-Aien priest fall into the dust as he scrambled out of the way. That would teach him to hurl spears at the Lord High Magician.

Chapter 40
A Game of Trust

Cathva told Kierce about the man Emperor Zelt appointed as Davitis's successor. He was everything Kierce had feared he would be; ambitious, experienced, a fervent advocate of Tay-Aien and a firm favourite of the Emperor. His arrival in Shehaios five years in to their Imperial alliance would effectively mark the end of Rainur's rule; what the Holders' Council would make of it did not bear thinking about.

The split was widening. The plans Rainur began to lay anticipated a breach with Kierce as much as a falling out with the Emperor, though he insisted to the last that Zelt would honour the agreement he had made. He attributed to him promises that Cathva told Kierce were interpretations of words to which Zelt attached a very different meaning. Her father rarely lied. His facility with the truth meant he very rarely needed to.

Kierce decided it was time he visited Arhaios.

For the past year and more, Caras had come as close as he believed he was going to get to being the Holder he had wished to be, governing a peaceful and prosperous community, albeit a slightly larger and more cosmopolitan one. He did not welcome Kierce's sudden interest in his affairs; neither did he welcome Kierce personally. The betrayal of a promise was to Caras a betrayal of friendship. His greeting was decidedly cool.

"You haven't come here because you've suddenly developed homesickness," he observed, once they settled alone in the small room that had been the heart of Leath's benign web. "So what do you want?"

Kierce was examining the multitude of small earthenware pots stacked around the walls of the room. Elani's interest in herbs and healing was beginning to take over the Holder's house.

"Elani is getting to be quite an authority on this," he observed. "She'll be challenging your Healer before long."

Caras said nothing. He sat and waited, arms folded. Kierce felt very much in the presence of the Chief of Oreath rather than an old friend. Caras's long held inclination to check Kierce's opinion before he made up his mind was missing. Kierce felt he would need to skirt carefully around accusations of pomposity.

"I need you to do something for me. Or more precisely, to not do something for me."

"What?"

Kierce sat down. "Rainur's called the Holders' Council to meet urgently."

Caras nodded briefly. "To discuss this new Imperial envoy."

"Before the Council convenes, Rainur will ask you to take command of the Shaihen army."

"Shaihen army?" Caras gave him a bemused look. "What Shaihen army?"

"The one Jagus has been training in Hieath."

Caras got to his feet and paced across the room in consternation. Kierce sat back more comfortably. That was more like Caras.

"Rainur is going to ask me to lead Jagus's men? What about Jagus?" He paused and looked critically at Kierce. "Jagus never gave his loyalty to Rainur, did he? He gave it to you."

"Exactly."

"So are you going to tell him to let me command his army?"

"Rainur's going to ask me to."

"And are you going to do it?"

"No," said Kierce. "I'm not. That's why I'm asking you not to do as Rainur asks you, either."

Caras turned on him coldly. Kierce saw the condemnation in his eyes as he read it in his mind. Caras could see the inevitable division coming, and his instincts were that the present King was far more trustworthy than the present Lord High Magician.

"You're going to drag me into your sordid fight with Rainur, are you?"

"Rainur's dragging you into it. I'm actually trying to keep you out."

"This had better be good, Kierce. Don't assume I'm on your side."

"If I tell Jagus to relinquish his men to you, I release him from any obligation to Shehaios. He's free to pursue his personal vengeance. Against Rainur, and against you."

"So you're protecting Rainur?" said Caras sceptically. "I find that a little hard to believe. Why has Rainur suddenly decided he can't live with Jagus's army? He's been willing to accept its presence up till now."

"But now he thinks he may need it and he doesn't want to have to rely on my support. He doesn't know all the details yet, but he does know that this new governor will bring with him greater authority than Davitis. You've heard of Tay-Aien?"

Caras gave him a rather sour look.

"I feel Tay-Aien's god in my bones whenever it rains," he said. "It was Tay-Aien's priest who broke my arm and several ribs. That said, of course, half our garrison here follow Tay-Aien's teachings. Men give his god one name, but it seems they use him for their own purposes, just as they did the ones who go by many names. Most of the book itself..." He shrugged. "His history teaches the same lessons for survival that our history teaches us. Breaking the rules of moral conduct," he added pointedly, "leads to division and conflict. Especially when it's those in authority who break them."

Kierce chose to ignore the comment. Tay-Aien's family-focussed morality was tailor-made for Caras.

"Tay-Aien's one god is the god of *as-caii*. Our people. It makes him our god as well."

"But we have none. We're the people of the Spirit. We're different. We're … " he hesitated, searching for the words.

"Right?" suggested Kierce, with a smile. "It's the nature of faith to believe you're right, Caras."

"Well, 'right' was never something that concerned you, was it, Kierce? Main chance, perhaps." He regarded Kierce with some contempt. "I must admit, you make a strange Tay-Aien priest to my mind. I can't think of anyone who shows less inclination to follow his teachings."

"Truth has many faces," said Kierce, serenely. "The problem is the Emperor's decree requiring everyone to follow Tay-Aien's god. You can't tell the Emperor he's wrong. And Rainur won't pretend to something he doesn't believe. He even had to convince himself he loved Cathva before he could marry her."

"*He* convinced himself!" exclaimed Caras in disgust.

"Oh, I *know* that I love her," said Kierce, ruefully. "I could wish that I didn't."

Caras paused, his fingers drumming an unconscious rhythm on his thigh.

"So you admit it. This is a private fight between you and Rainur?"

"No, Caras, it isn't," replied Kierce, impatiently. "Rainur's obstinacy is taking Shehaios towards a head-on conflict with the Empire. That would be fatal."

It was also threatening to take Imperial Commander Caras down a path that would make him a traitor to the Empire, but Kierce was not going to explain that to Caras. He had seen Volun's remains paraded through Vordeith, derided and mutilated, spat upon and left by the road into the city as a warning. He knew they would have preferred to do it to the living traitor had Caras not cheated them of that prize. The image of Caras himself undergoing such an end was not one he wanted to have to contemplate.

"I still don't see it," said Caras. "Jagus's dispute with Rainur is about him being too close to the Empire, not about being asked to fight it. Now, of all times, Rainur *could* trust his brother." He paused. "It's you he doesn't trust."

"Yes, it is," agreed Kierce candidly. "And since I've kept Jagus from attacking you or Rainur this long, I can keep him from using his warriors against the Empire if I want to. You, on the other hand, do what you believe to be right, and not necessarily what I tell you to do. Rainur knows that."

For some minutes, Caras remained silent, lost in thought.

"You're asking me to trust you when every rational bone in my body tells me to trust Rainur. What's set Rainur on this path, Kierce? He's played a clever game with Imperial power for a long time. Why does he find this one more deceit too much to stomach?"

Kierce hesitated.

"He fears the power of Tay-Aien's single omnipotent god. And he has no faith in the Lord High Magician."

Caras gave him a bemused look.

"Tay-Aien's god doesn't exist. I thought we'd already established that."

"He exists to those who believe in him. That makes him powerful."

Caras reflected on the answer, studying Kierce thoughtfully.

"And our belief in the Lord High Magician makes him powerful. The first thing I said to you when you told me you were Turloch's heir was that Rainur had to be able to trust you. You promised me he could. What happened?"

"Life," said Kierce, fatefully. "It happens to all of us. Even Lord High Magicians. Caras, the only wrong I've ever done Rainur is to steal his wife. I didn't do it out of any ill-will towards him. Rainur hates and mistrusts me, but I don't feel anything but affection and respect for him. It dismays me that he's destroying himself over this, especially since it's all so unnecessary. I know exactly how he feels about Cathva, and I know how I feel about Cathva. Rainur's in love with some perfect, beautiful ever-young queen of his imagining, whereas I … I can't think straight in her presence. And what's more, she damn well knows it." He passed his hand wearily across his face. "I don't know how to make you trust me, Caras, because you never have. But I am trying to save Rainur's neck as well as Shehaios itself, and I can't do it without your help."

Caras studied him, with intense suspicion. Kierce saw the legacy of countless small deceits and jokes coming back to haunt him. Caras never knew when he could believe him; now Kierce desperately needed his trust, there was no way left to convince him.

"You're very plausible," he conceded.

"I'm telling the truth."

"Which has many faces."

There was a heavily pregnant silence.

"Whoever leads Jagus's warriors, the problem remains the same. If Rainur defies the Emperor's governor—."

"He fears he may have to," interrupted Kierce. "But it won't come to that."

"Won't it?"

"No."

Caras waited, but Kierce remained silent. He was not going to explain further.

"If I do this," said Caras, quietly. "And you betray my trust, never ask me again."

With an inordinate sense of relief, Kierce stood up and grasped Caras's forearm.

"Thank you, Caras. This is for Shehaios. You will see it, eventually." He paused. "Don't defy Rainur. Prevaricate. He's lost his trust in me; I don't want him losing it in you as well."

"How long will I have to prevaricate for?" asked Caras, anxiously.

"I can't tell you. Not for very long. Steer us through the Holders' Council, I'll make sure Jagus isn't there this time."

"But once the envoy gets here …"

"If the envoy gets here I need to rethink."

Caras looked at him in surprise.

"*If* the envoy gets here?"

"That's the bit you don't want to know about, Caras." Kierce met his eyes in warning. "Believe me. You don't."

Just as the old envoy never reached Vordeith, his replacement never reached Shehaios. Crossing the plains south of the Shaihen mountains he found himself ambushed by a band of the *as-caii* warriors, lying in wait for him.

It was a curious attack to many people who reflected on it afterwards, Emperor Zelt among them. Not only had the Caiivorian bandits been uncannily well-informed about the movements of the new Shaihen governor, but they usually targeted valuable items which could be seized at minimum cost, not large Imperial wagon trains.

The new envoy certainly carried a valuable cargo. He had in his train several months pay for the Imperial Army in Shehaios, and the guard to go with it. It cost the Caiivorian bandits dear to steal it from him, the more so because of their determination to penetrate the Imperial defence far enough to lay murderous hands on the new governor of Shehaios. He was hacked to death under a welter of blows, and left among a field scattered with as many of Girstan's men as the Emperor's.

It was an exceptionally audacious attack, especially following so close on the heels of the one that had killed Davitis. Rainur was extremely alarmed by the news, and open to Kierce's persuasion that now was not the time to risk dissent within Shehaios by setting Jagus and Caras against each other. The immediate possibility of confrontation with the Empire had gone away and however appalled they both were at the manner of it's removal, it gave them time to reflect. This further proof of the banditry rife on his southern border reminded Rainur why he had made the alliance with the Empire in the first place, and put his differences with Kierce into a new perspective. Kierce's support through the crisis remained unfailing, and while they waited for the response from Vordeith, he and Rainur negotiated an uneasy truce. Rainur spoke again to Caras and they agreed to postpone the question of the leadership of the Shaihen army.

Caras and Kierce did not discuss the envoy's failure to arrive in Shehaios. Kierce was right. Caras did not want to know.

If Rainur was alarmed by the outrage against the Imperial governor, a few miles south in Mervecc Gascon was almost beside himself. The attack had not occurred on Shaihen soil, but they all knew the *as-caii* operated across the border and this represented a new level of boldness on their part. It was hardly surprising that a lone Caiivorian, dressed as a warrior, found in the mountains near to Mervecc was seized by Gascon's men and taken to their Holder with every expectation that he would give them permission to dispose of him without compunction.

Fortunately, Gascon recognised him.

"You should tell Kierce to give you some mark of his protection, Orlii," Gascon advised him. "These are dangerous times to be a Caiivorian in Shehaios unless you wear Imperial armour."

"Then perhaps I should do that, Lord Gascon," said Orlii, humbly.

"I think we're all going to have to do that before long," retorted Gascon grumpily. "I'll get someone to escort you to the Haven. I assume that's where you're going?"

"I go to seek my master, yes," agreed Orlii.

He found his master within the Magician's Tower. On the second floor, surrounded by images crafted by men of their world and of themselves.

Kierce thanked Orlii's Merveccian escort, and in turn he commended Orlii's courage in making the long and difficult journey from his captors in the mountains.

"So you escaped did you, Orlii?" commented Kierce with heavy irony that was lost on the Merveccian. "How wonderfully heroic of you. I'm quite overcome that you should be so dedicated to me."

"We nearly killed him as a bandit," admitted the Merveccian, slightly affronted by the edge of sarcasm in Kierce's tone. "Lord Gascon suggests you give him some token of your protection, Lord Kierce. He's likely to need it."

"Oh, I think Orlii carries all the protection he needs," said Kierce. "But thank Lord Gascon for his kind thoughts."

The Merveccian left, and Kierce contemplated the young man standing before him. Orlii was dressed in the plaid and rawhide armour that all Girstan's men wore. He carried a sword at one hip and a knife at the other, very much the adult of the boy Kierce had taken at Prassan. The Magician found himself as reluctant to interrogate his thoughts now as he had been then.

"I take it Lord Girstan is happy?"

Orlii smiled.

"He asks how many Imperial governors you would like dealt with, Master."

"Guard your tongue," rasped Kierce. "There won't be any more. Girstan has been paid in the currency he understands."

"Gold is not what he wants, Lord Kierce."

"I know it's not what he wants, I said it's what he understands."

Orlii hesitated.

"There will be more, Master."

"Of course there will. But killing them doesn't solve the problem. Killing Rainur might," he added under his breath. "I just needed a little time Orlii, so don't get carried away. Are you staying?"

"I am your servant, my lord."

"I thought you were Girstan's."

"He also is your servant."

Kierce gave a contemptuous snort.

"Until the Imperial army's pay runs out. Thrown out his Tay-Aien priest then, has he?"

"No, my lord. You are also a Tay-Aien priest. That's why Girstan believes you will deliver him to the land he has been promised."

"Land? Who promised him land?"

"Tay-Aien's god."

"Spirit defend me – the god who teaches peace and moral rectitude promises land to that bunch of murdering savages? Truth has more faces than I believed possible." He paused anxiously. "You do know I promised him nothing of the kind. He took his own reward. Our business is closed."

"I know that, my lord. Girstan believes what he chooses to believe."

Kierce cursed beneath his breath. However much he disliked it, he knew perfectly well that Girstan and his people were within the bounds of Shehaios. They were a part of the Whole Land. Orlii knew it too.

"Who knows what the future may hold," added Orlii deferentially. " Lord Rainur will not always be King. And you will not always be the Lord High Magician, Lord Kierce."

"I'd be surprised if Girstan is prepared to wait that long. I need to get us back in the protection of the Empire. And you'd better stay here." Kierce glanced at him. "Without the sword, please."

Orlii smiled and laid the weapon aside.

"Forgive me, master, I still have much to learn. I hope you will have many years yet to teach me. Unlike Lord Turloch."

"What could you have learned from Lord Turloch?" said Kierce derisively.

Orlii bowed his head.

"Just so, Lord Kierce."

Chapter 41
Messages from the Empire

In the spring of the following year, fresh messengers finally arrived at the Haven from Vordeith, delayed by a harsh winter and distractions of rebellion within the walls of the Imperial City. The Emperor's religious edict was stirring up passions all over his Empire, and it was not only Shehaios that was defying him. There were others wreaking havoc in North Caiivor as well as Girstan's lawless band; everywhere, shifting alliances formed between local kings and warlords and divisions of soldiers theoretically under the command of the Empire. What had been intended to bind the Empire together was threatening to tear it apart. Shehaios was a very minor part of Emperor Zelt's problems.

On the eve of his sixth wedding anniversary, Rainur sat in Prince Sartin's chamber, watching the boy sleep. The day had darkened early. Clouds covered the sun all day and now the rain was pouring steadily against the walls of the Palace. Sartin had been slightly feverish during the evening; a childhood disorder, probably caused by over-exertion during the day. He had been riding with Kierce, which was generally a pastime guaranteed to over-tire Sartin. He always wanted to do more. He managed the pony like a miniature satyr, and even on the very rare occasions he had fallen off, he seemed to have an ability to land on his feet like a cat. Like Kierce did.

Rainur couldn't remember when he first realised that Sartin was Kierce's son. He had gone on believing he could raise him as his own, moulded in his own image, the child born of Shehaios and the Empire, the heir he needed and wanted so much.

He held in his hands the parchment he had received from Emperor Zelt, containing not only his own fate but also that of the child sleeping in front of him. Yesterday, he would have done anything to protect that child.

Today, he had seen Sartin run to Kierce, as he always did. Rainur watched Kierce catch him and swing him into his arms, the child's straight, dark hair whipping round his face in the dampness and the wind. Rainur caught the impish smile on the little boy's face and he saw Kierce in it. Without any question.

Sartin would never, in any way, be his son.

He looked at the same small face, sleeping peacefully. He could no more harm the child than he could harm Cathva. Kierce was a different matter. If Kierce were not the Lord High Magician ...

He looked round as the chamber door opened quietly, but it was not Cathva. He didn't really expect it to be. He knew where Cathva was.

It was Tilsey.

She smiled at him, sitting in the dark with the child.

"He's peaceful now. He has been for hours. Leave him, Rainur. He's all right."

"I know he is." Rainur made no move. He stared back at the boy. "You've known since the night he was born, haven't you. When his father helped him into the world. What do you think he'll be, Horsemaster or magician?"

Tilsey set down the candle quietly and came over to him. She stroked his hair gently, moved to try and comfort him as she did the young Prince when life got too much for him. They had been close for more than a year now, from soon after Rainur finally banished his faithless wife from his bed.

"He's your heir, Rainur."

"Oh yes, of course, he's my heir." Rainur sank his head into his hands. "Kierce's son takes all I've worked for. Do you think he'll hold it?"

There was an agonised silence.

"I'm sorry, my lord," said Tilsey gently. "I don't know what to say."

"Even before—." He broke off. "The marriage was a lie from the first day. Even then, she was going to Kierce."

"It wasn't quite that way," said Tilsey. "You have to remember how little Cathva understood about Shehaios. About the Lord High Magician. He … ," she hesitated. She preferred to try not to speak ill of the Lord High Magician, but she found it difficult. She had very little time for him. He seemed to her to bring out the worst in the woman she had served and cherished so devotedly for so long. "The most generous thing I can say about Lord Kierce is that he took advantage of her ignorance. Others might care to give what he did a different name, when you consider how she feared him at the beginning."

Rainur sighed.

"Of course she did. My poor Cathva." He paused, looking at the Prince with pity. "And her poor little bastard. My wife is with child for a second time and her latest contribution to the Imperial family will have the same father as the first. Neither have anything to do with me."

Tilsey quietly guided his head to rest on the bulge of her stomach.

"Listen," she said. "Tell me. Do you have a son, or a daughter?"

Rainur folded his arms around her waist and held her tightly to him, burying his face in the body that bore his child.

"I have an heir," he declared softly. "A true, Shaihen heir. Not some bastard offspring of lust and illusion."

"Hush, Rainur. Don't speak of Sartin like that. He's a sweet, loving little boy."

"But he's not my little boy."

She drew back and looked into Rainur's face.

"He is still your heir. It's what he was born to be. I'm not your wife, Rainur. I'm very happy to bear your child, but your heir should be got between the king and the queen."

"He wasn't, though, was he? He was got between the queen and the Lord High Magician."

She hesitated.

"Lord Kierce gave him to you. I was there when he did it."

"And he's spent every day since trying to get him back. He promised me he would leave Cathva alone, too. Kierce lies. He cheats. He plays tricks. All the time, he moves between reality and illusion. I don't think he knows which is which any more." He hesitated. "This is one lie that's run its course. Everyone has assumed Sartin is my heir, but I've never named him as such. And now," he rested his hand on Tilsey's belly, "I never will."

Tilsey frowned anxiously. She had been a slave in Vordeith for ten years, most of them in the service of Cathva's mother and then Cathva herself. She knew the ways of Emperor better than Rainur did.

"Sartin is a child of the Imperial family," she said. "You can't disinherit the Emperor, Rainur."

He paused, and then picked up the discarded Imperial parchment.

"The Emperor informs me that he has bestowed on me the great honour of adopting Prince Sartin as his son," he said quietly. "I am to bring the Prince to Vordeith, where he will be raised as a true Imperial Citizen. In Vordeith, I am promised I will meet the new governor of Shehaios, the Prince's adopted uncle."

Tilsey's embrace became more protective, and she closed her eyes.

"No. Please tell me that's not what he says, Rainur."

"There's more," added Rainur, his tone still very calm. "The Shaihens who will be returning in the next few weeks from their five-year service in the Imperial army are to report to the Imperial Commander at the Haven, not to return to their Holdings. I am also instructed that all other Shaihen forces are to be brought under the Imperial Commander's authority forthwith, and when assembled they are to move south against King Bordred of North Caiivor—".

"He is to take Shaihen forces to war in Caiivor ?" gasped Tilsey.

"The Emperor believes we have already done so. He believes I arranged the previous envoy's death, Tilsey. It's written between every line of his letter." He got to his feet, and gently disengaged himself from Tilsey's arms. "Last but not least, he commends me to the counsel of the wise Lord Kierce." He looked at her. "What do you think the wise Lord Kierce will have to say to that? Will even Kierce be able to persuade Jagus to bring his warriors under the command of the Imperial army and take them to fight the Imperial army's battles?"

"Surely Kierce will stand beside you on this. These are impossible terms to meet."

"I think they're intended to be. I think His Greatness is dispelling the illusion that we ever had any choice. I opened the Gate to the Empire, Tilsey, and now, somehow, I have to close it." He paused. "I will go to Vordeith, and I will take Sartin. I'm not sure that isn't where he belongs. But I will not go until after your child is born, and I will not take with me the heir to the Shaihen throne."

"You can't go," said Tilsey, softly, with tears in her eyes. "You know you won't return."

"I don't know that at all. I believe I can convince the Emperor that his suspicions are unfounded, and restore his trust in me. But if I can't … I leave Shehaios an heir to the crown. I leave it a united Holders' Council. And I still have to believe I leave it a Lord High Magician. Perhaps without me, he will start healing the Whole Land instead of prostituting himself to the Empire."

"Not if you take Sartin with you. You know how he adores him."

Rainur smiled bitterly. "Yes. And why."

"He'll never let you take Sartin to Vordeith."

"Then he'll be defying the Emperor. Which he seems not to want to do. But it's time Kierce faced reality as well. We can't live the illusion for ever."

Chapter 42
Xemper

Kierce was unaware of the content of Zelt's message to Rainur, or the decision it had driven the King to make. The messengers from Vordeith came not only to Rainur and the Commander of the Imperial camp, but also direct to Kierce.

Intrigued, Kierce received his Imperial courier at the Tower.

The soldier entered, dragging with him a ragged prisoner in chains. Kierce looked askance at the encumbrance the soldier brought with him, but he said nothing as he led them into the smallest of the first level chambers, the room he had so often welcomed Cathva to.

He barely noticed its hedonistic splendour now. It was just a convenient room to use.

He watched the prisoner covertly as they made their way to it. The echo of his constant pain touched Kierce the moment he entered the Tower. The man walked with difficulty that wasn't entirely due to the shackles round his ankles; his face bore the scars of beatings and both the hands bound in front of him were crippled. His right hand had no fingers at all, and all those on his left were deformed. These were inflicted injuries, not defects of birth, and the scarring was still recent.

Kierce entered the room, closed the door behind his visitors and turned towards them. The soldier saluted him.

"Lord Kierce, I am sent by High Commander Hiren to bring you greetings, and to deliver you a message."

"High Commander Hiren?" said Kierce, with slightly ironic admiration. "He got his reward too, then?" He suspected Hiren appreciated his new title considerably more than Caras had appreciated his.

"Yes sir. High Commander Hiren is much respected in the Imperial City."

There was a pause.

"Well," said Kierce, shifting uncomfortably and giving the prisoner a distasteful glance. "Explain. What's the message?"

The soldier looked at him a little anxiously and hoisted his captive half a pace forwards.

"It's … well, it's him, sir."

Kierce frowned and the soldier continued to regard him apprehensively.

"High Commander Hiren … the Commander gave his message to this man, sir. This is Xemper, a traitor to the Empire and a condemned prisoner. But …he's the only one who knows what Commander Hiren wanted to say to you, sir."

"Then let him speak."

"Well – that's just it, sir. He can't speak. His tongue was cut out as punishment for speaking treason. He can't speak and he ... " he glanced at the man's tortured hands " ... he can't write. He can't communicate, sir, and I apologise, I don't understand."

"But he can think," interrupted Kierce quietly. He massaged his eyes wearily, recognising another player entering the game. Hiren was a very clever man. "Very well. Don't worry, soldier, I understand. Leave him with me."

The Imperial soldier looked even more baffled than ever, but his was not to reason why.

"I'll be outside should you need me, sir."

"I think I can manage," said Kierce drily. "Thank you."

The soldier saluted him and withdrew.

Steeling himself, Kierce turned to Xemper. The man's head was lowered, but his eyes watched Kierce with abject terror. He was utterly convinced that Kierce was going to kill him. It swamped every other thought in his head.

Kierce went over to him and put his hands around the manacles on the man's wrists. They came away like a cast slipping from a mould. The man's terror became mixed with confusion. Kierce bent down and applied the same treatment to the fetters on his ankles. By the time he straightened up, Xemper was prostrate at his feet.

"Stand up," commanded Kierce impatiently. "Better still," he gestured towards a nearby chair, "sit down. This could take a while."

The man stared at him.

"Sit down," repeated Kierce. "Yes, I do mean it, Xemper. I'm not going to hurt you. Not that there's a lot left to hurt," he added to himself. He crossed the room, leaned against the edge of the long table and contemplated the wreckage of a human being before him. Xemper edged himself cautiously onto the chair and sat as if waiting for it to bite him.

"Who did this to you?"

A confusion of images tumbled through Xemper's mind, most of them in Imperial army attire. Clearest among them Kierce recognised Hiren. High Commander Hiren had not got where he was today by being nice.

"Well, I'm sorry to do this to you, but I need you to think about Hiren," said Kierce. "At the moment you're so terrified of failing to give me the message I can't read the message. We could go round that circle for a long time. Relax. Free your mind."

He could see the man was going to need some help. Grasping the nettle firmly, he fixed his gaze on Xemper and went into his mind.

Gradually, the prisoner's eyes closed. His body sagged and his head lolled back. His breathing came rapidly, as if he were in a feverish sleep and occasional agonised sounds gurgled in his throat.

It took Kierce a while to sift a comprehensible story out of the jumble of horrors in Xemper's mind, but he eventually managed to piece it together.

The Emperor's persistent illness a year or two ago had reminded Imperial society of his mortality. That year and the one that followed, he had been plagued by plots and conspiracies, surrounded by pretenders to his title. Some were more serious than others, but none really threatened his position.

Hiren remained unswervingly loyal throughout all the shifting power-play, taking an active role in rooting out and dealing ruthlessly with the traitors. As a result he gradually moved into the inner circle of the Emperor's trusted men, and by now was one of the most powerful figures in the Imperial City. He commanded not only the Emperor's favour but also the trust and respect of the army.

He was also now the only remaining one of that inner circle who had not paid the required lip service to the cult of Tay-Aien. Kierce was not surprised. Hiren's dedication to his gods was practical and undemonstrative, but it was unshakeable. He had no more time for Tay-Aien than he did for Shaihen magic.

The Emperor's spell of poor health had, as Kierce knew from Cathva's letters, given him intimations of his own mortality as well. He had consulted various priests concerning the welfare of his soul and his prospects in the afterlife. He had forsworn the Games. He had moderated his appetites. He had endowed a rich temple to Tay-Aien's god and a foundation for penurious women. It appeared that he himself had fallen beneath the spell of the god his decree appropriated into the service of the Empire.

Kierce knew much of this already, but he was somewhat amused by Hiren's take on it. His view was muddied by the fact that Xemper himself was a fervent disciple of Tay-Aien and totally convinced that the Emperor's conversion was entirely hypocritical. It was nevertheless apparent that Hiren believed the old devil had experienced some real personal sea-change as he faced the prospect of his own death. The possibility of a religious fanatic at the head of the Empire was causing Hiren considerable alarm. Kierce smiled to himself. Poor old Hiren. Such unexpected developments.

Hiren was not alone in his concerns. Opposition to the Emperor's decree demanding adherence to his chosen creed was looking for a leader, if necessary a challenger to the Emperor's title.

Hiren had been approached. He had not turned it down. He sought to know what support he would have in the wider Empire, and knew better than anyone how important it was to secure the postern gate.

Xemper twisted and moaned in uncomprehending anxiety.

"He means Shehaios," said Kierce.

Hiren did not think he could save Rainur. Rainur's alliance with the Empire was inextricably tied up with his marriage, and the view from the Imperial City was that his wife dedicated her time to the temple of Tay-Aien while Rainur cast her aside in favour of a servant woman. Hiren may have known very well what it was that attracted Cathva to the temple, but he would not contradict the firmly held official view. It was doubly insulting to the current Emperor, because it was his daughter who was being thrown over, but it was not a situation any Emperor could tolerate, and Rainur's time was up.

If he were assured of Kierce's loyalty and support, however, Hiren promised to keep the touch of Imperial rule in Shehaios light. He would recognise Sartin as king of Shehaios, and Cathva and Kierce as holders of the government until the boy came of age.

Kierce was no longer smiling. Now Xemper's distress grew.

It was almost a personal, direct speech from Hiren that ended Xemper's message. He knew how much Kierce was ruled by his emotions and this was no business for the faint-hearted. The man who bore this message was a prisoner condemned to death. He had been spared solely to provide this one service, to convey a message that would bring disaster to both of them in the wrong hands. Once Kierce knew all he had to tell, the sentence should be carried out. Hiren would take a report of Xemper's immediate death in Shehaios as proof that Kierce could be trusted. If the man lived, he knew he had to secure his northern frontier against an enemy.

Which was why Xemper had from the start been so utterly convinced that Kierce was going to kill him. He was. He just hadn't known it until now.

Kierce withdrew from the contact carefully and gazed down at his feet, his hands gripping the edge of the table behind him. In the process of reading Hiren's message, of course, he had also read Xemper's own story. The treason he had been arrested for was preaching to the Imperial troops to lay down their arms and talk peace with their enemies. Not something that could be tolerated in the Imperial army, but the philosophy behind Shaihen politics for generations past. If such things were not said in the wrong place at the wrong time, they were never said at all.

He had to hand it to Hiren. He was nothing if not brutally honest. He intended to leave Kierce no doubt in the choice he was making.

The fact remained in Kierce's mind as stark as the day he had watched the Imperial army march into Shehaios. Shehaios could not fight the Empire. It lived within it, or it died.

Kierce stood up, looked into the fateful terror in the prisoner's eyes and went down on his knees beside him.

"I didn't kneel before the Emperor, Xemper," he said, quietly. "I will kneel to a man who has the courage to bear a suffering I could not have borne. You sought the truth and held it fast and it destroyed you. Not the whole truth. But still … " He gazed steadily on Xemper's bewilderment. "You know what I have to do. You've suffered that knowledge since you left the Imperial City. I have to surrender your body to the Empire. I have to make that choice, and nothing I say helps you or excuses me. But I do want you to know that I promise you immortality. To your people, I am a priest of Tay-Aien and this place you're in – this temple – has no name. Had no name. From tomorrow, it will be known as the temple of Xemper the Martyr. Your story lives after you,

Xemper. I will promise you that. It doesn't ease your pain, but it's all I can offer you. I'm sorry."

He bowed his head in a gesture of reverence, and then rose quietly to his feet. Xemper's eyes followed him in wonder.

"Thank you."

The words were a strangled grunt, but Kierce understood them. He closed his eyes for a moment against the gratitude in Xemper's face. Then he drew his hunting knife, seized Xemper's head and slit his throat with the speed and efficiency he would have used to despatch a wounded animal.

Like the injured hind, Xemper did not see the moment of his death coming.

Kierce opened the door and summoned the Imperial soldier.

"You can tell High Commander Hiren it's done," he said, tersely, glancing towards the body in the room behind him. "Though first I'd appreciate it if you cleaned up the High Commander's mess. Lord Xemper's body is not to be further abused. I will see a fire prepared for him in accordance with our customs. Make him ready to meet it, please. I'll send my servant Orlii to assist you."

He walked out with the blood on his hands seeping deeper into his soul with every step.

Chapter 43
Cathva's Last Letter

"To His Greatness Zelt an' Korsos, Twenty-Third Emperor of the Sacred Union.

Greetings from your most dutiful and obedient daughter Cathva, Queen of Shehaios.

Lord Rainur has shared with me the content of your letter to him, and I am overwhelmed by the generosity your Greatness shows towards our son.

The benefits he will gain and the wisdom he will learn from living within the City that houses our Great Emperor are beyond measure. We are indebted to your bounty.

My beloved husband wishes to convey Prince Sartin to you with all speed, but I write to beg Your Greatness's indulgence. Spare me my husband for a few short months more. I am once again large with child, and much fear the dangers which accompanied the Prince's birth. I dread my lord's departure at such a time—."

Cathva laid down the stylus abruptly.

"This is sheer madness, Kierce. All it will do is annoy him."

Kierce, standing behind her half dictating the letter and half writing it with her, laid his hands reassuringly on her shoulders.

"No, it won't. He won't take any notice, but he'll just think you're being a weak and foolish woman. Pregnancy is a great excuse to forget how to think rationally."

"But he knows it's not Rainur's child I'm carrying. He knows I no longer share the King's bed."

"Oh, I'm sure he does. That's no reason to admit it to him. As long as you and Rainur do not renounce the marriage, and I proclaim myself an adherent of Tay-Aien, that's all that's required." He began to massage her neck absently, sharing the little rill of pleasure he evoked just as unconsciously. He always found it hard to be near Cathva and not touch her. "Rainur's attachment to Tilsey is far more of a problem than your attachment to me. I must admit, I hadn't foreseen that. I forget how your people divide everyone up and build barriers between them."

"But I don't understand why we're doing this if it makes no difference. What's the point?"

"The point is to give reasons for delaying Rainur's departure for Vordeith. He wants to wait until after Tilsey's child is born – which will be about the time yours is born – and that suits me. Anything we can do to make it appear that he's not delaying because he doesn't intend to go is worth doing."

Cathva turned towards him, her face shadowed with anxiety.

"But even if the Emperor believed us – what does it gain us in the end? What do we do when the children are born, and we run out of excuses?"

"We see how the stones lie," said Kierce.

Cathva got to her feet and moved restlessly across the room.

"It's not enough, Kierce. You must understand that Rainur must never go to Vordeith. If he does, you've lost all semblance of independence. Proclaiming your adherence to Tay-Aien will no longer be enough, my father will not believe you. You will have a governor who will want to impose the law of Empire on your common people, and revoke the power of the Holders' Council – can you control the Shaihens' reaction to that?"

"I can control the Shaihens' reaction to nothing," said Kierce, quietly. "That's the mistake you made all along, Cathva."

He knew she wasn't listening. She was hardly even thinking straight. She was terrified of losing favour with her father.

She turned to face him.

"Kierce, if Rainur takes Sartin to Vordeith, you will lose me, too. I can't let him go alone. I will go back to Vordeith with him and do what I can to save us both."

Kierce paused for a long time, studying the ground. By both, she meant herself and her son. He knew as well as she did that this was the final throw in their game against the Emperor. Everything was at stake now, and every possibility had to be faced.

"Perhaps you should, if it comes to that. Sartin may need what protection you can give him." He reached towards her. He could not tell her that even if it came to a parting, he hoped it would only need to last until Hiren made his move.

Cathva brushed his hand away peremptorily.

"Do I mean that little to you, that you could let me go so easily?" she exclaimed indignantly. She paused, the brief moment of anger melting into despair. She took a step towards him and framed his face with her hands. She gazed into his eyes. "What's clouding that mind of yours, Kierce?" she said, softly. "Why can't you see what must be done?"

A thin mist of ice seemed to settle around Kierce's heart as he saw what was forming in her mind.

"No!"

She missed the hard edge beneath his quiet denial.

"Rainur has lost the Emperor's favour. Once lost, it's never regained. I still hold the Emperor's favour. You still hold the Emperor's favour. Rainur is the problem."

Get rid of the problem.

She knew she did not have to finish the thought aloud.

Kierce jerked away from her touch.

"No!" he repeated, thunderously. "I forbid you even to think that!"

"You don't need to kill him," persisted Cathva. "Do it the way you always do it. Make it happen. You were going to bring Jagus to the Haven?"

"I was going to send him after the *as-caii*," said Kierce curtly. "That's all. If he's already fighting one of the Empire's battles it's harder for them to demand his services to fight another."

"Send him as King," said Cathva. "Let him have Rainur first."

Kierce turned on her, his face dark with rage.

He felt the shock of her sudden fear. It was some time now since he had provoked that sensation. He levered it like a headlock, pinning her down with it while he poured his fury into her.

"Don't insult me with your father's voice!" He hurled the words at her so that they struck almost like blows. "And don't speak of Rainur as if he can be culled like last season's herd-leader! He is the Keeper of the Gate and the Head of the Shaihen Holdings, and I would sooner cut my own throat than kill him." He moved towards her, his anger dominating her without any need to lay a hand on her. "Yes, Cathva, you did misunderstand me. I have only ever taken from Rainur what had no value to him – a wife who didn't love him, didn't intend to be faithful to him, or support him, or do any of the things which a man might expect from his partner. I've loved you, Cathva. But I know what you are. You're your father's daughter!"

He turned and walked out of the room like a whirlwind leaving the landscape flattened behind him.

Cathva sank down onto the chair where she had sat writing the letter to her father, her hand resting on the bulge of the child she knew, this time, was without doubt Kierce's. His fury both startled and baffled her. The Emperor had granted Rainur the title King of Shehaios for a space, and now that was at an end. This was the way of those who chose to wield power. They rose and they fell, and only the Emperor continued. What they must do was to make sure his fall did not take Cathva, or Kierce, or Sartin down with him.

Kierce's towering passion took her aback. She hardly recognised the man who shared her bed, nor the one who amused Sartin with entertaining illusions. Both the fool and the hedonist disappeared. He even seemed physically larger. She had never seen him like that, not even in the Spring. Both the fool and the hedonist had been present in the Spring.

When she recovered slightly from the shock of his anger, she found herself impatient with Kierce's refusal to accept that taking Rainur's life simply saved the Emperor the trouble of doing it, and won back at a stroke the prospect of avoiding direct rule from Vordeith. It was the only way to preserve the authority of the Lord High Magician intact. Jagus was much easier to manage than Rainur. And he was not her husband. With Rainur gone, there was nothing to prevent her marrying Kierce. The union between Shehaios and the Empire would be stronger than ever.

She intercepted Orlii when he left the Haven a day later carrying Kierce's message to Jagus. She told him that he was also to inform the King's brother that the way of Shehaios and the road followed by King Rainur were parting. The Lord High Magician therefore unbound Lord Jagus from any promises he may have made regarding his own enemies when his freedom was returned to him.

Orlii hesitated. He knew his master.

"You are sure this is what Lord Kierce wants, my lady? There is no misunderstanding?"

"There is no misunderstanding," replied Cathva. "There will be retribution if you fail to obey me, Orlii!"

Orlii bowed his head.

"Yes, my lady."

Cathva hesitated.

"I know Lord Kierce is angry about what must be done. The Lord High Magician embraces all of Shehaios, and it pains him to sacrifice anyone or anything of the Whole Land. But for his sake as much as anyone's it must be done. I do know what Lord Kierce wants, Orlii." She moved closer to the servant and smiled at him. "He wants me."

The further Orlii travelled into Hieath, however, the more convinced he became that Cathva had misjudged it. He could understand the need to remove Rainur – he knew how much the King was frustrating Kierce's strategy for safeguarding Shehaios – but there were easier and more reliable ways than involving Jagus. He did not dare to disobey her, but he feared what she had done would bring Kierce's wrath down on both their heads. Orlii knew, because he had been there when Caras left Jagus in the Haven, and when Kierce restored his freedom, that release from the pledge he had made then freed him to seek vengeance on his despised captor as well as his brother. Jagus would attack the Haven through Arhaios.

Orlii did not want to be around Kierce when he discovered that Caras had become a victim of Cathva's plans. Neither did he want to be anywhere near Girstan if he discovered that Orlii had carried the summons to the army who were about to move against him.

For both those reasons, his return journey from Hieath took him through Arhaios with a warning for Caras. What Kierce would make of his compromise he was half afraid to find out. He returned to the Haven with a greater sense of trepidation for Kierce than he had felt since he cowered beneath Red Sky's hooves at Prassan.

Kierce was in the stone heart of the Tower, the majestic contemplative space he had recently dedicated to Xemper the Martyr. He had commissioned Brynnen to tell Xemper's story, the minstrel's art better conveying the passion that mere words struggled with. He confined his own contribution to a declaration of the naming and dedication of the Tower, a simple ceremony that caused a disproportionate reaction.

What everyone found incomprehensible, of course, was why Kierce had wielded the knife that killed the man to whom he was dedicating the Magician's Tower. It made no sense, and Kierce did not explain whether they were supposed to revere Xemper or condemn his folly. He simply ensured that the telling of the man's story included the manner of his death and the identity of his killer and left everyone to try and work it out for themselves.

When Orlii arrived, Kierce was tending a small flame which burned on a drystone cairn in the centre of the tower. Shafts of light from above formed a focus of brightness around it. It was a fire lit from Xemper's funeral pyre, and it had burned ever since.

Orlii came in through the ornately carved door and stopped just inside the temple. Kierce did not look round, and Orlii did not speak. He knelt.

"Are you paying homage to me, or to Xemper?" enquired Kierce.

"To you, Master," said Orlii. "I fear you may wish to do to me what you did to him."

Kierce turned to face him.

"Why?"

Orlii kept his head bowed.

"I try, my lord, but it is hard without your ability to read the thoughts of others. I could not see what you wanted."

"It was straightforward enough. I told you what message to take Jagus—". Kierce broke off. He read in Orlii's mind the invitation, almost the entreaty, to find out for himself rather than make Orlii speak it. For a brief, uncomfortable moment, he was reminded of Xemper.

He probed deeper into Orlii's memory. He saw him first speaking to Jagus, delivering the message and then, in confusion, he saw his meeting with Cathva before he went. He witnessed the words that passed between them, and then he heard again, clearly, what Orlii said to Jagus.

It was not anger that burned inside him. He was beyond anger. It was a cold, dead weight of betrayal.

Orlii sensed it. He began to tremble.

"I tried …" he began.

Kierce saw his dilemma, the divided loyalties to Cathva, to Girstan, to Kierce himself, the scheming and twisting and turning in Orlii's mind to try and please all of them. If he recognised what he saw, it did not prepare him for the quiet conviction buried in Orlii's head that he was heir to the Lord High Magician's title.

Orlii let out a low gasp of astonishment more than pain as he felt the sting of a lash across his shoulders. Kierce had not moved.

"Master, forgive me! I know I have much to learn and you many years to live. I don't read minds, but I know how people think, I guess what they want."

"You know nothing," hissed Kierce with suppressed rage. "You believe you could be trusted with Shaihen magic when you can't even be trusted to carry a message!" His voice rose to a shout. "Never trust a Caiivorian further than you can throw them!"

Orlii felt himself lifted off his feet and hurled across the temple. He hit the wall, knocking all the breath from his body, and slid down onto the floor, panting and shaking with fear. He knew the wrath coming at him was for Cathva as much as himself. He said nothing. He made no attempt to run, or defend himself. He waited while Kierce's fury ran its course.

"You don't even understand your own freedom. You think like a slave, you act like a servant, you know less than my horse knows of Shaihen magic. You are nothing more than an ignorant savage from a race of thieves and murderers!"

"Forgive me—."

"Forgive you!"

Kierce strode across to him, grabbed his hair and yanked his head up to look at the flame burning in the centre of the temple. "Ask that man your forgiveness. When I have an heir in Caiivor, he will come from men and women who sacrificed everything to hold firm their bit of the truth. Not from a conniving opportunist who veers whichever way the wind blows him!" He looked down at the stoicism in Orlii's face and thrust him away. "You are not my heir, Orlii. Any more than Cathva is Queen of Shehaios." He closed his eyes, struggling against the grip of emotion that threatened to explode out of him. "Cathva, how could you do this!"

He turned back towards the platform in the centre of the Tower, fighting to control what he could not allow to strike uncontrolled, and thrust his hand into the fire that burned there. He held it there until the pain broke through, and then snatched it away, holding it in his other hand until the seared flesh healed to a white scar across his palm. There was a long moment of silence.

"I'm sorry, Orlii." He spoke again in something approaching his normal dry tone. "You've always been terrified I'll do something like that. I shouldn't feed the nonsense in your head."

"I have always known what you could do if you chose," said Orlii humbly.

He couldn't see Kierce's face, the twisted smile that stopped just short of a howl of anguish.

"You don't have the first idea, Orlii. Believe me. You don't." He paused, struggling to keep his tone even. "And you are not my heir. No question about it."

"I am sorry," murmured Orlii, "I made a mistake."

"Nothing like the one I made," said Kierce, flatly. "I'd better go to Caras. My reputation will be in pieces around Arhaios by now. Just implore all the gods you know that Caras isn't."

Chapter 44
Oreath

Jagus had never made any secret of his desire to avenge the insult of imprisonment by taking Caras's life. The knowledge that Rainur had planned to give Caras command of his army only fuelled his resentment. Kierce's message was unexpected, but it did not take long for Jagus's forces to be on the move in response to it, and as Orlii had guessed, they headed for Oreath first.

Oreath, almost to a man – and woman – rose in support of their Chief. There were skirmishes on the border with Hieath where the people of some local Holdings tried to stop Jagus's march. Other Holders converged on Arhaios, forming a ring of encampments around the edges of the well-established Imperial Camp, populating the valley across the river from the Holding with their tents and lighting the night sky with their fires.

Many of those who gathered to meet the new enemy were men and women who had fought at Toshan. Caras spent his time schooling the rest into a cohesive force that would stand some chance against Jagus's trained warriors. He knew the strength of the foe he had to face had grown formidably since half a dozen Arhaiens snatched away his sword in Leath's hall.

The Oreathan chief was outside the Meeting House with three newly arrived Holders from the west when he became aware of the crowds parting to make way for the small, dark figure striding single-mindedly through them towards him.

He paused in his conversation to watch Kierce approach. He had never noticed before how unlike ordinary material the Magician's cloak really was. It was not so much black, it seemed to absorb light into it, and it moulded itself around the form of the man beneath it. For the first time in his life, Caras looked at Kierce and saw the Lord High Magician.

Caras steadied himself against something he had never expected to face. He knew Kierce had betrayed him. He didn't know how far.

"What do you want?" he demanded as soon as Kierce was within earshot.

He saw the shocked look of amazement pass across Kierce's drawn face.

"For Spirit's sake, I came to explain," exclaimed Kierce. "Why d'you think I came?"

A small wave of relief washed over Caras as he realised he was not facing a direct fight with the Lord High Magician.

"Explain?" he echoed contemptuously. "It's a bit late for that. I think Orlii explained it pretty comprehensively."

"I didn't—."

"Don't lie, Kierce, it sickens me that I can trust your servant better than I can trust you. I'm busy. If you've nothing to say to me, I've certainly nothing to say to you."

He made to resume his discussion with the Oreathans, who had moved back a pace at the Magician's arrival.

"I do have something to say to you. This is not my doing!"

Caras turned on him. "Not your doing? You never planned anything else! You set Jagus free. You gave him an army. You set him up to replace Rainur. And I let you do it – I even let you talk me out of taking command of Jagus's men when Rainur asked me to."

"Caras, that's really not the way it was."

"No? Then perhaps you'd like to tell me when I can bloody wake up!" Caras glared at him. "What are you here for? You want me to run away and leave Jagus a clear path to the Haven, perhaps? Just in case there's the remotest chance I might actually defeat him."

"I'm on my way to see Jagus now," said Kierce, quietly.

A renewed bitterness entered Caras's anger.

"Are you telling me I do have to fight you as well?"

"Of course I'm not, you idiot. I'm telling Jagus he made a mistake. I did not release him from his oath. Whether he'll accept it or not is another matter, but I did not ask him to kill Rainur, I will not stand by and allow him to kill you. Is that clear enough for you?"

Caras hesitated cautiously.

"It would be if I believed a word you said. How did Jagus make a mistake? Orlii took him the message, Orlii told me what the message was."

"But the message didn't come from me. At least, only part of it did. The *as-caii* he can have, if he can find them."

"I thought they were your allies."

"You thought nothing of the kind, Caras," snapped Kierce. "You knew what had happened to the Imperial governor. You said nothing. You knew there was no other choice."

"Did I? And how about that tortured creature they brought out of your Tower with his throat cut? Am I supposed to understand that, as well?"

"When you've finally negotiated your way up the valley, probably," retorted Kierce.

Caras turned away from him. He didn't dare let himself be deceived yet again by Kierce's plausibility. He hadn't won a game against him since they were both boys.

"Well, I don't have time now. There are people getting slaughtered in my name on my northern border, and the only way I can stop that happening is to take Jagus's challenge back to him."

"You really think I want to see Shaihen set against Shaihen like this? You think I feel the losses you've suffered on your northern border less than I felt the ones you suffered at Toshan?"

Caras paused and gave him a long, hard look. He could certainly see signs of the stress and exhaustion evident in the Kierce he had found wandering around the dunes of Toshan, but it did not evince the same sympathy and concern he felt then.

"So why are you doing it? Why do we have to go through all this? I'll tell you why. You're prepared to sacrifice Rainur, and me, and tear us apart like this just because you can't leave that bloody woman alone. I should have known what kind of a Magician you'd be the first time I saw you for what you are. When you took away the choice of the man trying to cut my throat!"

"What would you rather I'd have done?" exclaimed Kierce. "Let him kill you? Should I have left Cathva in fear of me and let Sartin die? Should I have let Volun attack Hiren and left all the warriors of Oreath to die at Toshan, too?"

"You're the Lord High Magician ..."

"Oh, I am the Magician now, am I?" cut in Kierce impatiently. "Not the trainer of horses, or the man who loves women, or the man you grew up with?"

Caras glared at him silently.

"Caras, I swear to you," Kierce insisted. "I don't want Rainur dead. I certainly don't want you dead. This is not my doing!"

Caras met his eyes, still full of the hurt of betrayal.

"No? Then it's the doing of that bloody Caiivorian whore you're servicing. Isn't it?"

Kierce had no answer.

Caras turned silently and walked away from him.

Jagus was Kierce's last hope, and he knew it was a forlorn one. Jagus had always believed unshakeably that Shehaios should remain completely independent, the Gate guarded against all incomers, and he saw himself as the Gatekeeper who would do that. It took little to convince him that his time had come; the movement of heaven and earth would not have persuaded him that he was mistaken in that belief. Kierce sat in the campaign tent of the Shaihen general he had created, steering as close as his pride allowed to pleading with him.

"I'm a man of my word, Magician," stated Jagus, "I would not break an oath once I've given it, but you're not asking me to keep an oath. You're asking me to renew the promise. That I will not do."

"But I didn't release you from the oath. I didn't send the message."

Kierce knew Jagus flatly disbelieved him. Jagus had never felt much respect for him, and saw his argument as mere vacillation. A sentimentimental weakness, like that which had subverted the Magician's power to the fond influence of a woman.

"Hold firm, Magician," said Jagus. "The time has come for sacrifices to be made. If, indeed, you are still playing to win."

"Jagus," sighed Kierce, "you don't even understand what the game is."

With Jagus's mind closed to him, there was nothing Kierce could do but try and establish to the men who followed him the authority Jagus himself no longer accepted. He rode with Jagus to meet the Holder's challenge which was the only alternative now to civil war in Shehaios. He knew it was the alternative Caras would choose.

Chapter 45
A Hero's Death

It was, in many ways, a good day to die.

As Caras rode through balmy summer sunshine in the peace of central Shehaios however, he could not help feeling it was a better day to be alive.

The northern reaches of Oreath, up to and over the border with Hieath, were the heart of Shaihen prosperity. It was soft fertile land, sheltered from the harshness of the mountain heights, washed by the western rains, a gentle landscape of fields, hedges and sprawling Holdings carved from swathes of ancient trees. The early summer sun lit acres of ripening crops and warmed the pale cattle that grazed around the Holdings, a landscape born of generations of peace and human toil.

It felt to Caras almost an act of sacrilege to be traversing the rutted dirt road from Arhaios to Hieath with an army at his back, yet he knew barely five miles ahead of him the army he had come to confront marched implacably southwards to meet him. In that army too marched the heirs to the Whole Land, the children of life.

The distance was closing with every step. This was the day on which the dispute would be settled.

He never entertained any illusions about the likely outcome of the fight. But it was only now beginning to come home to him how unprepared he was to make this the day he died. He wished he had taken better leave of Arhaios. He had said farewells, but even Elani's last fierce embrace had been swamped by the practicalities. He knew what a burden his death would leave her. He had named her his heir before he left, bequeathing her Oreath and Arhaios as well as three children. There was no-one else he could trust as well. The urgent words that clamoured to be said, the pressing need to pretend courage to his children and his people forced out the quieter need to fix the loved images of the place and the people he was leaving in his mind.

The sense of hopelessness in which he went made his departure so much harder than when he had left for Toshan. Then, he had ridden with Kierce and the Empire at his side. This time, he rode alone. Without the magic, he knew that whatever he did, the histories would sweep on without him, his sacrifice forgotten or even derided. Elani could offer him no explanation for Kierce this time, no sensible alternative to the course on which he was set. She could only hold him, and hope as he did for a miracle. Looking at the odds in cold blood, there was no other way he was going to defeat Jagus in single combat.

He looked on the wealth of the land around him for what may be the last time, and considered what hung in the balance against a superficial beauty with a corrupt soul and no heart that he could see. He wondered what had happened to the boy who had shown him the depth and complexity of the world he admired so much. The loss of Kierce himself was as hard to swallow as his treachery. Yet he did not dare believe the reassurance the Magician had attempted to offer him at Arhaios. He had to meet Jagus knowing he fought only with his own strength.

They met a few miles inside Oreath's northern border, Shaihen pitted against Shaihen across a mundane field of half-ripe barley. Caras saw Kierce riding at Jagus's side. He could taste the bitterness of his bile. If Jagus had offered Kierce as his champion in the fight, Caras felt he would have welcomed it.

But it was, of course, Jagus himself who rode forwards. Jagus fought his own battles. Caras matched him, until they were close enough to speak.

"Give me the road, Caras," said Jagus. "I'm on my way to the Haven."

"You'd like to think you are," retorted Caras.

"Will you argue with the Lord High Magician, then?"

Caras hesitated. He could almost hear Kierce saying, why not, you always do. Perhaps it was what he was thinking as he watched the exchange of abuse between the combatants from his place at the head of Jagus's men. But Caras had never understood what Kierce was thinking.

"I find myself doing all sorts of things I would once have thought I would never do," he answered Jagus with much greater confidence than he felt. "All I know is what I'm told. If you tell me it's otherwise, then we can talk, but as far as I know your intention is to kill your brother and appropriate his title. Both offend the Spirit of Shehaios. Brother should not kill brother, and heirs are nominated by those they succeed and approved by the people of a Holding. They don't appoint themselves."

"As you said," replied Jagus, "times change. Let me pass, Caras."

"You go through me," replied Caras implacably. "You know that. That's why you came."

"Well, I thought I would give you the chance to hide behind your men again," sneered Jagus. "But if you want to try your sword against me, nothing would give me greater pleasure."

Jagus dismounted and Caras cursed to himself. Whatever advantage he might have he held on horseback. Not on foot. But Jagus had chosen the ground and Caras could only follow suit.

Madred took Caras's horse for him. Caras tried not to see the hurt and despair in her eyes. She could see her brother among their enemy's men as well as he could.

Caras drew his sword. Jagus stood waiting for him.

They circled, weighing each other up.

"Are you sure you're ready to die, Caras?" Jagus taunted. "You don't have much longer to prepare yourself. I have been trained by the finest Imperial swordsmen of the Arena."

"I've done a bit of Imperial training myself," retorted Caras shortly. He didn't want to talk. He was watching for an opportunity that he knew in his heart was not going to come. Jagus had been notoriously good when he returned from the Imperial City and he had spent the past five years practising and honing his skill. Caras feared he would not even see the blow that killed him.

He made a play. Jagus blocked it and followed through. Caras deflected it clumsily, barely seeing it in time. It left him far too unbalanced to retaliate. He backed off, on the defensive, knowing that any moment his opponent was going to go in with a serious attack and the fight would be over.

Still, when the attack came, it almost caught him by surprise. It was even faster and stronger than he could have imagined; he retreated rapidly, every nerve straining to focus on his defence, drawing on every nuance of skill he could throw into the uneven fight. There was never the remotest chance of returning attack; the best he could do was to hold Jagus at bay, parry the blows, and fall back.

He seemed to do it for ever, the immediacy of death lending him a speed and stamina beyond anything he thought he could find within himself. All the time, he knew he was only reacting to Jagus. He took numerous small hits, none of them significant in themselves but all evidence of the dominance of Jagus's ability. It had to be only a matter of time.

Then suddenly, for no apparent reason, he sensed a weakening in Jagus's onslaught. Jagus disengaged and took a step back himself, as if he was tiring. Dazed with exhaustion and fighting with defeat in his face, the sudden hint of victory went to Caras's head. He launched himself at Jagus.

He didn't feel the sword thrust. He wondered why he could not see Jagus's weapon, and what had stopped his own assault. Then he looked down, and saw Jagus pull the blade from his body. He staggered, faintness flooding his head and weakness his body, and then he felt something grip him. It held him upright, as if something other than himself controlled his muscles. He raised the sword. He saw his enemy look at him in horrified astonishment. Jagus brought his blade up to meet the blow coming down towards him, but he was too late. Caras's sword bit deep into his shoulder at the base of his neck.

Jagus gave a gasping sigh and staggered. He dropped to his knees. Caras saw him begin to fall before the world grew dark and faded into a blind blackness.

Chapter 46
Collecting the Pieces

Kierce's return to the Haven came too late to save his daughter.

Every step he rode at Jagus's side he took in the knowledge that Cathva was fighting another lonely battle against her own body to bring their child into the world. Everything pulled him back to the Haven to throw his own strength into her battle, except the one thing that could save her, the simple fact that he was the Lord High Magician. Once Jagus refused point blank to turn back from what he had started, Oreath's claim on the Lord High Magician outweighed Cathva's.

Since even he could not actually be in two places at once, trying to do both ran the risk of failing to do either. He chose not to take that risk.

He had never intended to sacrifice Caras. Kierce took Caras's calm courage for granted. Caras had always been physically strong, and his strength had always been underpinned by his faith in the course he pursued. Kierce found it difficult to really appreciate what it felt like to know yourself to be the weaker party, to go in fear of death. His father had taught him from a very early age that the gift of *thinking man* always made him stronger than the biggest and most aggressive beasts and Kierce had never found it to be anything other than true. Caras's wild attack on Jagus had caught him unawares. He had never seen such a rash, unconsidered, blindly stupid bit of swordplay.

More than ever, Kierce felt the game slipping away from him. He had taken little rest since the Imperial messengers arrived, and it was beginning to tell on his strength. Part of the price for failing to maintain a distance was to find yourself keeping pace with events rather than being one step ahead. He was afraid he was falling one step behind.

Cathva's second labour was as long and unproductive as her first. By the time Kierce came to her, he was barely in time to save the mother. There was no hope for the child he delivered stillborn.

While Cathva lay racked with pain, the strength and life gradually draining out of her and her baby, Rainur's son slipped into the world with the minimum of fuss. He gave a lusty yell to prove he had arrived, then latched on to Tilsey's breast and got on with the serious business of life.

It happened that the King held his strong, healthy baby son in his arms when Kierce sought him out in the Palace. It was hardly surprising that Rainur took the opportunity to gloat. The Lord High Magician looked overwhelmingly human, his face gaunt and his eyes haunted by grief. If Rainur had wanted him to bear a little suffering, he had got his way.

"Congratulations, Rainur," Kierce greeted him. The irony would have come through better if his voice had been stronger. In fact he found it hard to speak at all.

"You have my sympathy, Kierce," Rainur lied, "It seems you chose the wrong moment to be away."

"Not my choice," said Kierce.

"Really?" Rainur turned towards him. "I'm surprised you're still here."

"Well, you always think the worst of me," said Kierce, wearily, sinking down onto a nearby chair. "I will have to go back. It's not finished yet."

"Not by a long way. Gascon and Colis are gathering their forces even as we speak – and if Onia were near enough to do any good, I suspect I could call on her as well. You're doing a good job of setting us at each others' throats, Kierce, what exactly does this have to do with the Lord High Magician's role?"

"Sod all," replied Kierce, shortly. "And tell Gascon and Colis to stop before it gets out of hand. The army I left in Oreath is coming to the Haven to do what the Emperor requested they do – put themselves at the disposal of the Imperial Commander."

"What?"

"Quite which Caiivorians the Imperial Commander takes them to fight, I leave to him and Tercien to sort out. But they will be Caiivorians, and not Shaihens."

"Him and …? Tercien is the Imperial Commander!"

Kierce smiled faintly.

"So is Caras. Had you forgotten?"

"But Caras is—."

"… lying in his tent feeling sorry for himself," finished Kierce. "Partly why I need to get back – hurling insults at me is bound to make him feel better." He looked steadily at Rainur. "You really think I would have let Jagus kill him, any more than I would let him kill you?" He shook his head. "You do always think the worst of me."

"You give me cause." retorted Rainur.

"I really don't, Rainur," protested Kierce mildly. He felt too exhausted to argue at any length. It was a great effort to take any interest, let alone pleasure, in the game when the only image in his mind was of a tiny, pathetic scrap of potential humanity. She could have been as beautiful as Cathva. She could have been as strong as Madred, as full of life and laughter as Sartin. She could have been his heir – Kierce did not see any good reason why the Magician's title should be a male stronghold. She would always have been his daughter. But she was destined to be nothing, never to draw breath in the world at all.

He forced himself to concentrate on the continuing argument with Rainur. He needed to go back to Caras with a clear idea of what was in the King's mind.

"Look, if you want to see this in terms of male rivalry, consider us even. You lost a son you thought was yours, I've just lost a daughter. The difference is, Sartin is still a living, growing, wonderful child. I can't believe you can love him one day and not the next, just because you find out he's not your son."

"It's not because he's not mine," replied Rainur. "It's because he's yours."

"He was never mine," insisted Kierce. "He was born to be your heir, a child of the Imperial Family, Cathva's son, the Emperor's grandson, the living fruit of your alliance. He is still all those things." He looked at the plump, healthy infant Rainur held. "I don't begrudge you your son. But don't make him your heir. Don't go to Vordeith. If you're going to defy the Emperor do it from here – you can lose a lot of communication between Shehaios and Vordeith. Like, exactly which Imperial Commander our warriors were supposed to report to."

"I don't need to defy the Emperor, I need to persuade him that he is mistaken in believing that I betrayed his governor."

Kierce sank his head into his hands.

"Rainur, listen to yourself. Persuade Emperor Zelt an' Korsos that he is mistaken? The Great Emperor is never mistaken. Even when he's wrong."

"Like you, you mean?" suggested Rainur acidly.

"I'm not in the business of right and wrong. My game concerns survival." He paused. "So does Zelt's. That's why he won't admit to any failure. His Greatness has to be unassailable. He won't listen to you, Rainur. He's already made his judgement and delivered his sentence. You won't even get anywhere near him. Don't go."

"I will not stay here and wait for the Imperial troops to charge me with the evil you did!" Rainur paused and took Kierce's lack of denial as confirmation of something he had hitherto only suspected. It sealed his belief that Kierce intended Rainur himself to be the victim of his next expedient murder. "I'm not deceived, Kierce. You may protect Caras, you'll certainly protect Sartin. It's me you intend to isolate. Well, you may succeed, but I won't make it easy for you by naming your son as my heir. I name my own, to the Holders' Council. So are you tearing us apart or are you uniting us?"

Kierce closed his eyes.

"So we all die together? I can't do that, Rainur." He sighed heavily. "Name your son as heir and you bequeath him dust. Whatever we can or can't persuade the Empire to accept, we can be pretty damn sure they will not accept the replacement of the Emperor's grandson – adopted son – by the child of a slave." He glanced at Tilsey. "I'm sorry, Tilsey. You understand what I mean."

"I do, Lord Kierce," said Tilsey softly.

Kierce looked back at her with disquiet. Tilsey understood all too well what he meant, she knew the ways of the Emperor intimately. He read with alarm the solution forming in her mind.

"I won't accept that, Tilsey," he warned.

"I know you won't, Lord Kierce." Tilsey's voice remained quiet, a habitual air of submissiveness acquired from hard experience.

"Accept what?" asked Rainur.

Tilsey's eyes remained on Kierce, and his on her.

"If the problem, my lords, is that the child you wish to inherit is not of the Imperial family … tell the Imperial family that he is." She turned to Rainur. "Only a very few people know at the moment that my child lived, and Cathva's did not. Announce it the other way round. As Lord Kierce says, much communication may be lost between Shehaios and Vordeith."

Rainur stared at her momentarily lost for words.

"You would give up your child?"

Tilsey smiled.

"What would I be giving up? Shaihens would know the truth as they have always known it. I cared for Sartin in every important way, I washed him, I dressed him, I sang the songs of Shehaios to him, I nursed him when he was sick – the fact that I do the same for Filas would not be remarkable. I would rather Sartin remained what he was always meant to be, but if you're set on making our son your heir, at least give him a chance, Rainur. Give him a claim to the Imperial family. Cathva has already claimed to the Emperor that the child she was carrying was yours."

"You would still need to explain to the Emperor why you were passing over your eldest son – the one he invites to be educated as an Imperial citizen – in favour of your youngest," interposed Kierce tartly.

Rainur gave him a cold look of calculation.

"I could perhaps tell him the truth. Sartin is your son, not mine. Once, had I told the Emperor my wife had been unfaithful to me, he would have despised my weakness in not keeping proper control of my household. But if I were to tell him Tay-Aien's priest raped his daughter within weeks of her arrival in Shehaios, executes Imperial prisoners in his temple and pays Caiivorian bandits to murder the Emperor's governor, how do you think he might react?"

Kierce met his eyes steadily.

"You want a real priest of Tay-Aien in my place?"

"I want the Lord High Magician of Shehaios in your place. But I'm not sure I'm going to find him as long as you live. Accept my authority, Kierce, or name your own heir, because I think my patience is done. You support me, or I denounce you to the Emperor myself."

There was a long and charged silence. Kierce studied Rainur and Tilsey standing side by side, and then got slowly to his feet.

"I have matters to attend to in Oreath," he said.

Chapter 47
Caras

Caras regained consciousness with such an overwhelming sense of Kierce's presence that he thought he was there. It was several minutes before his eyes connected properly to his brain and told him the face he was looking up at belonged to Madred.

He frowned at her. He was puzzled to know why her expression was one of such concern, and why she was bathing his face.

She smiled as she saw him looking at her.

"Welcome back, Caras. We missed you."

"Where have I been?" He tried to sit up, and Madred laid a gently restraining hand on his shoulder.

"Rest. Your body needs to understand it's been healed."

Caras lay back gratefully, startled by the dizziness in his head. He stared at the gloom of the hide tent over him, forcing his memory into life. He knew where he was. He remembered what had happened. And he knew Kierce had been there with him every step of the way.

"Jagus?"

"Jagus is dead."

"But there's his army – my own people—."

"They all wait on your word." The hurt had gone from Madred's eyes, and there was relief in the smile she gave him. "Kierce told Jagus's men they were under your command. They couldn't argue. You are a Holder, who won a challenge." Her smile broadened. "You're also an Imperial Commander. Kierce is a devious bastard, but you can't deny he plays a sharp game."

Caras closed his eyes. He sensed Madred's peace, and he found it difficult to recall the antipathy he knew he had felt for Kierce when he went to fight Jagus. He felt closer to him now than he ever had. He had a vague memory of an overwhelming presence within him, pulling together flesh that had been torn apart. His hand moved unconsciously to his stomach, just below his ribs. He felt the scar tissue running across his skin.

"He healed me."

Madred tried to smooth the frown from his forehead with her hand.

"Of course he did."

"Throws me into the fight and then puts me back together again," observed Caras, sourly. "Hard life being a gaming stone."

"I don't think he intended you to get hurt. You did … kind of throw yourself on Jagus's sword."

"Somehow, I knew it would be my fault." Caras opened his eyes. "Where is he?"

"He had to go to the Haven." Madred hesitated. "Cathva's labour had started."

"Cathva," Caras sighed. "Well, I suppose it's his child. Spirit defend us, is the world ready for the offspring of that union?"

He was feeling considerably stronger by the time Kierce returned to the camp on the northern fields of Oreath. In fact, when he looked at the Magician's face, he thought he was probably feeling better than Kierce was. Kierce looked utterly drained. Caras noticed this time that Orlii was still not with him.

"You should still be resting," said Kierce. Caras was sitting outside the tent receiving various messengers from the mass of men gathered in the surrounding field.

"I am resting," said Caras. "I can't lie around doing nothing." He looked at Kierce. "I think I should tell you to take your own advice. When did you last sleep?"

"When I last closed my eyes," said Kierce wryly. "But I haven't left half my blood in a field. Rest, Caras. There'll be more fighting to do one way or another. No way round it."

"Oh, I'm glad you didn't heal me for any sentimental reasons. That would have been hard to live with."

Kierce smiled wearily.

"I'm glad to see you so well recovered, Caras. You frightened me for a while. I've never seen such an idiotic move – I couldn't believe you'd done it."

"I'm sorry! Next time tell me I have magical protection and I might be a bit braver."

"I tried. You wouldn't bloody listen."

There was a pause. Kierce sat down beside Caras.

"Where's Orlii?" asked Caras.

"Ah. I fear he's gone back to his brothers, the *as-caii*," admitted Kierce. "I'm afraid I used Orlii badly as well. When I … found out what Cathva had done, I lashed out at what was nearest. What was nearest, of course, was Orlii. Do you know he believed he was my heir?"

"Not surprising," said Caras, "he virtually reads your mind."

"He does not!" exclaimed Kierce indignantly.

"He gets closer than anyone else." Caras glanced at him curiously. "Did you really not know what Cathva had done?"

Kierce sighed. "No, Caras, I didn't. Not until Orlii told me. I'm sorry to disappoint you, but I don't actually know everything. Just more than everyone else. I was so close to Cathva, and yet … I suppose I didn't want to believe she could do it to me." He paused reflectively. " Well, she has her punishment. Her healing will take a lot longer than yours."

"Her healing? Is she sick?"

"She lost the baby," said Kierce, quietly. "I didn't get there in time."

"You couldn't save your own child?" queried Caras in horror.

"Proof if you need it that it doesn't always go according to plan." Kierce gave Caras a bitter smile. "It was a girl. I always fancied having a daughter. Something about the way you and Alsareth—". He broke off and got to his feet. "This army, Caras. We have to decide what we're going to do with it."

"Is it one army, or two?"

"I think it's one. It has the makings of one, and in your capable hands I'm sure that's what it will become."

Caras paused reflectively.

"Which one of us killed Jagus?" he asked eventually.

"It was your hand on the sword."

"But not my strength wielding it." Caras looked at him with concern. "The Magician is not supposed to use his power to kill."

"That's why I have to keep you alive to do it for me," Kierce grinned. "Tell me, Caras, do you think Arhaios could cope with having all this lot billeted on it for a while?"

Chapter 48
Departure of a King

Rainur's mind was made up. He had told the Emperor he would come to Vordeith after the birth of his child, and two weeks after Filas was born he prepared to leave the Haven. Tercien gave him an escort of two Units of Imperial troops, and he took men from the Haven, from Mervecc and from Ccheven with him as well.

And he took Sartin.

He had told Gascon directly of his decision to name his heir, and messages had gone to Colis, Onia, Ered and Caras. He had not told them why he was not naming Sartin, only that he was naming Filas, the son just born to Cathva.

He wasn't sure of Caras. He knew Kierce was with him. He wasn't entirely sure what Kierce was going to do, but he did believe Kierce's fight was with him and not with Shehaios. If Kierce moved against him once he was gone, Rainur would do as he threatened and denounce him to the Emperor. If the Emperor moved against him as Cathva, Kierce and even Tilsey believed he would, he left Caras and Kierce with an army at Arhaios. Rainur felt the time for evasion was over. It was time to declare his hand.

What he was not expecting was for Kierce to appear at the Palace as they were preparing to leave. Red Sky was saddled, and carried a pack behind his rider. It looked as if Kierce was prepared for a journey. Rainur regarded him with misgiving.

"What are you doing here?"

"I'm coming with you," stated Kierce. "Sartin stays here."

Sartin looked at him in dismay. As far as he was concerned, his father was taking him on a wonderful adventure that only a boy big enough and brave enough to leave his mother and Tilsey behind could undertake. He was going to the glorious Imperial City to meet his mother's people. Kierce coming too was a joyous bonus. Kierce telling him to stay behind was devastating.

"Am I supposed to find your presence reassuring?" asked Rainur, coldly. "I think if I ride with you and I don't take Sartin, I won't make it past the Caiivorian plains."

"Then don't go at all. Either of you."

Rainur hesitated very briefly.

"There are two Units of Imperial troops waiting to escort us south from the Imperial Camp tomorrow," he said. "If I don't go to meet them, I strongly suspect they will come to meet me. The Emperor is expecting us."

He mounted his horse, and took hold of the bridle of Sartin's pony.

"Don't fight me over him, Kierce. I'm not leaving him here for you to play games of succession against Filas, and I'm not going anywhere in your company without him. You do as you wish, but Sartin comes with me.

Forgive me if I think your enthusiasm for protecting him is somewhat greater than your enthusiasm for protecting me."

Kierce hesitated. He could have taken command of both Rainur's horse and Sartin's pony, just as he could have physically picked Sartin up and carried him back to Arhaios. If he did that, he was saving Zelt the trouble of removing Rainur's authority. It was better than killing him. But not much. He decided to give himself the journey to the Gate to dissuade Rainur from this madness. What he was going to do then, he really didn't know. He was beginning to wish he was Turloch. It was much easier not to be involved, to play from a distance.

He urged Red Sky forwards and rode alongside Rainur, with Sartin between them.

He hadn't even begun to tackle Cathva yet. Her life was out of danger, but she was still barely aware of what had happened. He had hardly spoken to her. He wasn't sure he could, with any civility. He had helped her through the grim end to the labour begun under the cloud of his anger, he'd made it as easy as possible. There was no overt reproach in his words or his manner, but she had deliberately used his name and his authority to do something he had expressly forbidden, and he didn't know that he could forgive her for it. It had cost Jagus his life, nearly cost Caras his, and it had prevented Kierce being there to save his daughter.

They travelled the first day from the Haven with no untoward incidents, reaching the Imperial Camp by nightfall. Rainur's resolve remained as implacable as ever, and Sartin's excitement was undiminished.

The second night, they camped above the road on a good defensive site, with the Imperial soldiers augmenting their guard. Kierce knew there were Caiivorians around; he had caught glimpses of them through the day. They seemed to be a small band of observers rather than a war party, though he couldn't be sure. Until he was able to re-establish some communication with Orlii, he no longer had any direct contact with Girstan's forces. The Shaihen camp was on high alert for any sign of danger.

He was aware of the approaching horseman before the sentry's challenge rang out, and he was walking towards the man in the rawhide armour of Girstan's warriors as Rainur's guards checked him outside their encampment.

The Caiivorian's horse whickered joyfully at Kierce's appearance. He smiled, went up to the horse and scratched its nose in greeting.

"You've returned to us then, Orlii?" he welcomed its rider.

Orlii dismounted.

"I didn't know you were here, my lord. I came to Lord Rainur."

"Betraying your new allegiance already?"

"I am still your servant, Lord Kierce. I live with my people but I still serve you. Bid me return, and I will do so."

Kierce grimaced, still paying more attention to the horse than its master.

"If you think that being my servant gives you the powers you laid claim to, I'm inclined to think you're probably better off where you are. They haven't cut your throat yet. Come on, you'd better deliver your news to the King, he takes my word for nothing."

He turned back towards the camp and the sentries let Orlii pass.

They returned through the encamped Shaihen escort. On the way, they passed the horses, gathered near the centre of the camp. Red Sky grazed a little apart from them, knowing they were not his herd and he was not allowed to fight any of them. He raised his head and came trotting over as he saw Orlii's mare.

"It's late to be travelling," Kierce conceded. "Take shelter with us for the night. For your horse's sake if not for yours."

"Thank you, my lord," accepted Orlii. "That will make it easier."

He went to unsaddle the mare as Red Sky came up to nibble her mane and whisper sweet nothings in her ear.

"Look after her," said Kierce. "You know you have two horses there?"

"Red Sky's offspring?" said Orlii, with pleasure.

"If not I'll have two disgruntled stallions on my hands." Kierce turned away and indicated the fire burning beyond some bushes, in front of a large tent. "I'll be over there in front of the King's tent when you're ready."

He left Orlii to sort his horse out and hooked a pot of water over the fire while he waited for his former servant to join him. The light was fading fast and the temperature dropping as rapidly. He pulled the bearskin out of his pack and threw it around himself.

Orlii returned, and shortly after that Rainur emerged from the tent with one of the leaders of his escorting party. The Shaihen went off into the body of the camp and Rainur came over to the fire. Orlii scrambled to his feet at the King's approach.

"Orlii brings us news," said Kierce.

"My people – the as-caii – are in the hills around you, Lord Rainur," said Orlii. "I thought you should know. I didn't … I didn't realise Lord Kierce was with you."

Rainur glanced ironically at Kierce.

"Does this surprise us, Kierce?"

"I suspected they were there," Kierce deliberately misunderstood him. He glanced at Orlii. "Are they going to attack us? We have nothing they would want."

Orlii hesitated and met Kierce's eyes.

"You have the King."

Kierce looked at him sharply.

"So others think they can seize the crown by killing the king? Did you tell them this, Orlii?"

"I had no need to, my lord," said Orlii.

"Just as well I came then," said Kierce. Steam began to billow forth from the cooking pot, and he started to get up to fetch the herbs for infusion.

"Let me do it, Lord Kierce," said Orlii. "I know what it is you want."

"I want to sleep," sighed Kierce and subsided onto the ground. He was bone weary. He had slept only in fitful snatches ever since Xemper's arrival. The hot fire on his face was beginning to make his eyes droop.

"Is Sartin all right?" he asked.

"Asleep," said Rainur. "The sentries are keeping watch."

"You told them to keep their wits about them?"

"Of course." Rainur hesitated. "Where will you sleep, Kierce?"

Kierce opened one eye and looked doubtfully up at the sky. "Oh, it won't rain."

Orlii followed his gaze.

"Prediction?" he suggested.

"Wishful thinking," admitted Kierce. "But I can't be bothered to move."

He was vaguely aware that Orlii had scooped some of the tea into a beaker and handed it to Rainur. He was aware of Cathva's voice in Orlii's head. Something was chasing around the edge of his weary mind.

"I know what Lord Kierce wants. He wants me."

"I know what it is you want."

The cup had reached Rainur's lips before he scented the wrongness in it. By the time he was moving, Rainur had drunk deeply from it.

Kierce surged to his feet and hurled himself on the King, sending the cup flying from his hand and knocking the man to the ground. Rainur choked on his cry of alarm and went down with a crash. As he fell, a dreadful rasping came from his throat. He clutched at it with his hands. The blood drained from his face, his eyes bulged, and his mouth gaped, struggling to draw in the breath his body no longer knew how to take.

Kierce came down on top of him, fastened his mouth over Rainur's and began to draw the poison out of him. He tasted the bitterness on his tongue, and his muscles jerked in spasm as it entered his own system. He began to work against it, as he worked to draw it out of Rainur.

He knew as he touched Rainur's body that he was too late, but he would not give up. Sweat soaked him, and he shook with effort and fever, and still he worked to fight the poison in himself and to force Rainur's paralysed muscles to work. He breathed for him, pumped his heart for him, struggled to put the life back into him. He fought until the two battles, the one to keep his own body alive and the lost one for Rainur's life, finally overwhelmed his strength. He slumped to the ground by Rainur's body.

Orlii watched with racing heart. He had not intended to harm Kierce. He would not have believed he had the power to do so. Nevertheless, Kierce had fallen.

Orlii had never seen him helpless and vulnerable before. Orlii had never been free from his power. Now he was. In the heart of the Shaihen camp, he stood by the bodies of the Lord High Magician and the King of Shehaios, slain by his hand, he, Orlii, slave. His hand went to the tattoo on his chest, the symbol of his people. The sense of power tingled in his fingertips and surged through his heart. He could return to his own people in triumph beyond his imagining, conqueror not only of the enemy King he had promised them, but the Lord High Magician as well, the feared, powerful, untouchable foe. Shehaios lay before them for the taking.

Hesitantly he crept towards the bodies fallen one across the other. He reached out a tentative hand to touch Kierce's cloak. The Magician did not stir. Carefully, he released the clasp across Kierce's chest, pulled the cloak free and swung it around his own body. He shivered at the feel of it on his shoulders. The Magician's cloak. On his back. He reached out again, and his hand touched Kierce's shoulder. He paused. A lump rose in his throat. He had not intended to kill Kierce, the only human being he had ever felt anything resembling affection for since he was dragged from his mother's side. Grief that he had done this dreadful thing vied with the thrill of the power he believed he had inherited.

He struggled against it, and determinedly sought the staff at Kierce's side. He unbuckled the belt that held it, and pulled it free from Kierce's body. He stood up to fasten it around his own waist, turned, and found himself looking at Sartin, staring at him aghast, his eyes heavy with sleep and wide with disbelief.

"Go back in," ordered Orlii. "Go back in the tent."

"Those are Kierce's things," said Sartin, shocked. "You can't have them. Give them back."

Orlii took a step towards him. Noise would attract attention from the rest of the camp.

"Go back in the tent," he warned.

"Why has Kierce let you take them?" Sartin looked at the figures lying in such an extraordinary fashion on the ground and tears came into his eyes. "You can't have Kierce's things! I don't like you – where's Tilsey? Where's Mama?"

He looked at Orlii with his lip trembling, and Orlii knew what he saw. He had seen it himself, at the same age. Five years old. Looking at the man who had killed his father.

Orlii launched himself at the boy as Sartin sensed the danger in the man in front of him and turned to run. He almost slipped beyond Orlii's grasp; Orlii still held the staff in his hand and he swung it desperately at the fleeing child. It struck the side of Sartin's head, and he fell like a log to the ground. Panting with fear, Orlii looked down on him, and realised he looked at the future of Shehaios. He knew nothing of Filas. As far as he was aware, this was the sole heir to the Shaihen crown at his feet, the possessor of the Shaihen crown now Rainur lay dead behind them.

Suddenly, Orlii's mind cleared, and he knew what to do. He picked the boy up and dumped him down beside the fire. Then he went back to Kierce and Rainur, lifted Kierce's body almost as easily as he manhandled Sartin's and laid him down beside the child. Rainur was more difficult to move, but Orlii managed to drag him into the empty tent. He threw the furs over Kierce, and bent to pick up the child. He spun round as someone spoke behind him.

"All quiet?"

It was the leader of the watch, making a routine check. He suspected nothing. Orlii steadied his breathing.

"Fine. They're sleeping. I'll stand guard."

"All right, Orlii. Shout if you see anything. Good night."

He waited with his heart in his mouth until the guard was gone. Then he picked up Sartin and slung him over his shoulder, and slipped silently out of the camp.

Kierce came back to the body he had cleansed of poison to find it being significantly abused.

His hands were tied at the wrists. His arms were pulled above his head, and he was being dragged by them through dirt, rock and thorn in a distinctly painful manner.

He opened his eyes. A gout of mud flew into his face, and he shut them again, spitting dirt from his mouth. A rock thumped into his shoulder. He cursed, and with an effort, rolled over and scrambled to his feet.

A shout went up to his left, but it was to his right he looked. He was conscious of the horse at the other end of the rope which tied his wrists, but he was not fully in command of his faculties yet and in no position to influence it. He was conscious also, as he rolled up out of the dirt, of another body dragging alongside him, tied and trussed as he was. He looked, expecting to see Rainur.

He saw Sartin, a tiny forlorn figure coated in dirt and mud.

Kierce reached towards him with panic-stricken urgency, seeking some vital signs. There was nothing there. Sartin was not unconscious. He was dead.

Kierce raised his head and let out a cry of raw grief, loosing the ropes that held his wrists almost without thinking about it.

All around him, the as-caii were turning to see what was going on, shouting in surprise and alarm. They had fallen on the Shaihen camp and removed the corpses Orlii had promised them. Yet one now stood on the track in their midst, the ropes fallen from his hands as if they were webs of spider thread.

Orlii came back through the group he led to see what was going on. He halted abruptly at the sight of Kierce upright and very much alive. Kierce turned towards him. Orlii's heart quailed. In all the years he had watched and lived with the power of the magician he had never seen the terrible look he met in Kierce's eyes now.

Kierce looked at Orlii, clad in his cloak. In a second he read the story in Orlii's face, in Orlii's guilt, in Orlii's mind. One careless comment and Cathva's foolish schemes and this abomination had been born in Orlii's head, carried out with the dedication of a faithful servant. He gave another rending cry like some nightmarish beast that echoed from the depths of the rock to the skies above them, and sprang at Orlii. He dragged him from the horse, seized him by the throat. For a moment Orlii looked into that terrible face, and then Kierce placed his hands over Orlii's eyes, and nose, and mouth. Darkness closed down on him, all the fears of night rushing in on his soul, a stampede of demons let loose from his worst imaginings. His blood turned to fire in his veins, raging through his body. He tried to scream but no sound came. In terror and agony, the spark of life was squeezed from Orlii's soul.

Kierce's body recoiled as the life left the Caiivorian.

He released Orlii's corpse, tearing the cloak from him as it fell to the ground. He turned to face the rest of the *as-caii*. They gathered around him poised between menace and flight, unsure what to make of him. He knew he could not let them see how drained he felt. He was weakened and distraught and if they all turned on him now he was not confident that he had the strength or the will to resist them. He hardly cared whether he lived or died.

He stood summoning what resources he had left. He saw the carcasses of Rainur and Sartin still lying in the dust, dragging behind the horses of their Caiivorian conquerors. All he could do now was to save their bodies the indignity of the *as-caii's* triumphalism. He reached his hand towards them, and raised a fire to burn their humiliated flesh clean.

Caiivorians and horses alike started away from the sudden flames. Shouting and recriminations erupted among the startled warriors. They gathered around Kierce, cursing, waving fists and swords at him, each urging the others nearer, daring to try and be the first to harm the purveyor of Shaihen magic.

Kierce closed his eyes to them. Gathering his remaining strength, he let his body flow into the form of a bird, its plumage mirroring the flames that consumed the remains of his son and his King. Spreading his wings, he launched himself above the cowering Caiivorians and soared into the high clear air above the mountains.

Chapter 49
An End

The rain was falling steadily in Arhaios and on the army spread across the fields beyond the river, awaiting their Commander's word to move against the Caiivorian raiders.

Caras was still officially recuperating in the comfort of the Holder's house. He was playing twelve stones against Sheldo while his son looked on and Elani and Alsareth did something arcane with herbs, when there came a sudden thundering on the door.

Caras and Elani looked at each other; their son shot to open the door with Caras hastily following him, worried by the urgency of the knocking.

To his surprise, he found Madred outside, white-faced and soaked to the skin. Caras chivvied the child aside to let her into the shelter of the house.

"Madred, what on earth—."

"Praise the Spirit you're here, Caras," gasped Madred. "I was afraid you were down at the camp or … I don't know where. And I don't know who else to turn to."

"Calm down, Maddi," Elani came to join them. "What's happened?"

Madred looked from her to Caras.

"I don't know. You have to come, Caras. It's Kierce."

Caras gave a sigh.

"When is it ever anyone else. What's he done now?"

"No, you don't … I don't mean … he's here, Caras."

"Then why hasn't he come himself?"

Madred shook her head.

"No, I mean, he's … he's in the paddock. Among the horses. He won't move, he won't speak to me, he's … I don't know. He looks terrible. Something terrible has happened, and … he frightens me, Caras, I don't know what to do!"

Caras looked round at Elani. She held out his cloak to him and threw one around herself.

"Sheldo, you're in charge," she said, shortly.

They made their way through the lashing rain across the heart of the Holding to the Horsemaster's stables and the fields beyond. Caras saw the horses gathered at the far end of one of the fields, standing in a group around something. He and the two women squelched across the paddock towards them, and he was almost among them before he saw Kierce.

He was sitting on the ground, with his back against the fence, staring fixedly ahead of him. His cloak was pulled tight around him but Caras could see him shivering. There was something appallingly desolate in the tense crouch of his body and the grey emptiness in his face.

Caras moved quietly through the protective equine ring and bent down beside his erstwhile friend.

"Kierce?" he queried, tentatively.

Kierce did not respond.

"How wet do we have to get, Kierce?" asked Caras, gently. He paused. "Well, we will. We're not going to go away."

Kierce closed his eyes.

"They're all dead. Rainur's dead. I used my power to kill."

The words came out as disjointed fragments. Caras went very still.

Kierce opened his eyes again and gave him a look of pure rage.

"To kill the man who killed the King. You never trusted me, Caras, did you? Spirit knows, I tried to stop us ending up here!"

Shamefaced, Caras reached out and rested his hand on Kierce's shoulder. "I'm sorry ..."

Kierce did not seem to be listening.

"He killed Sartin," he whispered savagely. "He killed my son."

Caras stared at him.

"Sartin? Sartin is your son?"

"He was my son, my hope, the future. Gone. My little girl never even had a chance. Never drew a breath. So quickly. It was all over so quickly." He shuddered, a tremor that shook his frame with persistent violence.

"Kierce, come inside under cover," said Caras. "Get out of the rain and tell me properly what's happened."

Kierce said nothing for a moment.

"I can't," he admitted finally.

"Why not?"

"I can't ... I can't move." He gave a sort of a laugh. "I got this far and I can't get any further. Some Lord High Magician. Can't even move." He closed his eyes against the rush of emotion.

Caras hesitated, then moved forward and lifted Kierce onto his shoulder. He turned towards the Horsemaster's buildings. Madred came forward with one of the horses, but Caras shook his head. He carried Kierce into the house on his own back.

Elani went back to the Holder's house for her healer's herbs; Caras and Madred laid Kierce down semi-conscious on a rush bed in the Horsemaster's house where he had been born. They took off his sodden clothes, dried him, and covered him in rugs. They persuaded him to drink what Elani prepared. They did these things willingly for brother and friend, and none of them mentioned to each other the fear they felt that they had to do them for the Lord High Magician.

They took shifts to sit by him as the day closed into night, and they hoped that he slept. He was plainly exhausted way beyond even the Magician's strength; whether there was anything else wrong with him they couldn't tell. Elani wanted to send for the Holding's healer, but Caras would not let her. If the Magician could not heal himself he doubted anyone else could and he did not want others seeing Kierce in this condition.

In the early hours of the morning, Caras himself nodded off in the chair by Kierce's side, his own strength barely recovered from the injuries Jagus had inflicted. He awoke soon after dawn to find Kierce crouched over the hearth stirring distilled malt barley spirit into an oatmeal porridge.

Caras shook the sleep from his eyes.

"You frightened the bloody life out of us," he greeted Kierce, accusingly.

"Sorry," said Kierce, without looking round.

"We thought you were at death's door!"

"Went through it," said Kierce. He glanced round. "I'm the Lord High Magician. I heal myself."

He came back across the room and sat down on the edge of the bed with the blanket draped loosely around his naked body.

"I guess Maddi's still asleep?"

"Yes."

"Give her my apologies if I don't see her. I … I didn't mean to frighten her. I didn't know where else to go."

"You come here," said Caras, quietly. "Of course you come here. This is your home."

Kierce shook his head.

"Not any more. I must get back to the Haven. I don't know how, I suppose Maddi can find me a horse. I've … Sky's gone as well. I have to … I don't know what the *as-caii* will do next. I have to tell Tercien what's happened – Gascon – the Council… " He broke off with a grimace. "Cathva." He turned and looked at Caras. "But first I have to tell you. Coherently."

"Rainur's dead," said Caras. "I got that much." He hesitated. "Who killed him?"

"Orlii."

"*Orlii!*"

"Orlii. I should never have let him go on believing he was my servant. I should have …" He trailed off and stared into the fire. "I will never understand the Caiivorian mind. And now Rainur's dead, and Sartin's dead."

"You said … you said he was your son?"

The ghost of Kierce's wry smile touched his face briefly.

"Of course he was my son. Did you never even suspect it, Caras? Couldn't you add nine months to the night I met Cathva in the Temple of the Spring?"

"It was nine months from the day of her marriage too. How was I supposed to know?"

Kierce shrugged.

"You could have saved Rainur one heartache. He always believed he was the last to know." He paused, gazing distantly into the glow of the hearth. "Rainur's dead. Sartin's dead." He stopped again, and added softly. "Kierce is dead."

Caras started to protest, but Kierce over-rode him.

"The Lord High Magician lives. The Lord High Magician heals himself. But Kierce died on the mountain beside his son and his King." He looked at Caras. "It's a long time since this was my home, Caras. This time there was no question. I didn't use a knife, I didn't use you. The Magician's power killed Orlii and using it that way … that's why I'm not supposed to do it. Using the magic to destroy destroys something of the Magician as well. Using it to kill … "

He saw the baffled frown begin to creep across Caras's face. It was an expression familiar to Kierce ever since they were about twelve and he began to go where Caras could not follow him.

"I don't understand," said Caras.

Kierce smiled faintly.

"Caras, my friend, you never did. But you always know the right thing to do, and you do it without fail, whatever the cost. Sometimes …" He looked steadily at his rock, his touchstone, Lord of the Holding whose name meant Spirit of the Hearth. "Sometimes that's better than understanding."

Printed in the United Kingdom
by Lightning Source UK Ltd.
118808UK00001B/187-195